UNRESTRICTED ACCESS

JG ROBBINS

UNRESTRICTED ACCESS
A Novel
by JG Robbins

WEXFORD HOUSE PUBLISHING

Published by:
Wexford House Publishing
4800 Cox-Smith Road
Mason, OH

ISBN 978-1-7348529-1-2 (paperback)
ISBN 978-1-7348529-0-5 (ebook)

Editor: Parisa Zolfaghari
Cover by: Damonza

For my wife, Donna
Without your encouragement, the character Grant Markey
would still be a vague notion rattling around in my head.

UNRESTRICTED ACCESS

A GRANT MARKEY SUSPENSE/THRILLER

BY

JG ROBBINS

LIST OF MAIN CHARACTERS IN ORDER OF APPEARANCE

Grant Markey IV - The main character, with psychic powers.

Tony Russell - CIA Deputy Director and Grant's college fraternity brother.

Miss Doris Webb - Grant's housekeeper, friend, and family employee for many years.

Craig Clayton - CIA agent in charge, Grant's primary security agent.

Donnie Hambleton - CIA agent, member of Grant's security detail.

Karen Markey - CIA agent posing as Grant's cousin.

Angie Reynolds - FBI Special Agent posing as Karen's friend.

Yang Kexin - Assistant Deputy Chairman, Central National Security Committee, PRC. Li's assistant.

Allison Murphy - Agent of the PRC. Her maiden name was Allison Chen. Chinese parents.

Li Zhang Yong - Deputy Chairman, Politburo Standing Committee, PRC. Leader of the conspiracy.

Justine Aebischer - FBI Special Agent, FBI Jewelry & Theft Program.

Irina Rachkova - Russian GRU Agent (Russia Main Intelligence Directorate).

Wu Min - Computer programming genius and top official in APT10, the PRC cyberwarfare branch.

Hua Shuang - Minister, PRC Embassy, Washington, D.C., junior only to the PRC Ambassador.

Ryurik Vetrov - Russian billionaire oligarch.

General Wei Li Jie - Member of Politburo Standing Committee and foe of Li Zhang Yong.

CHAPTER 1

MY CELL PHONE rings just as I'm closing the office for the day. The caller ID shows a number with the Washington, D.C. area code 202. It's probably a nuisance call, but my gut tells me it's trouble. I want to ignore it, but I can't.

"Hello?"

"Grant, this is Tony, Tony Russell."

"Tony Russell from Ole Miss?"

"Well, yes."

I've dreaded this call for years, but the thought of it had faded away — until now. I heard Tony was working for the FBI or CIA; I don't remember which one.

"It's good to hear from you — I think — but it's been over twenty years. Why are you calling now?"

"Grant, I need to see you."

"Okay, I'm in Natchez this month. You know, the Spring Pilgrimage and all."

"Sure, no problem, I'll come to see you. Can you make an hour available day after tomorrow?"

"Yeah, what's it about?"

"It's too involved to get into over the phone. How about 2:00 p.m. on Thursday?"

"Okay, you can come to my office. Call me when you get in town, and I'll give you the address."

"I appreciate it, Grant. Look, I gotta run. We'll talk in two days. Bye."

The line went dead; he didn't even wait for me to say goodbye.

I don't like this; a call out of the blue from a guy I haven't seen in twenty years — and who has to see me right away. It sounds like trouble. I think I know what Tony has on his mind, but I don't understand why now.

The phone call from Tony Russell brings back memories of Ole Miss. I was the fifth generation of the Markey family to attend Ole Miss, but with no children, I'll be the last. My father told me if I studied hard, chose good friends, and kept out of trouble, my time at Ole Miss would provide the foundation for a happy and successful life. But with Tony back in the picture, I'm not so sure about happiness — even if there is success. Tony has that effect on people — everything is always about Tony — and screw everyone else.

Tony was chapter president of Tau Delta Pi when I was a freshman pledge. He was a big man on campus — one of the biggest. He was studying pre-law, was on the Dean's List, and was also involved in campus politics. I think he was student body vice president, maybe even president. He was popular with the girls, and there were plenty of beauties at Ole Miss. I was just a lowly pledge.

Our fraternity house was near the middle of campus on Fraternity Row. We had one of the oldest and most beautiful

Greek houses on campus but about as far away as you could get from Sorority Row and Rebel Drive, where the loveliest ladies lived — maybe all of a half mile on the other side of The Grove.

Trying to put Tony and Ole Miss out of my mind, I lock the safe and check around one last time to make sure I didn't leave any valuables on the desk. It's easy to do when you're dealing with gemstones. I had been examining several exceptional Ceylon cornflower-blue sapphires I just purchased from a dealer friend in Bangkok. Sadly, I couldn't attend the Bangkok Gems & Jewelry Fair this year — because of the dang Pilgrimage.

My longtime friend and fellow gem dealer Sammi Suriwatpong has been begging me to visit him in Bangkok. He claims to have discovered a new source for unusual and collectible African gemstones, which he wants to show me. Meanwhile, we continue to do business by courier — sapphires and rubies, mostly.

As I leave the office, I lock the two deadbolts on the entry door after setting the security system. The door appears to be wood, but it's actually several layers of steel sheet with a faux wood finish. A simple sign on the door says Natchez Trading Co. This space has been the main office of a Markey business since 1927, when the building was new. We have deep roots in Natchez.

Instead of the elevator, I take the stairs down from the third floor and exit into the parking lot in back of the bank. That's right, the bank. My family's bank, until my grandfather, Grant Markey III, sold it in 1988 to First Mississippi Bank. He said a small-town bank couldn't compete in the technology age with the large bank conglomerates. Even then, banks were investing in computer technology, and the small banks couldn't afford to keep up. Thankfully, when Grandpa sold the bank, he insisted to keep the building. It's in a prime location, right on Canal

Street, so First Mississippi Bank had to go along with his odd demand if they wanted the deal.

Getting into my car for the drive home, I can't help but think about the long trail of family history that brings me to this moment in time. My great-great-great-great grandfather, the first Grant Markey, arrived in Natchez in 1848 with his partner, John Jenkins. They were agents for the Bank of Virginia and soon set up the Natchez Planters & Merchants Bank. Adams County, with Natchez as the county seat, had potential and was the richest county per capita in the entire country by 1860.

After the Civil War, Grant Markey and John Jenkins bought the bank for pennies on the dollar. After John Jenkins died, Grant Markey became the sole owner.

Finally, in 1988, Grant Markey III, age sixty-two, sold out to First Mississippi Bank, who made an offer he couldn't refuse. The bank had been in the family for 140 years.

I could have walked home from the bank, only a few blocks over to Pearl Street, but I drove my car to the office today. I went to a meeting at noon concerning the Pilgrimage, which is scheduled to begin in only two weeks. My home is on the tour this year. My great-grandfather bought the house over seventy years ago from the original family's descendants. Once their spinster aunt died, the ownership had passed to another branch of the family who didn't want the mansion anymore. It needed a lot of work. My great-grandfather made another good business deal when he bought it along with all the contents, many of which turned out to be valuable antiques.

The house is much too large for me, but I can't let it go. There's prestige in owning a beautiful antebellum home in Natchez. But more than that, I love this old house where I grew up. Built by William Connolly in 1835, it doesn't compare with the magnificent mansions on Homochitto Street but is pleasing, nonetheless, with its classic pediment, four massive columns across the front, and the elliptical fanlight doorways at the main entrance and on the large upper balcony. Connolly named it Wexford House, in honor of his family's roots in County Wexford, Ireland.

I pull the car slowly around in back of the main structure and stop in front of the carriage house now converted into a garage. I notice that Miss Doris has set out some house plants to get a little sun now that warmer weather has arrived in Natchez.

Miss Doris Webb, now over sixty years old, has worked for our family most of her life, as did her mother before her. She now cleans house for me but also cooks and does the laundry. Miss Doris is here every day during the week but not on the weekend, unless I need her. She has her own family and grandchildren. She used to walk to work, but now her husband, Joe, drops her off and picks her up every day. They live in a small white frame house over on Briel Avenue only a few blocks away. She's a tall, thin black lady with silver hair, a quick wit, and a quicker smile. My parents are gone now, and Miss Doris is my link with the past, ever-present.

When I got married to my college sweetheart, Brooke, I thought we wouldn't need Miss Doris as much as before. Unfortunately, two years was all the time we were given to enjoy our marriage. Brooke was diagnosed with colon cancer, but it was already too late. Four years of surgeries and chemotherapy was a losing battle. When she died, a big part of me died with her; I've never recovered.

Miss Doris was here through it all, doing her best to make it as easy as possible. After forty years, we know each other inside and out. If I could, I would legally adopt her as my mother, and I think she feels just as strongly about me. We would do anything for each other, and we both know it.

I open the back door and enter the kitchen. Miss Doris is at the kitchen sink washing some pans in steaming-hot soapy water.

"Hello, Miss Doris."

"Hi, Mister Grant. Will you be eating at home tonight? I've already cooked some lima beans and mashed potatoes just as you like them, and it'll only take me a few minutes to fry a pork chop."

"Okay, that will be wonderful. What happened around here today?"

"That landscaping crew was here again, and they've got a lot to do to get ready for the Pilgrimage as best I can tell. Your grandfather wouldn't be happy with them. You know how particular he was about those rose beds."

I nod. "He was definitely a perfectionist, especially when it came to the roses. But these days, it's the lawn and the azaleas that most people like."

"They don't know anything!" she snorts. "If they only knew the effort it takes to keep up a place like this. Did you find out anything at that meeting today?"

"No, just the usual about ticket sales and docent training. It seems that most haven't been trained yet. But our lead docent is Mrs. Louise Bennett, and she knows as much about this house as we do."

Miss Doris harrumphs disapprovingly and throws her head back, looking over quickly at me to see my reaction, but there is none — intentionally. Miss Doris doesn't like Louise Bennett, though she would never admit it.

I continue, "It's amazing how she knows every detail about the antiques that were left by the Connolly family. I swear she must be able to talk to that old spinster's ghost."

Miss Doris says, "Well, she called today to tell me she's going to bring some of the new docents over here in two days for more training. She wants them to have everything down pat. And I heard Miss Sandy Brooks is going to be one of our docents. She's a beautiful young lady and nice, too. And she has those dark, smoky eyes and that lovely smile. You ought to get to know her, Mister Grant."

I just roll my eyes at her.

She adds, "I don't remember it being this much trouble to do Pilgrimage. It's been years since the last time the house was a participant."

The house had been part of the original Pilgrimage in 1931. And after my great-grandfather bought it, the house was a regular during the 1950s. But my grandfather didn't want the bother, and it dropped off the Pilgrimage for many years. Recently, the Pilgrimage Committee made an effort to add more houses to the tour, and they wouldn't take "no" for an answer, so I agreed. Actually, participating in the Pilgrimage makes me feel more a part of the community. These few weeks in the spring and fall are so important to the Natchez economy.

"My mourning period has to end sometime, Miss Doris. Plus, it's my responsibility as the owner of an antebellum house in Natchez."

"I'm sorry Miss Brooke isn't here. She would have enjoyed it so much."

"Yes, Miss Doris, but life has to move on."

I notice that Miss Doris nods her head, but not with much conviction, and then turns to look out the window to hide a tear, which she discretely brushes away with her hand.

I have the image in my mind of Brooke in the fabulous pale blue hoop dress that she wore to the Magnolia Ball the year before she became ill. It matched her eyes perfectly, which made her ecstatic. The thought makes me happy and sad at the same time.

CHAPTER 2

I SIT AT the kitchen table, enjoying my home-cooked meal, thinking about that phone call from Tony Russell. An incident over twenty years ago, the one I was sure would haunt me forever, has finally come back to do just that.

It was a Thursday afternoon at the Tau Pi house. All of us pledges were there after class, cleaning the floors and doing other chores. There was going to be a football game at Vaught-Hemingway Stadium against LSU on Saturday, with a big party scheduled afterward. Tony Russell and Raymond Watson were sitting in the dining room taking orders and collecting money for a liquor store run on Friday in advance of the game and party. If you were under twenty-one and wanted liquor, an older brother had to buy it for you. It was cheaper, and safer, if a couple of brothers made the eighty-five-mile drive to Memphis, where they could buy as much as they wanted, no questions asked. Lloyd McClusky and his buddy John Reid usually made the run, and Tony paid them to do it out of the ten percent service charge he collected on every order. They knew some girls at Memphis State and liked to go to Memphis every chance they got. Everyone knew that Tony got his cut for "arranging" the liquor run — the only question was how much he netted. Nobody knew the answer, but Tony always had money to burn, as he made the arrangements to provide the liquor for every party and, especially, every football weekend.

In the kitchen, the cook, George Albee, was preparing dinner and had several large pots of vegetables on the stove. He had just fried some bacon. His dishwasher and helper, Jimmy White, was setting tables in the dining room. Pledges were cleaning woodwork in the party room. Suddenly, George yelled, "Fire! Fire!" just as the smell and wisps of smoke started to become noticeable to the pledges. Everyone in the dining room and party room ran to the kitchen. George had a fire extinguisher and was trying to put out the fire. I was in the back of the pack but was tall enough that I could see George waving around the extinguisher, pointing it at the stove.

Tony yelled, "Call 911, call 911!" Pledge Frederick Boone made the call. Within a few minutes, sirens could be heard. George meanwhile had put out the fire, but the kitchen was a mess from the dry chemical extinguisher. Tony was trying to help George, who had gotten some of the dry powder in his eyes. Jimmy was helping him flush out George's eyes with water.

The Oxford Fire Department arrived within minutes. They saw the fire was out and started asking George what happened. George said he had just finished frying a pound of bacon to use in his black-eyed peas recipe and had gone into the pantry to make a list of what he needed to order for the weekend. When he came out, there was a fire raging on the gas stove, apparently from the bacon grease in the frying pan, but he couldn't understand why.

Suddenly, Tony started yelling from the dining room,

"Pledges, get out here, now! All right, which one of you bastards took it?"

"Took what?" Todd Green asked.

"The booze money, that's what! It was right here in a brown envelope," he said, pointing to the table.

We all looked at each other. Sam Luning shrugged his shoulders. Dave Farren shook his head. The rest of us just stared blankly, not fully comprehending what he'd just said.

"One of you little bastards took the money when we ran into the kitchen, and we're going to find out who. Line up over here," Tony said, pointing to the open space between the dining room and party room. As I got in line, I wondered what was going to happen next, but knowing Tony, I knew it wouldn't be good.

"Just stay right here. Raymond, keep an eye on them. We're going to search around to see if they hid the envelope anywhere nearby." Dennis Grisham gave us a stern look, as if he would attack if we so much as moved a muscle.

Tony, Lloyd McClusky, and John Reid started looking under the sofa and chair cushions, in drawers, trash cans, and the bathroom and the utility closet. They looked everywhere on the first floor but found nothing.

Tony said, "Okay, so you're smarter than we gave you credit for. Let's see if you have the money on you. Start taking off your clothes — now! Put them in a pile in front of you."

Shirts, pants, shoes, and socks came off until all fifteen of us were standing there in our underwear.

"Lloyd, you and John start looking through their clothes to see what you can find. Check their wallets, too, for large amounts of cash."

After a few minutes, Lloyd said, "No, they're clean."

I wasn't very happy, standing there in my underwear, but I knew better than to say a word.

Tony shook his head. "That's impossible, one of them is just a little smarter than us. But we'll stay here all night until the thief confesses. Okay, pledges, stand at attention. Let's start with Todd. Did anyone see him during the time we all ran to the fire and afterwards?"

Sam said, "He was right next to me the whole time, so I know he didn't take it."

The process went along like this for the next fifteen minutes, and everyone had an alibi, some having more than one person who could vouch for them during the entire time.

"So, some of you bastards were working together, then?" snarled Tony.

I was starting to get mighty tired of standing. I had visions of fainting like guys do in military school if made to stand at attention for too long. My mind was racing as I wondered who possibly could have taken the money if none of us pledges did. Then it struck me that the only person really not accounted for was Jimmy White. He was in the kitchen helping George, but he was also in and out of the dining room setting tables around that time. Jimmy was in his late twenties, with a skinny frame, long light brown hair tied in a ponytail, and tattoos on his neck and arms. Let's just say he wasn't the all-American type.

There was a chance I could find out if it was him, but I wasn't entirely sure. When I was younger, I'd been able to read my mother's mind, or more accurately, access her memory.

The first time I was able to do this with my mom I was ten years old. It was the week before Christmas, and I really wanted to know if I was going to get the new bike I wanted. One night, when my parents sent me to bed, I started thinking about that bike. I thought my mother and father probably talked about it in the kitchen while I watched TV after dinner. So I really concentrated, hoping that the few words I heard would allow me to know what was said. After a little while, I started seeing images as if I was sitting in the kitchen, talking to my father, and I realized I was seeing what my mother had experienced in her memory. My father said he'd taken the bike to my uncle's house to hide. He would bring it over here on Christmas Eve. That was all I needed to know. The next day, I snuck over to my uncle's house, peeked in the garage through the window, and saw it sitting there. I was afraid to ever mention what I had done.

I had known Jimmy for about two months and worked with him frequently on kitchen detail, so figured I might be able to sort of "tune in" to his frequency.

I concentrated really hard, trying to get inside his head at a point in time just before I remembered that the fire had started. Visions, like daydreams, were coming into my mind. I was definitely in Jimmy's head and seeing things as they happened from the time George was finishing up frying the bacon. Jimmy was getting a stack of plates from the drying rack at the dishwasher to take to the dining room. George was putting the bacon on a plate and turned off the gas burner. He said to Jimmy, "Don't worry about that frying pan, I need to collect the grease, but first I need to make my pantry order. I have to call it in by four o'clock, or they won't deliver tomorrow."

George disappeared into the pantry to begin checking inventory. Jimmy walked over, and after making sure no one was watching, turned up the burner under the pan of bacon grease to "High." Then he walked out into the dining room with the stack of dishes and began setting another table. Jimmy watched as Tony and Lloyd were taking the liquor orders and putting money into the brown envelope. About that time, George started yelling, "Fire! Fire!" and we all ran to the kitchen, including Jimmy.

George had made a mess with the fire extinguisher, and there was total chaos with all of us crowded into the small space.

Jimmy quietly slipped out through the back door, made his way to the exterior entrance to the dining room from the back terrace, and picked up the brown money envelope off the table. This took all of ten seconds, then he quickly made his way back out where his old car was parked. He opened the trunk, which was filled with junk, and he stuck the fat brown envelope underneath a big toolbox and carefully closed the trunk.

He then came back through the dining room into the kitchen, where he made a fuss trying to clean up George. About this time, the sound of the siren was getting closer. Jimmy had a pan of cold water and was dabbing a wet cloth at George's face. Then, the Fire Department was there, asking George what happened, and he was trying to tell them. That's when Tony yelled, "Pledges, get out here, now!"

I knew exactly what had happened, but what was I going to do with this information? And even more importantly, how could I obscure the way I had found out?

Jimmy came out of the kitchen and started picking up plates from the tables and making a big stack to go back into the kitchen. It was apparent that George was not going to be completing a meal for us tonight. I decided it was now or never. Jimmy was going to be leaving very soon, and it was obvious that he was in a hurry.

We were all still standing at attention in our underwear while the frat brothers were trying to decide what to do next.

I said to Tony, "Sir, may I speak to you a moment?"

Tony looked at me sternly.

"Oh, are you ready to confess?"

"No, sir, but I have a suggestion."

"All right, what is it?"

"Can I tell you privately, sir?"

"Okay, okay, come over here."

I followed him to a corner of the room and whispered, "I

think you ought to check Jimmy's car, and you need to do it now. He's ready to leave. And you need to look in the trunk under his big toolbox."

Tony looked at me skeptically, trying to figure out if this was some kind of trick. "And just how do you know this, Markey?"

With a shrug, I said, "I just think it would be a good idea, sir. I saw him in the dining room, and I know he parked his car around back. And sir, I don't know what he might do to me, so would you please not tell him? You can just say that you're expanding your search."

"Lloyd, John, come with me," said Tony. "Jim, you stay here with these assholes and keep them standing at attention." Tony and his posse went into the kitchen looking for Jimmy.

It seemed like forever, but Tony finally returned with the fat brown envelope in his hand, held high over his head.

"Guess what we found in the trunk of that rat Jimmy White's car. We didn't need the police over here asking questions about this money, so we just told him to get lost, or we'd beat his ass to a bloody pulp and to never come back here again. He was happy as hell we didn't call the police. All right, you boys can put your clothes back on now. And we're ordering pizzas to celebrate."

Tony came over to me.

"Markey, that was more than a lucky guess. If you don't tell me how you knew where the money was, I'll let everyone know you must have been in on it with Jimmy, but then changed your mind and let him take the blame."

I thought hard but couldn't come up with an answer I thought he'd accept.

"Tony, that's not true. I wasn't in on it. I think I was able to read his mind. I know it sounds bizarre but that's what happened. It only happened once before and I don't know how.

Please don't tell anyone. It'll ruin me. I'll be considered some kind of freak."

With a stern look on his face, Tony said, "I don't know whether to believe you, Markey. I still think you must have been in on it with Jimmy, but I can't prove it, so I'll just forget it. But I'll be watching you. And I didn't tell him that you told me. That'll just be between us. Maybe you can do me a favor sometime." Then his face softened as if he wanted my agreement, but I just shook my head.

Tony never mentioned that incident again, though he sometimes looked at me in a strange way, but then he graduated and started law school, and I didn't see him much anymore.

After more than twenty years, it seems that Tony finally wants to pick up where he left off with that conversation.

CHAPTER 3

TWO DAYS LATER, I'm at the office waiting for Tony's call and still trying to figure out why he wants to see me. If it's because he thinks I have some kind of singular ability to access another person's thoughts, then I have to be very careful. Except for the two occasions, one with my mother and the other with Jimmy White, I haven't tried to use this psychic ability again, if I even have it.

I can think of so many situations in which I could use it for my own gain, and no one would be the wiser. It would take a little work, but I could find out the financial results of practically any company before they were announced. Or I could find out the combination to any safe or secure vault in the world and sell that information to the highest bidder.

Knowing Tony, he might try to get me to do even more questionable things. But I know it wouldn't be right, and I wouldn't do it.

Then I think of the possible danger involved. What if someone found out I had psychic powers and tried to force me to use them for illegal purposes?

And, while not illegal, there are some things that we're just not supposed to know. That's why I always resisted trying to get into Brooke's mind. I didn't want to see the agony she was experiencing during her illness, or to find out thoughts she might have had about me that were not so flattering, especially while we were dating. Somehow, it just felt wrong.

My cell phone rings. It's Tony.

"Hello?"

"It's Tony, I'm in town."

"Okay, come to my office. It's in the First Mississippi Bank building on Canal Street. You can't miss it. Park in the back lot behind the building. I'm in Suite 301. It says Natchez Trading Co. on the door."

A few minutes later, the door buzzer sounds and the wall-mounted security monitor next to the door shows a powerful-looking man in an expensive charcoal pinstriped suit. He's noticeably overweight and his once-black hair is now salt-and-pepper gray, but it's definitely Tony Russell. Not precisely the Tony I remember, but definitely Tony. I open the door.

Tony smiles and sticks out his hand.

"Hi, Grant. Good to see you. You haven't changed that much." He isn't wrong. I'm slightly graying, but I'm still the slightly-taller-than-average, slim, and somewhat handsome guy who was a freshman pledge at Ole Miss over twenty years ago. The same can't be said for Tony.

Returning his handshake, I lie and say, "You haven't changed that much either." The only thing that's still the same, as far as I can tell, is that look in his clear blue-gray eyes that says, "I'm smarter than you, and don't forget it."

"By the way, I'm sorry about your wife. One of our college buddies just told me this week."

"Thanks, Tony."

I notice that Tony has only the slightest trace of a Southern accent now. His years in Washington, D.C. must have gradually softened, then expunged his accent, intentionally or not.

Tony has begun to look around the office as I motion him inside. The room is large and has a very high ceiling. It's decorated more like a home than a business office and has a lot of expensive furnishings. He seems a little confused. It isn't what he expected.

As I walk behind my desk, Tony gestures to the room. "This is an odd place for a business, isn't it?"

"It was my great-grandfather's office. And what better place to be located when you deal with valuables of various sorts than in a bank building?"

"Yeah, that makes sense," he says with a nod, still taking it in.

Trying to see it through his eyes, I follow his gaze. It's not really an office, it's almost a gallery or even a small museum. Oil paintings hang on the walls, and bone china figurines, sterling silver pieces, lacquered boxes, and ivory carvings are displayed around the room.

"My grandfather, after he sold the bank, really got interested in collectibles, as was my great-grandfather. My grandfather was involved in collecting paintings, watches and clocks, small antiques, and especially colored gemstones. He used to bring me here and show me what he had just acquired. He liked to go to New Orleans and to plantation country in Louisiana searching for antiques of the sort he wanted. He also made trips to China, Japan, and Thailand in search of oriental art. That's where he got interested in colored gemstones — in Bangkok."

"Well, Grant, it looks like you appreciate *objets de vertu*,"

Tony says, which is his way of saying collectible pieces of real quality. His gaze wanders over to my two safes, and I can tell he's interested — and impressed.

"Great-grandfather had the big safe installed back in the 1930s."

It is a Mosler safe, with a big black door decorated with Mosler Safe Co. in gold lettering. It has eight individual compartments inside, each with combination locks, manufactured in Hamilton, Ohio. He used to brag that a Mosler safe survived the atomic bomb blast in Hiroshima, and he was right. But Mosler went bankrupt in 2001, and it's difficult to find anyone to work on that safe now. I recently bought a new Hamilton Safe Co. steel plate model with electronic locks, also made in Hamilton, Ohio, by former Mosler employees, I imagine. I store my gemstones and watches in that one.

"I take after my great-grandfather and grandfather, I guess. I found a use for that degree in fine arts, after all. Tony, take a seat." As I sit down in my high-backed leather swivel chair, I point to a black leather armchair facing the desk, and Tony sits down.

"So, what brings you here?"

"You probably heard that after law school I took a job with the FBI. After a few years, I moved over to the CIA. At the time, they needed someone with my knowledge of financial investigations. They were trying to financially strangle terrorist networks. I've worked my way up to Deputy Director. My primary responsibility now is countering national strategic threats."

Tony looks around as if to see if anyone is watching, leans over the desk, and says almost in a whisper, "We have a serious threat that we can't crack. We have just enough information to know one of our global rivals is behind it and that something very bad is going to happen — and soon. That's why we need to take a different approach than we've ever taken before, and we need to do it fast."

He sits back and waits for my reaction, but I don't move or say a word. I'm still hoping this is unrelated to what I did in college, but then he looks me straight in the eye, and I know what's coming. That episode with Jimmy White is coming back to haunt me.

"I haven't forgotten what happened with Jimmy White and that booze money, though I'm still not sure how you did it. Just so you know, I kept my word and never told anybody. I still haven't, but I think maybe it's exactly what we need for this case."

His eyebrows raise, and I try to decide what I should do. We look at each other for a few seconds more, then I bring my hands up in defense.

"I just got lucky on that Jimmy White business. I don't think I can help you."

Maybe if I deny it, he'll leave it be.

"No," Tony shakes his head once, "there's no way you would have known he put that envelope in the trunk — and under the toolbox, except by some sort of extra-sensory perception; that is, unless you were in on it with him. And that theory doesn't hold water because Jimmy wouldn't have had the time or the need to tell you exactly where he put the envelope. And, if you remember, you admitted you had some kind of ability to read his mind, and I promised not to tell anyone. And after thinking about it, I don't believe you were lying. Don't you remember all that?"

With a sigh, I realize he isn't going to let it go.

"Tony, look, I've only had a couple of confusing experiences, and I don't really know what happened. There are a lot of people who make lucky guesses about things and then can never do it again."

Tony leans forward.

"But I think you have the raw ability. Our people can work with you to see what you can really do."

"Haven't you already worked with other people that claim to be real psychics?"

"Yes, but their abilities were minimal, mostly just false claims. Actually, we never found anyone who had credible and repeatable skills. The only skill they had, if you can call it that, was being able to make lucky guesses a small percentage of the time."

Shaking my head, I say, "I've got my own life. I'm just not interested."

"Unfortunately, that's not an option."

"Really, why's that?"

He's starting to tick me off now.

"If you have the psychic ability I think you have, it could be hazardous to our country if you fall into the wrong hands. And even though the chances are remote, we can't let that happen. We'll protect you, and we'll take the most extreme measures, if necessary."

I realize he means the CIA will take me out "if necessary."

What a jerk!

Tony hasn't changed a bit. More of his usual manipulation, though more refined now. In college it was less subtle, especially when using the fraternity pledges for his own purposes, like making us sell tickets for his weekly football or basketball raffle. And if we didn't, we knew he could blackball us from the fraternity, so we had to go along.

"But how would 'the wrong hands' even know about me?"

"I'm frequently followed by foreign intelligence services. Even though I took two days to get here by a circuitous route and I'm confident that I'm not being followed, there's no guarantee. So the CIA is going to be a part of your life from now on, whether you want us or not."

Did he purposely come here to compromise me?

Trying to gather my thoughts, I sit there, glaring at Tony.

Am I going to cooperate or not? I'm not sure of the alternative. I don't really want him or anyone else to know what I can or might be able to do. I actually don't even know myself. Whatever path I choose, my life has changed.

"So you're ruining my life, and if I don't cooperate, the CIA can just make me disappear, is that it?"

"It sounds so harsh when you say it like that, Grant. We'll make it as easy as possible for you, and I guarantee you will be rewarded beyond your wildest dreams."

I feel my face getting flushed as anger fills me. I stand up with my fists clenched.

"No, Tony, I don't have to do anything for you — or anyone else. And I think it's time for you to leave." I won't be bullied or manipulated by Tony or anyone else.

Tony stays seated. Seeing I'm angry, he puts up his hand and says, "Just hold on a minute. Don't take what I said the wrong way. It's just that the stakes are very high. Our national interests are at play. Don't you want to help your country?"

I tell him, "Look, I don't work for you. The U.S. government has vast resources. Surely, you can find someone else to happily do what you want. Now get out."

"Okay, I'll leave, but let me make you an offer. I've already told you we'll reward you beyond your wildest dreams. We'll do that, but maybe we can do more — and we do have vast resources. What else do you want? What could we do that would motivate you to work with us? Just name it. Think about it. I'll check back in a few days."

Tired of his games, I say, "Don't hold your breath, Tony."

"Okay, just think about it."

With that, Tony stands up, walks over to the door, then

turns around. "You'll like working with us. We're the best in the world at what we do."

"Get out, Tony."

He says, "Bye, Grant," as he opens the door, slips out, and closes it behind him.

I decide to go to the gym to work out before going home. Maybe punching the heavy bag while thinking of Tony will release some of my stress.

Two hours later, after my workout, I actually do feel a little better.

CHAPTER 4

THE NEXT DAY, I decide to take a drive out to Ashland. There's a spot out there overlooking the river where I go when I want to think. The large barges moving slowly down the river are somehow soothing to watch. So I decide to stop at the usual place and watch the river traffic while I think about the visit from Tony.

I pull the car to the left side of the isolated gravel road, get out, and lean against the fender of the car, looking across the river to Louisiana. On the other side of the road behind me is a large field that will soon be planted in cotton or soybeans. The rotting corn stover from the fall harvest still litters the field.

I'm a person who cares deeply about our country, and it's an insult for Tony to insinuate otherwise. But I'm not really sure I can help the CIA, and I don't want to screw up my life. Working with the CIA does sound exciting, even if I have to work with Tony, but I like my life just the way it is. Well, I like how it could have been, with Brooke. Right now, it feels like I'm in a holding pattern. I still enjoy my existence, but I'm not getting anywhere. I guess that's something to think about, too.

And there's something else that really bothers me — and the conversation with Tony made me think about it. It started when my mother came home crying one day when I was a teenager. She said a woman she met at a charity benefit told her she heard that my great-grandfather, John Markey, stole a piece of jewelry worth a fortune, and if that wasn't enough, a plantation as well, from her husband's great-uncle.

My father got angry and told her it wasn't true and to just ignore such talk. I was shocked that my great-grandfather was being called a thief and asked my father to tell me what this was all about. He said the story had been circulating in Natchez for nearly seventy years. He said it was small-town talk that was kept alive by people jealous of our family's success. He was right about that because later I was taunted by another student who said our family were crooks. I settled that dispute with a punch to his gut, then his nose, which doubled him over, bloodied him, and shut him up. Many of my classmates witnessed it, and I was never bothered about this again.

My father told me after the stock market crash in 1929, when no one had any money, my great-grandfather had many visitors at the bank asking for loans using land as collateral. He turned all of them down. The bank had been run conservatively for many years, which gave it a margin of safety during the Great Depression and allowed it to remain solvent. He wanted to keep it that way.

However, a plantation owner, Jacques Devereaux, from St. Francisville, Louisiana, came to him in 1930 with a request and a unique offer. His primary plantation, Chantilly, was located outside St. Francisville, but he also owned a smaller plantation near Natchez, called Pontotoc Bluffs. It was almost 3,000 acres, located less than ten miles north of Natchez, overlooking Gibson Landing, on the other side of the river.

Devereaux owed delinquent taxes on the Pontotoc Bluffs plantation and wanted to borrow enough money from the bank to save the plantation from being auctioned by the county. My great-grandfather told him the bank would not make such a loan but that he would personally loan him the money if he had sufficient collateral, excluding the land. The plantation owner offered as collateral a piece of jewelry, which was comprised of a sizable Burmese ruby, 20.9 carats, cushion cut, pigeon-blood red, possessing perfect clarity, and set into a pendant surrounded by a double row of flawless diamonds, fifty in all. The piece originated in Paris, and Devereaux's grandfather had bought it for his wife in New Orleans during the 1850s as an extravagant gift during the cotton boom.

John Markey was already a collector of jewelry and *objets d'art* and instantly realized the significant value of the ruby. Also, Devereaux provided a recent appraisal, which was required for an insurance policy, which John Markey purchased, and added to the cost of the loan. Unfortunately, due to the state of the economy, the appraisal was significantly depressed but covered the taxes owed many times over.

My father went to his desk, opened the bottom drawer, and pulled out a yellowed envelope from which he produced the appraisal and also a carbon copy of the loan agreement. He handed the documents and the envelope carefully to me, saying, "Read for yourself."

I read them, and the content was just as he said. But there were also sharp black-and-white close-up photographs of the pendant, front and back. The appraisal listed the weight and dimensions of the individual gems and the overall piece. The appraisal stated the setting was embossed on the back with a French eagle mark, indicating it was 18k gold, as well as the hallmark of the Parisian jeweler, Mellerio dits Meller. It also stated, "The pendant hangs from a hinged bail enhanced by four small diamonds and secured with a lock and figure-8 safety catch." All of these details could be seen in the photographs.

My great-grandfather agreed to keep the ruby pendant as collateral until the plantation owner was in a position to repay the loan; there was a time limit of seven years, after which the loan could be renegotiated. The loan was made at a fair interest rate of 5%, which was the prevailing market rate. John Markey was happy to earn a safe 5%, well collateralized, while waiting to be repaid. And the plantation owner, Mr. Devereaux, was just as happy to sign the loan papers and receive the desperately needed cash.

The ruby pendant was put into a safe deposit box in the Natchez Planters & Merchants Bank vault for safekeeping. After about three years, John Markey decided to examine the pendant. He wanted to see how the diamonds were set, because he had recently been told by a jeweler in New Orleans that the old French method of setting small gems was superior to American methods, and he wanted to understand why.

When the safe deposit box was opened by John Markey in the presence of the senior bank teller, it was empty. The ruby pendant had been stolen! The Natchez police, the Mississippi Bureau of Investigations, and the insurance company commenced investigations. Unfortunately, the theft was reported in newspapers all over the state, and in every edition of the *Natchez Democrat* for weeks, spawning many theories, most of them pointing to John Markey as the thief.

John Markey was interrogated, investigated, his house searched, and he was harassed for months. He was the prime suspect, but so were other bank employees. After two long years, the investigators gave up and admitted they had no leads. At that point, the insurance company paid the proceeds of the policy to my great-grandfather, who owned the policy. After another three years, Mr. Devereaux concluded that due to the state of the economy, he would never have enough money to pay off the loan due to his other obligations. Therefore, my great-grandfather offered to buy the plantation using the proceeds of the insurance plus an additional amount of cash. Mr. Devereaux agreed as this would allow him to focus on operating his larger Chantilly plantation.

Unfortunately, many townspeople in Natchez, including relatives of Devereaux, said John Markey stole the ruby and then cheated Devereaux out of the Pontotoc Bluffs plantation. All my family members, who knew the facts, vehemently disagreed. And more than anything else, there would have been no reason for John Markey to open the safe deposit box if he knew the pendant was missing; he would have waited as long as possible, waiting to see if Devereaux defaulted on the loan. If that happened, a theft wouldn't have been necessary. The accusation of John Markey didn't make any sense. But you can't tell that to small-town people once they make up their minds.

And the worst thing was that Brooke was asked at a volunteer event by one of the upper-crust society ladies of Natchez "if I was ever going to let her wear that Devereaux pendant because I must know where it's hidden." Then I had to explain the whole thing to Brooke, and that made me angry.

A dream of mine would be to redeem our family's reputation. The only way I can see to do that would be to locate the ruby pendant and find out who stole it. Maybe by using the "vast resources" of the U.S. government, it can be done. So, perhaps I do have something to discuss with Tony, after all. My only hesitation is I'm afraid that I'm going to open Pandora's box with the extra-sensory stuff.

Actually, where I'm standing right now is part of the former Pontotoc Bluffs plantation. It's a combination of open farmland and wooded tracts. There was no plantation house — ever. There was only a small overseer's house, now abandoned, and slave quarters, now completely dilapidated and partially falling down. After assuming ownership, my great-grandfather rented the land to neighboring farmers, and that has continued to this day.

I look out across the Mississippi River and see the orange sun setting in the far distance. Now that I have a flicker of hope to resolve an important family issue, it seems to me that tomorrow will be a much better day. But I don't want to appear too anxious to help, so I'll wait for Tony to make the next move.

CHAPTER 5

FRIDAY, MARCH 22
WASHINGTON, D.C.

Tony Russell sits at his desk, trying to decide what to do. This was the first time in his career that he was indecisive. With a shake of his head, he decides to review what he knows and what he doesn't.

He knows that the intelligence community has assessed there is a significant national security threat brewing, based on sources that had never been willing to share information with the U.S. before. He knows these sources are from inside China. And he knows from those sources that the threat might be only weeks or months away from being launched.

They said they were willing to give information because they thought it was not in China's national interest and because a high-level official, who could pull it off, was behind it. But they were not willing to provide names or detailed information; they were scared for their lives. He also knows that unless they provide more information, the U.S. has no way to find out the details. That's where Grant Markey comes in.

The CIA sources said the threat was being coordinated through the Chinese Embassy in Washington. It would be impossible to penetrate the embassy with all their sophisticated electronic defenses. But they might be able to narrow down who in the embassy is involved by identifying embassy visitors and surveilling embassy staff. And if Grant can use his extra-sensory skills, he might be able to find out what exactly they are planning. That is, if Grant actually does have such skills.

But the biggest unknown is the type of threat; it could be anything. The fact that the CIA's unidentified sources were so concerned makes this an urgent situation.

The most important thing Tony knows is that he needs to move fast; there isn't a lot of time left.

Tony had always moved fast, at least one step ahead of everyone else. He had climbed to the #2 position in the CIA. He realized that the top job usually went to a politician. But if he was outstanding in his job during these difficult times, he might just be able to make the jump when the current Director retires or a new administration comes into office.

After all, it didn't hurt that he had been the single person responsible for squelching the Russian takeover of Belarus two years ago. Tony himself had been present in Gomel when Russian operative Sergey Yahontov was captured and the Russian network dismantled. This prevented the planned assassination of the Belarus president, Alexander Lukashenko, which would have led to Belarus becoming a puppet of Russia. Since neither Belarus nor Ukraine are members of the EU or NATO, they've been under intense political pressure from Russia.

Tony was privately and personally thanked by President Lukashenko. Unfortunately, he was also now on the radar of the Russian intelligence services. He knows this because of the Russian-style bugs that are found planted in his home and car on a regular basis.

A text interrupts Tony's thoughts. It's CIA Director Kohl's administrative assistant telling him to call the Director. Tony calls the Director's private number.

"Mr. Director, it's Tony," he says when Director Kohl answers.

"Yes, thanks for calling. I'm wondering how it went with your friend down South."

Tony says, "He's hesitant. He would rather not get involved. But I leaned on him pretty hard. I think he'll come around, but he might have some demands."

The Director says, "Do whatever you need to do; this is too important. Agree to anything, but don't actually act on his demands until we verify his capabilities and confirm he's cooperating."

"Understood, sir."

"Keep me advised, Tony."

"Yes, sir."

Tony knows how to play the game. He would get in touch with Grant and try to arrange another meeting. That would give Grant two more days to stew over his choices and decide on the price of his cooperation, if he had a price.

Bringing up Grant's number, Tony texts, "I'll come back to see you on Monday, okay?"

Grant texts back, "Fine, whatever."

CHAPTER 6

Around 10:00 a.m., the door buzzer sounds at my office. I look at the monitor, then let Tony in.

"Thanks for seeing me today, Grant," Tony says. "What have you decided?"

Raising my eyebrows, I say, "I've decided you need to leave me alone."

I need him to sweat a little so he'll agree to my terms.

"Grant, I've already told you we can't do that, so what will it take for you to feel okay about working with us?"

"Well, there's only one thing, in addition to being 'rewarded beyond my wildest dreams,' which you already promised."

Tony looks at me appraisingly. "What's that?"

"My great-grandfather was accused, but never convicted, of stealing an extremely valuable piece of jewelry from a safe deposit box right here in the bank. It ruined his and our family's reputation. We know that he wouldn't have done it. If you'll arrange to use the 'vast resources of the United States government' you brag about to find the jewelry and the actual thief, then I'll work with you."

"When did this happen?" Tony asks.

"In 1932 or 1933."

His eyes open wide in disbelief, and he says, "You've got to be kidding. You mean you want an investigation of something that happened almost ninety years ago?"

"No, I'm not kidding, that's the deal, take it or leave it," I say, crossing my arms.

I think Tony will have to find a way to make this work for me, because he's desperate. But knowing Tony, then he'll try to get away without fulfilling his end of the bargain, so I need to be careful.

"You mean we've got to find the jewelry and identify the thief before you'll help us?" he asks.

"No, I mean you've got to launch a serious investigation. And if I'm not satisfied at any time with the effort or progress, I quit."

The incredulous look on his face turns thoughtful, and I can almost see the cogs turning in his mind.

"The FBI has a special section that investigates cases like that, but I'll have to get approval from the FBI Director."

"Assuming you can confirm that, then I'll work with you, but I'll quit at any time if I'm not happy with how things are going."

"I guess we can't force you to cooperate," Tony says.

"And I want to have this in writing, Tony."

"What for?"

"Because we need to have an understanding. And I want to be able to feel that I have a firm commitment from you."

"Okay, then draft something and I'll review it," Tony waves a hand in the air, "but you've got to demonstrate that you actually have extra-sensory powers."

I nod. "So if we can agree, what's next?"

"Who occupies the other offices on this floor?"

"Nobody, I own the building. The bank occupies the bottom two floors, and I have the third floor. Suites 302 and 306 are empty. I use Suites 303 through 305 for storage."

"What's behind those doors?" He points to two doors along the wall between my office and Suite 302.

"The door on the left is my private bathroom. The door on the right is a closet."

"Okay, we'll occupy Suite 302. And if you decide not to work with us, we still think we ought to be right next door for your own safety."

I don't like the sound of that.

"Who is we?"

"I'll send some of our people to begin working with you as soon as possible. We're going to need a lot of your time. You'll probably need to travel a fair amount, so you need to cut back on your business — no more new customers. You can keep appointments already scheduled with old customers to avoid suspicion, but we may even need to cut back on that. Don't worry, you'll be paid well. Will $30,000 a month be enough to keep you going?"

I'm thinking that Tony wouldn't throw out his best offer, so I need to up the ante.

"I'll think about it, but I sometimes make a lot more money than that when I sell a rare collectible."

"I didn't say you couldn't do any business, just be selective. If you need to take on new customers for important sales opportunities, you can do it. Just don't let it interfere with our work."

"I'll put it in the agreement," I say.

He says, "Fine, include whatever you need to make this arrangement work."

"So, how long is this 'arrangement' supposed to last?"

"Well, the situation we've been talking about needs to be resolved within the next couple of months. But we'll want you to be available any time we need you in the future."

"In other words, you're going to pay me a retainer, is that it?"

"You can call it that."

That's exactly what I want to call it. I want to be paid full time, not just when Tony wants to "use me."

"What exactly am I going to be doing?" I ask.

"That depends on what we find out about your capabilities. We think that we'll be identifying foreign operators who might be involved in the threat, and we'll use you to try to find out if that's true and to identify more leads on who's behind it and exactly what's involved. If you have to be within line of sight or no more than some maximum distance away from a subject, that's going to complicate things and will take more time. We really are going to have to feel our way along."

I ask, "Okay, what else do I need to know?"

"Actually, one more thing. We need to have security with you twenty-four hours a day, so there'll be some agents around. They'll be inconspicuous, of course."

I imagine two men in ill-fitting suits and sunglasses trailing behind me as I run errands, and shake my head.

"Inconspicuous in a small town like Natchez? I doubt that."

"We'll get started in a few days after we sign your agreement, if we need to do that," says Tony.

"Yes, you'll need to do that, Tony."

"Well, you'll have a new tenant in Suite 302. Let's call them Canal Street Investments, Inc., okay? You can add them to the directory in the lobby. They'll be coming and going regularly, so they'll need a cover. As soon as we're all in agreement, you can have your janitor clean up Suite 302. Your new tenants will be in touch when they get in town. Our man, Craig Clayton, will be in charge."

"And if I have questions, how can I contact you?"

"Just tell Craig, he'll contact me, and then I'll call you. Let's handle it that way for now."

He gives me a 601 number for Craig; it's our original area code. These bastards are really professionals. All new phone numbers in Natchez have been given a 769 area code since 2005. The 601 area code was split several times before 769 came into existence, but 601 is still active in much of Mississippi. They're obviously doing everything possible to give these guys a local cover.

"Okay, Tony, I'll work up an agreement and you can check on the jewelry investigation. I'll text the draft agreement to you, if that's all right."

"Yeah, that's fine, and do it as soon as you can. I gotta go now. Grant, I'm sure we'll do just fine working together. Unless you need me sooner, I'll be talking to you again in a few days. Meanwhile, work with Craig. It was nice to see you again."

"Tony, I wish I could say the same — about it being nice to see you, I mean."

"Don't worry, we'll take care of you. I can let myself out."

"Yeah, right, Tony. We'll see."

Tony gets up and walks to the door. He turns and starts to say something, but then he just smiles at me and leaves.

More of Tony's mind games, what an ass!

When the door closes, I lean back in my chair, trying to process everything that just happened. I'm glad I didn't mention the Pilgrimage. Tony would have shut that down immediately if he realized I'd have strangers touring my house. Well, that's an issue for another day.

CHAPTER 7

Sitting at my desk, I wonder where all this is headed. Tony seems to be willing to agree to anything to get me on board. For my part, I'm interested in the jewelry investigation, so it might be worth it to get involved — if it clears the family name. I decide to put Tony to the test by drafting up an agreement that will push the boundaries.

I think about it for a while and then list out the conditions. Satisfied with what I'd come up with, I open up my laptop to draft the agreement. It's a quick process, and soon I'm printing out a copy to look over.

Personal Services Agreement

Grant Markey, IV (Grant) and Anthony Russell (Tony) agree as follows:

Grant Markey will provide personal services to Tony Russell for investigative work and agrees to certain conditions.

Tony Russell will provide remuneration for such services and agrees to certain conditions.

The agreement takes effect immediately when signed by both parties and it has no expiration date.

CONDITIONS

Grant agrees to be available at any time requested by Tony to perform any personal service he is qualified to perform, so long as it is not illegal or immoral.

Grant agrees to provide office space to Tony in the First Mississippi Bank Building, owned by Grant.

Tony agrees to pay Grant a retainer of $40,000 per month, payable on the last day of each month. Grant is also eligible to receive success payments for each completed assignment. The amount of such payments will be determined by Tony. The retainer will be increased annually, using the month in which the agreement is signed as the first month, by the change in the CPI-U index.

Tony agrees to pay all Grant's travel expenses. Grant's travel arrangements will be commensurate with that expected as a top-tier private sector consultant, typically first-class or business-class accommodations.

Tony agrees to provide all security staff and related equipment at all times, 24 hours a day, whether Grant is on assignment or off.

Tony will arrange for the FBI to initiate an investigation into the theft of the Devereaux ruby pendant. The FBI investigation will continue as long as this agreement is in effect or until the ruby pendant is recovered, delivered to Grant, and the thief identified. The investigation will include, as necessary, investigation of foreign nationals and following leads in locations anywhere in the world. Tony or his employer will bear the costs associated with this investigation.

Tony will pay for any medical costs that may be incurred by Grant in connection with performing the personal services in performance of this agreement.

TERMINATION

This agreement may be terminated by either party for any reason, at any time, by giving direct notice. In such case, the retainer payments will convert to termination payments, at the same rate as specified above, for a period of six months from the date of termination.

DISPUTES

Grant and Tony agree that in case of disagreements or if any issue arises not specifically covered in this agreement, they will make every effort to resolve such dispute in good faith in the spirit of the agreement.

/signed/_________/date/_____/signed/_________/date/_____

Grant Markey, IV   Anthony Russell

I feel pretty happy with it. but I'm not sure if Tony will try to bargain or not. If Tony signs it, he's committed to payments of at least $240,000. That will show how serious Tony is about all this. As long as Tony gets the FBI investigation underway, I'm happy to cooperate with him. The other remuneration is just gravy, but I'd never let Tony know that.

I text a copy of the draft to Tony and tell him that I'm ready to start at any time. On second thought, I add, "Tony, remember this party is all your idea, not mine. I'm happy to walk away."

CHAPTER 8

THE NEXT MORNING, Tony was at his desk early, as usual. Tony had been on his way back to D.C. when he saw the text from Grant come through. He read the attachment and wasn't too happy. He tossed and turned all night trying to decide what he would tell CIA Director Kohl, who had to approve the agreement.

"Mr. Director, I'm back from Natchez. He's playing hard to get. But rather than risk an outright 'No,' I asked him to tell me what it would take for him to work with us. He came up with a list, actually, a personal services contract between me and him. I'll send it over to you."

"A contract?" the Director asked.

"Yes, and it's insanely precise and demands a big retainer plus an FBI investigation into something that happened ninety years ago," said Tony.

"Is he crazy?"

"No, but I think the investigation is what he really wants, so he's insistent on that."

"Send over the contract so I can see it," said the Director.

"Okay, it's on the way now."

After a minute, the Director said, "Is this guy a lawyer?"

"No, but he's smart and very detail oriented. He's always been that way."

"You know if you sign this, you're committing us to pay him for six months even before we know what he can do."

"We already decided we are committed to using him if he's the real deal, Mr. Director, right?"

"Yes, of course, we don't seem to have any other alternative approach that can break the case. But if we don't pay, what's he going to do, sue us?"

"He's testing us, Mr. Director. If he has extra-sensory powers, he'll be worth every penny. If not, we rolled the dice and we lost."

"Well, then go ahead. There's no sense quibbling over the details. We can still decide not to pay him. I'll talk to the FBI Director. No, I'll call and give the Director the general picture and tell him that you'll call him with the specifics. Hold off on calling him until I tell you."

"Yes, sir."

"Goodbye, Tony. This better work out."

"Thank you, sir. It will."

A few minutes later, a text from the CIA Director popped up, "Call Lambert now."

Tony checked his contact list and found the private number for FBI Director Lambert and tapped the number on his phone, initiating the call. He could hear the number ringing.

Director Lambert answered, "Yes, Tony. Director Kohl told me you would call. What's this about?"

"We're trying to work out an arrangement with a special

resource to help us with the urgent security threat we talked about last week in the DNI meeting. One of the conditions for his cooperation is an investigation into a theft that occurred in 1932 or 1933. His great-grandfather was accused of stealing a rare and extremely valuable piece of jewelry from a bank vault, and it tarnished his and the family's reputation, though he was never arrested. The jewelry never turned up and could be anywhere in the world. Our candidate has a good description of the jewelry, including an old appraisal and photos, and it's unique and would be easy to identify."

Director Lambert said, "This is an odd request, but we do have a section that deals with international jewelry thefts. It was set up to combat international jewelry theft rings, but we have contacts now in almost every country, so we would be in a position to do a thorough investigation. Who knows, it might even turn up."

Tony said, "He also wants to know who stole it."

The Director said, "Really? Unfortunately, that will be harder than finding the jewelry. The agent in charge of the program will have to figure out where to start. Is this really that important — a ninety-year-old theft?"

"Yes, sir, I'm afraid it is."

"Okay, then, the CIA will owe us a favor, Tony. I'll have the agent-in-charge contact you."

Well, at least I can tell Grant that we agree to his terms, then we'll see what else he asks for.

Tony texted Grant, "We agree. What's next?"

Grant texted back, "Sign two copies, notarized, and then I will sign. You can keep one copy and I'll keep the other. Then we can start to work and the clock starts on the agreement."

Tony thought, *Bastard*, but texted, "Okay."

Then Tony thought to himself that actually he's pretty happy; he's got Grant on the hook, his boss has agreed to pay, and the FBI will take care of the jewelry investigation. And he has a chance to be a hero in the eyes of the Director, the DNI, and even the President, if Grant works out like he thinks he will. What's not to like?

CHAPTER 9

I AM IN my office catching up on e-mails while I wait for Craig Clayton. Tony had texted to say that Craig would be bringing signed copies of the agreement that morning.

A little while later, when the door buzzer sounds, I walk over to the door, check the screen. It's a tall guy about my age, wearing slacks and a sport shirt. I use the speaker, just to be cautious.

"Who's there?"

"It's Craig Clayton."

I open the door, shake hands, and wave him in. He seems friendly enough.

He holds out an envelope and says, "I'm supposed to deliver this to you."

I open the envelope and take out the signed and notarized copies. My signature line is still blank on both forms. That means I can still back out. But if I do, I'll lose the only real opportunity to solve the Devereaux jewelry mystery and clear my family's name. On the other hand, if I sign, my life will be totally changed, and probably not for the better. However, I can quit at any time, right? What the hell, I'll sign!

"I'll need to go downstairs to sign and notarize it at the bank."

"Okay, I'll go with you," he says. I shrug my shoulders and nod my head in the direction of the door.

We walk down the hall toward the elevator.

"Craig, so we're going to be neighbors, right?" I ask.

"We're going to be more than neighbors. I guess Deputy Director Russell didn't explain very much, did he?"

"Of course not, that's Tony. He would leave that to you."

We take the elevator down and go through the lobby to the bank entrance. We enter, and I wave to the assistant manager, Susan Emerson, an attractive, petite, thirty-something, with dark blonde hair and hazel eyes. She's also a part-time fitness instructor at the gym I use. She was friends with Brooke and was her personal trainer before she got too sick to go to the gym. Susan rises behind her desk, flashes a beautiful smile, smooths her skirt, and asks, "Grant, what can I do for you today?"

"Hi, Susan. I need to have these documents notarized. Oh, this is Craig Clayton. His company will be relocating to the building, on the third floor next to me."

"Nice to meet you, sir. I hope you'll be doing your banking with us. I'd be happy to help you open your accounts."

"Yes, I'll have to come talk to you about that sometime soon, Susan," Craig says.

"Have a seat, Grant, and I'll get my notary stamp," Susan says.

She goes to a cabinet behind her desk and gets out a rubber stamp and ink pad.

"Okay, Grant, go ahead and sign your documents, and I'll stamp them."

I sign, and she stamps and adds the date and her signature. "I don't need to see your ID, I know you."

I say, "Thank you, Susan."

"You're welcome, come see us more often," she says.

I smile, put the documents back in the envelope, and leave the bank with Craig right behind me.

"See you soon, Mr. Clayton," Susan says with a smile.

Craig nods, and we leave the bank lobby.

He says, "You didn't have to tell her all that."

"Yes, I did. She'll see you coming and going, so it's better to tell her now. The other bank employees will know within the next fifteen minutes. This is a small town."

When we're back in my office, Craig says, "Can we sit down and talk?"

Nodding, I motion to the chair across from me before I sit down behind my desk.

I take one copy of the signed document out of the envelope, put it in my desk drawer, and hand the envelope with the other copy back to Craig.

"According to Deputy Director Russell," Craig says as he sits down, "we're going to set up a command post in Suite 302. Our first priority is to check out everyone and everything around here to make sure we don't have any unwanted visitors that might have been trailing Tony and stumbled onto you. But first let's take a look at 302."

"You're going to do all this before I even complete the extra-sensory testing?" I ask.

He says, "Yes, the Deputy Director doesn't like to waste time. And he tells me he's already committed to paying you a lot of money, so he wants to protect his investment. The cost is minimal in his mind. That's how he thinks," replies Craig.

I say, "Okay, it's not my money being spent — I don't care."

I'm not surprised — Tony has never been good at waiting.

I give Craig the key to Suite 302 and lead the way out into the hall.

"The key also fits the lock on the bathroom door down the hall," I tell him.

"Thanks, we'll make some copies of the key. I'll introduce you to the others when they arrive. We might change the lock, though. We don't want anyone to be able to get in here and snoop around. Your door has electronic locks with a keypad, so that's probably okay," Craig says.

He uses the key to open the door to Suite 302, and we walk in and look around. The office is the same size as mine and has one closet but no bathroom.

"Your office is on the other side of that closet, right?"

"Yes."

"Good, we're going to add a door in the back of the closet so we can get quick access if we need it."

"Wait a minute, I've got valuable items stored over there. I need more protection from intrusion than an ordinary wood door." I can feel my face turning red, and I think Craig can tell.

"Okay, then. We'll make it a reinforced steel door with deadbolts. Does that satisfy you?"

"Maybe, but I need to see it," I say curtly. He looks at me as if I offended him.

"We'll send over our own guys from Jackson to do the work. They're also going to install some electronic security equipment. And not just here, in your office, too."

I just roll my eyes. He doesn't like that, either, but doesn't say anything.

"In a day or two, we'll bring in a team to work with you to find out what type of extra-sensory perception you actually have, if you have any at all."

"And if I don't have any?" I shouldn't have said that, but I just wanted to see his reaction.

"Well, that's up to Deputy Director Russell. I'll be back tomorrow to start working on the office upgrades. We'll be bringing in some extra furniture, too."

"So am I being followed?"

"Yes, for your own protection."

"And what about at my house?"

"Yes, we're outside, but we won't be a nuisance. You won't even know we're around. But we're thinking about setting up shop in your carriage house. How would you feel about that?"

"I have a housekeeper during the day, and I don't want her to get suspicious." I feel my face getting red again.

"Okay, we won't push that for now. Let's see how the ESP testing goes and then decide. I'll see you tomorrow, Mr. Markey."

"You might as well call me Grant. It sounds like we're going to be spending a lot of time together, but if you're doing construction here tomorrow and over the weekend, I probably won't come to the office, so I'll give you a key to the front door of the building."

He just smiles, nods, and walks out the door, down the hall, and disappears around the corner.

After I watch him leave, I go back to my desk and make a phone call to let the bank manager know there will be a tenant in the building this weekend.

Then I slump down in my chair and wonder what surprises they have in store for me next week.

CHAPTER 10

AFTER THREE DAYS of construction, including the weekend, the office upgrades and security system installation are complete, and the crew in Suite 302 is ready to start evaluating me. I had the feeling that those three days would be the last relaxation time I'd have for a while. I already canceled appointments for the next few weeks with the excuse of being too busy due to the Pilgrimage.

I arrive at the office at 8:30 a.m. and Craig Clayton is waiting in the hallway. I wondered how long he had been standing out there.

The moment he sees me, Craig says, "Are you ready to start to work? By the way, here's your front door key."

This guy wastes no time. He follows me into my office. I give him a long look, wondering if they're always in such a rush, before noticing the new steel connecting door. It has the deadbolt on my side, as promised.

"Let me see what you did to my office first."

The new door doesn't match the other doors, but that's okay. Then I notice what looks like an exposed nailhead in the door frame. When I look closer, I see it's not a nailhead, it's a tiny camera. I frown at it, not too happy.

"So you take away my privacy, too?"

"We need to see what's going on over here so we can provide protection."

"What's the earpiece for?" I ask, motioning to the bud visible in his ear.

"We have people outside to provide a perimeter of protection, just in case. They can communicate with me." That answers the question of how he knew exactly when I was coming up the elevator.

"I assume you have my office bugged and can hear any conversation over here, right?"

"Yes, when we feel we need to. The microphone is right over here," and he shows me where it's located behind one of the large safes.

Frustrated that any privacy I had to conduct business had disappeared, I ask sarcastically, "Did you put a camera in the bathroom, too?"

"No, we cut you some slack on that."

I resist getting angry, but just barely.

"Okay, then let's get started," he says. "You might as well open the connecting door. And the key is on your desk."

I open the door connecting to Suite 302. Sitting at the desk is a woman, nicely dressed in a blue suit, about fifty years old, and a man, casually dressed, around forty years old, sitting in a chair in front of the desk. The woman is wearing glasses, has dark brown hair, and has the look of a serious professional.

Craig motions toward the two.

"Grant, this is Dr. Cynthia Dehner. She'll conduct the

testing. And this is CIA officer Donnie Hambleton; he'll be a participant in the testing. This is Grant Markey."

Donnie Hambleton is a contrast to Dr. Dehner. He has dark blonde hair, with a slightly amused look on his face. When he stands, I see he's of average height and a little on the muscular side.

As soon as we all shake hands, Dr. Dehner gets down to business. "Our objective is to find out what extra-sensory skills you have and try to define as much as we can how they can best be utilized. In the classical definition of ESP, there are six types: telepathy, clairvoyance, precognition, retrocognition, medium-ship, and psychometry.

"Based on what I've been told about you by Deputy Director Russell, I think you may have a form of telepathy, and that is what we will be primarily testing. We may test for other forms of ESP if the initial test results take us in that direction. For the initial testing, you and I will go into your office. Craig and Donnie will stay here."

We walk back over to my office, and she shuts the connecting door.

"Before we begin, why don't you give me examples of experiences that may indicate you have ESP."

I tell her about my childhood experience involving my mother and the college experience with Jimmy White that was witnessed by Tony Russell, and she takes some notes as I talk.

"Thank you, that was helpful. Let's start with a simple test. This is called the Zener Test. I have twenty-five cards with five different images that I'll show you: a star, a circle, a cross, a square, and wavy lines. I'm going to shuffle the cards, pick up a card, and think of the shape. You take about ten seconds to try to receive my transmission of the image and tell me what shape you think I'm telling you by telepathy. I'll keep score."

I nod. "Let me see the images, so I have an idea of what I'm trying to receive."

After she shows me each image, we start. She picks out the first card and keeps it hidden from me. After a few seconds, I say, "Star." She goes through the entire deck, keeping score.

Honestly, I felt like I was just guessing.

"Okay, now I would like you to do the same thing with Donnie."

"Aren't you going to tell me how I scored?"

"Don't worry about that right now. I want to see if you score the same with a different person. That will tell us if your extra-sensory reception is greater or less with different people." She brings Donnie into my office, and we do the same thing, and he keeps score.

I again felt I was just guessing. I wonder if Donnie has ever done this before and why he was chosen to be a participant. He strikes me as someone who does what he does very well, but I wonder about him; something doesn't seem quite right. Maybe I'm overthinking everything. When we finish, Donnie leaves, and after a minute or so, Dr. Dehner returns.

"Good, let's move on." Dr. Dehner would be an excellent poker player. Her face isn't giving anything away as far as my results are concerned.

"For this next test, Donnie'll stay in the other room. He's thinking and focusing very hard on something specific. I want you to take some time and try to determine what it is."

This is suddenly getting much more difficult. Guessing one of five shapes was a piece of cake, even if I didn't have a clue. Donnie could be thinking of absolutely anything. I bury my head in my hands and try to concentrate very hard.

I finally say, "I'm not getting anything."

Dr. Dehner says, "Maybe you are, but not enough to be sure. If you can, just take a guess because it might not actually be a guess, you just aren't getting it consciously."

After a while, I do take what I consider to be a guess.

"I'm getting an image of a gun. Yes, that's what I believe he's thinking about."

But I'm not sure if it's what I perceive he's thinking about or if it's just what I would be thinking about if I were him.

She writes something down. "Okay, now let's try something different. Donnie was checking his e-mail when you got here this morning at 8:30 a.m. Can you tell me who he got e-mails from?"

I concentrate very hard again. This time, I do start to get something. In my mind, I can see Donnie's smartphone in front of me showing an e-mail from Johnny Hambleton on the screen. Then he goes to another e-mail from Russ Brownell. Then he opens another e-mail, this one from Howard Perez.

When I tell Dr. Dehner, I'm pretty certain her eyes light up briefly. She talks to Donnie, and when she comes back, she says, "That was good, now we're going to try something different. Donnie is going down the street to the coffee shop. After about ten minutes, we'll do another test. Just relax for a moment."

I wonder what's next, but mostly I'm surprised I was able to connect with Donnie to get that e-mail information. I don't know how I did it, but it wasn't that hard.

Ten minutes later, Dr. Dehner says, "Okay, Donnie is at the coffee shop. Can you tell me what he had for dinner last night?"

"It would help me if you told me what time he ate."

"Why is that?"

"Because I think I have to access his thoughts according to a particular time as a reference point."

"Try it first without knowing the time."

I concentrate very hard on figuring out what Donnie had for dinner last night, but I'm not getting anything. So I finally make the assumption that he ate at 6:00 p.m. and focus on that. I see Donnie driving and thinking about the directions to the Natchez Tavern. Also, he has someone in the car. It's Craig

Clayton! I decide to skip ahead to 6:30 p.m. They're sitting at a table in the Natchez Tavern. Donnie is eating grilled catfish and french fries. Craig has pasta and garlic shrimp. They're talking about Dr. Dehner, and they aren't very complimentary, but I'm not going to tell her that.

I tell her what they both were eating and where they were eating, and that I had to guess twice at the time to get the connection with Donnie. She seems to almost smile, but not quite.

If she were less professional, I think she would've rubbed her hands in glee.

Gathering her notes, she stands up. "I'll be back in just a minute. You can take a break."

While she does whatever she's doing, I decide to take a bathroom break and get a soft drink from the small refrigerator behind my desk.

When Dr. Dehner comes back, she hands me a photo of a man. "You don't know him, but that's the point. See if you can find out anything about him by just thinking about him."

I shake my head, like, *You really expect me to be able to do this?*

"Can you give me a hint, maybe his name?" I ask.

"Try it first with just his image."

I try, but I get nothing. "I need something to go on."

"His name is George Morgan."

Again, I receive nothing.

"Okay," she says when I tell her. "Now I want you to meet George Morgan. Let me bring him in."

George Morgan walks in and sits down; as I stick out my hand, Dr. Dehner's arm shoots between us. "Don't shake hands, not yet. Actually, don't even talk to each other. We'll do that later."

So we just sit there and stare at each other. This is so strange.

George is a black man, about thirty years old, a little on the heavy side. He's wearing jeans, a purple LSU hoodie with gold lettering, and scuffed brown work shoes that are more like boots.

Dr. Dehner says, "Grant, I want you to see if you can tell me what George was doing at 9:00 a.m. this morning."

I close my eyes and concentrate really hard. This testing is wearing me out mentally. After maybe thirty seconds, in my mind I see George sitting at the coffee shop down the street having a cup of coffee. Donnie walks in the door and sits down with him.

I tell Dr. Dehner what I saw. She nods her head and smiles just a little. She says, "Okay, I think you can take a long break now. It's almost lunchtime. We don't want to draw any attention, so just go ahead and do what you normally do and come back around 1:00 p.m."

When I get back to the office after lunch, Dr. Dehner is waiting with a new round of testing. She's sent Donnie and George across the river to Vidalia, Louisiana. She tests to see if I can connect with them at that distance. I can. And she's actually smiling now.

She wants to see how far back I can access their memories, so we try progressively further in the past. When she calls them to verify the information I'm getting, it's confirmed to be accurate. It seems there's really no limit to the information I can access in their memories.

I can do more than I thought, and it concerns me because now I realize that Tony was right; I might be a valuable commodity or a danger, depending on who's side I'm on.

CHAPTER 11

THE NEXT MORNING, Dr. Dehner says she has a few new things to work on today. Donnie and George are gone, but the doctor brings in a man I haven't seen before. She introduces him as Diego Garcia. We shake hands — after she says it's okay — but she says he can't speak to me. We look at each other for a minute or so. He is a small Hispanic man, in his thirties, slim, with lively black eyes, brownish-red skin, and a wispy mustache. He is dressed in workman's clothes, a uniform of some sort, but no company name or logo is visible. I wonder for a moment if all these people are part of the security team that Craig mentioned. Dr. Dehner seems satisfied that we've had enough time to check each other out and leads him back to Suite 302.

When she returns, she has a yellow notepad in her hand. She says, "We'll get to Diego in a moment."

After studying her notepad, she says, "Your mother has passed on, correct?"

I'm pretty sure I know where she's going with this. I've never tried to connect to my mom since she passed away. I was always afraid of what might happen. Being able to talk to my mother from the grave would seem to take away my independence, making me feel like a child again, at least, that's my fear. And it would open one more door into the unknown. Taking a deep breath to fortify myself, I say, "Yes."

She must've noticed because she studies me for a second. Then she says, "Have you ever tried to access her memory since she's passed?"

Shaking my head, I say, "No, I was afraid."

But I really didn't want to tell her why. She appeared to start to ask me, then changed her mind.

"Do you mind trying now? We need to know if it's possible."

With another deep breath, I nod. I'm still afraid of what's going to happen, though.

My palms start to feel damp, and I wipe them on my slacks before closing my eyes. I concentrated harder than I ever have before, but after a few minutes, nothing happens. Not even a twitch of a memory. I tell Dr. Dehner that I'm not able to make a connection with my mother. She makes a note on her pad. She looks disappointed.

She says, "Okay, I would like you to try to connect with Diego. He was talking with his friend, Eduardo, last night at 8:00 p.m. See if you can find out what they were talking about."

I concentrate on Diego, thinking especially about what I can remember about his face. After less than a minute, I start to get something. I notice that each time I am able to connect with someone, the image I get seems to be a little stronger and now blocks out everything else.

Diego is talking with another man, who I assume is Eduardo. They are talking about World Cup soccer. They are talking in Spanish. Diego says he likes Chivas, and Eduardo likes América. Diego says he hopes to see a match in Mexico City this year. I tell Dr. Dehner, and she is really smiling now. I can't believe I was able to understand them. I've never learned Spanish!

Dr. Dehner and I complete several more tests before she says she thinks she now has enough information to draw some conclusions. When she's written everything up, she brings her laptop and places it on my desk.

"I think you should take a look at my report before I send it Director Russell."

She seems to be seeking my approval. I see a bit of excitement in her face. As an expert in the field of psychic studies, according to Craig, she has probably never seen anyone with actual extra-sensory powers.

I read the report, which is open on her computer screen.

Deputy Director Russell,

My findings and conclusions are as follows:

1. *Grant Markey has conclusively shown he has telepathic abilities.*

2. *His ability is currently limited to accessing the memory of a subject with whom he has had direct contact. In other words, they have been in the same space at the same time, but speech or physical contact is not required. The exact limit of distance has not yet been determined.*

3. *Grant's ability to reconnect does not seem to be limited by distance and spans at least several miles.*

4. *Once Grant has made a connection with a subject, then he can access the same individual's memory at will.*

5. *Grant cannot read a person's current thoughts. The thoughts need to have been transferred into long-term memory, or perhaps only into short-term memory, before he can access them.*

6. *He can understand information from the subject's memory even if in a different language.*

7. *He seems to have the ability to recall information precisely as the subject experienced it. More testing is necessary to determine the level of detail that is available.*

8. *A subject does not seem to be aware that Grant has obtained information from the subject's memory. In other words, this is a stealth skill.*

9. *Grant seems to be able to access a subject's memory only based on a particular point in time. In other words, he cannot search a person's memory for a specific topic or event. He needs to have a time reference.*

10. *The subject must be living. Grant cannot communicate with the spirit world.*

11. *My theory is that he can detect the brainwaves being transmitted from each subject as a unique frequency. However, in a much more complex way than a simple frequency. The analogy is like a radio with presets. Once he has a "preset" with a subject's individual setting, he can access that subject again simply and quickly by returning to the corresponding "preset," which is a reference point for him.*

12. *I believe that he is only able to access the portion of the brain which stores memories after they have been transferred from the active sensory memory in the prefrontal cortex to storage in the neocortex,*

hippocampus, and amygdala. It seems this transfer takes different lengths of time to complete for each individual, from seconds to minutes, perhaps longer. Researchers do not agree on the mechanism or the time required to transfer memories from active to short-term to long-term memory. But this is why Grant can't tell what a person is thinking. He can only access what has gone into short- or long-term memory. However, he may be able to develop the ability to access active memory in the future.

13. *As far as understanding other languages, I theorize he must be receiving information at a more elemental and universal level than language, maybe similar to bits and bytes in a computer, rather than at the program language level.*

14. *There has never been, up to now, any person with proven telepathic ability, but Grant Markey definitely has it. These skills are totally unique so far as I know.*

Further evaluation is required to better understand Grant's full capabilities. I would be happy to continue this work if you request it.

Cynthia Dehner, Ph.D.

/signed/

I tell her the report is accurate as far as I can tell. I ask her who is going to see the report besides her, me, and Tony. She says Tony is the only person who might share it. I tell her I want to make sure it is kept confidential. She says, "Talk to Deputy Director Russell."

I'm sure Tony will never take a chance on me falling into the wrong hands. My psychic ability is both a blessing and a curse. I'll probably never have a normal life again, though I can hope for it, but it's what I signed up for, so I have to deal with it. Anyway, I'm getting paid generously, getting the FBI investigation I wanted, and can quit at any time, according to our agreement. I might just do that if the FBI investigation comes to a conclusion. I can't see myself doing this forever, maybe a couple of years. There have got to be other people out there with the same abilities as me. It's Tony's job to find one, which I'm guessing he'll try to do, just to keep them out of enemy hands — and to have a backup in case something happens to me.

Dr. Dehner thanks me for the opportunity to evaluate me, and then sends her report to Tony, packs up her things, and leaves the building. Craig comes over to my office just to touch base and wrap up things for the day.

He says, "You really showed some amazing skills in the testing. Tony will need to review the results with Director Kohl and Director Lambert, perhaps even with DNI Nelson. There will be only a very small group of people who will know about you. It can't be avoided when you deal with the government. They need to approve the strategy on how and when you will be used as a resource. For example, to decide if you'll be allowed to travel overseas."

I hadn't thought about this possibility. I don't like the idea of Tony or anybody else telling me where I can and can't go. I have a business that requires me to travel out of the country in search of rare gems and *objets d'art*.

CHAPTER 12

THE NEXT WEEK is uneventful. Craig spends his time making security arrangements and leaves me alone. He says Tony's waiting for new information on the national security threat that will require my involvement.

This morning, Craig comes to my office just to kill some time. He asks for recommendations on restaurants he hasn't tried in the area, especially across the river in Vidalia.

Suddenly, Craig puts his hand to his earpiece and listens intently. He lifts his left arm and talks into his sleeve. "Okay, got it."

He motions me over near the door on the side next to the monitor.

"There's a FedEx guy with a delivery to the building, but he might be an imposter. He arrived in a car, not a delivery van. If he comes to your door, play along with him, but don't open the door. Stall him."

Craig hurries over to Suite 302, and I see him open the bottom-left desk drawer and pull out a gun case. He gets out a pistol and a silencer, which he quickly screws on, then goes toward the door to Suite 302.

Within a few moments, I hear the elevator door open and close. Then the buzzer at my door sounds, and I can see a man in a FedEx uniform on the monitor. He's a short, white male in his late twenties or early thirties, wearing a long-sleeved FedEx shirt and a FedEx hat, with a large envelope in his left hand.

I say, "Who's there?"

"FedEx," the man says. "Got a delivery for Grant Markey."

"You can leave it by the door."

"I need a signature."

Knowing I need to stall, I say, "Just a minute."

I look over through the connecting door into Suite 302, but I can no longer see Craig. I'm guessing he went to look out his door to check out the FedEx guy. Then I hear a loud *thump* and quickly turn back to the monitor. I see Craig standing over the FedEx man's body.

I rush to the door and open it. "What happened, who is it?"

Craig says, "This guy was going to kill you and me both. He had a gun in his hand under the envelope. But I was a little faster." He motions to the blood pooling on the hallway floor. "Do you have any towels or anything?"

"The janitor's closet down the hall. I'll look in there." I quickly go to the closet and find rolls of paper towels, several mops, and cleaning supplies.

Meanwhile, Craig is talking to someone on his security device. In a minute or two, Donnie Hambleton exits the elevator with his gun drawn.

"Let's see if he has any ID on him. We need his car keys, too. He was by himself, right?" asks Craig.

Donnie nods once in the affirmative. "I didn't see anybody with him or following him."

Craig searches the body and takes out his wallet. He doesn't have a phone on him.

"Well, here we have Mr. John Michael Demarge of Lane, Idaho," Craig says, handing the ID to Donnie.

"Donnie, run a check on him. Let's find out exactly who he is."

I look from them to the body on the floor. "Aren't we going to call the police?"

"No, we're not," Craig says, giving me a hard look. "That would bring too much attention, and we don't want that. We'll handle it as being related to a national security incident. As such, we don't want to alert the bad guys. Let's lock the body in the bathroom until we figure out what we're going to do with him. Grant, get the key."

Not liking that scenario, but not knowing what to do about it, I go and get the key. At least there are no other tenants on this floor to worry about.

When I return, I see that Donnie and Craig have already dragged the body down the hall. I open the locked door, and they move the body inside, carefully laying paper towels where there might be any blood oozing from the wounds. They lay his weapon on his chest before I lock the door, and we all head back to Suite 302.

"Grant, we need some help figuring out where we can dispose of the body. How about a good spot around here where we can dump him in the river?" Craig asks.

I never thought I'd hear anyone say those words to me. What have I gotten myself into?

With a small shake of the head, I say, "I'll tell you anything you want, but I won't touch the body. I don't want to get mixed up with that."

"Okay, we don't know this area, so we at least need some information from you."

"There's no place I know where you wouldn't be seen. There are docks along the river, but they're public, or on commercial property — you would have to break in," I say. "But there are some big lakes around here."

"No, dumping him in the Mississippi River would be much better."

"How about dumping him into a river that feeds into the Mississippi?" I suggest.

"Yes, that might work." Craig nods thoughtfully. "Where are you thinking about?"

"The Homochitto River runs through very rural and mostly inaccessible areas and dumps into the Mississippi about twelve miles south of Natchez. I know a place down there — a fishing camp. A friend of mine owns it."

Now I'm also going to be involving my friend Ollie in this. I keep getting in deeper.

"Does he have a boat?" asks Craig.

"Yes, why?"

"Because if we throw the body off the dock, most likely it will eventually float to the surface, and we can't be sure that the current will carry it downriver like it would in the Mississippi. Do you have access to this fishing camp?"

I hesitate for a moment. I quickly decide the worse option is to be caught with the body right there at the bank, so I say, "Yes, but I wouldn't go there without asking. We don't do that around here. Besides, there are people that live along the road and they watch out for each other."

"Okay, can you ask your friend if you can take some guys fishing there later today or tomorrow — and ask if we can also use the boat?"

"Yeah, I'll give him a call."

I'm starting to wonder if I should've asked for more money.

Craig gives me a firm look; he can probably sense my reluctance. I didn't think I'd be helping cover up dead hitmen right off the bat. Or at all.

"Grant, you need to stick with us until we're sure how we're going to protect you against another assassin."

I nod, and he looks at me a moment longer, as if trying to discern if I really agree, before turning to Donnie.

"Donnie, go to Walmart and buy the largest cotton sleeping bag you can get. Make sure it's cotton, not polyester fill. Also, get some cotton rope, about ¼-inch diameter, and something to cut it."

"I've got a knife," Donnie says.

"Okay, then just the sleeping bag and rope."

⸎

While Grant was on the phone with Ollie, the man who owns the fishing camp, Craig calls Tony.

"We've got a problem. Someone hired a gunman to knock off your man, Grant Markey, and me along with him. Fortunately, Donnie spotted him and I took him out. His driver's license says he's John Michael Demarge of Lane, Idaho. We're working on how to dispose of the body," Craig says.

"Okay, get rid of him. We'll try to find out who he is and who hired him. We don't want the police involved. It'll bring too much attention. I'll send some reinforcements to Natchez. It sounds like someone had inside information on our operation and decided Grant Markey was important enough to eliminate. We'll be working to find out if our communications are compromised, or if there's a traitor among us," Tony replies.

"I would check out Dr. Dehner and everyone involved with the evaluation," Craig says.

"Yeah, that makes sense. Talk to you later."

Hanging up, Craig turns to Grant just as he finishes up his call with Ollie. "What did your friend say?"

"He said we can use his place. I have to go over and get the gate key," Grant says.

"Take Donnie with you."

⧟

By now it is mid-afternoon. Donnie is back from Walmart. He says he got what Craig wanted. He also has information about John Michael Demarge.

"He was a member of American Patriots, a well-known sovereign citizen group that hates the federal government. They have a large compound in the woods of Idaho where about thirty of them live with their families. They'll take on assaults, assassinations, and other dirty work if it's intended to hurt the federal government. It's unlikely he knew who he was working for, or why he was hired to kill us, except that we are federal agents. They need to earn money to survive, and this is one way that also suits their purposes," Donnie says.

"I checked out the car he was driving. It's a rental from Jackson-Evers airport. We'll have to get it back and, according to the paperwork, it's due today," Donnie says.

Meanwhile, Donnie and I go to get the gate key from Oliver Briggs. Since Donnie is one of my bodyguards, I figured I should get to know a little more about him.

"Where are you from, Donnie?"

I ask him about his life growing up — he's from Quincy, Illinois. He'd been married once but now is divorced. "The wife couldn't stand me being gone so much."

"Were you in the military?"

"Yes, before the CIA. I was in the Army, Special Forces, and served in Afghanistan."

"Have you worked with Craig before?"

"I've worked with Craig a long time, he's a friend. Saved me a few times. And I've returned the favor more than once. I like the excitement and the money."

I wonder about that answer. I thought he would mention patriotism, and I'm a little worried about the loyalty of someone who was primarily, or only, motivated by excitement and money. But if Craig thinks he's okay, then I have to accept that. He knows him.

Oliver Briggs's office is on Franklin Street just east of Commerce. Ollie's an attorney and had bought one of the old brick storefronts, formerly a clothing goods store, which he converted into office space. It's only about four blocks from the courthouse, where Ollie spends much of his time on behalf of his clients. He's known as a lawyer who can get a client out of serious trouble if arrested for DUI, possession of drugs, or disorderly conduct. It has earned him a good living, as it did for his father.

I got lucky and found a parking space directly across the street from Ollie's office. Donnie decided to sit in the car and watch the street with his weapon drawn while I went inside. I was back in less than ten minutes, carrying a black case.

"What's in the case?" Donnie asks.

"A Humminbird Helix fish finder. Ollie said we could use it. Actually, it'll come in handy, even if we don't do any fishing."

I drive back to the bank and park in the lot behind. The total trip only took about twenty minutes. Natchez is not a big town.

"Did he want to know who you were taking out to the fishing camp?" Craig asks when we arrive at the offices.

I shake my head. "No, he just wanted to remind me there are alligators out there and with the warm weather, breeding season will start any time now. When that happens, they get aggressive."

"Wonderful, just what we need," Craig says. "The alligators may get a meal, which might not be such a bad thing, unless it's us!"

"Donnie, get the sleeping bag and the rope. And bring your knife, too," Craig says. He'd decided it would be better if we put the body in the sleeping bag before moving it to the car.

While Donnie is gone, Craig asks me, "What time does everyone leave the building?"

"As far as I know, everyone is gone by 5:30 p.m. The bank closes at 5:00 p.m. and it takes them a little while to close up for the day."

"Okay, then let's go turn in the car at the airport and come back here around 8:00 p.m. It should be dark. Then we'll move the body to our car and go out to the fishing camp."

When Donnie comes back with the large Walmart bag containing the sleeping bag and the rope, Craig tells him of our altered plan.

"You're going to drive his car and turn it in, so put on a ball cap and sunglasses. And here's a pair of gloves to wear while you're in the car. There's no sense in leaving fingerprints. We should arrive at the airport before 5:00 p.m., so the sunglasses will be okay. We'll follow you in my car and pick you up at the terminal. Let's get your suitcase on the way out of town so you can act like you're heading to your flight after you turn in the car."

"Okay, sounds like a plan," says Donnie.

I'm quiet as they figure out the plan. I can't help but wonder if we're going to get caught with the body. It's all I can think about. Well, that and Miss Doris. I better let her know I won't be home for dinner — and maybe not for breakfast in the morning. I made the call before we drove over to Donnie's hotel.

Donnie is staying at the Hotel Vue, so it only takes five minutes to get there from the bank. He runs in and gets his roller bag and puts it in the trunk of John Demarge's rental car. He gets his Atlanta Braves ball cap and sunglasses, and changes into jeans and a lightweight blue hoodie.

We leave in a caravan onto US-84 East, then turn north on US-61 toward Jackson. About two hours later, we arrive at the Jackson-Evers Airport.

Donnie drives to the rental car return while we stop at the cell phone lot and wait for him to let us know he's ready to be picked up. I ask Craig, "How long will we wait for Donnie?" and "Wonder what the chances are that he'll be caught turning in Demarge's rental car? And if he is, what does that means for us?" In my mind, I can see things going downhill fast if that happens.

Craig says, "Don't worry, it's all going to be okay."

After about ten minutes, Craig gets a text from Donnie and we head to the terminal. When I see Donnie standing at the curb, I sigh in relief. Craig pops the trunk and Donnie puts his roller bag inside, then gets in the back seat.

Craig says, "Any problems?"

Donnie replies, "No, everything went smoothly. Mr. Demarge returned his car and went to the terminal to check in for his flight."

They decide it would be a good idea to get back to the bank, babysit the body, and wait for darkness before making another move. On the way, we stop in Brookhaven at Walmart. Craig sends Donnie in to buy three of the brightest flashlights he could find, plus one small flashlight, and extra batteries. Then Craig turns to me and says, "We've got to make a purchase, too."

I have no idea what we need, but I shrug and follow Craig into the store. Craig gets a cart and heads directly to the sporting goods section. "We need to do some weightlifting."

I have no clue what he's talking about, so I just let him lead the way. We end up in the aisle with weights. As I watch, Craig looks over the selection and picks up two ten-pound weight plates and puts them in the cart. Then after pondering the selection some more, he grabs two fifteen-pound kettlebells and puts them in the cart, too.

It takes me a few seconds of staring at them in confusion before I understand.

Craig says, "Now we need some duct tape," and I follow him to the home improvement area, where he selects a big roll of silver duct tape.

So I realize we're not going to just dump Demarge in the river, we're going to bind him up and weight him down, just like in a movie.

I just keep getting in deeper and deeper — all because of Tony. It doesn't make me very happy — it scares me.

Then I come back to the moment and hurry to catch up with Craig heading to the front of the store. We check out and meet Donnie back at the car.

When we get back to the bank, it's almost dark. The bank is closed, but I have the key to the front door. We enter the dimly lit lobby and ride the elevator to the third floor. We'd left our purchases in the SUV; we wouldn't need them until later. Craig checks the bathroom door to make sure it's still locked. It is. He unlocks the door and looks in to make sure John Michael Demarge is still there. He is.

While Donnie goes to Suite 302 to get the sleeping bag, rope, and knife, Craig and I figure out the best way to get Demarge into the bag and bound up for his journey to the river. We finally decide it would be best to drag him out into the hallway, where there's more room to work. Craig unwraps several feet of paper towels and wraps them around Demarge's neck to keep the blood from seeping onto the floor or getting onto our clothes as we handle the body. He also stuffs more towels into Demarge's shirt at the site of the chest wound.

When Donnie returns, he unrolls the sleeping bag next to the body. The bag is quite a bit longer than Demarge, which is precisely what Craig wanted.

"Donnie, unzip the bag and open it up, but first, take your knife and make slits in the outer cover. We want water to be able to get in and soak the cotton batting."

Donnie begins making slits in the cover of the sleeping bag, then turns it over and makes slits on the other side.

"I think that's enough," Craig says. "Grant, help me lift Demarge onto it."

Craig grabs the body under the armpits, and after hesitating, I grab his legs at the ankles. This is definitely more involved than I'd hoped to be. As soon as I touch the body, I feel like I've crossed some invisible line, but Craig assures me that what we were doing is okay and it "would be treated as a national security incident." I'm wondering if I should've included some sort of protection from prosecution for things like this in my agreement with the CIA.

After we place the body in the bag, Craig says, "Donnie, cut about eight feet of rope. Mister Demarge needs an extra belt." Donnie smirks as he starts cutting the rope.

When they've secured the rope around the body, Craig folds the open side of the sleeping bag over Demarge, and they zip it up. He's totally inside the bag. They then take some more rope and wrap it around the outside of the bag at the ankles and tie it with a slipknot. Then they do the same around his waist and his chest.

"Okay, then let's load him up and go. It's dark outside," Craig says. "Donnie, get the gun. Wipe it off, remove the silencer, and wrap it in a rag or paper towels, or a bag. See what you can find. We'll dump it in the river, too," Craig says.

Donnie unscrews the silencer and wipes both it and the gun with a rag he found in the janitor's closet. He then wraps them in the soiled cloth and hands me the bundle. "You can take it to the car," he says.

I have the feeling this is all routine for Craig and Donnie, but this was not the time to ask. This is like a bad dream that won't go away. I'd almost been assassinated, and I'm just glad to be alive. And I remind myself that we don't yet know if John Michael Demarge had any accomplices. I didn't think I might be killed my first day on the job! If Demarge had other helpers, they just might try to make sure I'm the one going into the river.

CHAPTER 13

BY THE TIME we arrive at Ollie's fishing camp, it is completely dark. On our way out of Natchez, we stopped at Bill's Bait Shop to get fishing licenses and bait. We had to make sure our trip appeared legit.

At the entrance of Ollie's fishing camp is a brand-new galvanized chain-link fence, with a double gate about twelve feet wide and eight feet tall. The fence appears to run about thirty feet wider than either side of the cabin, all the way down to the river bank.

I have the key to the gate and, with help from Donnie holding a flashlight, get the padlock off and the gates open. Just at that moment, the headlights of a vehicle appear on the gravel road, not far away. It sounds like a diesel truck and skids to a stop about four or five car lengths behind the Suburban. The headlights are still on, so I can't see who the driver is, but I hear the person get out of the car and shut the door.

"All right, you boys put your hands up, or I'll blow you to pieces, and I mean right now!" a gruff voice says.

"Johnny Ray Rutherford, put that damn shotgun down, you crazy bastard! This is Grant Markey. Oliver said we could use the place, and we have the key."

"Mister Grant, is that really you?"

"Yes, you crazy son of a bitch, put that gun down and step out where we can see you," I shout. Thankfully, Johnny Ray does as I order him.

"Mister Oliver asked me to watch his place for him, Mister Grant. Nobody but troublemakers come down here to the Hom-uh-chit-uh at night, sir, so I watch it for him," Johnny Ray says.

"Yes, Johnny Ray, and you do a good job." An idea came to me, and I say, "I've got some money here for you, $20. I want you to get in your truck and go back down the road and watch to make sure nobody comes down here to bother us while we're night fishing. We don't want any trouble here. Understand?" Maybe with Johnny Ray as our lookout, we won't be bothered again.

"Yessir, I'll do a good job for you, Mister Grant, I sure will."

"I know you will, Johnny Ray. Now, we're going to pull our vehicle inside and lock the gate so nobody can get in here until we leave. You understand?"

"Yessir, nobody is to come down here to bother you, right?"

"Yes, thank you, Johnny Ray. Here's your $20," I say, taking a step forward to hand him the money.

Johnny Ray beams a semi-toothless grin on his unshaven face, which strangely complements his ragged bib overalls, frayed red plaid shirt, and muddy work boots, but not the brand-new New Orleans Saints ball cap perched on his head of scraggily grayish-brown hair. The new NFL cap is a little odd for a sixty-something in overalls; a dirty John Deere hat would have been more appropriate.

"Johnny Ray, these are my friends Craig and Donnie. You help them out if they ever need it, okay?"

"Yessir, Mister Grant," Johnny Ray says as he continues to admire the twenty-dollar bill.

"All right, then. Get on down the road so you can watch out for trouble," I tell him.

Johnny Ray climbs up into his rusty old Dodge Ram truck after he carefully reaches across and leans the shotgun against the passenger seat. He waves, quickly backs out, and takes off down the road, spraying gravel.

"Is that guy someone we should worry about?" Craig asks as Johnny Ray drives away.

"No, he's harmless," I say. "And if he should happen to see something, no one would believe him. He used to hang around downtown, for years, directing traffic, shouting at drivers. Everyone knows him; he's a local character. He lives down the road in an old shack on a farm that Oliver Briggs owns. He survives on a small welfare check, and Ollie gives him a little money every month to watch the farm and the fishing camp. And Ollie lets him use that truck; he doesn't have a driver's license. He'll do anything Ollie tells him to do — or anyone else with a twenty-dollar bill."

Once Donnie pulls the Suburban inside and parks between the cabin and the dock, I close and lock the gate behind us.

Then we go over to the dock and get the ring of keys from Ollie's hiding place underneath.

There's a padlocked metal box on the cabin's covered porch where Ollie stores gasoline cans for the boat.

The cabin doesn't have electricity, so I light the Coleman lantern once we're inside. There's a stack of fishing poles leaning in the corner and a tackle box sitting on the floor next to it.

There are four beds in the single room as well as a few cabinets, a table and four chairs, and a counter made from a sheet of plywood; all pretty typical for a primitive fishing camp. And there's an outhouse behind the cabin about forty feet away, just inside the fence.

Craig says, "Now that we've seen the place, let's sit down for a minute and work out a plan." He motions to the table, and we all sit. "Grant, I think you ought to start the boat and make sure it's running properly. If it's not, we'll have to figure out something different to do with the body. If it is, then we'll bring the body in here and make the final preparations before putting it in the boat."

"Okay, that makes sense. Donnie, come with me." We go to the dock, and while Donnie holds the small flashlight, I check out the boat and start the engine. The Mercury 150 hp engine roars to life and, after half a minute, idles smoothly. I shut it off, and we go back to the cabin to tell Craig the boat's good to go.

Craig says, "Okay, let's bring the body in here."

We open the back of the Suburban and pull the sleeping bag out of the back onto the tailgate. While Craig slides the body out, Donnie lifts the middle and I grab the head end of the bag, and we slowly carry the body into the cabin and lay it on the floor. Donnie goes back to the Suburban for the other supplies and places them next to the body.

Craig unties the ropes from around the bag, unzips it, and opens it wide. The paper towels are soaked with blood, but the bleeding seems to have stopped.

"Donnie, cut four pieces of rope; two of them about five feet long and two about three feet long. Tie the two plate weights to the rope around his waist but on individual ropes close to his waist, one in front and one in back. Then tie the kettlebell weights to the rope on his waist, but let them rest near the bottom of the bag. Actually, tie a piece of rope to secure one kettlebell to each leg," Craig says.

Donnie ties the weights as Craig instructed. Once Craig is satisfied, he zips up the sleeping bag.

"How long will the weights keep him from floating?" I ask.

Craig just shrugs his shoulders. "There's no way to know. Anywhere from a few days to a few weeks, possibly. The weights plus the water-soaked sleeping bag should keep him down pretty well until the bag and ropes start to rot. But that's fine; we want Mister Demarge to be found eventually. It's cruel for his family not to get closure if the body stays missing — and when discovered, a strong warning to the American Patriots to stay away from these kinds of jobs."

I watch while Craig and Donnie duct tape the bag several times around, making sure it'll stay closed for as long as possible.

"Can I make a suggestion?" I ask. When Craig nods, I say, "Let's put him in the back of the boat. It's a Lund Crossover XS, which is a pretty big fishing boat, and it has a casting platform on the back next to the outboard motor. It would be pretty easy to lift the body and push it off the back platform — much easier than trying to dump it over the side."

"Okay, that makes sense," Craig says. "Let's carry him to the dock and get him in the boat. Donnie, go take a look around to make sure no one is out there, then we'll get it done. Grant, take the fishing poles, bait, flashlights, and the fish finder to the boat and get everything ready to go."

In a few minutes, Donnie comes back and reports all is quiet and there are no visitors that he can detect, including Johnny Ray Rutherford.

"Okay, take Demarge's gun to the boat, then come back, and we'll carry him to the dock," Craig says.

When Donnie comes back, they again lift Demarge as

before, but now it isn't so easy to carry the body with the addition of fifty pounds of weight. It takes them a minute or two to cover the fifty feet to the dock. They lay the body on the dock's edge, next to the boat. Craig climbs into the boat, and I hold the small flashlight while Donnie helps Craig move the body into the back of the boat. As soon as Demarge is in the boat, I breathe a sigh of relief. Now we should be able to easily get him out into the Mississippi and dump him right down to the bottom.

Once we're all set, I start the boat, letting it idle while I cast off the lines. Then I slowly back the boat away from the dock. Once we're away from the dock, I turn, then put it into forward gear, give it a little gas, and move out into the Homochitto River. The river is fairly shallow, though this is the time of year when it runs higher than normal. Still, it's rarely more than twenty feet deep until it empties into the Mississippi River only a little over a mile away. The fish finder shows the depth at seventeen feet as we move toward the Mississippi River. Ollie's boat has the required red, green, and white navigation lights so we can be seen by other boats, but so far there are no other boaters to be seen.

Donnie asks, "Grant, was Ollie serious about those alligators?"

Actually, I find this kind of humorous.

"Yes, keep your hands in the boat and you'll be okay," I say. "Shine your big flashlights on the bank on either side so we can see where we are." Craig and Donnie shine the flashlights on the muddy river banks. The river is about two hundred feet wide at this point but will get wider and deeper as we get closer to the Mississippi. The water is calm, at least at the surface.

It's partly cloudy, and the waxing crescent moon casts just enough light as it goes in and out of the clouds to reflect off the water, but not enough to see exactly how far we are from the shore. I motor slowly toward the Mississippi. It's a good thing we all are wearing ball caps and light jackets because it's starting to get chilly on the river.

Gradually, the reflections on the water widen and lengthen until we can see the convergence of the Homochitto with the Mississippi River. At this point, the mighty Mississippi is about a half mile wide.

There is an unusual situation at the junction of these rivers. On the other side of the river is a loop in the river that used to be the main channel but was bypassed as the river changed course sometime during the last two hundred years. The state boundary followed the old channel above this point, and that leaves the new channel entirely in Mississippi for about two miles. But south of where the old loop intersects the new channel, the old boundary between Louisiana and Mississippi is in the middle of the river starting right where we enter the Mississippi and southward from there. I suggest we dump the body in the area of the shared boundary, preferably on the Louisiana side. If the body is recovered in Louisiana, it might slow down the investigation, as the authorities on both sides of the river are not known for cooperating with each other. Craig thinks this makes sense and tells me to head across to the Louisiana side if I think it's safe to do so.

"Do you see any navigation lights up or down the river?" I ask, trying to spot any myself.

Donnie and Craig both scan up and down the river. They both say, "No, nothing." I can't see anything either, so I increase the speed of the boat to 15 knots, and we head across the river.

"What's the minimum depth you want?" I ask.

"Fifty feet, at least, preferably more," Craig says.

"Okay, we're at sixty-three feet, but if we need to get closer to the Louisiana side, it might be a little more shallow," I say.

"Go ahead," Craig says.

"I see lights in the distance, maybe a barge," Donnie says

suddenly, pointing to the south. Following his finger, I spot the navigation lights. They're quite a ways off in the distance and appear to be moving slowly.

"Donnie, get rid of Demarge's gun," Craig says. Donnie drops the gun and silencer — tied inside a plastic Walmart bag — over the side as we cruise along.

The Humminbird Helix displays the water depth as sixty-seven feet, and we were clearly on the Louisiana side of the river, though still five hundred feet from the shore.

Pulling the throttle back to an idle, I say, "Okay, how about right here?"

Craig says, "This seems okay to me. Let's get the body up on the casting platform, feet first."

We all grab the body and lift it up onto the platform, then slide it over the stern. The duct-taped sleeping bag slides silently into the water, and the heavily weighted end drops down first, causing the head of the bag to pop up out of the water. But then the bag slowly sinks out of sight into the dark water as we all watch.

Craig and Donnie act like this is business as usual. "Let's get out of here," Craig says.

I feel the same way as the bag — like I'm sinking. I wonder if this episode is going to come back to haunt us, but I'm counting on Tony to prevent that from happening.

I open the throttle and turn the boat in a wide circle, heading back over to the Mississippi side.

The barge in the distance is getting closer, but we'll be long gone by the time it gets to our location.

After returning to the fishing camp, we decide it's better if we go back to town now, so we pack up and leave. We pass Johnny Ray Rutherford, who's sound asleep in the truck about a mile from the fishing camp. Twenty bucks doesn't buy much protection, even in Adams County, Mississippi.

CHAPTER 14

CRAIG SAYS, "TONY wants to talk with you. Call him on the secure phone I gave you yesterday." I find his number in the Contacts app, put in the security code that Craig assigned to me, and initiate the call.

It only rings once before I hear Tony say, "Grant?"

"Yes, I'm here, Tony."

"We're going to step up your security. We don't yet know who hired Demarge, but we'll find out. They may make another attempt, but we'll be waiting for them.

"I've just talked to DNI Nelson — the Director of National Intelligence — and the FBI Director, as well as our CIA Director. Since we're going to use your skills inside the U.S., we need to work jointly with the FBI because they're responsible for domestic investigations. They're going to provide special agents to work with us. And we want you to have someone who can be with you twenty-four hours a day on protective duty without creating undue suspicion."

I say, "So are you telling me Craig is going to move in with me at my house?"

He says, "No, even better, two women!"

I must have misunderstood what I just heard.

"Would you explain that, Tony?"

"We know your grandfather had a brother, your great-uncle, who moved to California and made a fortune in real estate. His son had a daughter, your second cousin, Karen Markey. She still lives in California. We're going to send an agent to Natchez who will assume her identity. The cover story will be that she's decided to trace her family roots and has come for an extended visit. And she's going to be bringing a friend with her, Angie Reynolds. Karen is a CIA officer. Angie is an FBI special agent."

"Won't it be easy for anyone to figure out that Karen isn't my real cousin?"

"Most foreign services would be able to penetrate any impersonation. But this is primarily for the locals in Natchez, so they won't question why you have two female houseguests. Did the real Karen Markey visit Natchez as a child?"

"Yes, she did, but we were small children."

"That's good, so there's no way your housekeeper, Miss Doris, will know she's not for real."

"I guess that's right. But what about my real cousin?"

"We have her under surveillance, so we'll know if anyone contacts her and starts asking questions."

"You mean you're monitoring her phone calls?"

Only Tony could dream up something as slimy as this, but having an agent impersonate my cousin is kind of ingenious.

"She'll never know unless she's approached, and then we have a fabricated story ready to tell her — and anyone else — if our cover is blown."

"I won't even ask about that, but when will the agents be here?"

"They should arrive together tomorrow afternoon. You better tell Miss Doris today."

Now he's got me lying to Miss Doris. Where will this end?

"Okay, I'll tell her. What else?"

"You'll need to be ready to travel on short notice. We'll talk again after Karen and Angie are settled. Talk to you soon. Bye."

I turn to Craig, sitting in the armchair in front of my desk, and say, "I guess you know this already, right?"

"He told me earlier this morning. We're also going to bring in some electronic equipment to set up a secure VPN for all of us to use here at the office and at your house. You need to tell Miss Doris to expect some AT&T technicians to come to the house to upgrade the internet service."

"Okay, I'll do that, but she isn't going to like the short notice on having houseguests."

"Well, just tell her you didn't know yourself."

A look of concern comes over Craig's face, and I brace myself for whatever he's about to say. It looks like he starts to say something and hesitates, but then he says, "And one more thing. We think you ought to have a gun. You'll most likely never, ever have to use it, but if you get into a bad situation, you'll be glad you have it. You have a lot of valuables in your office, so you should have one anyway. I'm happy to take you to buy one and get you set up with the training so you can qualify for a Mississippi enhanced concealed carry permit."

Now I have to be my own bodyguard? Does that mean they aren't sure they can stop another attempt?

"Is this really a good idea?"

"Do you remember Tony saying that you're a valuable asset that we can't let fall into the wrong hands?'

"Yes, but I'm counting on you guys to protect me."

"I don't count on anybody, and neither should you."

At that, Craig gives my shoulder a brief squeeze. "For your

own protection, you should have one. That doesn't mean you'll ever use it."

I shake my head once, but I already know there's no way around it.

"Okay, I guess that makes sense. Shooting at targets sounds like it might be fun."

Even though I'm trying to make light of it, seeing the dead and bloody body of the assassin, who had every intention of killing me, has me good and scared.

Then, slowly standing up, Craig says, "No time like the present. Let's drive over to Jackson right now. You can apply for a permit at Highway Patrol Headquarters, and we can go on over to the gun shop after lunch."

"Well, okay, but I need to return the keys and the fish finder to Ollie Briggs. And I need to stop first and buy him a good bottle of scotch."

I can tell Craig isn't too interested in wasting any time getting to Jackson, but he says, "Yes, we may need to use his fishing camp again."

I say, "Not to dump any more bodies, I hope."

Craig says, "You never know." I cringe.

We stop at the Franklin Street Package Store, just down the street from Ollie's, and I buy Ollie a bottle of Bunnahabhain 12-year-old single malt scotch whisky.

While Craig waits in the car and watches up and down the street, I return everything to Ollie; he's very happy with the scotch.

"Did he ask about the fishing?" Craig asks when I get back in.

"I told him we caught a few small catfish and threw them back. And I told him Johnny Ray was doing a good job of watching the place. He'll let us use it again."

Before we leave town, I call Miss Doris to let her know

we'll be having houseguests. She was none too happy. Especially when I couldn't tell her how long they were staying. With that and the Pilgrimage, she was worried, and rightly so, about how we'd handle everything.

And I was still wondering how to handle Tony and the CIA. The Pilgrimage had become the last thing on my mind. For our first year back on tour, that probably wasn't a good thing, and I felt an obligation to put on a good showing because I had made the commitment.

❧

After applying for my concealed carry permit and getting some of my favorite barbecue for lunch, Craig and I head over to Crosshairs Shooting Range and Gun Shop. When we walk in, a tall guy with sandy hair behind the counter, wearing black pants and a black t-shirt with the crosshairs design on the front, waves to Craig and calls us over.

After Craig shakes hands with the man, he says, "Grant, this is Randy Lewis. Randy, my friend Grant has decided to join the good guys and get a handgun and an enhanced concealed carry permit. You need to help him choose a gun and holster. I'd suggest you stick to 9mm handguns, though. Maybe a Glock."

Randy looks me over and then tells me he thinks either a Glock G19 or G26 would be the right choice for me. He brings out two guns from under the counter. I notice Randy has USMC tattooed on one forearm, and Semper Fi on the other. I'm guessing his expertise with guns started in the Marines.

He first shows me the G19. It has a fifteen-shot magazine and is lighter than I expected. He says it has a polymer frame, but it's powerful and accurate. I handle the gun and it feels good in my hand.

He then shows me the G26 and says it is a little smaller, has a ten-shot magazine, and is easier to conceal. I handle the G26, and it feels okay, too, but the grip doesn't feel as comfortable as the G19.

He thinks the choice might depend on how they feel in my hand when I shoot. Since my hands are large, then the G19 might be better because it has a more extended grip. I say that either one would probably be just fine, depending on the holster and how it fits. I ask Craig what gun he carries. He says the G19M, a government issue that is almost identical to the G19 that Randy just showed me.

Holding both guns and weighing them in my hands, I say, "I think I'll go with the G19, but can I shoot both of them before deciding?"

Randy says, "Good idea."

He enters some info in his system, I assume to check out the guns to Craig or me, and hands the G19 to me and the G26 to Craig. He says, "Craig, why don't you take Grant to the range and let him shoot — then he can decide."

We walk over to the firing range, which is not busy. After putting on the safety glasses and earmuffs, Craig shows me the proper stance, then how to hold the gun with two hands, sight the target, and slowly squeeze the trigger, which has a built-in safety. I fire the first shot with the G19 and barely hit the target. The amount of recoil surprises me. I try again, and this time it feels better, and my shot is closer to the bullseye. In total, I fire about twenty rounds with each weapon. I like the G19 much better than the smaller G26.

After I tell Randy my decision, he runs the background check online with NICS, and it's approved in about thirty seconds. There's no waiting period for purchasing a handgun in Mississippi, and I can take the gun with me today.

"Do you know where you want to carry the gun?" Randy asks as he leads me to the display of holsters.

Starting to feel overwhelmed, I shake my head.

He suggests inside the waistband behind my right hip in what they call the four o'clock position.

He also recommends buying a holster belt. It's a steel core belt that will not sag with the weight of the gun and holster. The holster has clips that go over the belt, or I can get loops. I wind up buying the G19, an IWB holster with leather loops, the gun belt, and a thousand 9x19mm ammunition rounds. I also purchase a biometric handgun safe, gun cleaning supplies, earmuffs, and shooting glasses. Tony's going to be receiving a hefty bill for reimbursement. After all, they're the ones who wanted me to have a gun.

Once I'm settled with my new supplies, we head over to the range with the rented G19 for me to use. Before I can use my new weapon, I have to clean it, according to Randy.

That's enough for me today. But before we leave, I register for the five-hour enhanced carry permit class required to get that endorsement on my concealed carry license. Meanwhile, I'm going to have to come back to practice in the range to pass the fifty-shot qualification test that's part of the class requirement.

On the drive back to Natchez, I turn to Craig. "So why aren't you guys just providing a CIA weapon to me? That would be much simpler, wouldn't it?" He laughs and says, "You aren't a government agent, so you can't have one. But your G19 is almost exactly the same except for a few small differences, like the shape of the hand grip."

I nod, but it's got me thinking. Another reason not to supply a CIA-issued gun to me is if something goes wrong, it can't be traced back to them.

CHAPTER 15

FRIDAY, APRIL 12
NATCHEZ, MISSISSIPPI

THE NEXT MORNING when I get to the office, I'm determined to make the day somewhat normal. Since Tony blew into my life, my own work has been sadly neglected. I settle in behind my desk, preparing to call one of my regular clients who's been waiting to hear from me, when Craig walks in.

"Good morning! I was just about to make a business call, but you can stay while I'm on the call. I'll only be a minute."

Craig nods and takes a seat across from me as I dial the number. When she answers, I say, "This is Grant Markey, Mrs. Ambrose."

She says, "Yes, I have been wondering when I would hear from you."

"I've been looking for a suitable green gemstone for your pendant, and I think I have several that will work for you if you'd like to see them."

"Tell me about them."

"I have a tsavorite garnet, oval cut, 8.13 carats, with striking green color and clarity. It is a rare stone from Kenya. It's slightly less scratch-resistant than emerald, but since you want to use it in a pendant and not a ring, it will be splendid. You'll never find a better color. I also have an Ethiopian emerald, 7.30 carats, square cushion cut, also great green color, but with a little less clarity than the tsavorite. Tsavorite has more brilliance than emeralds. They would both be lovely in a pendant, but I favor the tsavorite."

"What's the price for each?"

"They're both expensive, but within the price range we've been discussing. I think you ought to see them first, decide what you like, then we can discuss the price, if you like either or both of them. I don't think anyone will have a finer green stone, Mrs. Ambrose. I think I've told you that right now high-quality green and red gemstones are very costly because the Chinese favor these colors. Prices are not going to come down because of the high demand from China and the scarcity of high-quality stones of this size."

"All right, then. Let me talk to my husband, and we'll schedule an appointment with you soon. Thank you, Grant."

"Goodbye, ma'am."

After I hang up the phone, Craig looks at me, curiosity in his eyes. "Can I see those gemstones?"

Shrugging, I say, "Why not?" and open the safe and pull out a full tray of gemstones, each in its own clear acrylic container. I put the tray on the desk and turn on the overhead spotlight.

I can see Craig's jaw drop right before he says, "Wow!" I show him the two gemstones I discussed with Mrs. Ambrose. "I've never seen anything like these in person before. I probably shouldn't ask how much these would cost."

Shaking my head, I say, "You really don't want to know,

but I hope Mrs. Ambrose's husband is having a good year in his investment business."

"Where do you get gemstones like this?"

"I buy most of them from dealers I know in Bangkok. I buy a few from dealers in the U.S. who can't move them, so they look for a wholesale buyer like me. I usually sell to collectors or to jewelers looking for something unique. Mrs. Ambrose is a special case and a good reference for me with her circle of high net worth friends."

I put the tray of gemstones back in the safe. While the safe is open, I pull out my new Glock handgun, which I'd placed in there yesterday, and set the box on my desk. Then I close the heavy door and lock the safe.

Craig shows me how to disassemble and clean my new G19. It's a simple weapon, breaking down into only four components, not including the magazine: the frame, barrel, slide, and recoil spring. The gun frame contains the trigger and other mechanical parts.

Craig says, "Maybe you should wear the IWB holster and gun around the office to get used to it?"

"Okay, that makes sense." So I take off my belt and put on the steel core belt, then put the loops on the belt and attach the holster to the loops. Craig helps me adjust the position of the holster to four o'clock. Then I put the gun in the holster and take it out a few times. It still feels a little awkward, but I think I'll get used to it.

Craig says, "There's something else I forgot to tell you yesterday. Tony insists we have passcodes for every operation. He says you never know when you might need one, and he wants us to be ready. We have several pairs of passcodes and counter-codes that we'll use. The first pair is scepter and lance; the second pair is oatmeal and okra; the third pair is bourbon and sugar.

"If you just need verification of something — you use them

in this order, such as scepter, answered by lance. Oatmeal and okra is just a spare set, used the same as scepter and lance. However, if you are under duress, use the last pair, bourbon verified by answering sugar. On the other hand, if you want to communicate that the other person may be in danger, then reverse the pair. And if they are in extreme danger, use the last pair but reversed — sugar, which is verified by bourbon. Understand?"

"Yes, I think so," I answer.

Craig says, "Tony always says not to worry, we'll know when we need to use them. We have never had to use passcodes yet, but they could come in handy someday, so don't forget."

Even though I hope we won't need them, I recite the words over and over until I'm sure I have them. Knowing Tony, I probably will need them. Yes, definitely.

While we wait for the two other agents to arrive, I try to get some regular work done. People have already started noticing something is different because I got an e-mail from a friend in Natchez asking where I've been lately. I tell him I'm busy getting ready for the Pilgrimage and with my business. I've got to get back to a more normal routine, or there will be more questions coming.

Around 3:00 p.m., I hear voices next door. We've been leaving the connecting door open, making it easier for Craig to communicate with me. I decide to go over to see what's happening.

As soon as I appear at the threshold, Craig says, "Grant, come meet Karen and Angie."

I smile and extend my right hand, wondering if I'll ever know their real names; I decide it's better not to know. It would just create confusion — and possibly danger — for them and for me.

The smaller of the two women firmly grasps my hand. "Hi, I'm Karen."

She's about medium height and weight, maybe a little smaller, almost petite, and appears to be in her late thirties, with pale blue eyes, light brown short hair, and a cleft chin.

The other woman says, "I'm Angie Reynolds." She's taller and curvier than Karen but about the same age. Her jet-black, shoulder-length hair perfectly frames her face. I wonder if her hair is dyed. I like the way it looks. She has green eyes and a dimple in her left cheek. There's something about her presence that I instantly like; I can't exactly define it, but for me — it's there.

Karen and Angie are both attractive but not so striking that they would draw immediate and unusual attention. I guess that's perfect for a government agent.

Karen says, "Let's discuss our cover story before we meet Miss Doris. Tell us everything you remember about Karen Markey."

I suddenly realize Suite 302 is functionally complete with four desks and a chair for each, but not really suitable for a group discussion.

"Let's go over to my office and sit down." They all follow me, including Craig, and we all take seats in comfortable leather chairs around the conference table.

I tell them what I remember, which isn't much, just the visit when Karen was a child, maybe around six years old. Then I share what I know about my great-uncle, which also isn't much, either.

I ask what they know about the real Karen Markey, and Karen gives me the details she has, from education to employment.

Once we've gone over all the details, including their cover story, Karen and Angie follow me to Wexford House. When we enter, Miss Doris is waiting for us in the kitchen. She has a big smile on her face and says, "Miss Karen, do you remember me?"

Karen smiles and gives her a big hug and says, "Yes, Miss Doris, I think so, but that was a long time ago."

"Yes, and you were just a small girl. You have grown up to be a lovely lady," Miss Doris says.

"Thank you, Miss Doris. Meet my friend, Angie Reynolds." Angie smiles, and the dimple becomes more pronounced.

They say hello to each other, and Miss Doris invites them to sit down at the kitchen table while getting some lemonade.

As she bustles around the kitchen, Miss Doris says, "I've been trying to think of your mother's name, and it just won't come to me."

I'm startled by the question, my eyes widen involuntarily, and I quickly look at Karen, wondering how she'll answer. Karen calmly says, "It was Christine, Miss Doris."

"Oh yes, now I remember."

This is the first sign that Karen is more than a bodyguard; she's a professional undercover agent.

"I've prepared the guest rooms for you, ladies. If you don't find everything you need, just let me know. I'll be here in the morning to fix breakfast. I hope you like Natchez. And you're here just in time for the Pilgrimage. This year, we're one of the houses on tour," she says proudly.

For a second, Karen gives me a frown, letting me know she's not happy. I'd never told Tony we would be on tour, so obviously, Karen didn't know either. I give her a weak smile, and she gives me another frown. I guess she'll be telling Tony, and I'll have to deal with him.

Dinner was a fantastic meal of fried chicken, grilled catfish, mashed potatoes, green beans, and buttery biscuits. Afterward, I take Karen and Angie upstairs and show them their rooms.

Once we're alone, Karen turns to me, raises her eyebrows,

and says sharply, "Why didn't you tell us about the Pilgrimage tours?"

"Because Tony would have told me to cancel and I couldn't do that. I made a commitment. And I didn't know someone was going to try to assassinate me. Besides, it's only for eight days during the next month."

She says, "It's going to make it more difficult for us — letting just anyone have access into the house. They could check the layout and test our security measures." She sighs. "We'll just have to deal with it, I guess — unless Tony makes you cancel."

"Well, I can't do that," I say. Now I'm really getting angry. If Tony doesn't want anyone to know I'm working with the government, they need to respect my prior commitments. I shake my head, but I don't say anything more — for now. This whole arrangement with Tony keeps turning my life upside down, more than I ever imagined.

CHAPTER 16

MISS DORIS IS busy in the kitchen when I get downstairs. I asked her to work this morning, since it was the ladies' first weekend with us. I haven't seen Karen and Angie yet. The smell of fresh coffee should entice them down soon. Miss Doris says, "Karen and her friend are very nice. Any idea how long they're staying?"

"No, I guess it depends on how they like it here; they don't seem to be in any rush to get back to California. And they should stay long enough to do the Pilgrimage tours, so at least a few weeks, anyway."

When the ladies arrive in the kitchen, Miss Doris asks them what they'd like for breakfast. I can see she's ready and willing to cook anything they want, but they both say they only wish to have coffee, yogurt, and fruit. I know Miss Doris is disappointed, so I ask for scrambled eggs, bacon, and toast. She gives me a smile and starts cooking. While we all have breakfast, I ask the ladies what they'd like to do today. They say a tour of Natchez would be helpful so they can get their bearings.

We say goodbye to Miss Doris but head to the office, taking both cars, instead of taking a tour. I unlock the door to Suite 301, and they go over to Suite 302. By the time I go over there, they're telling Craig about the "Pilgrimage problem" and discussing what they should do about it. They decide to beef up surveillance, but I don't hear them say how. I wonder if they took shifts last night standing guard. I really can't understand how I could draw so much attention from the wrong people when I haven't even done anything yet.

We spend the rest of the day touring Natchez in my car. We drive through the downtown area and past all the big mansions, which I encourage them to visit during the Pilgrimage, starting tomorrow. Karen says, "As interesting as that would be, we're not here for that. We need to stick with you unless you're with Craig or Donnie." I realize now how much things have changed for me. I'll never be alone again, at least not until this — whatever this is — is over. Since they don't want to draw any more attention than necessary, they've decided not to stick around the house during the Pilgrimage tours. And they don't want me to be there, either.

Actually, I believe they're right. It would be a convenient way for an assassin to make an easy attempt on me. There would be so much confusion in a crowd; it would be easy for a killer to escape. And until we know more about who hired Demarge, I won't feel safe.

We make a quick stop back at the office before going home. Craig is still there.

Craig says, "Tony wants you to make a trip soon. It seems there was an important meeting recently in Washington, D.C., at one of the foreign embassies."

I ask, "Which embassy?"

Craig says, "The People's Republic of China. We have some intelligence indicating the meeting was very important, but we don't know what it was about. He's waiting until they get a line on when and where you can get exposure to one of the principals. Until he tells us he's ready, we sit tight right here."

CHAPTER 17

CRAIG CALLS ME and suggests he and I go over to the shooting range for some practice. He says the ladies can stay in Natchez and get settled. And he wants me to wear my IWB holster so I can start getting used to it. When we arrive at Crosshairs, his friend, Randy, is behind the counter and greets us with a wave and a smile. Craig gives me instructions on shooting technique. My accuracy is gradually getting better. He thinks before long, I'll be ready for the enhanced concealed carry fifty-shot qualification test.

When we leave Crosshairs, we head back to Natchez, but today Craig takes a new route, turning west off I-55 onto MS-28 at Hazlehurst. Craig says, "We don't want to be too predictable with our routine. Demarge might still have friends around here."

MS-28 is a two-lane highway cutting across rural Mississippi over toward Natchez. There are no towns along the forty-six miles between Hazlehurst and the intersection with US-61 twenty miles north of Natchez. There are a few farms along MS-28 where they're raising cattle, but it's mostly just pine forest. The only traffic we encounter are a few logging trucks, pickups, and older cars, mostly all headed in the opposite direction. As we get further from Hazlehurst, the road has some sharp curves and steep embankments with deep gullies and ravines. Of course, there is thick kudzu, which has wholly covered the trees along the roadside in some places. It hasn't changed much since I was a little boy driving along here with my parents on trips to Georgetown, Mississippi, to visit my mother's family.

I ask Craig, "How much gas have you got in this guzzler?" referring to the Suburban. "There's not a gas station until you get to US-61."

He says, "We're fine, this thing's got a huge gas tank, and we're still half full."

We talk about handguns, and Craig explains the differences between Glock, Ruger, and Sig Sauer.

Then, looking in the rearview mirror, he says, "It looks like we've got company."

I pull down my visor and look in the mirror. A large black SUV, a Nissan Armada, has come out of nowhere and doesn't try to pass us. It's almost on our bumper.

Craig says, "There are two guys in there. Their best move would be to pass us, which we don't want."

He edges the Suburban over into the center of the road, blocking them from passing. At the same time, he speeds up, though the road is starting to get curvy, and the signs say to slow down.

Then the Nissan tries to go around, but Craig forces him further to the left just as I notice the passenger stick a handgun out the window. He fires but misses. Heart racing, I get my gun out in case I need it, but I really hope I won't need it.

Suddenly, the driver tries to go around on the right, but Craig easily blocks him.

Craig says, "You better get down, it's too dangerous to try to shoot out your window. I'll handle this."

Thinking that's probably a good idea, I slouch down in the seat, though I keep my gun out.

Craig is still partially in the left lane, and the Nissan can't get around. The Nissan's passenger takes a few more shots but doesn't hit anything.

Then, a loud *bam!* as the Nissan rams the back bumper of the Suburban. The impact throws my head back against the seat. Craig lets out a grunt, but says nothing else; he's focused on the road.

We're going faster now, and Craig is swerving to the left and then to the right, keeping the Nissan behind us. As we round a curve to the right, the Nissan makes an effort to go around us on the left.

I don't hear any more gunshots and can't stand not seeing, so I raise my head barely above the dashboard, trying to look in the visor mirror, when I see it coming toward us.

Craig jerks the steering wheel to the right, and the Nissan is by itself in the left lane but is facing an oncoming fully loaded log truck. We just barely miss the log truck by inches.

The Nissan isn't so lucky. They don't see the truck until it's too late. I hear the crash as the log truck and the Nissan collide.

I look in the visor mirror in time to see the Nissan flip and go off the side of the road and down the steep embankment. The log truck swerves back and forth, but the driver retains control and comes to a stop crossways in the road.

Then I hear the explosion. The Nissan's gas tank ruptured in the crash, and the fumes ignited.

By this time, Craig has the Suburban stopped halfway off the road, at the edge of the embankment. We see the Nissan is in a ball of flame amid the black smoke.

Craig says, "Nothing we can do here. Let's go!" and pulls away. I see the driver of the log truck climbing down out of his cab.

Once we're a few miles down the road, Craig says, "We'll have our Jackson field office see what they can find out about the Nissan's two occupants. I bet it's unlikely they'll be able to identify them. It seems someone wanted to finish the job Demarge started. We need to be doubly careful now."

I'm shaking and feeling kind of sick to my stomach. Is this how it's going to be from now on? Thank God I'm with Craig.

"Who do you think it was, Craig?"

"It might have been whoever hired Demarge. They probably met him at the airport when he arrived in Jackson and gave him his instructions. They might have even been waiting to pay him off when it was over. But when he didn't get in touch, they knew something was wrong and decided to take over themselves — or they could have hired these guys from a different source. I doubt the American Patriots would have sent someone else without knowing what happened to Demarge. And since it's been four days, I think they hired a couple of hitmen from a different group. I hope we can identify the bodies, but I'd say the chances are slim with the fire."

I nod in agreement and say, "Yeah, unfortunately, that makes sense."

We make the rest of the trip in relative silence, watching the road for any new attackers. Fortunately, there aren't any.

As soon as we get safely back to Wexford House and tell the ladies what happened, Craig calls Tony.

After Craig gives Tony the details, Tony says loudly enough

for me to hear even though he's not on the speaker, "We're still trying to find out who's behind the assassination attempts. Tell Grant we'll do everything possible to protect him." Then he changes the subject, and I can't quite hear what he's saying.

After listening for a few minutes, Craig says, "Yes, Director, I understand," and hangs up.

"We're taking a trip to New York as soon as we can arrange it, maybe tonight," says Craig.

"I thought you said the meeting was in Washington, D.C."

He says, "That's right, but something changed, and that's about all Tony told me. And all of us are going." Craig doesn't say anything more, but I can tell he's deep in thought. I know better than to ask for more.

At least I can finally do something useful instead of just shooting at the gun range.

Later, Craig tells us that one of the subjects in the embassy meeting in Washington, D.C. had gone on to New York. Tony has information that the man purchased a ticket to the Metropolitan Museum of Art. The tickets are valid for three days. The plan is for us to stay close to the museum, and when we hear he's there, we'll hurry over and try to get close enough for me to make a mental connection.

Craig booked us into two suites in The Surrey Hotel, East 76th Street, about seven blocks from the museum, which sits along Fifth Avenue on land carved out of Central Park by the city in 1871. From the hotel, it's only five minutes by taxi.

I call Miss Doris to tell her we are going on a trip. Explaining why I'm making an impromptu trip to New York when the Pilgrimage is about to start, and having her believe me, was more challenging than expected. This was despite the fact I told her a gemstone dealer called me to say he had some extraordinary stones that I might like. She was even more bewildered about why Karen and Angie would make the trip with me. I told her we were going to make it a mini-vacation and stay several days.

CHAPTER 18

THE MORNING AFTER we arrived at the hotel, Craig gets a call from the front desk, telling him a messenger has delivered a package. Once it's brought to the suite, Craig opens the large brown envelope and studies the contents.

He hands me a stack of 8x10 photos of the man we'll be trying to intercept at the museum. Craig says, "This is a photo of Yang Kexin of the People's Republic of China, the Assistant Deputy Chairman of the Central National Security Committee. He's our subject and was one of the principals in the meeting at the PRC Embassy in Washington. Yang made a special trip to Washington for the meeting, so we know it was important. He met with Minister Hua Shuang, second only to the PRC Ambassador, Han Zemin."

The photos show a fairly tall man, about fifty years old, medium build, with black hair and a round, pleasant face. Yang is in several of the photos walking with another man. This man is much bigger, with black hair, about thirty-five to forty years old, muscular, with a square face, eyes not much more than slits, and a menacing countenance. I assume this man is his bodyguard. Craig agrees.

Craig says, "They're staying at the Ritz-Carlton Hotel overlooking the Pond at the south end of Central Park. They can get to the Met in about ten minutes if traffic is good, so we have to be ready to move quickly.

"You three are going to the museum, and I'm staying here to coordinate the operation. You need to download an app called W-T onto your iPhones. It'll allow us to talk to each other, like walkie-talkies. Use your AirPods. Karen and Angie, don't take your weapons; and your museum tickets are in the envelope."

Craig gets another phone call. He says, "Yesterday morning, Yang went to the PRC Consulate on 12th Avenue. He then returned to the hotel, had lunch, and visited the museum for a couple of hours in the afternoon. He spent most of his time in the Asian Art gallery on the second floor. We'll have to stay ready because he could leave his hotel at any moment. And luckily, he only has one bodyguard with him."

Not having anything else to do, I play out in my mind how the museum visit might go. I want to get relatively close to Yang for at least a full minute. I also hope there are a few other tourists around, just enough so that Yang won't notice me. We've never tested how a crowd of people affects my ability to connect with a subject.

I ask Craig, "The meeting at the embassy — exactly when did it take place?"

He says, "Last Tuesday, about 10:00 a.m., the best we can tell."

We wait and wait. Around noon, the maid knocks on the door and wants to clean the room. We decide to go have lunch. The Café Boulud opens at noon and is the only restaurant in the hotel, so we head downstairs. I order fontina ravioli, the ladies order the baby gem lettuce salad with chicken, and Craig orders mushroom risotto. We all hope we don't get a call telling us we need to leave before we finish our food. Unfortunately, Craig's phone rings partway through our meal. When he hangs up, he says, "Yang is at the Met. He and the bodyguard went to the restaurant on the fourth floor. He'll be there for a while, so no rush."

We go back to the suite to wait for another call. While we're waiting, Craig pulls out some sort of electronic equipment and scans the suite for bugs and doesn't find any. Since it's April, the weather in New York is not exactly warm. While we wait, we gather our jackets, check out our phones to make sure the walkie-talkie app is working, and make sure we have our Met tickets.

I happen to realize that I haven't heard a word about the Devereaux investigation that Tony promised to begin. I ask Craig, "What's the status of the Devereaux investigation? You know about that, don't you? I think I should see some action on that before I do anything for Tony."

Craig says, "Yes, I know about it. Tony has someone from the FBI Jewelry & Gem Theft unit scheduled to contact you. This sudden trip postponed the contact until we get back to Natchez."

I involuntarily frown, which Craig can clearly see. I wonder if Tony is jerking me around. It wouldn't surprise me. If I find out he is, then I'm done with this.

"I want to talk to that agent as soon as I can. I want that investigation to get underway. That's part of the deal," I tell Craig.

"I'll make sure Tony knows you're anxious about it."

I give Craig a stern look but don't say anything more.

Just before 1:30 p.m., Craig gets another call. "Yang has left the restaurant. It's time for you three to get over to the museum. When you arrive, I'll let you know where Yang is in the building."

We go downstairs and ask the doorman to hail a taxi. Within a minute, a cab is at the door, and we're on our way to the Met. As we turn the corner onto Fifth Avenue, the imposing figure of the Met is visible. The building is two million square feet behind the beaux-arts facade.

Karen pays the taxi driver, and we ascend the three tiers of stone steps to the main entrance, where we quickly pass through security. Karen goes through first, then Angie, and I'm last.

This is the first time I've been here, and it's impressive. The Great Hall's scale, the height of the ceiling, and the size of the archways separating the main hall from the galleries are imposing.

Angie tells Craig we're past security and inside the Museum. He tells us to proceed through the Great Hall to the Medieval Sculpture Hall and wait. It's a central location. He says Yang is in the Lehman Collection, and he wants us to wait to see where they go next because the galleries are small in that section of the museum. He prefers to make contact in a larger gallery where we are less likely to be noticed.

In a few minutes, Craig tells us Yang and his bodyguard have come out of the Lehman Collection and have stopped at the restroom in the French Decorative Arts area, south of our location. He says we should continue to wait but be ready to move quickly.

We consult our maps of the museum to see where he is.

Soon after, Craig tells us to start moving south toward the Modern and Contemporary Art Galleries. We enter the main gallery and immediately see Yang and the bodyguard.

We quickly realize why they came to this particular gallery. It houses the immense and iconic silkscreen portrait of

Chairman Mao by Andy Warhol. They're standing in front of it, discussing the painting excitedly in Chinese.

There are other visitors in the gallery, including a family with two teenage girls. I'm starting to feel anxious about what we're doing. Up until this point, using my extra-sensory skills didn't seem particularly dangerous — the two assassination attempts resulted from my connection with Tony, not from using my skills. But looking at Yang's intimidating bodyguard, I'm starting to think this was a bad idea.

What if they notice us? What if this will just bring more assassins to my doorstep? And maybe this even puts Miss Doris in danger, which I hadn't even thought about before.

Taking a deep breath, I steady my nerves. Luckily, the bodyguard is focused on the family, who are now right next to Yang. As the bodyguard's attention is split between Mao and the family, I take the opportunity to move a little closer.

Suddenly, Yang hands his phone to one of the teenagers. He asks her to take his photo with the bodyguard in front of the Mao portrait. The older girl takes the phone and directs them where to stand. She tells them to smile, which neither does, and she takes several photos. She shows Yang, and he wants her to take some more shots but with just himself this time.

While Yang is getting his photo taken, the bodyguard's attention moves around the room. We feign interest in the Mao and move even a little closer. As soon as I feel the bodyguard's eyes on me, my heart starts racing.

Am I going to faint? I feel like my legs are starting to tremble. The thought occurs to me that the bodyguard has a gun and probably will use it.

Luckily, Yang takes the phone back and distracts the bodyguard with the photos. They both are obviously happy with the images and thank the girl.

I had more than a minute to make a mental connection

with Yang, but I was somewhat distracted, so I won't know if I was successful until we get back to the hotel, and I have a chance to concentrate. Yang turns and leaves the gallery with the bodyguard right behind.

I almost stagger to the visitor's bench in the gallery. I have to sit down for a minute, the stress of the encounter proving almost too much for me. A thousand scenarios of how this could have gone wrong play in my head. Angie and Karen take a seat, also. They look quizzically at me. I nod, and Karen tells Craig we made contact with Yang.

After a minute to catch my breath and with the bodyguard gone, I feel much better. I ask if we can look at the Vincent Van Gogh paintings on the second floor before leaving. They say yes, and we head upstairs. I already looked up the location this morning on the Met website.

The elevator is right outside the gallery we've just left, so we take it up. The paintings are in Gallery 825, which is not far away. Van Gogh's *Self-Portrait with a Straw Hat, Sunflowers, Oleanders, Cypresses, Roses, Bouquet of Flowers in a Vase*, and a few other Van Gogh paintings are on permanent display. The most extensive collection of his work is at the Van Gogh Museum in Amsterdam, which I hope to visit someday, but this opportunity to see even a few real Van Gogh paintings makes the trip worthwhile for me. I've been interested in Van Gogh since my fine arts classes at Ole Miss. After taking about half an hour to view the Van Gogh paintings, I feel much better. I'm ready to leave, and so are the ladies.

We grab a taxi outside the Met and head back to the hotel. When we get to the room, Craig is anxious to know how it went. I tell him it seemed to go okay, but I don't know yet. I need some time alone to concentrate. He says okay, and I go to my bedroom while they wait in the suite's living room.

Sitting down on the bed, I close my eyes. Maybe it'll be

easier to connect with Yang when I first saw him before going further back. That would have been around 2:30 p.m. Images of the museum started to fill my mind — but nothing from Yang. I try to concentrate even harder — still nothing!

Maybe the distractions from the other tourists in the gallery were just too much, or perhaps it was the stress from feeling a threat from the bodyguard. Or maybe I need to be closer to Yang to make a connection. After all, during the evaluations with Dr. Dehner, I was always very close to the subjects, most times actually touching them briefly and talking directly with them.

I come out to the living room of the suite. Craig, Karen, and Angie all look at me with anticipation. I shake my head no.

Craig, with a surprised look on his face, says, "Really?"

I try to explain to him what I think happened. Then I say, "Look, I think I need to try again, but this time get a little closer, if possible."

He says, "Okay, let me find out where he is." He gets on his phone and makes a call. He hangs up and says, "Yang went from the Met to the Guggenheim."

I exclaim, "Oh, that's good. I know the Guggenheim, and it's not far from here, either. But I don't want him to recognize me, or us, from the Met. Can you have one of your guys go to the gift shop downstairs and buy a Yankees ball cap and an NYC sweatshirt for me? Ladies, did you bring sunglasses and hats?"

Karen says, "Sunglasses, yes, hat, no."

Angie says, "Same here."

"Okay, that'll work. As soon as the ball cap and sweatshirt get here, we can go."

About five minutes later, a bellboy knocks on the door and hands a bag to Craig. He tips him and hands me the bag. It contains a Yankees ball cap and a gray sweatshirt with New York in black script across the chest.

"That'll do," I say as I grab it from the bag and start removing the tags. I remove the price sticker from the ball cap, too.

"Let's go. We'll use the walkie-talkie app, Craig. Are your guys in the Guggenheim? Will they be able to tell us where Yang is in there?"

"Yes, they can do that."

The Guggenheim Museum is just north of the Metropolitan Museum by about five blocks, between 88th and 89th Streets. We take a taxi up Madison Avenue, turn left at 89th, and again at 5th Avenue. The cab lets us off in front of the Guggenheim.

"Before we go in, let's talk about this. Have you been here before?" I ask. They shake their heads no.

"Okay, it's like a big open atrium. The art exhibits are hung on the outer wall or on pedestals along a wide spiral walkway that encircles the atrium with about six spirals. The idea is to take an elevator to the top and walk down the walkway, enjoying the exhibits. It's bright and noisy in there. I think it will be better for me if I intercept Yang as he leaves the building. He's less likely to recognize me there than if we try to catch up with him along the spiral walkway. We'll wait at the bottom in the main lobby. You ladies need to maintain some distance from me to make it harder to recognize us as a group they saw at the Met. When they leave, I'll follow them out the door and get as close as I can, and then break off in the opposite direction out in front. You two follow them out, but well behind me — you got it?"

They nod yes, but I can tell they don't like it as it will minimize their ability to protect me. I say, "Don't worry, the bodyguard's not going to do anything right there in a busy public place."

I wonder why I said that, since I've been the one who's been worrying so much. I want to prove my bravery, I guess.

We go inside, buy our tickets but hang around in the lobby area. I ask Craig on the walkie-talkie app, "Where are they?"

He says, "A little more than halfway down, but they are moving along."

"Okay, thanks," I reply.

After about twenty minutes, I spot them at the beginning of the last spiral just above the lobby. It won't be long now. The large oculus in the middle of the dome lets a lot of light shine down into the atrium, and the sunglasses are needed. Since the building is constructed of concrete, the sound bouncing off the hard surfaces makes it quite noisy. Both things combined provide a perfect cover if you don't want to be noticed.

I move over between the pedestrian ramp descending to the lobby floor and the main entrance. I see Yang coming. I judge the distance and start strolling toward the revolving door so that I'll get there just before he arrives. I enter the door first, then Yang, and his bodyguard is last. The revolving door is relatively small, definitely only enough room for one person at a time and no room to move to the right or left at the exit point.

As soon as the door reaches the point that I can exit, I step out. Yang is in the compartment right behind me. I suddenly drop my phone and stoop to pick it up. He crashes into me, and we both go down in a heap. The bodyguard is blocked inside the revolving door.

I try to get up, but he is laying on me. I say, "Sorry, but I dropped my phone," as we both struggle to stand up.

He says, "Excuse me. Very sorry, very sorry."

I say, "That's okay, are you hurt?"

By that time, the bodyguard has pushed his way out of the door and is helping Yang. He hurries him away, talking in Chinese. I turn and walk in the other direction to the corner of 89th Street. In a few seconds, Karen and Angie are there next to me.

"Why did you do that?" Karen says. "That was too danger-ous. What were you thinking?"

"Well, I had to get close to him, and that seemed like a good way to do it." I smile stupidly.

"Well, I guess it worked, then," Angie says, smiling.

"Totally unexpected, I have to admit," says Karen.

I feel much better now — like I redeemed myself somehow. And it felt good to actually do something.

When we get back to the hotel, Craig wants to know how it went. I tell him it was good — even better than at the Met. Angie and Karen look at each other and at me but don't say anything.

Craig says, "Good, glad to hear it."

I go to my bedroom while they wait again in the living room.

Sitting down on the bed, I close my eyes. I decided to try again to connect with Yang at the Met. Images of the museum start to fill my mind. Yang is walking toward the Modern and Contemporary Galleries and is talking to his bodyguard. I can hear that they're talking in Mandarin, but I can understand them.

Yang says, "Li Qiang, I want a photo of the Chairman's portrait to show my family what I've seen on my cultural tour in New York."

The bodyguard says, "The guidebook says it's over here."

Once they enter the gallery, Yang looks at the massive 14.7-by-11.4-foot portrait and says, "Why would the artist paint such a portrait of someone he doesn't know and cannot possibly understand?"

Li glances around the room before looking down at his guidebook. "Because he only paints famous people and Chairman Mao was the world's most famous and enigmatic person in 1973."

Then Yang hears the family approaching and turns to look at them. As he does so, he briefly notices me, Karen, and Angie but gives us no thought. He then pulls his iPhone from his pocket and gestures to the teenage girl to ask if she will take a photo. The girl takes several images, then Li steps away, and the girl takes several pictures of Yang by himself in front of the portrait. He thanks her and turns away. He doesn't look in our direction again. Then Yang and Li walk away.

I go out and tell Craig that I have made a connection to Yang Kexin and ask if he can find out where Yang is at the moment. It's not important where he is now, but the information will help me understand my capabilities. He sends a text message and gets a reply. "Yang is back at the Ritz-Carlton, about a mile away."

I tell Craig that it will help me to see a photo of Hua Shuang, so I know if I am connected to the correct meeting. He says he'll get one. Within a couple of minutes, he receives a file photo by text message of Hua Shuang, which he shows to me.

After telling him I'll see what I can do, I go back to the bedroom and concentrate on making a connection again with Yang. I try to index back to last Tuesday at 10:00 a.m.

Yang is sitting in an office, apparently at the PRC Embassy, across the table from Hua Shuang.

Hua says, "Why did you make the sudden trip to Washington?"

"Deputy Chairman Li Zhang Yong has decided it is time to implement Plan 23-2."

"What is Plan 23-2? I don't keep up with such detailed plans at the National Security Commission."

Yang glances around the room. "Can we talk of such details here, Hua Shuang?"

With a dismissive wave, Hua says, "The PRC Embassy has the strongest electronic security anywhere. You can speak openly here."

"Plan 23-2 will cripple the United States banking system," says Yang.

"Such a significant plan needs the approval of President-General Secretary Xiong Fu Wen and the Politburo Standing Committee. Does Li Zhang Yong have their approval?" says Hua with a look of disbelief on his face.

"The Deputy Chairman says he has the authority he needs," replies Yang confidently.

Hua shakes his head and impatiently asks, "Why are you telling me all this? What do you want?"

"The cyber defenses of the major banks and the clearinghouse for financial transactions are robust. Our cyberattack group, APT10, has not been able to penetrate them. So we need to recruit IT personnel in those institutions to infect their systems with our software. We are willing to pay large bribes to get this done. Money talks in the United States. We want you to facilitate the hiring of these mercenaries. We suggest you use Allison Murphy. She helped us when we needed information from the Indian embassy."

"What's the deadline to get this done?" asks Hua resignedly.

"Li Zhang Yong tells me there will be a small trial run of Plan 23-2 in Thailand soon, no later than next month. So we need these individuals hired and ready to go by that time. If the Thailand test is successful, we will be ready to execute here whenever Deputy Chairman Li decides."

"How much money can we spend?" Hua shifts in his chair, obviously uncomfortable with all this.

"I have $200,000 for you to pass on to Allison Murphy.

You can promise as much as you need. And you can make substantial up-front payments. But we don't plan to make the final payments, if you understand what I mean."

Yang notices that Hua suddenly stiffens.

"What about Allison Murphy?"

Yang leans forward, turning an angry glare on the man across from him. "We cannot leave a trail, Hua Shuang."

"Yes, I understand. Does the Ambassador know about this?" Now Hua is starting to sweat.

"No, and he is not to be told. Do you understand?" says Yang forcefully.

"Yes, I understand," he says submissively.

"Thank you for your time. Please keep me informed through our most secure communications channels. I will be going to New York for a few days and then heading back to Beijing." He stands to signal the meeting is over.

When Craig told Tony what I'd discovered, Tony suggested we celebrate this success in finding out the details of the threat. I'm relieved I was finally able to connect to Yang but can't understand why I wasn't successful the first time.

We left at 8:00 p.m. for dinner at Le Bernardin on 51st Street, a French restaurant specializing in seafood. We were lucky to get reservations. When we arrive, the restaurant is almost full, but we're guided to a lovely table at the window. We order caviar and oysters with a glass of Dom Perignon 2009 each. Karen and Angie order lobster, Craig orders scallops, and I order black bass; each dish is exquisitely prepared. We drink a bottle of William Fevre Chablis Les Preuses Grand Cru 2016.

Angie keeps us laughing with her stories about her first trip to NYC as a special agent.

"I was in Queens and asked someone if I was in Newark. They thought I was crazy," she says. "Then, the next day, I was trying to get to Brooklyn and wound up in Harlem!" She laughs, and her laugh is contagious. I couldn't help but laugh with her. There's something about her sense of humor that I find captivating.

We decide to skip dessert and just have some coffee. Afterward, we take a taxi back to the hotel and arrive at 10:30 p.m.

I'm beginning to like this style of living.

CHAPTER 19

THE NEXT DAY, while Karen, Angie, and I visit the Museum of Modern Art to see Van Gogh's *Starry Night*, Craig calls us and says he found out Hua Shuang is in New York on business. He's at the PRC Consulate and has gone out to lunch with one of the consulate staff. They are at 44 & X, a trendy restaurant in Hell's Kitchen, not far from the consulate. If we hurry, we can have lunch there, and I can make contact with Hua, which may be useful later.

We quickly exit MoMA and catch a taxi to 44 & X. Within ten minutes, we're seated three tables away from Hua and his associate. This is perfect, as Hua has never seen any of us before, so we don't have to be too careful. I feel more relaxed than yesterday because Hua doesn't have a bodyguard, unlike Yang. The restaurant has a varied menu, but we all order sandwiches, which should be served quickly. While we're waiting, I study Hua. He's a typical bureaucrat; nothing unusual in his appearance. After about fifteen minutes, Hua and his companion leave the restaurant. We finish our sandwiches soon afterward and go too.

In the afternoon, we walk from the hotel through Central Park over to The Dakota, a famous landmark apartment building in New York. On the way, we stop at the "Imagine" mosaic in the Strawberry Fields section of Central Park dedicated to John Lennon. He lived at The Dakota for the latter part of his life before being murdered outside the building in 1980. I love this part of New York — Central Park, the famous buildings surrounding it, the carriages in the park, and the potential to see some real celebrities.

After we return to The Surrey, I try to make a mental connection with Hua. He's talking with the other man from the consulate. He never notices that we're seated nearby, I note with relief. In Mandarin, they're discussing an issue related to processing visa applications, which sounds like typical consulate business. I report to Craig that I can contact Hua whenever needed.

I am relieved that I had no problem connecting with Hua. Maybe the trouble accessing Yang was an aberration.

Tony calls, and Craig puts him on the speaker. "I want to share our objectives so we're all on the same page.

"1. Our primary objective is to block Plan 23-2 from being successful in the U.S.

"2. Find out who is involved in carrying out this plan and arrest them.

"3. Capture the malware so it can be studied, and a countermeasure developed.

"4. Determine who in the Chinese government has authorized this attack.

"We think it's best to let the plan more fully develop. I'm

speaking for DNI Nelson, Director Kohl, Director Lambert, and myself. We'll start digging for information on Allison Murphy, and we'll get it to you as soon as we can. Any questions?"

Craig says to Tony, "So, our primary objective is to get the intelligence. But we might be instructed to do other things, too. And you'll coordinate between the CIA and the other agencies to make sure we accomplish the four objectives. Is that right?" The rest of us nod our heads in agreement.

"Yes, that's it," says Tony.

As we make our way back to Natchez, I think about Allison Murphy and the IT mercenaries. They will die if they're successful. But if we stop them, they'll go to prison for a very long time. I convince myself that they're involved in criminal activity. Because of that, they should know the consequences, so my conscience is clear.

And I'm still waiting to find out if it was the Chinese, Russian, Iranians, or someone else who hired Demarge to take me out. Tony says they're trying to find out. I sigh. I wish I had never met Tony.

CHAPTER 20

WHEN WE ARRIVE home, we tell Miss Doris about visiting the Met, the MoMA, and all the lovely restaurants. I also lie and tell her I bought some gemstones that are being shipped. She looks at me as if she knows I am telling a white lie, just as if I was seven years old again. I hate to mislead her, but I'm not sure if telling her what's going on won't put her in danger, and I never want that.

While we were gone, the house hosted two tours in the Pilgrimage. Miss Doris says they were both busy and that we had a lot of visitors in the house. As best she could tell, Mrs. Louise Bennett and the docents did an excellent job. I wasn't planning to be a docent, but I was planning to be at the house when I could — greeting visitors. I guess that's out now — damn Tony!

I'm still thinking about the Pilgrimage and whether any foreign agents were at my house when I arrive at the office the next morning. I open the connecting door to Suite 302 and find Craig bent over behind one of the desks.

"What are you doing?" I ask before placing my things down on my desk, leaving the connecting door open.

"Sweeping for bugs. I'm going to send a team to sweep the house, too, so tell Miss Doris some people are coming by to fix the WiFi."

I sigh inwardly, wondering what my life has come to that I have to worry whether my home and my office are bugged. Then I pick up the phone and tell Miss Doris what I'm supposed to.

I ask Craig, "So what's next?"

He says, "We're trying to get information on Allison Murphy. She seems to be the logical trail to follow. We are also monitoring Hua Shuang's phone calls. We can't listen in, but we can get the metadata, meaning the incoming and outgoing phone numbers, times, length of the call, etc. We're also watching Yang Kexin."

"See what you can find out about the Devereaux investigation, okay? You said Tony made arrangements for someone to contact me, but it hasn't happened."

Craig says, "Yes, I'm going to talk to Tony about that this morning."

I nod and sit down at my computer to respond to e-mails. I've got work to do, and I can't suddenly cut myself off from the world.

I can hear Craig on the phone over in Suite 302 but can't make out what he's saying.

The meeting at the PRC Embassy was the first time I've used my extra-sensory powers for real. I wonder if I missed anything in the conversation between Yang and Hua. I think about it, and without any effort, the memory pops right up in my mind in the same detail as before.

The ease of recall surprises me. I haven't accessed Yang's mind — the memory came from me — I can tell the difference.

I don't know how, but it might be significant that once I access memory from another person, I store an exact copy of the subject's memory in my own mind. I go over the entire Hua-Yang meeting again, but I can't come up with anything new. The reason this might be important is if I have stored a segment of a subject's memory, and they died, I would still have this memory for future use. I try it with my mother's memory of the bike incident, and it's the same.

Craig knocks, comes through the connecting door, and says, "Wear your gun around the office today. You need to get used to it. By the way, you're going to get a call about the jewelry investigation any minute."

In a few minutes, my secure phone rings. I answer, "Hello, Grant Markey speaking."

"Good morning, my name is Justine Aebischer, Special Agent-in-Charge of the FBI Jewelry & Gem Theft Program. Deputy Director Russell asked me to call you. He gave me a general outline, but I need to discuss the details. FBI Director Lambert told me to give this our highest priority."

"Thank you for calling, Justine. May I call you Justine? You can call me Grant."

"Yes, that's fine. I understand you have an appraisal document and photos. Can you send me the originals or copies of equivalent quality? I'll send you the address, and you can send them by FedEx."

"Yes, I can do that."

"Does the bank have any records from that period?"

"I don't know, I'll have to ask. What are you looking for?"

"A list of the safe deposit box numbers and their owners between the time the pendant was placed in the box and when it was discovered missing. Also, I'd like a list of bank employees."

I'm impressed. Justine really sounds like she knows what she's doing.

"And I would like to know the relatives of Mr. Devereaux who lived in Natchez at that time, if you know. If you don't, we can search various databases to try to find out," Justine says.

"Okay, I'll let you know what I can find. I assume you have the secure e-mail address that Deputy Director Russell has set up for me?"

"Yes, I've got it. You'll have mine when I send you my mailing address. And you can call me on this secure phone number."

"Thanks, maybe we can talk in a few days," I say.

"Yes, sounds good. Goodbye."

I'm happy when I hang up, not only because it seems there's going to be a real professional effort to solve this case, but also that Tony appears to be holding up his end of the bargain. I just hope it stays that way.

At noon, we decide to walk down the street and around the corner to the Cotton Alley Café. Craig checks the place out and asks the greeter if we can sit in the corner. She says we can, and seats us on the opposite side of the room, away from the counter and the cash register. Craig wants to sit with his back to the wall, facing the front of the cafe.

"Why are you so particular about where we sit?" I ask.

He says, "Because someone wanted to kill us, and they might try again, even in a public place, though doubtful. But I also want to see if anyone is showing unusual interest in us."

His eyes sweep the cafe and outside through the large plate-glass windows in the front. After a minute, he seems satisfied and studies the menu. We both ordered iced tea, unsweetened. After our server brings the drinks, Craig orders the fried chicken sandwich, and I order the club sandwich.

I realize I know next to nothing about any of the people

who've invaded my home and office. "Craig, where are you from? I recognize the accent, but I can't quite place it."

"I grew up in Milan, Tennessee."

"You're tall, did you play basketball?"

"Yes, for the Milan Bulldogs. We had some good teams. Regional champs when I was a senior."

He still looks like he could play, though I imagine he was a bit thinner, almost rawboned, in those days.

"Where did you go to college?"

"UT, the University of Tennessee — studied finance and international business." Then he whispered, "That's what got me into the CIA, along with good grades."

"Ever married?"

"No, but came close a couple of times. I guess I never stayed in the same place long enough."

"How long have you known Tony?"

"About fifteen years. Tony was my first Case Officer Supervisor. We hit it off and have been working together ever since."

Just as I was about to ask another question, Craig's phone rings. He answers and listens intently. After he hangs up, he levels a look at me, and I can tell I'm not going to like whatever he's about to say. "That was a member of the crew who went to your house. They found a bug — actually, they found two bugs. One was in the dining room, and the other one in the south parlor."

I'm so surprised, I almost drop my sandwich in my lap. Someone going into my home and planting bugs means I really am a target now. I'm none too happy about the invasion of my privacy, and I'm sure my face shows it.

"And did they remove them?"

He shakes his head. "No, we don't want them to know that we know. We might be able to use it to our advantage later."

This is not something I wanted to hear.

I ask, "Do you know who planted them?"

"Our guys say the devices are generic, so it could have been anybody."

"Any guesses?"

"Well, it could have been the Israelis, the British, the Iranians, the Russians, or the Chinese. They're all aggressive about planting listening devices like that. But for my money, it was the Russians. And I imagine the bugs were planted by the same people who wanted to kill us."

"But why would they bug my house?"

"The office is too secure, so your house is their best bet. And because they want to know why Tony came here to see you. The Russians hold a grudge against Tony because he always gets the best of them."

I just shake my head.

Tony's involvement always makes everything so complicated.

"How long will they keep this up?"

"As long as they want. They could stop at any time. If they decide you're not a threat to them, they'll quit. But it seems like they already decided you are."

"Do you think they followed us to New York?" I ask.

"Possibly, but I doubt it, though they might have put someone on our tail when we arrived."

In a way, I hope they did because unless it's the Chinese, the other intelligence services would have concluded based on our actions in New York that we're not interested in them.

"And if the Chinese followed us?"

"Then we might be headed for trouble, because if they saw you at the Met in the same room as Yang, then again with you at the Guggenheim, they know we're after them for something."

But at least they likely don't know why. Only Yang and a few others know about their secret plan.

I quietly ponder the possibilities, of which there are too many to count.

"How do you know we aren't being tailed right now?"

He laughs and says, "We have our people watching to see if we're being followed, and as you can tell, I'm watching, too. So far, the answer is no."

But we could be a target of assassination at any time.

I vow to myself to start wearing the Glock at all times as soon as I receive my permit.

I'm starting to think I never should have agreed to any of this. Damn Tony.

CHAPTER 21

CRAIG SAYS, "CLEAN your gun. You need to be able to do it blindfolded." I grumble but get out the supplies, put on blue nitrile gloves, and take the gun apart on a silicone mat to keep my desktop clean.

While I'm cleaning the gun, there's a knock on the door of Suite 302. It's a UPS delivery. Donnie has called to tell him the driver came in a real UPS truck. Craig opens my door and peeks down the hall to make sure the driver doesn't have a weapon drawn. Once he's satisfied, he asks the driver who he's looking for. The driver says, "Craig Clayton," and Craig says, "That's me." He signs for it, takes the envelope, goes over to Suite 302. The ladies stop looking at their computers while he opens the envelope.

"Interesting," he says, then looks up at everyone. "We have something to work with here."

Taking off my gloves, I head into Suite 302 as Craig passes around several photos of a Chinese woman.

"This is Allison Murphy."

I look at the photo. "She doesn't look like a Murphy to me."

He says, "Her maiden name was Chen, her parents are naturalized citizens from China. Allison was born here. She has a degree in computer science from Georgetown. She worked for the Department of Defense for a few years, then started her own IT personnel contracting business out of her home in Arlington, Virginia. She supplies IT contractors to the government and to private industry. One of her major client groups is the financial industry. She takes a cut of the contract, usually twenty percent, and the contractor gets the remainder. She has a loyal group of employees who have been with her for a long time; each employee makes at least twenty percent more than a direct employee of the hiring company. Her husband, Dr. John Murphy, is a professor at the Institute of Political Science."

"What's next, then?" I ask.

"For now, we wait. We need to make sure Allison is involved in this before we take any action. We'll be analyzing her phone's metadata as well as Hua's. We're also tailing him."

After the bank opens for the day, I decide I better find out about the safe deposit records. I ask Angie if she'll go with me because I know I'm not supposed to be without protection. She says, "Sure, why not?" We take the elevator to the first floor and walk through the lobby to the bank entrance. When we go inside, several people say hello, but the bank manager, David Feldman, comes out to greet us. He's a handsome, forty-ish-year-old man with thick black hair who transferred to this branch from McComb about two years ago. He probably thinks of me as the landlord that he needs to keep happy.

"Grant, what can I do for you today?" says David.

"Hi David, let me introduce Angie Reynolds. She's a friend of my cousin, Karen. They're visiting me for a while."

"Hi, Angie."

"David, I came down to find out if you still have any of the old bank records in storage."

"What do you need?"

"Actually, I'm interested in the safe deposit box records from the 1930s. I want to investigate a mysterious disappearance from a safe deposit box that happened while my great-grandfather ran the bank."

"Well, I don't know about that, but we have boxes of old records stored in Suite 206. We don't have any of the old account transaction records, but we have boxes of miscellaneous ledgers. Let me ask Susan Emerson to take you up there, and you can look around to see what you can find."

"Okay, that sounds good," I say.

"Just a moment, then." He walks over to Susan's desk, and they talk for a few seconds. She grabs a set of keys from her desk drawer, and they walk back over to us.

"Susan will take you upstairs, and you can take a look. Happy hunting." While I'm introducing Angie, David leaves and returns to his office.

Susan says, "Anything that happened in the 1930s was way before First Mississippi Bank was involved, so we don't care if you look at the records or even take them."

We go up to Suite 206, and Susan unlocks the door. Old cardboard boxes are sitting on racks of steel shelving. The boxes have writing on them with dates and descriptions of the contents. They smell musty, and the room is dusty, too.

"I suggest we look for boxes that are dated 1930 or 1931 and are labeled as 'Safe Deposit Boxes.'" Angie and Susan nod, and each takes a set of shelves, and I do, too. After a few minutes, Susan says, "Here are boxes dated from 1930 to 1935."

Angie and I stop what we're doing and go over to her to take a look. One of the boxes says, "1930-35 — Safe Deposit Logs."

I say, "Let's look inside this one."

I pull open the flaps of the box. Inside are bound ledger books — one for each year. I open the 1930 ledger. It has two sections. The first section is a list of all the safe deposit box numbers from 100 to 199, along with the renters' names. The second section contains in chronological order the individual occurrences of renters signing for access to their box. Each entry lists the date of access, the box number, the initial of the bank representative who gave access, and the renter's signature. I notice that my great-grandfather, John Markey II, had two safe deposit boxes, 103 and 178. I have no idea why or if that has any significance.

I then grab the 1931, 1932, and 1933 ledger books. They are organized in the same fashion.

I tell Susan, "I found what I was looking for. Can I take these ledgers with me?"

She says, "Yes, David said that would be fine."

We go back downstairs, and I thank her and David.

On our way back to Suite 302, I decide to make digital scans of the Devereaux pendant appraisal and the accompanying photos. I print out a copy of the scans, and they look to me to be as good as the originals. I send them to Justine Aebischer by e-mail, ask her if the scans are good enough or if she still needs the originals. I tell her about the safe deposit ledger books and ask if she wants me to send them to her.

Justine says she wants the ledger books as soon as possible and says she can work with the appraisal scans for now. After reading the appraisal and studying the photos, she says that the pendant is stunning and would be highly desirable in the world of illegal jewelry sales. She thinks she will ask a certified jewelry appraiser to update the appraisal value.

I feel better now about everything Tony's putting me through now that the Devereaux investigation is actually getting started.

CHAPTER 22

THURSDAY, APRIL 25
NATCHEZ, MISSISSIPPI

THE NEXT WEEK is best described as boring, but I can see the signs of tension increasing on Craig's and Karen's faces. I surmise this is because they don't know what's going to happen next, and they don't like the uncertainty. But Angie doesn't seem to be affected. She says her theory is that China won't do anything in Thailand until they have their plan in place in the U.S., and Allison is the key over here. So she thinks nothing is going to happen until Allison makes a move. That makes sense to me.

I'm beginning to appreciate Angie's old-fashioned common sense.

I spend my time getting used to wearing the Glock, going to target practice, and cleaning the weapon. My enhanced carry class at Crosshairs is coming up soon, and I want to pass on the first try. The Pilgrimage continues, and every day that the house is on tour, we get a full report in the evening from Miss

Doris. Meanwhile, I try to ignore the bugs but still wonder who planted them.

Maybe I should have dropped out of the Pilgrimage after all. If we weren't a part of the tour, it would've been more difficult for someone to plant the bugs and get familiar with the house's layout. I wonder if they're going to come back while they have the chance during the Pilgrimage. At least there haven't been any more attacks on my life. I wonder why.

I've been able to spend some time phoning my contacts in the world of collectibles. We discuss new items that have come on the market and the results of recent auctions. Some of them ask where I've been lately. I tell them I've been busy with the Pilgrimage. I don't know how long that excuse is going to wash.

Finally, after a week of waiting, Craig comes into my office and says, "Well, things are starting to move. Allison and Hua met in person at the Ritz-Carlton in Arlington. The interesting thing is that Hua and Allison both brought identical Nordstrom shopping bags to their luncheon and discreetly switched them. We suspect he gave her a bag of cash to pay off the mercenaries she's lining up.

"Tony wants you to see what you can find out about Hua's meeting with Allison. He wants to know specifically what instructions he gave her, and anything else you can learn. The meeting happened at noon sharp yesterday at the hotel's restaurant, Fyre."

I nod my head, and Craig returns to his office, closing the connecting door behind him. Leaning back in my chair, I concentrate on Hua, trying to focus on noon yesterday.

After a few seconds, I begin to get images. Allison Murphy is sitting at a table in the corner of Fyre. She's a slight young woman with long black hair and a porcelain complexion. She's dressed in a suit and sitting very erect in her chair. She's all business. It's relatively quiet in the restaurant, as it's not very crowded, even at noon. Still, people in the adjoining lounge create enough background noise to prevent being overheard. She smiles as Hua sits down and places his shopping bag right next to hers.

"Did you have any trouble getting here, Allison? Traffic was awful today."

They're speaking in Mandarin, but once again, I can understand them.

"No, it's a short ride using Uber, and I didn't have to find parking."

The server comes over and takes their drink order, gives them the luncheon menus, and scurries off.

"What can you tell me about your new employees?" Hua asks.

"Well, Nathan Kleiner was the easiest to bring on. He's employed at J.P. Morgan in New York; his wife spends money like water, and he'll do anything to keep her happy. Thomas Karlsson was a little more difficult, but in a similar, actually worse, situation. He's got a gambling problem, needs the money desperately, and says he has a debt collector threatening him. He works at The Clearing House systems and data center in McLean, Virginia. They're both concerned about getting caught, but they each say they have a way to get the job done — but it won't be easy, which is their way of saying it will be expensive. They think I'm paying them to install software to collect transactions from a couple of accounts to catch a rich hedge fund client's embezzler. In other words, they're going to be the good guys and catch an embezzler."

"Do you trust them not to rat you out if they get caught?"

The server comes back with their drinks, takes their food order, and hurries away.

"No, but they're both brilliant; they won't get caught. They'll set it up to make it look like someone else did it, probably their boss or someone in the office they don't like. They know we'll provide the malware to them on a flash drive. How they'll get it into the system, I don't know. That's their value-added trade secret. Company executives and managers think their systems are secure because they're spending a lot of money on security. But they don't understand that it all depends on the computer geeks' integrity that operate and monitor the systems. If my guys can't get the malware into the system themselves, if they have a friend in the security group, it will get done, don't worry. And if they think they're doing nothing wrong, just installing some monitoring software to catch potential embezzlement, it's easy."

Hua studies Allison, wondering how she can be so sure.

"How much did you promise them?"

"I told each of them I would pay $25,000 now and $25,000 later, but I expect they'll both ask for more after I give them the initial payment. And don't forget my payoff."

"I thought you were doing this for ideological reasons."

Allison smiles.

"I am, but there's nothing wrong with making a profit commensurate with the risk. That's the capitalist way, right?"

"Okay, there's $200,000 cash in the bag. You keep the extra $100,000. You can promise Karlsson and Kleiner up to $100,000 each, and you can have another $250,000 if you get this done — it's that important. But the money will only be paid after we know the malware is installed and operating. We'll provide the flash drives to you when we're ready. It could be any time within the next month. Any questions?"

"After I get the flash drives, I'll need some time to get them into their hands, so assume a week before they're ready. But I'll confirm the timing with each of them when I deliver this payment. And I know how to contact you if I have questions."

Allison seems to be quite happy with herself. Is it because of the money or something else?

The server brings their salads. They make small talk while they eat. Hua pays the check, and they each pick up a bag from the floor before saying their goodbyes.

Bringing myself back to the moment, I make a few notes to record the names and amounts and timing, then go to the connecting door and call the crew over.

Once Craig, Karen, and Angie come into my office, I tell them what I found out. Seeming pleased, Craig leaves the room, taking my notes with him, presumably to call Tony.

When he comes back, he says, "We're being instructed to sit tight for now. We'll tail Kleiner and Karlsson as well as Allison. Yang Kexin is back in China, and we're watching him as much as we can, though our people have to be very careful operating in Beijing."

I shrug my shoulders. Craig and Karen go back into Suite 302, talking logistics, but Angie hesitates.

I wonder why she's standing there, though I'm not against it. There's something about her that I feel drawn to. Maybe it's her looks, perhaps it's her quick wit. I don't know.

She shifts her weight, obviously weighing whether to say something or to stay quiet.

Well, if I'm interested in her, I better find out if she's already taken.

Before I can talk myself out of it, I ask, "Does your boyfriend know you're in Natchez?"

At first, she seems surprised, then smiles and says, "I don't have a boyfriend — or a husband."

I can't help but smile in response. "That's what I was wondering. Thanks for clarifying. Now, what was it you were going to say?"

Angie chuckles slightly, and I can tell the question relaxed her. She tilts her head and says, "Why is it that you don't seem to have tried to read any of our minds? I guess I should say our memories, especially Tony's? I assume you could if you wanted."

"I value my own privacy, so I respect the privacy of others."

"But you don't seem to be bothered by reading the minds of some people."

"Those people, in my opinion, are criminals or at least suspected criminals. I think they've given up their right to privacy by their actions."

"You wouldn't use your unique power in other situations?"

"I don't think so, but I'm still trying to figure this whole situation out." Tilting my head slightly, I ask, "What would you do?"

"Well, for example, if I was married and thought my husband was cheating on me, I think I might use it."

I nod. "You could be right. It's a moral dilemma. I'm sure there are other situations like that. It seems like too much to even think about right now. I just want to get this case, if you can call it that, over and done, so I can get back to my former life."

"I hate to tell you this, but I doubt that's ever going to happen. Your ability is too valuable, and if we're not using it, someone else will want to, and that puts you in continual danger."

The thought has crossed my mind before, but I still hope they'll find someone with better abilities than mine one day. But I just say, "Yes, I'm worried about that."

"Well, for now, don't worry. We're the only ones who know what you can do. And we're here to protect you. But it doesn't hurt for you to get comfortable using your Glock."

Patting my holster, I say, "I'm getting ready for the enhanced carry test next week."

Angie grins this time as if she thinks this is funny. She probably thinks I don't know how to handle a weapon and might shoot myself.

"Well, we definitely want you to pass that test. Maybe we can go to the range sometime. I need to practice regularly myself."

She seems interested in spending time with me without Karen or Craig. I like that idea!

I almost blush.

"Okay, we'll do that soon."

I wonder if she's flirting or what? I hope so.

CHAPTER 23

STICKING HIS HEAD in my office, Craig says we all need to talk. I wave him in, and the ladies follow.

After making himself comfortable in one of my leather chairs, he says, "We know the initial link to Demarge. It was Dr. Dehner's boyfriend, a guy named C.T. Brasfield. The FBI has been investigating Dr. Dehner as a possible leak and ran across Brasfield. They questioned him. He admitted he's been sharing her research with an individual who's been paying him for the past two years. Brasfield wasn't in the picture when she got her clearance."

Karen asks, "So who's been paying him, and why?"

"He says he was approached in a bar by a man who called himself Dr. George Reed, who knew that Brasfield had a relationship with Dr. Dehner. Reed said he was a researcher in the same field. He was willing to pay for any information Brasfield could provide about her work. He said he needed to keep up with developments in parapsychology, a field in which Cynthia Dehner is a recognized expert. Brasfield said he needed the money to pay alimony to his ex-wife plus his kids' college expenses."

As Craig's words sink in, so does worry. I shift uncomfortably. "You mean he shared Dr. Dehner's evaluation of me?"

"Yes, afraid so, Grant. He says he stole the report from her computer when she was working at home." Craig continues. "Brasfield says Reed told him to leave both sun visors down in his car whenever he had information. Reed would eventually call Brasfield on his cell phone, usually from a different number than he used before. By the way, there is a Dr. George Reed at Georgetown, and he is a professor in the same field as Dehner, but this was not the real George Reed.

"If Brasfield had desirable information, Reed would arrange to receive it, usually by text message. Reed would then send him a payment electronically using Venmo or Zelle. We assume Reed was passing this information on to one of the foreign security services, but we don't know which one. We believe that foreign security services make it their business to know if anyone is found to have legitimate extra-sensory skills anywhere in the world. The CIA does the same thing. The U.S. wants to know if Russia, China, or Iran has someone with proven extra-sensory skills working for them. It makes sense they want to know if someone working for a foreign service can read the mind of the highest officials in their government."

Craig continues, "The bad thing is we don't know which security service George Reed was working for. My guess would be Russia, as that would be their style, but we don't know. Tony says the FBI and CIA are trying to find out."

"So, we obviously need to stay on alert for another assassination attempt," says Karen with a look of concern on her face.

"Yes, that's for sure. We need to be armed at all times. And Grant doesn't go anywhere alone," says Craig.

I ask with genuine concern, "But why hasn't there been another assassination attempt?"

"Tony says they have been thinking about that, and there are several possible explanations, all of which you aren't going to like," admits Craig.

I frown and say, "Such as?"

"Well, if they watched us in New York, they saw we were interested in the Chinese, so it's probably not China. They would've made another attempt by now. That brings us back to Russia, Iran, Israel, or others. Seeing that we are interested in China, maybe they decided it gives them time to see how this plays out and plan a kidnapping instead of an assassination. That may be why there was an initial assassination attempt instead of a kidnapping; they couldn't quickly develop a plan to get you out of the country. So they decided that permanently getting rid of you was just as good or even better than the status quo. The other explanation is that they're working on another assassination attempt. Tony thinks 'they,' whoever 'they' is, will watch and evaluate before they decide what to do and are probably working on both options."

Thanks, Tony, thanks a lot.

"But I've got more news," Craig says. "Tony, Director Kohl, and DNI Nelson think the focus now needs to be on what happens in Thailand. They don't believe anything will happen here until the Chinese test their Plan 23-2 in Thailand. And they don't think Thailand will come into play until Kleiner and Karlsson accept Allison's payment. Also, the Chinese won't give Allison the flash drives until they see the results of the Thailand test. We don't understand what they can do in Thailand that won't alert the banking industry worldwide. We want to see what the malware will do, even potentially capture it, before we shut them down.

"This means we need to be ready to leave for Bangkok very soon. We'll have a few days' notice. We can enter Thailand as tourists, so we don't need a visa in advance unless we plan to stay for an extended period, which we don't. But for entry, your passport has to have at least six months before expiration, so Grant, check yours tonight. The passports for you ladies will be here in a few days. You should pack to stay at least a week."

At the mention of Bangkok, I straighten. I may not have gotten to the Bangkok gem show this year, but maybe I can squeeze in some visits with my gem friends while I'm there.

I ask, "Can I contact a business friend and tell him I'm making a trip to Bangkok soon and will plan to see him? I assume you'll want me to act normally and to have a legitimate reason to be in Bangkok."

Craig thinks about it for a few seconds and nods. "Yes, you can contact him." After a brief pause, he continues, "And one more thing. A body was found floating in the Mississippi River down by Morganza, Louisiana. It was a male, and the body had two bullet holes. That's all we know. No doubt it was Demarge. At least his family will have closure now."

Demarge's friends will have revenge on their minds, but they might only know that he had a job in Mississippi and nothing more. That's what I'm counting on.

CHAPTER 24

I DRIVE OVER to Pearl with Karen and Angie to attend the handgun safety course required for the Mississippi Enhanced Carry Permit. Randy greets me as usual and directs me to the counter, where I pay the $107 fee for the class. Karen and Angie are not allowed to apply for the permit because they've not been residents of the state for at least a year, and Mississippi will honor their license from their home state. But as federal officers, they don't need a concealed carry permit anyway.

Randy then points me to a crowded conference room with about fifteen other people also attending the class. We sit in class for three hours, listening to a canned presentation by a certified instructor whose name I didn't catch, but it doesn't matter.

Then we go to the firing range and take the three-yard and seven-yard firing test, taking twenty-five shots at each distance. I score about in the middle of the pack but good enough to pass. I qualify to receive the IC (instructor certified) sticker for enhanced carry on my Mississippi Firearms Permit, which looks like a driver's license with my photo, home address, birthdate, issue, and expiration date and imprinted with the slogan "Mississippi, the Hospitality State." There's something ironic to me about mixing guns and hospitality.

On my next trip to Jackson, I will take the document, which certifies I passed the handgun safety course, to the Highway Patrol Headquarters in Jackson to get the IC sticker. After I do that, I can take a concealed weapon anywhere in Mississippi except police/sheriff/highway patrol stations, jails/prisons, courtrooms, and "places of nuisance." The instructor told us this means places of prostitution, lewdness, or where controlled substances are unlawfully used. It seems to me that "places of nuisance" are where you need a weapon for protection, but then I'm not a politician deciding such things.

Now, I have a gun and a concealed carry permit. I still don't know if I could ever use the weapon other than at the shooting range. Craig says I'll be able to if I'm in a life-or-death situation. I hope I never find out, but I'm afraid I will.

On Monday morning, Craig has big news. "Allison has paid Kleiner. She made the trip to New York this weekend and made the payment in a Brooklyn coffee shop. But Karlsson is in the Virginia Hospital Center with kidney stones. He's been there for two days. I don't think Allison will be taking a bag of cash to the hospital. We don't know how much longer he'll be there. And he probably won't be going anywhere for a couple of days after that. So we don't think anything will happen in Thailand or here until Kleiner and Karlsson are primed and ready. If the Thailand test is successful, they won't want to give anyone time to figure out what happened before they strike."

He continues, "But that's not all. Li Zhang Yong is in Bangkok; he arrived yesterday and has a reservation at the Oriental

Hotel for two full weeks. We suspect Li wants to be close to the action when Plan 23-2 is activated. The plan's actual timing probably hasn't been set, so he's making sure he's covered and doesn't have to change hotels. He may even want to enjoy a few days of vacation in Bangkok. We need to be ready to leave as soon as we can make our travel arrangements." Craig turns to me. "Grant, you need to —"

"I know, tell Miss Doris that the ladies and I are taking a gem-buying trip to Bangkok."

Actually, I'm pretty excited to be making the trip to Bangkok. And I'm pleased the jewelry investigation has started. And even better, Tony owes me a check tomorrow, April 30.

CHAPTER 25

Suvarnabhumi International Airport is about twenty miles east of the city. Once we get through passport control, pick up our luggage, and then pass through Thai customs, we finally enter the arrival hall, where hundreds of limo drivers and family members wait for arriving passengers. Craig has made arrangements for a van from the Oriental Hotel to meet us. The uniformed driver is standing along the rail separating us with a sign displaying the hotel name and logo and "Mr. C. Clayton" in large letters. When we go outside, we're hit in the face with unbelievable heat and humidity even though it's 10:30 p.m. Welcome to Bangkok!

Fortunately, it's late enough that we don't have to fight the insufferable Bangkok traffic, which could take us two hours or more during the day to reach the hotel. It only takes us forty minutes tonight. It feels strange to have the van driving on the left side of the road and the steering wheel on the right. Many countries in Asia drive on the left side.

Our Mercedes van turns onto a side street, Soi Charoen Krung 40, leading to the Oriental Hotel entrance. The van climbs the inclined drive and stops at the covered entrance. The uniformed staff greets us with smiles and the traditional Thai greeting, the wai, a slight bow with the palms pressed together and the fingertips at about chin level.

Craig, Karen, and Angie don't know what to expect and exit the van with anticipation. I only know the Oriental from a luncheon I attended here many years ago. It's located on the banks of the Chao Phraya River. We enter the vast lobby, which is breathtakingly beautiful, decorated in Thai style with a soaring ceiling, tropical plants, luxurious furniture, and soft lighting. The lobby has a floor-to-ceiling glass wall on the side that faces the gardens, pool, and river. The Oriental has been a Bangkok landmark since 1876, though most of the existing buildings were built in the twentieth century. It has long been considered one of the best hotels in the world. I'm definitely looking forward to staying here, especially if Tony's paying.

We check in and are taken to our two-bedroom suites on the River Wing eleventh floor, looking north over the Chao Phraya River. Craig tells the ladies we'll call in the morning but that we should have breakfast in our suite to avoid running into Li Zhang Yong until we're ready. They agree, and we all crash for the night. I toss and turn, partially from jet lag but also from anticipation. I finally fall asleep and wake up at about 10 a.m., which is 10 p.m. at home.

When I come out to the living room, Craig is sitting, drinking coffee. He still looks tired.

"Breakfast should be coming soon," he says. "Karen and Angie will be over in a few minutes."

I look out the window overlooking the Chao Phraya River at the many brightly colored boats making their way along the river. These are the so-called river taxis. Some of these boats carry as many as 150 people on their way to work, school, or shopping. It's fascinating to watch this scene. There are two piers that I can see from the window where the river taxis are taking on and letting off passengers.

There are also some smaller boats, carrying maybe a dozen passengers each. These are long-tail boats, given the name because of the long propeller shaft extending from the back. Tourists can hire a long-tail boat for a ride on the river and tours up the narrow canals, called klongs, that run off the river. I hope Karen and Angie have time to take a long-tail boat ride while we're here — and Craig, too, if he wants to go, but based on New York, he doesn't like to do touristy things.

Karen and Angie knock at the door and, after checking through the peephole, Craig lets them in.

Craig says, "We missed Li this morning. He had breakfast on the Terrace."

The Riverside Terrace is at ground level right at the river's edge and serves breakfast, lunch, and dinner, buffet style. I've heard it's one of the most enjoyable experiences at the hotel.

Craig says, "Li had two bodyguards with him and was given a table away from the crowd. The hotel must know he's a VIP. He left for the PRC Embassy in a private car. We'll have to catch up with him tomorrow. And Karlsson is still in the hospital. Since we have nothing on schedule today, I suggest we get out of the hotel. What would you like to do?"

Karen says, "I'd like to do some sightseeing."

Angie says, "I'd like to shop."

Since it's already 10:30 a.m. and we haven't yet had breakfast, I suggest we go to the Grand Palace after eating. They all agree, but then Craig says, "I think I'll just stay here at the hotel. I have a few things to do, and I've really got jet lag. Maybe I'll go out later today or maybe tomorrow."

I suggest that to get the most out of the Grand Palace visit, we should hire a tour guide. Karen and Angie agree, so I call the concierge after we eat breakfast. I make arrangements for us to leave the hotel at 12:30 p.m. to meet the guide at 1:00 p.m. I also tell them the dress code requirements, as explained by the concierge — a regular shirt or polo shirt and long pants for men and skirts and a blouse with sleeves for women. The concierge says it's a place for tourists to show modesty and respect. The Grand Palace is a large complex of buildings, so navigating it and understanding what we see will be easier with a guide.

At 1:00 p.m., we meet the guide, a friendly Thai woman, about thirty years old, named Sriwat Jaiyong. She speaks passable English and says she studied in Australia for two years as a teenager.

The Grand Palace is a mind-blowing smorgasbord of buildings, pavilions, and statues. The buildings range from traditional Thai to combined styles with Thai rooflines and Italian Renaissance facades. Many of the buildings are covered in gold leaf or colored tiles. The tour's highlight is the Temple of the Emerald Buddha, Wat Phra Kaew, constructed in 1783, the holiest Buddhist temple in Thailand. It houses the ancient Emerald Buddha — a green Buddha statue twenty-six inches tall carved from a single jade stone. The King of Thailand comes to the Temple three times per year, corresponding to the changing seasons, to change the cloak around the statue, providing good luck to the nation during the upcoming season.

The smell of incense is heavy in the air, as many Thai people are lighting incense sticks and meditating at the temple. Combined with the 97-degree Fahrenheit temperature and the high humidity, the three of us are noticeably uncomfortable. We're ready to go back to the hotel for a cold drink when the tour is over.

Sriwat tells us she will be happy to be our guide on other tours. She then calls the driver to take us back to the hotel. I noticed the entire time we were on the tour that Karen seemed to be surveying the crowd to see if we were being followed. But it was hard to tell for sure what she was doing because of her oversized Givenchy sunglasses, but she didn't act like she spotted anyone. When we get in the taxi, I ask her, and she says no. Angie says she agrees; no one was following.

I'll take that as a good sign I don't have to worry about an assassin here in Bangkok.

When we return to the hotel, Craig has photographs to show us. The primary subject is Li Zhang Yong. He's a short, stocky man in his early fifties with black hair and a square, pockmarked face. He is fearsome-looking. He's wearing casual clothes, trying to look like a tourist, I suppose. There are also photos of his bodyguards, younger, taller, thinner, and better-looking, but not the type with whom you would want to have an altercation.

Craig says, "Grant, we think you should try to get close to Li tomorrow morning at breakfast on the Terrace. He's been going there every morning around 8:00 a.m., and he stays about thirty to forty-five minutes enjoying the food and the view of the river."

I ask, "Craig, you said, 'We think.' You mean you and Tony?"

"Yes, I forgot to tell you, Tony is here. Well, not really here in the hotel, but in Bangkok."

Oh no, Tony always brings trouble. I feel my heart sink. What if the Russians are trailing him and find me?

"Why?" I ask.

"He wants to assess the impact of Plan 23-2 for himself. If the impact is too great, then they'll go ahead and arrest Kleiner and Karlsson and not let it go any further. But they would rather not do that. They would prefer to catch them with the flash drives so our people can analyze the malware."

I wonder why Tony would come to Bangkok if he knows

he's regularly being followed by foreign security services, as Craig has said. It seems that he just likes to be at the center of the action, just like in college. It's hard not to love and hate Tony at the same time.

"When are we going to see Tony?"

Craig says, "Soon, I think. We need to make sure we won't cross paths with Li prematurely. As soon as we believe he's not going to be arriving or leaving the hotel for a while, we'll go see Tony. He's staying nearby at the Shangri-La Hotel."

CHAPTER 26

WE HAD TO wait for quite a while. Finally, Craig gets a call from Donnie, who's part of the security detail downstairs. Craig says, "Li has gone with a group from the embassy to the Pagoda Chinese Restaurant in the Marriott Marquis Hotel. They have a private room, and Li is holding court. He'll be there for several hours, maybe longer if the liquor starts to flow."

We leave the hotel and take a taxi to the Shangri-La. Actually, we go to the more exclusive and private Krungthep Wing of the hotel with its own lobby, bar, and pool. Tony's suite is on the twelfth floor.

He greets us by saying, "I bet you're surprised to see me here!"

I say, "Yeah, you're full of surprises, just like always." Tony laughs, but I'm not smiling.

We sit down, and he asks if we'd like a drink. We all decline, and Karen says, "Too early, maybe later."

Tony says he and the CIA Director and the DNI have decided to let Plan 23-2 in Thailand proceed. "It's our only chance to learn what this is all about." When I learn they haven't alerted Thai officials, it crosses my mind that they're playing a perilous and dangerous game.

Tony says they think the plan is moving slowly because the Chinese want to have everything ready to go quickly in the U.S. if the Thailand test works. But they can't do that until Karlsson is out of the hospital and has accepted his bribe. Our experts also speculate that the software must need to have an internal clock set to a specific date/time for the malware to be activated. This is because the Chinese haven't been able to penetrate the firewall and other cyber defenses, so they can't start it remotely. It must already be set like a time bomb when they make their malware installation.

I think they're going to an awful lot of trouble to test it here.

"Tony, why are they testing Plan 23-2 in Thailand?" I ask.

He says, "The U.S. provides Thailand with financial software for its central banking network. So, we think APT10 believes they're testing the U.S. cyber defenses, like if the software will be detected or not in our system and whether it will function as they desire. They also want to see the public's reaction if they can take the system down."

"Won't disrupting the United States financial system hurt the Chinese as much as it'll hurt us? We're their largest customer, and they own a trillion dollars' worth of our treasury bonds."

Tony says, "I always knew you were smart, Grant. That is the one question we can't answer. We don't think it makes sense, either. There must be some reason we haven't yet identified. We're hoping you can help us find out."

I can only nod my head. I really hope I don't have problems connecting with Li. If I do, I doubt I'll pull off a stunt like I did with Yang; I don't expect Li's bodyguards to allow anything like that. He's too important, and I imagine, too well guarded.

Tony says, "Let's go to dinner. I've made a reservation here at the hotel in the Salathip Restaurant."

We go downstairs, accompanied by Tony's bodyguard, who Tony introduced only as Ron, and walk outside along the Krungthep Wing pool located next to the river. We eventually emerge on the softly lit main grounds of the Shangri-La Hotel, filled with tall royal palms and smaller bush palms surrounded by many lush tropical plants, all in bloom. The Salathip is a beautiful Thai-style pavilion in the center of the hotel grounds. We're seated inside, away from the heat, although some groups are seated outside on the terrace next to the river. We're all served a bowl of tom yum goong, a spicy Thai soup, and then platters are brought to the table with various salads, curries, seafood dishes, and fried rice. We have an excellent French wine that Tony orders. For dessert, we all have mango and sticky rice. The food is delicious, and I'm really enjoying the evening. And if that's not enough, we're treated to a little show with Thai music and costumed Thai dancers, plus I get to sit next to Angie.

This almost makes me forget why we're in Bangkok in the first place. Almost, but not quite.

CHAPTER 27

AT 7:45 A.M., we are waiting to go to the Terrace for breakfast as soon as we hear Li has made his appearance.

Craig gets a call at 8:10 a.m. and listens for about a minute. He says, "Are you sure?" His face turns grim at the answer.

Hanging up, Craig turns to us. "I've got news, and it isn't good. Li went to the Terrace for breakfast, but as soon as he was seated, Yang Kexin showed up. Apparently, he's coordinating the Plan 23-2 test here in Bangkok, just like in the U.S. We can't take the chance on Yang recognizing you from the Met or Guggenheim. We're going to have to wait for another opportunity."

I'm really concerned that Yang or his bodyguard will recognize me. They've seen me twice.

"And that's not all," says Craig. "Donnie spotted a female Russian agent shadowing either Li or Yang. He recognized her from Singapore. It might just be their normal surveillance of an important Chinese official, but we can't be sure. And we don't know which one she's watching. We'll have to be careful around her. So we can't go anywhere until they've all left the hotel."

At 9:15 a.m., Craig gets another call.

"They've left the Terrace, and the Russian left, too. Li went back to his room, and Yang left the hotel. The Russian followed Yang. They may be more involved in this than we thought. Anyway, you all can go to breakfast. You ought to get to enjoy the Terrace at least once on this trip. I'll stay in the room. It's probably best if all four of us aren't seen together."

When we get to the Terrace, we ask to be seated at the railing next to the river. It's pleasant at this time of day, but that won't last long. There are umbrellas at each table to shield guests from the sun.

After we order drinks, Karen says, "It would be nice to come here as a real tourist sometime. I mean, not having to worry if you're being followed or that someone might try to kill you at any moment."

Angie says, "Yes, but then we'd have to pay for it on our own. Let's enjoy a free trip as much as we can. It's just like what you see in a travel magazine."

I smile and say, "I think I can get used to this; it's better than a travel magazine," pointing to the hotel, then to the river.

Karen asks, "Where do you stay when you come to Bangkok?"

I respond, "At the Royal Orchid Sheraton. Not far from here, and nice, but no Oriental or Shangri-La." Then I ask, "Why didn't Craig join us?"

Karen says, "He's all about the mission and not that much for socializing. You'll get used to him. He's got your back, you can count on that."

I like hearing that.

We get up from the table and walk over to the smorgasbord to peruse the extensive offerings. We try all the Thai fruits:

pineapple, jackfruit, mango, rambutan, papaya, pomelo, mangosteen, banana, lychee, and more. Karen and Angie go to the egg station and order omelets while I go to the waffle station. We then finish up with pastries and coffee. We enjoy watching the large and small boats on the river.

Angie says, "You know, we need to find a gift for Miss Doris."

That's very thoughtful of Angie. One more thing I like about her.

Karen agrees and says, "Grant, you know what she likes, so help us out."

I say, "Okay, there's plenty to buy around here. We'll look when we go out to see my friend Sammi. He told me he'd be available any time we can drop by his office."

When we go back to the room, Craig says that Li has a reservation for three people at the Authors' Lounge for tea at 3:00 p.m. He says he talked to the concierge and was able to get us a reservation as well. Hopefully, Yang won't join Li for tea. Craig doesn't seem to think that's likely.

We decide now might be a good time to go to the embassy to pick up our weapons. We couldn't bring our own, since we took a commercial flight over.

Once we know the coast is clear and Li is gone, we take a van taxi to the U.S. Embassy on Witthayu Road, also known as Wireless Road. The embassy is a huge, white concrete building with small windows, constructed in 1996 to the security standards developed after the Beirut Embassy bombing in 1983; the thick concrete walls will withstand a severe bomb blast.

The driver asks if we want to go to the embassy or long-time Ambassador Arthur Debowy's residence across the road. He says the Ambassador frequently hosts meetings there, so it's a frequent destination from the hotel. It's barely visible in a tropical compound of about five acres. He tells us it was built in

1914 as a private home and has been the United States Ambassador's residence since 1947.

Craig says, "The embassy." The driver pulls into the drive, and we get out. We must pass a thorough security check before we can even get into the lobby of the building. We have to wait in the security area until the CIA Station Chief comes to the entrance to let us in. Chief R. A. Parker is a friendly, fiftyish-looking man of medium height with blond hair and broad shoulders. He takes us upstairs to his office and gives us each a Glock G19M, two ammunition clips, and an IWB holster. Chief Parker also provides a box of supplies for cleaning. He has official permits for the weapons, each with a photo, undecipherable Thai writing, and an official-looking embossed seal.

So, they can give me a government-supplied weapon after all? I was right that they wanted to disassociate me from the CIA if they could. It's just not convenient here.

Parker says, "Take care of these weapons. I don't want to have to replace them. And I don't want to have to bail you out of a Thai jail."

I say, "I've heard about Thai jails, and we don't want any part of that!"

I'm thinking about the Thai jail scenes in the movie *Brokedown Palace*, which makes me cringe.

We wait a few minutes in security for a van taxi and get back to the hotel in about twenty minutes, in plenty of time for the tea. Fortunately, we don't run into Li as we make our way back to our rooms.

When we get back, Craig says that Donnie was able to identify the Russian agent following Yang. He was able to get a photo of her with the help of CIA Chief Parker.

Craig shows us the photo and says, "Her name is Irina Rachkova. We need to be on the lookout for her. She may switch from following Yang to following us. We know she's always involved in the Russians' most important covert operations. She's a skilled operative and a killer."

She has the appearance you would expect for a Russian agent. She has a thin face with high cheekbones, has short blonde hair, is slim, and is above-average height.

I say, "I'll put either Angie or Karen up against her any day!" They both laugh.

We decide to read up on the afternoon tea in the hotel guide as we wait. The Authors' Lounge is in the oldest part of the hotel. The lounge is named in honor of authors who have stayed at the hotel or just hung out in the bar, including Joseph Conrad, Somerset Maugham, Noel Coward, James Michener, Barbara Cartland, Ian Fleming, and John Le Carré. It sounds like a fascinating place.

At 3:00 p.m., Craig gets another call. "Li has invited the PRC Ambassador and his wife for tea. You can go down now."

I breathe a sigh of relief that Yang and his bodyguard won't be there.

CHAPTER 28

Everything inside the Authors' Lounge is painted white, including the wicker furniture. Combined with the large glass skylight, it's exceptionally bright inside. The only color in the room is from the tropical plants and the green floral accents on the cushions; even the floral arrangements are white. The dual twin staircases meet at a balcony landing at the second-floor level, and flowers hang over the railings. The opening under the stairs leads to another section of the lounge. Some of the guests are busy taking photos. The pianist plays softly on the white grand piano, under the stairs but slightly to one side.

Karen, Angie, and I are seated in the corner of the garden room and have a somewhat clear view of Li and his guests in the far corner. We arrange ourselves so that I have the best view of Li, who is not quite facing our direction, but I can see his face.

We order one each of the Western, the Oriental, and the Vegetarian tea set menus. We choose our favorite teas and wait for the food to be served. Li's group just had their orders brought to the low table in their furniture grouping's center. I notice one of Li's bodyguards peeking around the corner of the doorway to make sure all is well.

When I'm sure the bodyguard's attention is elsewhere, I study Li's face. Li looks as intimidating in person as he does in his photo. Though he might be enjoying himself, it's difficult to tell it. He must hate social settings like this. The ambassador's wife chatters on endlessly. Li makes an attempt to smile — if you can call it that.

Karen and Angie are enjoying the lovely food and the beautiful room, but I'm anxious to go. I have all I need from Li. I'm uncomfortable thinking that Li might recognize me in the future, so I want to limit my exposure to him and the possibility that he'll remember me. Maybe I'm just paranoid, but I can't help it.

As soon as Karen and Angie have finished their food, I whisper that we need to leave, and they look disappointed but nod in agreement. I get the bill, ask Karen to sign for it, as I want to remain anonymous, and we leave. I don't think Li and his party have noticed us.

When we enter the suite, Craig looks up from his laptop. "How did it go?"

It went well if he didn't notice me.

"It went well. I think I can connect with Li whenever you want me to."

"Okay, why don't you try now?"

I nod and head into my room to get rid of distractions. Sitting down on my bed, I remember that Craig got a call at 8:10 a.m. saying that Li and Yang were having breakfast on the Terrace, which seems to be a good time to focus on.

I try to relax and concentrate on Li, recalling his face and mannerisms. I focus and begin to receive images of Yang Kexin sitting on the Terrace across from Li.

"When did you arrive in Bangkok, Yang?" asks Li.

"Yesterday, Mr. Deputy Chairman."

"Are you staying here at the hotel?"

"No, I'm staying at the W Hotel on Sathorn Road."

"Yes, you seem to enjoy the pleasures available nearby in Soi Patpong. And Nana Plaza, and Soi Cowboy, as well, if I recall."

He says, with a slightly embarrassed look, "I'm only acting like a typical tourist."

Li waves his right hand dismissively. "What's the situation in the U.S.?"

"We've recruited the two mercenaries we need, but one of them is hospitalized, sir. We don't know how much longer he'll be there, probably several more days. He had a very painful kidney stone attack. In the meantime, we can only wait until he is released. Then our agent will make the payment, and if all is well, we can proceed. It will be probably four or five days until we know we are ready there."

Li growls. "I am tired of waiting. Couldn't you find someone else?"

"No, sir." Yang shakes his head. "He is part of a small group of IT analysts that work in The Clearing House. It would be too risky to try to recruit someone else now."

"And what's our situation here in Thailand?"

Yang says, "We have our mercenaries ready to go. One is an employee of the Bank of Thailand, which operates the banking clearing and transaction systems, BAHTNET and ICAS. These systems handle all transactions between banks and all check clearing in the country. We also have one ready at Krung Thai Bank. We've decided that, for a limited test, Krung Thai Bank is well suited. We've set up the malware to affect only the operations of Krung Thai Bank in Chiang Mai, where they have nine branches and a network of ATMs. We plan to set the malware to be effective from 7:00 a.m. until 1:00 p.m. the next day. That should give us enough information to know how well the malware functioned and the disruption's social impact. It will correct itself, and then the malware will self-destruct, so they will never find out what happened. As you know, we plan to eliminate the two mercenaries."

Li says, "Excellent, Yang. Who will activate the malware?"

"Mr. Deputy Chairman, I was instructed two days ago by Wu Min how to set the internal timer before sending the flash drives to do their work."

"Speaking of Wu Min, did you ask him if he has taken care of our business in Hong Kong?"

"Yes, Mr. Deputy Chairman, he says the new accounts are open, just as instructed."

"Well, that is good, but I want the account numbers as soon as possible. Wu Min will be rewarded handsomely if our larger plan goes well. I'll leave for Phuket tonight for a few days of relaxation; I cannot wait idly in Bangkok. You know how to contact me when you're ready to proceed. I want to be here when it happens."

"Yes, Mr. Deputy Chairman, I'll let you know at least a day in advance."

"Very well, Yang Kexin, let's enjoy breakfast and this fascinating view."

After their conversation is over, I make a few notes and go back to the living room area of the suite.

Craig writes some notes, obviously to give Tony.

"Oh, one more thing. I have the name of the programmer at APT10 — his name is Wu Min. And Li mentioned something about a larger plan. In response, Yang told him Wu Min had opened new accounts in Hong Kong."

Craig looks puzzled but writes it all down.

With Li going to Phuket and their plan on hold, I realize that I finally have time to visit my friend Sammi Suriwatpong, the gem dealer. Smiling, I give him a call and tell him I brought my cousin and a friend to Bangkok, and I'll see him in the next day or two.

CHAPTER 29

LI KEPT HIS room at the Oriental when he left for Phuket, so we know he'll definitely be back, but for now, we decide to take it easy today. We all go to the pool after breakfast and order lunch while there, then go back to the room at about 2:00 p.m. to rest. We're still trying to get over our jet lag.

After a short nap, I get on the computer and ask Justine what's been happening on the Devereaux investigation. She says she's chasing some leads but doesn't have anything yet. I am anxious to see some progress.

We decide to have dinner on the Terrace, then go to a night market before meeting Tony at the Long Bar in the Shangri-La Hotel. The entire evening is a treat for all the senses. But it also feels to me like the calm before the storm. I keep waiting for the other shoe to drop. The assassination attempt still has me on edge.

After dinner, the taxi drops us off at the night market, and we make our way in from the street, looking at the merchandise as we go. The bazaar is bustling. There's a generous supply of clothes and knock-off goods, from purses to watches — and a surprising number of food stalls. Apparently, a lot of local people come here just for the food.

After the appropriate amount of haggling over the price, Karen and Angie each purchase several sarongs, wallets, and other small leather goods. I buy several t-shirts, and Craig purchases a powerful LED flashlight at a modest price. We finally decide to leave the night market and walk to the Krungthep Wing entrance of the Shangri-La, only about five blocks away.

We walk about two blocks and turn onto a small side street on the way to the hotel. Craig and Karen lead the way, with Angie and me following carefully to avoid twisting an ankle on the narrow, broken sidewalk. Angie's telling me how much she's enjoying Bangkok so far.

I'm amazed how readily Angie shares what she's thinking; it's easy to talk with her. She makes me comfortable in a way I haven't felt in a long time.

We're only a few blocks from the night market's intensity, but it feels like a different world. The street is quiet, and I take a moment to enjoy strolling slowly next to Angie. I think about reaching over and holding her hand, but I decide this isn't the right time.

Tires suddenly screech against the pavement behind us. A motorcycle, its engine revving wildly, shoots out of the alley we passed a few yards back and comes straight toward us. For an instant, I wonder why a motorcycle taxi would be driving crazy like that. But then I notice the two men are wearing black pants, black long-sleeve shirts, and black helmets with the visors down. They're also wearing shoes instead of the typical flip-flops. This is definitely not a motorcycle taxi. My heart begins to race as I realize they're not slowing down. As we jump out of the way, I see the glint of a barrel pointed at us. Fear grips me, and I feel myself freeze.

Bang, bang, bang, bang, bang. At least five shots from a semi-automatic pistol whistle past at almost point-blank range. The noise jolts me, and we dive for cover as the shots ring out. Karen, Angie, and Craig all have their weapons drawn before I even think to get mine out. They yell, "Don't shoot, don't shoot!" as the motorcycle heads down the street toward a crowd of people at the intersection. A shot might hit one of the civilians.

As soon as the danger's passed, Craig asks me, "Are you okay?"

I say, "I'm okay, just scared." But I hope he doesn't notice my hands are shaking.

We get to our feet and put our weapons away. Karen asks, "Did any of you see anything? I was blinded by the headlight until it was past us."

I tell them what I saw, which was nothing useful.

"Maybe someone was trying to send us a message," Angie says.

We warily walk the remaining few blocks to the hotel and call Tony from the lobby. A few minutes later, he meets us at the Long Bar. We all gather in a seating area away from the bar. He sees we are shaken and asks what happened.

"We got shot at on our way over here, but the guy missed," Karen says. "We were lucky, the motorcycle they were riding was right on top of us."

I wonder if we were followed all the way from Natchez. But I assume they were Thai people on the motorcycle, so I'm confused. Then I think maybe they weren't Thai; maybe they were Chinese. Nothing I'm coming up with makes me feel better.

Tony frowns and says, "Any idea who it was?"

Karen shakes her head. "No, do you have any idea?"

Tony says, "Maybe it was just a Thai gang that doesn't like foreigners and wanted to scare you away from their neighborhood."

I wonder why Tony would say that. To me, it seems to be much more likely it was the Russians or Chinese or another country's security service.

Craig says, "Possibly, but more likely it was a Chinese hit. And missing at close range doesn't make sense unless they didn't want to hit us. But it doesn't make sense to scare us because they know we won't just up and leave if we're on a case. Maybe it was the Russians letting us know they have their own operation underway and don't want us to get in the way and mess it up."

Tony says, "Well, if that's true, there'll be another incident to make sure we get the message. But if you keep to the heavily traveled areas and hotels, you should be safe. And that includes me, too. Tell me what happened with Li."

I fill him in on what I found out. He thinks a minute and says, "We need to be ready for action when he comes back. We don't know what's going to happen next. Grant, keep mental track of Yang so we know the status of their U.S. plan and the timing for their attack here. He seems to be the one coordinating the operations for Li." He sits back for a second, seeming deep in thought.

He adds, "I also don't understand why Li thinks this is important enough for him to spend this much time away from Beijing. See what you can find out."

CHAPTER 30

I DECIDE TO stay in the room today, order room service, and figure out what I can do to answer the questions Tony asked. The best place to start might be to rethink Li and Yang's discussion on the Terrace yesterday. Craig has promised to keep quiet so that I can concentrate, and I've already put a "Do Not Disturb" sign out for the maids.

Once I settle in, it only takes a few seconds for me to pull up the conversation in my mind from Li's perspective.

"When did you arrive in Bangkok, Yang?" asks Li.

"Yesterday, Mr. Deputy Chairman."

"Are you staying here at the hotel?"

"No, I'm staying at the W Hotel on Sathorn Road."

Of course not, you don't want me to know what you're doing when out of my sight.

"Yes, you seem to enjoy the pleasures available nearby in Soi Patpong. Nana Plaza, and Soi Cowboy, as well, if I recall."

"I am only acting like a typical tourist."

I can only hope typical Chinese tourists would not disgrace themselves like you.

This time I can actually capture Li's inner thoughts, but I have no idea how. I didn't do anything differently. Maybe my telepathic ability is evolving with practice. Actually, that's kind of exciting. I decide for now not to tell anyone about the change in my powers. I'm not sure whether enhanced abilities are beneficial to me or just create more danger. I need time to decide.

"What's the situation in the U.S.?" Li asks.

"We've recruited the two mercenaries we need, but one of them is hospitalized, sir. We don't know how much longer he will be there, probably several more days. He had a terribly painful kidney stone attack. In the meantime, we can only wait until he is released. Then our agent will make the payment, and if all is well, then we can proceed. So it will be probably four or five days until we know we are ready there."

Li growls. "I'm tired of waiting. Could you not find someone else?"

Yang always has a problem, not a solution. I need to get rid of him when this is over.

"No, sir, he is part of a small group of IT analysts that work in The Clearing House. It'll be too risky to try to recruit someone else now."

"And what is our situation here in Thailand?"

Yang says, "We have our mercenaries ready to go. One is an employee of the Bank of Thailand, which operates the banking clearing and transaction systems, BAHTNET and ICAS. These systems handle all transactions between banks and all check clearing in the country. We also have one ready at Krung Thai Bank. We have decided on a limited test that Krung Thai is well suited. We've set up the malware to only affect the operations of Krung Thai Bank in Chiang Mai, where they have nine branches and a network of ATMs. We plan to set the malware to be effective from 7:00 a.m. until 1:00 p.m. the next day. That should give us enough information to know how the malware functioned and the social impact of the disruption. It will correct itself, and then the malware will self-destruct, so they will never find out what happened. As you know, we plan to eliminate the two mercenaries."

Li says, "Excellent, Yang. Who will activate the malware?"

"Mr. Deputy Chairman, I was instructed two days ago by Wu Min how to set the internal timer before sending the flash drives to do their work."

I hope you wrote out the instructions. Nothing can go wrong, or it will be your neck!

"Speaking of Wu Min, did you ask him if he has taken care of our business in Hong Kong?"

"Yes, Mr. Deputy Chairman, he says the new accounts are open, just as instructed."

Finally. We're running out of time.

"Well, that is good, but I want the account numbers as soon as possible. Wu Min will soon be rewarded if our larger plan goes well. I will leave for Phuket tonight for a few days of relaxation; I cannot wait idly in Bangkok. You know how to contact me when you're ready to proceed. I want to be here when it happens."

"Yes, Mr. Deputy Chairman, I'll let you know at least a day in advance."

You better not intentionally delay so you can spend more time in the go-go bars and seedy hotels. "Very well, Yang Kexin, let's enjoy breakfast and this fascinating view."

Maybe if we watch the river, I won't have to listen to you anymore.

❧

Later, I ask Craig if he can get any information on Wu Min, since he's apparently a key figure in all this. Craig says he'll try.

Heading back into the bedroom, I decide to go through the same conversation from Yang's point-of-view.

After playing it in my mind, I see that Li and Yang obviously don't like each other. That could help us. Nothing was discussed about interference by us or any other intelligence service. If they suspected it, I would expect them to have addressed it, unless one of them wanted to hide it from the other. I'm guessing that rules out the Chinese from conducting the motorcycle attack. But if not them, who?

Exhausted, I look at the time — almost noon. Since we have nothing to do, I decide today would be a good day to visit my friend and gem dealer, Sammi Suriwatpong. His office is located in the Jewelry Trade Center (JTC) on Silom Road, very close to the Oriental Hotel.

"Craig, you liked the gemstones I showed you. How about going with me to see my friend Sammi? He says he has some fabulous stones to show me."

Craig looks up from his laptop and shakes his head.

"I need to find out what I can about Wu Min. Maybe next time. Karen and Angie will probably want to go."

I don't have to ask Karen and Angie. They're my protection, and I can't go anywhere without them. But I ask anyway. "Ladies, how about going with me to see some gemstones?"

"Absolutely," says Angie.

"And sometime, I'd like to go to a shop where I can get some clothes made," Karen adds.

"I have another friend, Jesse, who can do that, or I recommend someone else if you want dresses," I respond as we head out.

We decide to go directly to the JTC by taxi and eat lunch in the food court. Angie has som tam (papaya salad); Karen has pla goong (prawn salad). I have pad thai (fried noodles). They all have salty, spicy, sweet, and bitter flavors that make Thai food unique.

All during the meal, I watch my surroundings for anyone suspicious but don't see anyone. Karen and Angie don't seem too worried, though.

After lunch, we proceed to Sammi's office on the 45th floor of the office tower.

On the ride up in the elevator, I ask, "Do you think we're being followed?"

Both Karen and Angie say, "No!"

I say, "Maybe that's too bad because visiting a gem dealer reinforces my cover." They both smile at my theory.

Sammi's office's door has a sign that says simply, "Siam Trading Company, Limited." The wholesale gem dealers tend to keep a low profile, letting the retail jewelers in Bangkok have the spotlight with their extreme marketing techniques.

Sammi's assistant, Miss Arunee, greets us at the door with a wai and shows us into Sammi's private office. Sammi jumps up from his desk, says, "Grant!" and gives me a big hug.

He bows and wai's Karen and Angie. Sammi is short and round with a big smile and medium-length black hair. I think he's about five years older than me. He wears a traditional Thai silk banded shirt, untucked at the waist, and khaki pants.

Sammi says, "Grant, it has been too long. How are you?"

I respond, "Sabai dee mahk khap," which means I'm well.

I introduce Karen as my cousin and Angie as her friend. Sammi greets them warmly.

I say, "Sammi, you told me you have some new sources of

gems in Africa, so I came to take a look. Also, you know I'm always looking for collectible sapphires and rubies."

"Yes, my friend, I have a new source for gems from Africa. Let me show you." He opens his large safe and pulls out several trays.

"Here's a spessartite garnet from Nigeria. This one is 22.4 carats." It's a bright-orange color, cushion cut, very clear and sparkling. Actually, there's a whole tray of spessartite of different sizes and shapes.

He says, "I can get equally good quality in any size up to about 30 carats, my friend. How do you like it?"

"Let me take a look." I pull out my jeweler's loupe and borrow his locking tweezers to examine the gem carefully. The color is spectacular. It is bright orange, uniform, with deep saturation. The clarity is good, with no obvious inclusions; the cushion cut is well done and exhibits significant brilliance. It is an exceptional stone for this type.

Sammi says, "Chaawp reu mai chaawp."

I translate for the ladies. "He asked me, do you like it or not?"

"Chaawp maak maak."

To the ladies, I say, "I told him I like it very much!"

Then, "Yes, Sammi, I know someone who would like it. What's the price?"

"You should be able to sell it for $1,500 per carat, maybe more, but I would sell it to you for $1,000 per carat."

That's $22,400 — I don't think many customers could afford that. And that's only for the stone.

I think it's a fair price, but I don't want to act too anxious to buy. "Do you have the gemological report for this stone?"

"Yes, of course."

While he's looking for the report, I hold up the stone to

Angie and Karen, who were not close enough to have a good look. They nod that they like it too.

Sammi hands me the GIA colored stone lab report. I read through it, take a photo with my phone, and give it back.

"The photo will help me remember it. Let me think about it. What else do you have?"

"Here is a rhodolite garnet from Mozambique. This one is 10.7 carats, oval cut, unique purple/red color, usually described as raspberry red. I can also get these at this quality up to about 15 carats," says Sammi.

I go through the same routine with the loupe and the tweezers. I also ask for the GIA report and take a photo.

"Very nice; how much is this one?"

"It should sell for $1,200 per carat, but I will sell to you for $900 per carat."

"It would make a very nice pendant."

I show it to the ladies, and they agree. Angie seems more interested than Karen, but I'm not sure. Maybe raspberry red is not her color.

He then shows me trays of pink spinel from Mahenge in Tanzania, green tsavorite from Kenya, emeralds from Ethiopia, and pink padparadscha sapphires from Madagascar. We go through the same routine as before to examine the stones. I photograph the GIA reports of the gems in which I have an interest.

Karen seems more interested now, especially in the pink sapphires.

He then says he has some other gems to show me. He pulls a tray of electric-blue zircons from Cambodia, which he says he will sell at an exceptionally reasonable price. They are lovely and not expensive. Karen seems especially interested in the zircons. Maybe blue is her color.

Sammi asks the ladies which color gems they like. Karen

says pink or blue, and Angie says blue or orange. Sammi says, "Maybe Grant will buy one for you as a remembrance of Thailand." We all laugh, and I hope that means Sammi will kick in a choice gemstone for each of them if I make a large purchase.

After another look at the trays, I think of some past customers who might be interested, especially Mrs. Ambrose and her friends. "I'll let you know after I have a chance to check with some potential customers, probably when I get back to Natchez. Is it possible to hold the spessartite and padparadscha for two weeks?"

"I would be happy to do that, my friend."

We agree that if I want to purchase, I can wire the money as in the past, and he'll ship using Brink's.

"Grant, it was so good to see you again," Sammi says. "Maybe next time it will be in Natchez!"

"If you come to Natchez, you can stay with me," I tell him. "I'll give you a tour and take you to New Orleans."

He smiles wide and says, "I would like that very much!"

Sammi bows and wai's Karen and Angie.

We all say goodbye to Miss Arunee, and she waves to us as we leave.

As we get on the elevator, Angie says, "That was an experience. I'll probably never see so many valuable gems in one place in my life, and not one of them was a diamond!"

We all laugh, and I say, "That's what I love about Bangkok!"

When we get back to the hotel, Craig has information about Wu Min. The photo shows a young man in his early thirties, tall and thin. He is a Ph.D. graduate of Tsinghua University, majoring in computer science and technology. The CIA believes he is a manager in APT10, leading their sophisticated hacking operations. He lives in Beijing and is not married.

Craig says, "Karlsson's been released from the hospital, too.

He'll probably need to stay home for a couple of days, which will delay Allison's payoff; we're watching them both. Tony still thinks nothing will happen until Allison's part of the operation is ready. Li is still in Phuket, so nothing is imminent here."

All we can do is wait.

"Tony's also asking if you've found anything new from Li or Yang."

I shake my head. "Nothing yet, but I'm working on it." Honestly, I don't quite know where to go next. But it gives me satisfaction to be in control of the situation for once, and not Tony.

Let him sweat a little.

CHAPTER 31

I **AWAKEN EARLY** and lie in bed, thinking through the whole situation. I wish I were back in Natchez, eating breakfast with Miss Doris and going about my routine — just as before I got that phone call from Tony.

Well, nothing I can do about it now. It seems I'm stuck in this new reality unless I quit, then I may be stuck anyway.

After I get dressed, I check with Craig. "Anything happen last night?"

He says, "No, not a thing."

"Well, then we have another day to kill in Bangkok until the Chinese are ready."

Angie and Karen come over to the suite. Room service delivers our breakfast, and I ask the ladies, "Do you want to go shopping today?"

They both say, "Yes."

"Craig, how about you? There's safety in numbers!"

He scrunches up his face, then says, "Okay, I'll go along today."

I suggest we first visit my friend and tailor, Jesse Gulati, and his son, Victor, at their shop called Rajawongse Clothier. They specialize in men's clothing but also make blouses and blazers for women. Their shop is on Sukhumvit Road next to the Landmark Hotel. I suggest that afterward, we go to a jewelry shop in Siam Square.

We take a van taxi to the Landmark Hotel. It's the closest place to stop and let us out safely near Jesse's shop, which is only a few hundred feet away.

When we get to the front of the shop, I lead the way by climbing the five black marble steps to get up to the entrance. These shops were built above street level to prevent flooding from monsoon rains. Sewers in this part of the city would not take the water away quickly enough — and the streets would flood in a matter of minutes.

As soon as I step inside, Jesse greets me. "Grant, how are you? It's been a long time, my friend!" Jesse never forgets a name, and I'm sure Victor doesn't either. Jesse and Victor are Sikh and wear traditional turbans.

"Jesse, yes, it's been too long. How is your family?"

"They are all excellent, Grant. And now I have more grandchildren."

"Jesse, I'm so glad to hear it. I brought my friends with me today. This is Karen, and her friend Angie, and our friend Craig." There was no reason to tell Jesse and Victor that Karen is my cousin.

Victor says, "If you are a friend of Grant's, you are a friend of ours."

I say, "Please show them around your shop and tell them

what you can do. I'll look at fabrics for a new suit while you're doing that."

Jesse proudly shows them around the shop, showing them photos of his celebrity customers — Presidents George H. W. Bush, George W. Bush, Barack Obama, etc. Jesse brags how many generals, admirals, ambassadors, and other government officials are regular customers. Victor mentions all the Secret Service and law enforcement agents who are customers. He says this is because he and Jesse are experts in fitting a blazer or suit to hide a gun. That gets our attention.

Jesse asks, "How long will you be in Bangkok, Grant?"

I tell him, "We don't know. We might have to leave on short notice, but I expect we'll be here at least two or three more days."

Jesse says, "Okay, if you place an order today, then I will have it ready for a fitting tomorrow, and the finished suit or blazer in two days. If you can't come here, I will come to your hotel, my friend."

Victor asks what color and style of cloth we would like. I say, "I'm looking for a dark blue or black fabric with a chalk stripe."

Craig says, "I'd like a gray fabric with a blue pinstripe."

Karen sees samples of blazers and likes the subtle plaid fabric. She tells Victor, "I want a plaid like that in blue."

And Angie says, "I want a blazer in a dark fabric, blue or black. Show me your options."

The shelves are stacked with bolts of cloth all the way to the ceiling. Jesse and Victor climb on ladders, pulling down bolts of cloth to show us.

They lay out the bolts of cloth on the large cutting tables in the middle of the shop. We each make our selection.

I pull Jesse to the side and tell him we all want to be fitted so that we can hide weapons. I tell Jesse that the others are federal agents and I have my own weapon, too. His eyes get very big, and he nods his head.

Jesse and Victor begin the process of taking our measurements, which they've done thousands of times; it doesn't take long.

Jesse says, "Can you come here after 3:00 p.m. tomorrow for a fitting?"

I say, "Yes, but if something interferes, I'll call you. What time do you close?"

"We close at 8:00 p.m., my friend."

"Thank you, Jesse and Victor. We'll see you tomorrow."

We leave the shop and walk back over to the Landmark Hotel to catch a taxi to Siam Square. As we walk to the hotel, I discreetly look around to see if we're being followed. I don't see anyone, but I'm on the watch for motorcyclists with black helmets. Karen, Angie, and Craig all say we're not being followed, but I want to check for myself — as if I would know.

We get caught in traffic on Rama I Road as we near CentralWorld, very close to Siam Square. Motorcycles creep ahead between the lanes of traffic, and I can feel my palms start to sweat. We're sitting ducks in this traffic, but luckily only the regular motorcycle taxis pass by us. We can see the famous Erawan Shrine at the corner. Today, we get a treat, as there is an elephant on the sidewalk in front of the shrine. His trainer, called a mahout, is selling bananas to tourists so they can feed the elephant.

Angie thinks it's funny. Karen asks, "How do the elephants manage to get around in all the traffic?"

I tell her, "They come from their camps outside the city early in the morning before the traffic gets awful, and they just block traffic behind them as they walk down the street. Sort of like garbage trucks might do at home."

We watch tourists flock around the elephant. We finally

get through the intersection at Ratchadamri Road and turn left onto Henri Dunant Road. I tell the driver to stop and let us out on the perimeter of Siam Square.

Wuthikrai's shop, Siam Jewelry International, is right on Henri Dunant. We don't have to navigate the maze of shops on the side streets inside Siam Square. We enter the shop, and I see Wuthikrai in the back with a customer. He says something to his wife, and she takes over with the customer as he comes out from behind the counter.

Wuthikrai Boonvarute is a very tall man by Thai standards, over six feet. He's obviously an ethnic Chinese, as is about half the population of Thailand.

He says, "Welcome, Grant. It has been a long time!"

I say, "Yes, I wasn't able to make it to the Jewelry Fair this year."

Wuthikrai says, "It was bigger and better than ever."

"Did you have a booth?"

"Yes, primarily to make connections for jewelry manufacture, my specialty."

"Wuthikrai, these are my friends, Karen, Angie, and Craig. I wanted them to see the beautiful jewelry available in Thailand."

Wuthikrai says, "I'll be happy to show them what we have on display and also give them an idea of what we can make." I turn to the others and ask, "Is there any certain type of jewelry you want to see?"

Angie says, "Yes, rings, bracelets, and necklaces." Karen nods in agreement. Craig doesn't say anything; he's watching out the window to see if we're being followed, I guess.

I suggest they might be interested in sapphire jewelry, since that would be the real bargain.

Wuthikrai shows them a large display of sapphire rings of all sizes. Many of them have a center sapphire and are flanked by two smaller diamonds. The settings are made from 18k gold, which is the typical setting used in Thailand.

He also shows them a whole case of sapphire bracelets, made with links of matching gems, again with 18k gold settings. Wuthikrai has a shop in the back of the store where his employees turn out the handmade pieces.

Karen and Angie also examine the sapphire pendants and peruse the assortment of gold necklaces. They like everything they see!

Meanwhile, Craig admires the antique ivory chess sets he knows he can't bring into the United States. Karen decides on a striking sapphire pendant encircled in small diamonds. Angie chooses a lovely sapphire ring with two smaller diamonds flanking the center sapphire. Wuthikrai gives both Angie and Karen excellent bargains. The ring needs to be sized, and Wuthikrai tells us he can send it to the hotel tomorrow.

After Karen and Angie pay, Wuthikrai says, "Grant, up to now you have bought finished pieces from me, but I can make any kind of custom setting for your clients, and you can supply your own gems. And you know we can copy anything just from a photo."

"Yes, and with Brink's, FedEx, and UPS all doing business with jewelers and gem wholesalers in Bangkok, there are more delivery options than before. I'll keep you in mind. It's getting more expensive to have custom jewelry made in the U.S.," I respond.

Miss Yaowadee finishes with her customer and comes to greet us. She has black hair, cut short, and has a sincere smile on her round face; she is wearing a lovely Thai silk outfit. She has the perfect personality for dealing with foreign tourists who might be hesitant to buy jewelry in Bangkok. She wai's all of us and says, "Hello, Grant, it's nice to see you again. Who are your friends?"

"This is Karen, Angie, and Craig. This is their first time in Bangkok, and I'm showing them the best places to shop." Miss Yaowadee wai's again as a gesture of thanks.

"We'll take good care of your friends, Grant," says Miss Yaowadee.

"Yes, I know. That's why I brought them here — despite the traffic." We all laugh about the terrible traffic, which is a fact of life in Bangkok.

Wuthikrai and Miss Yaowadee escort us to the door and wave to us as we leave the store and go out into the blazing heat.

As we wait to get a taxi, I look around. I feel like someone's continuously been behind me ever since the motorcycle shooting.

"Craig, have you noticed anyone following us today?"

"I'm not sure. I thought I saw someone suspicious standing across the street from Jesse's shop, but I haven't seen him since."

I'm glad I have my three bodyguards with me today.

As I check to make sure my weapon is ready to go in case I need it, Chief Parker's warning about not winding up in a Thai jail pops into my head. I really hope I don't have to use my weapon.

CHAPTER 32

IF I'M GOING to find out about Li's motives, I need to find more meetings between him and Yang. The only way I can do that without knowing exactly when they've met is to sample over some time in ten- to fifteen-minute increments. I decide to go back in time about two weeks, start at 8:00 a.m., and work through until 5:00 p.m. That would be thirty-six segments per day to check.

Unless I get very lucky, this will take some time, but that's okay because Tony's paying me a retainer of $40,000 per month, and I like to earn my pay.

I start with Li's memory on Monday, two weeks ago. As I suspected, Li was in his office. He's reading, and it's nothing important. So I check ahead fifteen minutes, still nothing. Again, and again, still nothing. I finally get to the end of the day without learning anything, so I go ahead to Tuesday. More of the same on Tuesday, and Yang has yet to be seen. Wednesday morning starts out the same way, but then it changes.

Yang is in Li's office at 10:30 a.m. Li asks him, "Did you find out what Councilor Chua thinks of General Wei Li Jie's chances if President Xiong steps aside?"

I hope he made inquiries as I instructed him.

Yang says, "Councilor Chua believes the General will be nominated by the President as his successor both as President and General Secretary."

I was afraid of that.

"Did you find out any more about the President's condition?"

Yang says, "It appears the President is getting weaker. He's secretly getting chemotherapy for lymphoma, but he has no plans to step down."

It's actually good if he can hang on for a while longer to give me a little more time.

"We need to move quickly. The General is not the right man to lead the country. He's too philosophical, too honest, and too timid. He believes the military's purpose is to only defend the country. I believe it is to drive foreign powers out of Asia. He will be a weak leader. He thinks China can win the economic struggle with the United States, but I know better. I must be selected to succeed the President. And to do that, we need to immediately implement Plan 23-2."

If I can pull off a successful attack on the U.S., it will give me the support I need in the Politburo to succeed President Xiong. I will announce to the Politburo that APT10 has taken down the United States financial system. We will leak it to the Western press if President Xiong does not allow China to take credit. When the Politburo sees that the United States has been damaged, they will be celebrating. There might be a temporary disruption in China, but the United States will suffer much more. They are more dependent on their financial system and public confidence in it than we are.

Yang says, "Yes, Deputy Chairman, I will make arrangements to go to the United States immediately. I will need to take enough cash with me to grease the wheels, at least $200,000. Can you arrange for it?"

I have more than enough already here, but it's best you don't know that.

"Yes, come here to the office to pick it up, say tomorrow at 2:00 p.m."

I will have him watched to make sure he is not double-dealing with the General.

Yang says, "Yes, Deputy Chairman," and leaves the office. *Plans are finally underway.*

Deciding to take a break, I walk out to the suite's living area to get coffee. Craig is there, and I tell him what I've learned. When he calls Tony to relay the information, he ends up handing the phone to me.

"Grant, this is Tony. What did you find out?"

"Li says the President has lymphoma and is very ill. Li wants to replace him. But General Wei Li Jie has the inside track, according to Councilor Chua. Therefore, Li needs to do something to gain the favor of the voting members of the Party. That's the reason behind the planned attacks."

Tony says, "Chua is a member of the Politburo Standing Committee. Any candidate for President would need Standing Committee support. Li and General Wei are both members, and there are only four others, not counting the President. The Standing Committee's recommendation would carry the most weight with the twenty-five Politburo members, which in turn control the 2,987 members of the National People's Congress, who actually elect the President.

"Good work, now we need to find out about the bank accounts in Hong Kong and why they're important."

I tell him, "Okay, I'll work on it."

Tony says, "We're running out of time, Grant. We can stop the financial attack, but we want to eliminate Deputy Chairman Li once and for all, or he'll continue to be a threat to the United States."

"I understand."

As long as they can't tie Li's elimination back to me, I don't care. That'll be Tony's problem to handle. But I assume "elimination" means Li will be jailed, not killed. But with Tony, you never know.

I hang up and give the phone back to Craig before heading into my room. I think I can work for another hour or two today, then I will have to give myself a break. This mental work is too exhausting.

I decide to pick up the next scheduled meeting between Li and Yang. I only have to spend a few minutes concentrating, and I begin to get images.

Li is sitting at his desk with stacks of cash in front of him. He's preparing a receipt for Yang to sign.

The receipt says, "I, Yang Kexin, acknowledge receipt of $200,000 from Deputy Chairman Li on this date for carrying out Plan 23-2."

Knowing I have this receipt should make him think twice before betraying me.

Yang is escorted into the office by Li's secretary.

At least he's on time.

"Deputy Chairman, I'm scheduled to leave tonight for Washington, D.C."

Li says, "That's excellent. The payoffs need to be made as soon as possible. I have the $200,000 here. You're going to sign for it, as usual."

I don't want Yang to be able to say if he's caught that he doesn't know anything about what's in the pouch and place the blame solely on me. He needs to be reminded that he's up to his neck in this.

Yang counts the money and nods his head in agreement.

Li puts the money in the diplomatic pouch and affixes an embossed official plastic seal, which can only be removed by breaking it. Yang signs the receipt.

"Do you have an appointment with Minister Hua?"

"Yes, Deputy Chairman, only a matter of hours after I arrive."

Finally, he does something right.

"And let me know immediately when the money has been transferred to Allison Murphy. Tell Minister Hua it is extremely urgent."

"Yes, Deputy Chairman."

"Have a safe trip, Yang."

If you don't do as I say, there will be hell to pay.

"Thank you, sir."

I decide to back up fifteen minutes before the scheduled meeting time with Yang to see where Li got the cash.

Deputy Chairman Li is sitting at his desk with a ledger in front of him. It lists numbers and amounts. It appears these are some sort of reference numbers. Li flips through the pages. There's a page for each reference number. On each page, there are amounts listed in Chinese yuan.

Li looks though the ledger book, scanning the entries, and thinking about each one.

101-20151112   ¥6,000,000
Xi controls critical delegates in the Politboro.

102-20151206   ¥6,300,000
Zhou will be loyal.

201-20151220   ¥3,500,000
Guo bears watching.

103-20160107   ¥7,500,000
Chua is very influential in the Standing Committee.

104-20160323   ¥6,500,000
Liang has his own ambitions.

202-20160418   ¥3,350,000
Xu is greedy. He will be asking for more.

203-20160515   ¥3,500,000
Yu controls the delegates from the North.

204-20160627   ¥4,000,000
Shen will be loyal as long as he is paid.

205-20160712   ¥4,500,000
Fang is expendable, but I need him now.

206-20160730   ¥4,500,000
Qin needs to support his large family.

207-20160815   ¥4,000,000
Xue has to feed his gambling habit.

208-20160909   ¥4,500,000
Tao has a lot of debt; he needs money.

209-20161124   ¥4,250,000
Qiao is young and ambitious, and has money problems.

210-20161217   ¥4,500,000
Dai's vote is for sale to the highest bidder.

211-20170123   ¥4,500,000
Hao wants to move up in future years.

Obviously, each reference number corresponds to a person, and based on Li's thoughts, it appears they are all Chinese politicians. My guess is these are payments he has made to each of them; more accurately, these are bribes. He will give them political cover to support him as Xiong's replacement by successfully executing Plan 23-2, but the bribes will ensure their support.

I notice that he doesn't look through the entire ledger, however, so there may be other entries that I haven't seen.

Closing the ledger book, he turns and puts it into a drawer in the safe. He opens another drawer in the safe and pulls out bundles of cash, each with five banded stacks. From what I can see, each stack comprises a hundred $100 bills, about a half-inch thick, secured in the official mustard-colored bands. He takes four of the bundles of five stacks each, totaling $200,000, from the safe. There are plenty more bundles still in the safe. He opens another drawer in the safe, inspects a QSW-06 military pistol with a silencer, and then places it back in the safe.

At that moment, Li's secretary announces Yang has arrived for their meeting. Li shuts the safe and locks it.

Now I know that Li is behind a bribery scheme to gain the support of those who will elect the next president. I have their names and the amounts they've been paid. I also know Li keeps a ledger book in his safe with all the details. But I don't know where he's getting the money to pay out millions in bribes. I might be able to find out how to get into the safe. I'll try that next, but now I'm too tired. I need a break.

After a couple of hours, I decide to pick up where I left off with Li. I get nothing — no images — nothing! This hasn't happened before; I try again — still nothing. I try to connect with Yang — nothing. Now I'm starting to worry. If I can't connect with anyone, then I'm useless to this operation. It will be a quick and disappointing end to my new career.

Angie is in the living area on the couch, reading a magazine. She says, "What's the matter?" seeing the look on my face.

"I can't connect with Li, or anyone else. I don't know what's wrong. Maybe it's transient, or maybe it's not. I never really understood how I could do it, so my psychic ability could have left as quickly as it came. If I can't do it when I want, what good is it?"

Laying the magazine aside, she pats the couch and says, "Come sit down and let's talk about it."

I sit down next to her. "How am I going to explain this to Tony?"

She says, "You're not going to — at least, not yet. You need to just relax; it's probably nothing, maybe just stress. You've been doing a lot of memory probing lately.

"Why don't you see if you can connect with me? Then at least you might find out if I find you attractive or not!"

"I already know the answer to that. I can look in the mirror. Who wouldn't find me attractive?"

We both laughed, but I take her advice and try to make the connection, but it doesn't work.

I frown and shake my head.

"Well, just lay your head here in my lap and relax while I massage your forehead and temples."

"Okay, maybe that'll help."

I like feeling her touch and just being close to her.

After a while, Craig and Karen come back from the gift shop and ask what we're doing.

"Grant's got a headache, so I'm trying to help make it go away."

"Did you take anything for it?" Karen asks.

"No, I didn't have anything."

"I have something for a headache. I'll get it."

"Okay, thanks."

After taking the two Tylenol, I lie on the couch for a while, thinking what I'm going to do if I can't "do my job." Most of all, I'm not happy that Angie and I were interrupted, even though we weren't doing anything.

And if my psychic ability can just come and go without warning, I'm not dependable and really no good for this type of operation. I would like to know one way or the other. I'm not looking forward to explaining this to Tony; he'll think I'm just making excuses. I'm confused. Finally, I decide to just give it time and see what happens.

CHAPTER 33

JUSTINE AEBISCHER WALKS out of the Grand Hotel du Palais Royal, carrying a black leather briefcase, and takes a taxi to the shop Mellerio at 9 Rue de la Paix, right next door to Cartier. She had decided the most logical place to start the search was with the Devereaux pendant's original manufacturer.

Exiting the taxi, Justine looks at the windows along the Mellerio storefront before entering. There are large color photos of the collections of jewelry, watches, and silver items. There will be no smash and grab here. She appears to be just another customer, dressed in an attractive and expensive black pants suit, which is flattered by her tall, slim figure but adorned only with costume jewelry. The look of simply a woman shopping is spoiled by the briefcase, which dwarfs her small leather purse.

She is buzzed into the store and is greeted by a man, impeccably dressed in a charcoal pinstriped suit and expensive

Hermès red jungle-pattern tie. She notices his pink, gold egg-shaped Montre Neuf watch, which must have cost a fortune.

She says, in perfect French, "Monsieur Jacques Mellerio is expecting me. Justine Aebischer."

A distinguished-looking man in his sixties with gray hair emerges from the back room. He says, "Madame Aebischer, it is a pleasure to meet you. May I see your identification?"

She says, "Certainly," and produces her FBI badge.

He says, "I have been doing some research since I talked with you about your case last week. Thank you for sending me the appraisal and the photos. I think I have some old but useful information for you. Please, come to my office, and I'll explain."

Justine follows him into the back. His office is relatively large, containing an antique desk, leather chairs, a small conference table, and a workbench with adjustable high-intensity lighting fixtures typically used by jewelers.

They sit at the small conference table.

He says, "May I call you Justine?"

"Yes, of course, may I call you Jacques?"

They both laugh. He says, "We are both members of a small club of people who regularly are searching for valuable jewelry. I am searching for gems to turn into items to sell and you to recover them if they are stolen. Unfortunately, jewelry theft has been part of the business for centuries. We must always be cautious.

"Justine, I may have a lead for you. My grandfather mentioned a fabulous ruby pendant when I was a teenager and first learning the business. He said someone brought it into the store for a repair, and he tried to purchase it, but the owner would not hear of it. I thought it must have been in the 1970s. We had been victims of fraud in the past, so my grandfather began a policy of photographing every piece that came into the store for repair, beginning in the 1960s. We still have the old files and photos. I began searching and found these photos from July 23, 1973."

He hands her two photos, front and back. She opens her briefcase and pulls out the appraisal and photos that Grant had given her. The piece appears to be the same in all the photos. He also had a description of the piece with the overall weight, which is precisely the same. The documentation says the owner brought in the piece to repair the security clasp.

Justine asks, "Who was the owner?"

He replies, "The record says M. Georges Lang, 38 Rue Fabert. That is in the 7th Arrondissement. I checked, and unfortunately, 38 Rue Fabert is now an office building. But you might be interested in how he would know to bring the pendant to us. I checked our records and see that he was a regular customer. He had earlier bought many expensive pieces. So he knew our hallmark and saw that the pendant had originally come from us. I would imagine since he brought it to us for repair, he was not aware it had been stolen. But where he bought it is a mystery. However, I can say for certain that he was very wealthy. I hope this information helps you, Justine."

She says, "Yes, it does very much. But if M. Georges Lang later sold this piece, where would he do that?"

Jacques says, "If he didn't know it was stolen, he would probably have tried Sotheby's at 76 Rue du Faubourg Saint-Honoré in the 8th Arrondissement."

A solid lead, finally!

Even though it's not much to go on, Justine feels hopeful now that she's found out this much.

"Thank you so much, Jacques," Justine says.

"Happy hunting, Justine. Come visit any time."

Leaving Mellerio, she hails a taxi right outside.

After getting in, she says, again in perfect French, "Take

me to Sotheby's on Rue du Faubourg Saint-Honoré." The taxi driver nods, and in about twenty minutes, they're there.

She hands the driver twenty euros, exits the taxi, and goes inside Sotheby's.

When Justine steps inside, a nicely dressed receptionist greets her.

Justine says, "I'm here on official business. Is your manager available?" She flashes her badge so quickly it would have been impossible to identify which agency she was representing.

The woman takes her to the office of M. Claude Dupuis.

"Sir, this lady is here to see you on official business," the receptionist says.

Claude Dupuis stands behind his desk, slightly startled. "I'm sorry, I missed who you are representing."

He is wearing a double-breasted gray suit and blue patterned tie. He has thick, long, sandy hair combed straight back from his forehead. Judging from his smile, he is a friendly salesman type, very used to dealing with wealthy customers who have valuables to sell.

Justine says, "The United States FBI, Jewelry & Gem Theft Program. I'm Special Agent Justine Aebischer."

M. Dupuis's eyes widen slightly, and he says, "Your French is so perfect. Did you learn in America?"

Smiling, she says, "My parents are Swiss."

"Oh, I see," M. Dupuis says, motioning for her to sit. "What can I do for you?"

"I'm trying to locate a stolen piece of jewelry that could have been auctioned in Paris. It might have been sold by a M. Georges Lang sometime after July 23, 1973. I have a description of the item. Can you help me?"

"Perhaps. All of our records have been computerized. We opened in Paris in 1968, so we might have handled this transaction.

Let me see if we have any record of a sale for M. Georges Lang." He starts making entries in his computer. In less than a minute, he says, "We have several sales for M. Georges Lang, whose address was 38 Rue Fabert. Just a moment while I print the sales records."

Justine smiles.

Maybe this will be easier than I expected.

"Yes, M. Lang auctioned a diamond bracelet in 1986 for 600,000 francs. Then he auctioned a Cartier diamond necklace in 1992 for 550,000 francs. And finally, a ruby pendant in 1995 for 30,000,000 francs."

"Yes, the ruby pendant is the piece of interest. Do you have a description of the piece?"

"We have a written description and photographs. Just a moment while I pull up the file."

The documents come up on the screen. It only takes a few seconds for Justine to see it is the same pendant. She almost jumps out of the chair.

"I assume you know who bought the pendant?" Justine asks.

"Yes, it was a Mr. Ryurik Vetrov of New York, USA. I believe you would call Mr. Vetrov a Russian oligarch. It was bought by him on June 3, 1995."

"Do you have the exact address in New York?"

"It was 1 West 72nd Street, New York, New York."

"And did you require M. Georges Lang to provide any proof that he was the owner of the piece?"

"Yes, of course. He provided a Bill of Sale from M. Pierre Rousseau of Paris, France, dated May 15, 1973."

"And the address of M. Rousseau?"

"The record says 44 Rue Fabert, Paris, France. That is in the 7th Arrondissement."

This is too easy. No one's trying to cover their tracks — unless all these buyers had no idea it was stolen.

"So, they were neighbors?" Justine asks.

"Apparently, and wealthy ones, too."

"May I have a copy of the records?"

"Yes, of course. Just a moment while I print them."

Justine puts the copies in her briefcase and leaves Sotheby's after thanking M. Dupuis for his help.

He says, "I hope you find the pendant, Justine. If you do, please tell me. I would be very interested to hear the full story."

"Yes, I will. Again, thank you so much."

Once back in her hotel room, she logs in to the Interpol website and enters a request for information on M. Georges Lang, M. Pierre Rousseau, and Mr. Ryurik Vetrov with their last known addresses.

She also sends an e-mail to Grant.

It says, "Grant, I found a sale of the Devereaux pendant in 1995 at Sotheby's in Paris for 30 million French francs (about $6 million in 1995). Likely worth much more today, if we can recover it. Trying to find the current and past owners. I will give you more details as I get them, but this is significant progress. Justine."

CHAPTER 34

I'm happy after receiving Justine's update. I'm glad someone besides me is holding up their part of the bargain. But I still can't connect with Li, and Tony is asking for more information, so I'm not as happy as I could be. I decide to just try to relax, and maybe the problem will take care of itself. I'm not going to say anything about it to Craig or Karen.

We're still anxiously waiting for Li to return to Bangkok; we know nothing will happen until he returns. While eating breakfast, I say to Angie, "We're supposed to go to Jesse's shop today for a fitting. Why don't we do some sightseeing on the way? If you agree, we'll see if Craig and Karen want to go." Craig and Karen are still getting dressed.

"Sightseeing? Aren't you worried about another attack?" she asks.

"No, I've got a great security detail," I say, smiling.

"Yeah, I've heard. Especially that cute but deadly FBI agent," she laughs.

"Yes, I'm getting very dependent on her. I'm thinking about hiring her permanently."

"Haha, you wish!" she says.

"Well, what about sightseeing?" I ask.

She says, "Sounds like fun!"

When Craig and Karen show up for breakfast, I ask them, and they agree. About a half-hour later, we're ready to leave.

We just have to stay in public places — that's what Tony says.

We take a taxi to Wat Pho, which is not very far away and just south of the Grand Palace. This temple is home to the famous giant, gold-leaf covered reclining Buddha, about 150 feet long; the crowd enters the building at the feet and progresses toward the head, where we exit. The admission cost is only a hundred baht, and the temple is crowded both with tourists and worshipers. The air is heavy with the pervasive fragrance of smoldering joss sticks.

After we leave Wat Pho, we take a boat from the Tha Tien Pier across the Chao Phraya River to Wat Arun. The boat ride costs only three baht. Wat Arun is also known as the "Temple of Dawn" because of the pearly reflection of light off the colored glass and porcelain surfaces. Visitors are allowed to climb several levels of steps but not all the way to the upper levels. We climbed two ranks of the steep steps, which was enough for me and the others.

On returning to Tha Tien Pier, I decide to make a stop at River City Bangkok, a shopping mall near the pier, to buy a gift for Miss Doris. We shop in several stores and find a beautiful Thai Benjarong vase, about eight inches tall, in Angkor Antiques. I know Miss Doris loves decorative items like this, especially if no one else in Natchez has one.

We then decide to head toward Jesse's shop after eating lunch at the Grand Hyatt Erawan on Ratchadamri Road. We eat in the Erawan Tea Room, which has only a small crowd, as the lunch hour is past. We choose some Thai specialties to share: por pia goong (deep-fried prawn spring roll), gaeng phed ped yang (duck with red curry sauce), gai hor bai toey (deep-fried chicken wrapped in pandan leaf), and gaeng kiew wan gai (green chicken curry). It was all very flavorful, but I thought the duck curry was the best. While I enjoy the distraction of a good meal, afterward, I wonder if or when another assassination attempt is coming.

By the time we finish lunch, it's almost 3:00 p.m., so we take a taxi to the Landmark Hotel. From there, we walk a few hundred feet to Jesse and Victor's shop. When we enter, as usual, it's like Jesse hasn't seen us in years. I wish I could be half as enthusiastic and happy as Jesse is on his worst day.

Jesse says, "Grant, I am so happy to see you and your friends today. We have everything ready. We just need to see if we need any adjustments to make your new clothes fit perfectly."

Then he says in a low voice, "Do you have your weapons with you?"

I say, "Yes," and he says, "Good, then we won't have to make any guesses."

Jesse says, "Victor, please get the clothes for Grant and his friends — Karen, Angie, and Craig." Jesse never forgets a name!

Victor brings out the clothes from the back room. Craig and Karen use the two tiny changing rooms in the back while Jesse chats with Angie. Then Jesse goes to work while Victor takes over the chatting.

Craig's suit requires a minor adjustment to the jacket, and Jesse also measures for the pant cuffs. Karen's blazer is too big, so it will take a little more work. Then Angie and I take over the small changing rooms and take turns in front of the mirror in the back of the shop while Jesse inspects, tugs, marks, and pins the material just so until he's satisfied. Angie's blazer fits nicely. Since we don't use the bulky radios that were used in the past, it's easier to provide the extra room needed for our weapons.

Jesse tells us we can pick up the finished clothing tomorrow, or he can send them to the hotel. We ask him to send the clothes over in case we need to leave on short notice and don't have time to get back to the shop.

Jesse says, "Come back again on your next trip to Bangkok, my friends. If I'm not here, Victor will be here to take care of you."

We shake hands with Victor and Jesse and hurry back to the Landmark Hotel to catch a taxi. We are careful to time our arrival at the taxi stand to avoid the first or second taxi just in case a foreign agent is masquerading as a driver. Craig even goes inside the hotel, waits, and then comes back out so that we take the fourth one in line.

༄

That evening, I walk out to the living room to see that Craig, Karen, and Angie don't look happy. I ask, "What's going on?"

Craig says, "Li has returned from Phuket, and Allison Murphy has made the payoff to Karlsson. That means Plan 23-2 is ready to proceed. Yang has also returned and checked back into the W Hotel. Tony expects that Yang will program and deliver the flash drives tomorrow unless Li has decided to delay. We should expect the malware to be activated the day after tomorrow at 7:00 a.m."

"Well, then, I don't understand why you look unhappy," I say.

Karen says, "Because Tony has decided to go to Chiang Mai himself to see what happens when Plan 23-2 is activated at the Krung Thai Bank."

"Wouldn't he be spotted if he goes there?" I ask, thinking of the gunman the other day.

"Exactly."

No wonder they don't look happy.

Since Li's back at the hotel, we have to wait until he leaves again before we can do anything.

When we get the call that he's gone out for dinner, we decide to get away and meet Tony for dinner. He's made reservations at the New York Steakhouse in the JW Marriott Hotel on Sukhumvit Road, not far from Jesse's shop. We're all ready for some American food. And we want to talk with Tony.

When we arrive, Tony's already seated at a large round table with a bottle of wine. Menus are there, water is poured, and wine glasses are waiting. With its dark wood, beamed ceiling, oversized leather chairs, and black-and-white 1950s-style photographs, the room really does radiate the feel of a New York steakhouse.

Tony welcomes us with, "Well, I think we're finally going to get real action day after tomorrow, and I'm going to Chiang Mai to see it for myself."

I ask, "Don't you think it'll be risky for you to be there?"

He says, "No, I don't think the Chinese will know who I am, but they know better than to bother me if they do. You could call it professional courtesy. Besides, I'll have a team of our agents with me."

Great, that's just what we need, a shootout in Chiang Mai.

Karen asks, "Is there anything we can be doing here?"

He says, "You can go out and about and observe anything unusual, but I don't think you'll see anything here. Grant, you should continue to try to find out what you can from Li or Yang."

Angie gives me an anxious glance, not knowing what I'm going to say.

I say, "Sure, I'll keep working on that."

I don't know how much longer I can stall before he finds out my psychic powers are gone!

The server comes to the table, pours the wine, and takes our orders. Karen orders lobster, and Angie orders lamb chops. Craig and I order U.S. Prime beef filet, but Tony wants to try the Australian beef filet. The server prepares the Caesar salad tableside with plenty of anchovies.

Once the server leaves, Craig asks, "Tony, what do you expect in Chiang Mai?"

"I think the first thing will be that the ATMs won't work. Then, when the bank branches prepare to open, they'll see that their computer systems are not working, and the branches may stay closed."

After that, he doesn't know how the public will react but will be closely monitoring.

"But won't the Chinese have agents monitoring, too?" asks Angie.

"Tony, you just don't look like a regular tourist, so you'll be conspicuous. It seems like you're taking a lot of risks. Can't you just arrange with the Consulate in Chiang Mai to report on what happens?" I ask.

Tony shakes his head. "We don't want anyone else to know what's going on."

He always has to be at the center and in control.

I say, "Okay, but I'd keep as low a profile as possible in Chiang Mai. You know that Chiang Mai is only about 50 miles from Myanmar, 100 miles from Laos, and a little over 200 miles from China, right? They could kidnap you and have you out of the country pretty fast if they wanted."

Tony replies, "They don't want to create a diplomatic problem. They'll leave me alone."

I nod my head.

I hope so, Tony. I hope so.

"Tony, on another topic, there's something I've been thinking about. Allison Murphy told Hua how smart Karlsson and Kleiner are and that they'll never get caught. That worries me. What if they're arrested when they arrive at work, and they don't have the flash drives on them. Have you thought about that?" I ask and wait for a reply.

"What do you mean?"

"Well, she just said that she doesn't know if they'll actually use the flash drives or some other method to get the malware into the system and that they might use accomplices. And they know getting it past security will be the first order of business. You don't really expect they'll have the flash drives in their pockets when they go through security, do you? Will you have arrest warrants and search warrants ready for their homes and their places of work?"

"Yes, we'll do that," he says.

"I was wondering if they evade initial detection, then what will you do? My suggestion is to let me have a chance to see them in person, then I can probe their minds later if necessary. So, I guess that will require a quick trip to New York and D.C. before their plan goes into effect. If not, then I'll need to see them right after they're arrested. But that will be hard with them being in two different locations." I wait for Tony to respond.

Come on, Tony, use your head.

Karen adds, "Grant's on to something, Tony."

Tony looks at her for a second, then says, "Yeah, that's a good idea. I want you all to go to D.C. after we leave Bangkok. Then we'll decide what to do about Karlsson and Kleiner. And thanks for reminding us they may use other methods; we'll start working on 'probable cause' so we can get the warrants," he says with a worried look. "Thanks for that input, Grant."

"I'm just trying to earn my retainer, Tony," I say with a smile.

Tony doesn't return the smile. He frowns instead.

CHAPTER 35

AFTER A LEISURELY breakfast on the Terrace the next morning, enjoying the view of the river for perhaps our last time, I tell Craig I'm going to do a little mental work while I'm still feeling fresh. I'm hoping that with a few days' rest, I'll be able to connect with Li this time. Closing the door to my room, I lie down on the bed and concentrate on Li. I try to resume my search where I left off — before Li counted out the money from the safe.

This time, I'm finally able to make a connection!

Hopefully, I'm back on my game for good!

Li is talking on the phone about a foreign policy issue with Zhou, one of the Standing Committee members. When he finishes the conversation, he hangs up and turns in his chair to face the safe on the floor behind his desk. The gray safe is about three feet tall, two feet wide, two feet deep, and has a combination lock. It is obviously old, looks very heavy, and is probably fireproof. Li leans over and spins the large dial to the right several full turns. I watch closely as he spins the dial first right, then left, then right again. He turns the handle and the safe pops open. Now I have the combination: R27-L16-R33. With that, maybe Tony's team can eventually get the evidence they need to put away Li and other key players.

I still don't know the source of cash for the bribes. Li is getting a lot of money from somewhere, but from who? I suspect Yang or Wu Min has the answer. I only have access to Yang, so I have to start with him. During the conversation with Li, Yang mentioned that he had seen Wu Min two days earlier when he instructed him how to program the malware on the flash drives.

I need to start there. I start at 8:00 a.m. and check fifteen-minute increments, two days earlier than their conversation on the terrace. The first five increments reveal nothing. Then, at 9:30 a.m., Yang walks from his West Building office to the edge of the lake in the Zhongnanhai complex called the "Southern Sea." Zhongnanhai is the walled complex where Chinese central government buildings are located.

I must talk with Liang before my meeting with Wu Min. Liang has promised me more money, but he's not delivered. There he is now.

Yang approaches a tall man of medium build and bows slightly.

"Hello, Liang Wang Yong."

He's smiling; that's a good sign.

"Hello, Yang Kexin."

After greeting, they walk together along the edge of the lake. "I'm going to Bangkok tomorrow night to see Deputy Chairman Li," Yang says.

"Since he's in Bangkok, his plan must be coming together," says Liang.

Yang looks around, then says, "Yes, in a few days there will be panic in the streets."

"Why did you want to see me today?" asks Liang.

Yang says, "I've given you the information exactly as I promised your 'friends,' but I haven't seen the payment you promised."

I don't trust the Russians at all.

Liang says, "Yes, and they are pleased. I'm told they'll deposit the $500,000 as promised into your account this week."

"I understand there are sometimes delays, but I've been worried," says Yang.

They insist on handling all payments through the Russian Commercial Bank in Cyprus. It's my account, but they could probably transfer the money out of the account any time they decide.

The $1,100,000 on deposit is still not enough for the risk I'm taking. I wonder how much the Russians have paid Liang.

"Liang, I'm taking huge risks by helping you. If I'm to continue, I need assurance of more money in the future."

"There'll be more money coming, but only after Deputy Chairman Li becomes President — which is the Russians' immediate objective.

Then we can threaten to expose the bribery scheme that brought him to power. He'll realize if he kills us, there will be others to take our place. He will then just have two choices: resign or come under the control of our Russian friends. If he refuses to fall under Russia's control, then one way or another, I will succeed him, and our friends will be just as happy. In that case, you will be handsomely paid also," replies Liang. "You understand that Russia wants to control China, and this is their plan, but we'll never let that happen. We'll double-cross them, just as they would do to us. In the meantime, we'll play along and take their money."

"But what about General Wei Li Jie?" asks Yang.

He is a more logical successor to Xiong than Liang.

"Our Russian friends will take care of the General. They consider him to be too dangerous and completely incorruptible," says Liang.

They'll probably poison the General or arrange an "accident."

"One more question for you. I'd like to start taking funds now from the RCB account. How can I do that?" asks Yang.

"I'll have to check with our 'friends' and let you know. Typically, you would have to go to the bank and withdraw money in person, but I suspect that it is too risky an option for you."

Yang nods.

If Li found out I went to Cyprus . . . It's definitely too risky.

"Okay, please check and let me know. Actually, having some of this money in my hands will make me feel more comfortable to continue."

"I'll do that. Have a good trip to Bangkok, and give my regards to the Deputy Chairman."

Not likely.

"Goodbye, Liang."

I will see you sooner than you like if I don't get my money this week.

Now I have a few more pieces of the puzzle. Liang is working for the Russians, expecting, with their help, to become President in the future, after Li. Yang has also been recruited by Russia and is being handled by Liang. But I still don't know what the Hong Kong account is about or who's funding Li's bribes. It could be Russia, trying to compromise Li and eventually get him out of the way, or it could be someone else. I'll work on that another time; it's already late in the afternoon.

Craig, Angie, and Karen are all in the living room when I enter. I ask, "What's new?"

Craig says, "Li is back in the hotel. Tony is in Chiang Mai, and Yang is back at the W Hotel. We think he delivered the flash drives today. So now we're all just waiting."

Angie gives me a questioning look. I nod my head, and she smiles. She understands my psychic powers are back.

No one has anything else to say, so I ask, "How did you ladies enjoy the pool?"

Karen says, "It was great! The water was warm, and the pool attendants brought us cool face towels and drinks. We also talked with a nice couple from Mason, Ohio, here on vacation. It was nice for us to talk with someone besides you two."

I ask, "Did they ask why you had guns hidden under your towels?"

Angie laughed. "Fortunately, they didn't notice."

I decide to tell them what I learned from Yang about Russian involvement. Then I add, "That might explain why our people saw the Russian agent shadowing Yang."

Craig says, "This definitely complicates things. If the Russians want Li's plan to be successful, they'll certainly try to prevent us from spoiling it if they know we're involved."

All this gives me more to ponder.

Why would the Russians shadow Yang if he's already in their pocket? And do the Russians know we're here, or not?

CHAPTER 36

THE NEXT MORNING during breakfast, Craig writes something down and shows it to us.

"Station Chief Parker is sending over a technician to sweep our suites for bugs, now that we know for sure the Russians are involved," it says.

We talk aloud about options for sightseeing during the day while we write notes to each other about what we are really going to do. Craig gets a call from the front desk and says he'll be right down to the lobby. Using hand signals, he asks Karen for her room key. He also writes a note saying he'll meet us in the Authors' Lounge. We all leave the suite.

A few minutes later, Craig meets us in the Somerset Maugham section of the Authors' Lounge. The Ciao Terrazza restaurant serves breakfast here if you prefer to sit inside and not on the terrace.

Craig says, "The technician will sweep both suites. Since the Russians are involved, we need to be more careful."

Angie says, "If they've planted a bug, what do they already know?"

"It depends on when it was planted, and we don't know that. We have to assume the Russians know everything that was said."

"Tony said we should go out and see if anything unusual is happening around the banks and ATMs. Any ideas where we should go?" asks Karen.

"Let's go over to the CentralWorld shopping complex. There are a lot of banks and ATMs around there," I suggest.

"Sounds good. Let's wait until the early afternoon," Craig says before answering a call. He listens, then hangs up. "No bugs."

We are all shocked, then relieved.

"That doesn't mean they aren't aware we're here. We still need to be careful about what we say in the suites. And they could make a plant at any time."

After we get back to the suite, Craig changes his mind and thinks I should stay at the hotel to remain safe, with Angie as my bodyguard. Karen will go with him to CentralWorld. Even though I know staying in is safer, I can't help the disappointment that shoots through me at not getting out of the hotel. It'll at least give me a chance to do some more mental work and then be with Angie.

I tell Angie what I'm going to do. She seems a little disappointed. She thought we could at least talk and keep each other company while Craig and Karen were gone. I tell her we can talk later.

Leaving Angie in the living room, I go into my bedroom to resume with Yang after his meeting with Liang.

I again check in fifteen-minute increments. At 2:30 p.m. I see that Yang is with Wu Min, and they're sitting in front of Yang's laptop. There are two flash drives on the desk.

Wu says, "I need to show you how to set the start and stop times for the worm attack. We included this feature, so the attack's timing can be decided right up until the time the malware infects the system. Unfortunately, we can't penetrate their firewall and do it remotely, so we have to do it this way."

Yang says, "Wu, I don't need to know how it works, I just need to know what to do. Show me or tell me."

"Okay, first insert the flash drive into the USB drive. Go ahead," says Wu.

Yang inserts the flash drive.

"Now, see the menu. One of the menu items is called Timer. Highlight that and hit enter."

Yang does it.

Wu says, "Now, there are two segmented fields on the screen, Start and Stop. Each field has sub-fields with individual entries for MM/DD/YYYY and HH:MM. The Hour field uses a twenty-four-hour time format. Understand?"

"Yes."

"After you fill all the fields, hit Enter while holding down the Control key. This allows the flash drive to be removed without loading the worm. If you are ready to load it, then just hit Enter, and the Start and Stop fields cannot be changed. The next time the flash drive is connected to a computer, it will load and the screen will show an Execute option. At that point, highlight Execute and hit Enter twice, and the worm is activated and will start and stop at the times that were set."

"So, once I get the times set and give these devices to my agents, I tell them all they need to do is connect the flash drives, allow the malware to load, highlight the Execute field, and hit Enter twice. Right?"

"Yes."

That seems simple enough.

"Thank you, Wu. Now, the Deputy Director wants to

know if you had any problems establishing the new cryptocurrency accounts."

"No problem. I opened two accounts in Hong Kong this week at the same bitcoin exchange, Xuobi," says Wu.

"Xuobi was able to buy the valid ID documents required to open them. I'll send you the account numbers later. You'll need to tell me how much to transfer into the new accounts."

"I'll do that as soon as you give me the new account numbers. Deputy Chairman Li is the only one who knows which account belongs to which person, so he will have to let me know. He wants to keep us in the dark as much as he can — the bastard — though we are taking as much risk as he is. Actually, we are taking more risks because he somehow will blame us. But if his plan is successful, we'll share in the success," says Yang.

"We've named our price, and he's paid it — so far," responds Wu Min.

Now I know that Li, Yang, and Wu are involved in a bribery scheme using a crypto-exchange in Hong Kong to make the payoffs. And only Li knows all the details, which he probably has recorded in the ledger he keeps in his safe. But there is still the question of where the money is coming from to fund the bribes. And Yang and Wu don't seem to trust Li.

I go back out to the living area of the suite. Angie is there, but Craig and Karen are not back yet from CentralWorld.

She says, "Everything good?"

I reply, "Yes, and now I know how to activate the malware."

She asks, "But do you know how to deactivate it?"

That's really a good question because I don't think you can deactivate it.

"Well, no," and we both laugh.

Is that gallows humor?

I ask, "Exactly what's Tony going to do in Chiang Mai?

Angie rolls her eyes, then says, "Probably just draw attention to himself, and then to us."

I shake my head. "That's what I'm worried about. Why can't he just let us do this?"

She says, "Oh, so now you're a street agent?"

I laugh, "Well, I want to do more than sit around a hotel room."

She smiles and says, "Hotel rooms don't have to be boring."

I am surprised by this. Well, things could get interesting if we ever have any privacy.

"Yeah, well, Karen and Craig will be back any time, so it will have to stay boring for now," I reply.

Angie makes a pouty face, and I laugh.

Then Angie says with a disappointed look, "I was hoping to go to Chiang Mai. My friend told me it's a wonderful place. Maybe next time."

Then she asks, "Have you ever considered living in Bangkok?"

I tell her, "Yes, but after I'm here a few weeks, I always get homesick for Natchez. I've never really considered living here full time, but I like to visit."

Angie says, "I can understand that. Natchez is a more homey type of place."

I ask Angie, "So what's going to happen after this operation is over? Am I going to get my life back? I may never be allowed to come back to Bangkok if it's up to Tony, that is, unless there's another investigation here. But he might agree if I pay for my own security, and you could do that job. Anyway, that's a thought." I smile and wait for her reaction.

"I'd like that," she says. "From what I can see, the DNI is going to designate you as a critical national security asset. That means you're going to continue to have round-the-clock protection. And you will be 'activated' as needed on important cases involving national security. I think you'll be able to travel, though."

At the mention of round-the-clock protection, I ask, "Does that mean Karen is going to stay with me indefinitely?"

"I don't know. But the FBI is supposed to be in charge of domestic intelligence. Karen is CIA, so probably not. That's why I was sent to Natchez."

"I wish you could play the role of my cousin. Nothing against Karen, but I'm more comfortable with you," I reply. "Couldn't we figure out a scenario where she leaves, but you stay?"

"Well, I'm afraid it's too late for that — unless we get married." She smiles.

"Well, that's an idea that has some appeal," I respond, laughing. "And what about Craig?"

"He'll most likely stick around for a while. At least, that would be my guess. The other agents in the background who you don't see will be rotated."

Sighing, I say, "So I'm stuck in this scenario forever?" I try to imagine living this way for the rest of my life. Part of me wonders if I should've asked for more money. Too late now. Though I can always try to renegotiate while threatening to quit as a last resort.

"That's my best guess. But you will be handsomely rewarded," says Angie.

"That's what Tony said."

I'm not entirely sure if he meant it, though.

She must have noticed the worry on my face, because she says, "From what I know, you can believe him."

What's better: freedom or living in a gilded cage? I know freedom; now I'm going to experience the gilded cage. There had better be a lot of gilding.

❦

When Craig and Karen return in the late afternoon, they tell us that nothing happened, neither here in Bangkok nor in Chiang Mai. Apparently, the operation has been delayed for some reason.

Craig's phone rings. When he hangs up, he says, "Something is going on. Li went to the W Hotel to see Yang, and he didn't look happy. Grant, give them a few minutes, then see what you can find out from Li."

I go back to my bedroom and concentrate on making contact with Deputy Chairman Li. After a few seconds, I see that Li is in Yang's hotel room.

"My observers in Chiang Mai say the malware is a failure, nothing is happening. The bank is operating normally, and so are the ATMs. What went wrong?"

He better have an explanation.

Yang says, "I know. Everything was done as instructed. The malware didn't work. We need Wu Min to investigate."

So, he is going to blame Wu Min, just as I expected.

"Send for Wu Min. I want to see him here in Bangkok tomorrow afternoon. I will meet him at the Oriental Hotel in the Authors' Lounge at 2:00 p.m. Then I will meet with you at the embassy at 4:00 p.m. And talk to your agents here in Bangkok and make sure they executed their instructions exactly. I will see you tomorrow afternoon, and we will decide what to do next."

When I tell Craig, he says, "That explains why nothing happened; their plan misfired."

He calls Tony and tells him the malware didn't work, that Li is very upset, and that they're bringing Wu Min from Beijing to resolve the problem. Tony tells him to expect they'll try again in a day or so. For now, he'll stay in Chiang Mai.

After Craig gets off the phone, he says, "We have time to kill."

In a few minutes, Craig gets another call from Tony.

After he hangs up, he says, "Tony got a call from the Director. The Federal Reserve reported they got an urgent call from the Bank of Thailand. Their BAHTNET and ICAS systems went down this morning a little after 7:00 a.m. These systems handle all bank transfers and check clearing in Thailand, and they're asking for technical assistance. The general public wouldn't notice problems with these types of transactions for a few days. That's why we didn't see anything unusual today here in Bangkok. So part of the malware did work, but Li and Yang don't know that.

"Tony wants you to establish a mental connection with Wu Min. If you're in the lobby when he arrives from Beijing, you'll have about fifteen seconds' exposure, maybe more, while he walks through on his way to the Authors' Lounge. Is that enough time? If not, we can go into the Authors' Lounge ourselves." Then he shakes his head and says, "No, you should go with Karen or Angie. A vacationing couple in the lobby or the lounge will draw less attention."

I'm not sure I like the possibility of Li recognizing me if I go back to the Authors' Lounge!

I respond, "That's not a lot of time, but it might be enough."

These developments mean that nothing will happen until Wu Min arrives tomorrow. He'll probably work late tonight trying to figure out what the hell happened, especially since Deputy Chairman Li will be looking for someone to blame. I bet Wu Min would like to know the Bank of Thailand attack was successful; it was just the Krung Thai Bank attack that flopped.

Later, we get a call from the front desk saying the clothing from Rajawongse Clothier had arrived. The bellman brings the garment bags to the suite. A note attached from Jesse says that if there is the slightest problem with the suits, he will come to the hotel himself. Fortunately, the fit is perfect for both Craig and me. The ladies have their clothes from Jesse delivered to their suite, and theirs fit perfectly, too.

When the ladies come to our suite that evening, we discuss what might be happening during the next several days. We conclude that the Chinese would make another attempt to disrupt the Krung Thai Bank operations, probably the day after tomorrow. We also decide it would be better if we ordered room service tonight and stayed out of sight.

CHAPTER 37

SUNDAY, MAY 12
BANGKOK, THAILAND

THE NEXT DAY, we wait around until Wu comes to the hotel. Craig says Li left for the PRC Embassy after breakfast, so we decide it's safe to have lunch at Lord Jim's. The restaurant is on the second floor of the hotel, facing the river. There are six beautiful curved tan leather banquettes, all empty, in the room's center, but we ask for a table near the windows. There were not many people in the restaurant at lunchtime. There was an enticing seafood buffet, so we all decided to make it easy and order the buffet.

Once everyone has their food, I ask, "Are you all ready to go back to Natchez?"

"Bangkok is great," Karen says, "but yes, I'm ready to go home."

Surprised, I say, "It's interesting that you consider Natchez as your home."

"You know what I mean!" She waves a hand in the air. "Living in a hotel doesn't feel like home."

Angie adds, "And Miss Doris makes us feel at home."

I have to agree with that; she sure does, and I miss her cooking.

After lunch, we go back to our suite to wait for Wu. We already decided it will be less conspicuous if Karen and I sit by ourselves in the lobby when Wu arrives. We agree that we should try to avoid Li. He'll probably arrive before Wu, so Karen and I browse the Louis Vuitton shop across the driveway from the lobby entrance to kill time. It's close enough to quickly move to the lobby after Li has gone into the Authors' Lounge.

At precisely seven minutes until two o'clock, we leave the Louis Vuitton shop, cross the driveway, enter the hotel lobby, and wait. Li has hopefully already passed through the lobby on his way to the Authors' Lounge. We sit on one of the couches in the middle of the space, facing the front doors, as if we're waiting for a car to pick us up at the entrance.

Wu arrives at two minutes until two o'clock and exits the taxi. It takes him a minute to pay the driver. Wu is wearing a light tan suit with a green tie and has a black briefcase in his right hand. He is tall and thin, just as in his photograph. He enters the lobby and asks one of the greeters for directions to the Authors' Lounge. The greeter shows him, and Wu walks briskly past us on his way to see Li.

I'm pretty sure that was enough time to make a mental connection. I concentrate on the image of Wu's face in my mind, figuring if it wasn't enough time, we could go into the Authors' Lounge. Choosing a time several hours ago to focus on, I receive images within a few seconds. He's flying in first class and is finishing his breakfast. He's thinking about what he's going to tell Li. I decide that's enough verification for now.

When we're back in the suite, Craig gets on the phone and gives Tony an update.

I wait until a little after 4:00 p.m. and then try to connect with Li, starting when their meeting is scheduled to begin.

Yang, Wu, and Li are sitting in an office at the PRC Embassy. It appears the meeting is between Yang and Li, with Wu primarily as a spectator.

Li says, "Wu explained the possible problems with the malware. He says there are only four things that could explain the failure:

"1. Your agents did not load the malware.

"2. The malware did not work as intended.

"3. The malware was detected and removed.

"4. The malware was not programmed correctly with the start/stop times."

Li rules out the software as the problem, as it has been tested repeatedly. "I doubt your agents would be so foolish as to not load the malware after accepting our money. And I believe Wu when he says it cannot be detected. So, I am only left with the choice to blame you for incorrectly setting the start/stop times. Wu Min has brought two more flash drives with him. I want him to set the malware times on both drives so there is no mistake. Tell your agents they need to load the malware again."

Yang listens, the look on his face becoming increasingly worried. "But sir, they have taken great risks to do it once. They will demand more money to do it a second time."

"You may give them another payment. I will make arrangements for it. Tell your agents they must load the malware again before noon tomorrow. I want the malware to be active from noon tomorrow until noon the next day. That will be enough of a test. We are getting short on time," says Li.

"Sir, I will try to get in touch with my agents immediately."

Don't try, do it! No excuses!

"Tell them there will be serious consequences if they do not carry out their instructions to the letter by noon tomorrow."

"I understand, sir."

"Wu, is there anything else that Yang needs to know?"

"No, sir. I can prepare the malware now if we are finished," says Wu.

"Yes, Yang can show you to a laptop here in the embassy that you can use. Meanwhile, I will arrange for the cash to be given immediately to Yang. Yang, contact your agents and arrange times to give them the money and the new flash drives. You will meet with them separately, of course."

"Yes, sir. I will do it tonight."

"And please confirm to me when you have made the hand-offs successfully to the agents, no matter how late. Do you understand?"

"Yes, sir."

At this point, I stop and come out to the living area. I tell Craig what I've learned. Li is blaming Yang, and Wu will be programming the malware for the next attempt tomorrow. Craig calls Tony to bring him up to date.

I decide to review the meeting in the Authors' Lounge between Li and Wu. I go back into the bedroom and relax. It doesn't take long to connect mentally with Wu. He tells Li essentially what Li repeated to Yang, but Wu also explains how the malware works and what could have gone wrong.

Wu tells Li, "Once the malware is activated, it begins creating millions, potentially billions, of false transactions in the banking system. In this regard, it's like cancer in the body, out of control. Eventually, it overwhelms the system with the sheer number of transactions, and the systems overload and shut down. However, the fraudulent transactions contain a specific identifier so that when the timer stops, the false entries are instructed by the malware to self-destruct but leave everything else as it was before. Then the malware itself is erased without a trace."

Wu is confident nothing can go wrong with the malware once it is activated. He did say that it was possible that the software code to limit the impact to the Chiang Mai branches might not have worked as planned, so he will remove it. Therefore, the next attack in Thailand will affect all Krung Thai Bank branches across the entire country.

Second, the U.S. attack plan is to set the Start timer but not the Stop timer. The worm will remain active until the authorities figure out how to neutralize it. Wu thinks this will take several weeks and will cripple the U.S. banking system, at least temporarily, maybe permanently. The more important result will be the loss of confidence by the American public in the banking system.

Third, within APT10, they call the malware "the Sputnik worm." They have written it so that if detected, isolated, and analyzed, there are characteristic signs of Russian malware. They are sure that Russia will be blamed. Li is pleased with that. He even smiles, but to me, it looks more like a grimace.

CHAPTER 38

WHEN WE ARRIVE at the Terrace for a late breakfast, it's just starting to warm up outside, and the morning crowd has left except for a few late risers.

There are still crowds of people on the river taxis, many of them college students, wearing uniforms, as is required in Thailand. The girls wear plain or pleated blue or black skirts with a white blouse, and the boys wear black trousers with a white shirt and a blue or black tie.

Both Chulalongkorn University and Ramkhamhaeng University are not far from the Oriental Hotel. Many students come from the other side of the river or from outer suburbs using river taxis. Of course, the students have no idea of the drama that will be taking place in the financial system in Thailand during the next twenty-four hours. They may never know unless they try to use an ATM. We don't precisely understand what's going to happen, either. But we'll find out soon enough.

As before, I'll stay at the hotel with Angie while Craig and Karen go to CentralWorld. We know the attack is set to trigger at noon.

We order room service for a late lunch. This time we take extra precautions. When room service arrives, I wait in my bedroom with my Glock — ready for action — and watch through a crack in the door. Angie answers the door, and the usual room attendant delivers the food and sets it up in the living area. Today we decide to have Thai food. Angie ordered ba mee ped haeng (egg noodles and duck), while I ordered pla kapong neung manao (sea bass with lime garlic sauce). We both chose khao neeo mamuang for dessert (mango and sticky rice). The food was delicious.

We wonder what is happening in Chiang Mai but don't want to bother Tony. He likes to communicate through Craig, so we wait. While we're waiting, we notice from our window the French Embassy next door. The historic Embassy/Ambassador's Residence faces the river. Right behind it is a new modern Embassy building, clad in pure white porcelain, and is prism-shaped. It is startling. We heard from our tour guide, Sriwat, that at night they project silhouettes onto the building of passing tourists superimposed onto the literary text of famous travelers, in French, of course. We need to remember to look at it tonight. There is always something unusual, unexpected, and surprising to be found in Bangkok.

Angie and I kill time by playing gin rummy. She beats me badly.

"You should figure out how to use your psychic skills at cards. Otherwise, you'll lose every time. You've got no card sense."

And we laugh that I could never be a casino dealer as I keep dropping the cards when I shuffle. She makes me smile and feel happy — and I think the feeling is mutual.

Spending time with Angie relaxes me in a way that I haven't

experienced in a long time. Even then, the stress of the situation seeps through. We continue to be careful what we say because we can never be sure the suite is not bugged. We also keep our weapons ready, just in case.

Late in the afternoon, Craig and Karen return. They say the Krung Thai Bank ATMs around CentralWorld were not working. The Krung Thai Bank branches were open, but customers were milling around, so there were obvious problems.

Craig calls Tony to report what he has seen. Tony says the Krung Thai Bank ATMs are not working in Chiang Mai. And there are a few people lined up at the banks there, too. He will be checking tonight to see if the bank has been able to fix the issues.

It appears the Chinese malware is working as designed, at least so far.

I hope my psychic skills keep working, too.

CHAPTER 39

AROUND 9:00 A.M., Craig's phone rings, and he practically jumps to answer it. He'd been prowling around the room since 7:00 a.m. He was obviously worried at not hearing from Tony if the path he wore on the carpet is anything to go by. "Tony, where have you been?"

Craig says, "What?" There's something about the tone of his voice that has the rest of us at attention. He sounds worried. "Hold on, I'm going to put you on speaker. Karen, Angie, and Grant are here. Okay, you're on."

"I was shot at last night," Tony says, "and I returned fire. I hit him with one shot, and he died on the spot."

"Where did it happen?" Craig asks.

"Near the Night Bazaar, while we were checking out the ATMs. Suddenly this guy jumped out of the shadows and started shooting."

A chill runs up my spine, and I wonder if this is connected

to the guys on the motorcycle. Tony seems to have too many enemies. Chinese, Russians — it's too confusing.

"The police came quickly and arrested my bodyguard and me. Fortunately, they allowed me to call the consulate and talk to the Consul General. She'd given me consular papers, so I had diplomatic status, which helped. And she talked to the chief of police to expedite our release."

"Who was the shooter?" Karen asks.

"That's the strange thing. The shooter's papers said he was from Myanmar. Since Myanmar and Thailand aren't exactly friendly, we probably won't get more information. So we don't know if he was a hired gunman or just a fanatic who didn't like my looks."

"Probably working for China or Russia. You aren't exactly popular with either country," Craig says.

"Yes, I wish we knew," Tony says. "I'm going to lay low in case he had friends here. I'll try to get back to Bangkok tonight. You all should be careful, too."

"We'll be careful. Karen and I will go back out to see what's happening this morning. The attack is supposed to end at noon."

Tony says, "I received a report that the Thai authorities informed the Fed last night that the same problems have resurfaced with the check clearing and bank transfer systems. They also reported the Krung Thai Bank transaction problems. The Thais asked the Fed for help, since their systems are practically a carbon copy of our U.S. systems."

"Let us know when you're back in Bangkok, and we'll compare notes," Craig says.

"Will do, stay safe," replied Tony.

When Craig hangs up, we speculate why Tony was attacked, but we really have no good explanation. It might have just been random violence, but none of us believe that. Craig and Karen leave for Siam Square.

I want to try and find the source of Li's bribe money before Tony asks for an update, so I retire to my bedroom to do some mental work while Angie stands guard in the living area. He's paid out over ten million in bribes, so he's getting a lot of money from somewhere. Could it be from the Russians?

I doubt it, from Yang's conversation with Liang, but who knows what kind of double-dealing is going on behind the scenes.

I decide that the best place to start is with Li's memory a few days before his arrival in Bangkok. I reason that if Li asked Yang whether Wu had opened new accounts in Hong Kong, it must be recent and possibly something to do with a new round of bribe payments. If this doesn't work, then I'll explore Wu's memory around the same period.

I decide to start five days before Li arrives in Bangkok and gradually work my way through the morning in fifteen-minute increments, finding nothing of interest. The afternoon also yields nothing, just a continuous stream of meetings. I wish I had more time because some of them seemed interesting, especially discussing what the Chinese are doing in Tibet. I move to the next day and work my way through Li's morning.

By lunchtime, I've found nothing, and I need a break.

Angie agrees we should order room service, but we also need to let the maid clean the room. We go to The Verandah — a small restaurant in the hotel — taking our weapons, of course. We sit outside under an umbrella because it's a little too warm to sit in the sun.

Angie orders pad thai (fried noodles), and I order a club sandwich. We enjoy the view, although the boat traffic plying the river has slowed considerably since the morning rush. It is a delightful break, and we stay an extra half hour to give the maid service more time. To complete our lunch, we order an assortment of macarons for dessert.

As she picks up a pink macaron, Angie says, "Have you ever used your power to read my memory?" She shifts in her seat, and I notice her cheeks begin to turn faintly pink. She asked me this once before, but this time it feels like she wants to know if I've tried to find out how she feels about me.

I actually like the fact that she's interested.

I tell her, "No, I don't think it's right to do that unless I'm engaged in official business."

She asks, "What if you thought you were in danger, and accessing my memory might help eliminate the danger?"

I stop for a moment, furrow my brow, and consider her question. "I don't know; I haven't thought through all the potential situations."

While we walk back to the suite, I'm still pondering our conversation, wondering how interested she is in me.

We linger in the hallway until a guest walking down the hall passes by and gets into the elevator. Angie enters the suite first with her weapon drawn, just in case, and quickly checks out the suite before signaling that it's safe for me to enter.

I go to my bedroom and pick up where I left off before lunch with Li and check through several hours with no result. But then I have success.

It's now the late afternoon, and Li is finishing up a meeting. His guest leaves, and I realize he's thinking about the bribe money. He decides to open the safe and pulls out the ledger book. He turns past the list of officials and the amounts he has paid and stops at a page that contains another list.

Beijing Consulting Services 01-486754

China Industrial Bank

Sino Life Insurance

DongLiu Motor Group

Sino Petro Works

State Electric Corporation

Mobile Telecom Corporation

TSAI Motor

Beijing Construction Corporation

WAF Telecommunications Group

Guanghai Development Group

Development Bank of China

China Chemical Group

Dalian Heavy Construction Co.

Shanghai Semiconductor Corp.

Xuzhou Manufacturing Company

Changzhi Agriculture Group

Chengdu Industries

He takes a few minutes to stare at the list while thinking of the people he deals with at each company. He puts the ledger back into the safe, closes the heavy door, and locks it — spinning the combination lock numerous times.

I'm guessing there's a separate page for each company further back in the ledger, with the amount each has contributed to his scheme. But I'm puzzled by the first entry on the list, Beijing Consulting Services. It's a services company, not a significant corporation, unlike the others. I also realize that the other companies are heavily reliant on the Chinese government in one way or another.

The number after the name makes me think this is the account number associated only with this company but not the others. I try to imagine how this would make sense. The only scenario I can think of is that Beijing Consulting Services sends each of the other companies a phony invoice. Then they pay the invoice into that account. In other words, Li is getting kickbacks on government contracts he controls — or as a retainer to protect their interests. The payments go into a Beijing Consulting Services account.

Well, that seems to exclude the Russians from being involved, at least in the bribery scheme. I write down the list of companies and the suspected account number. I need to find out more about this when I have a chance — from either Wu or Yang.

Hearing Craig and Karen, I go out to the living area. They say that the Krung Thai Bank branches were closed and the ATMs were not working this morning. Then, a little after 1:00 p.m., the bank branches reopened, and the ATMs started working. That makes sense because if the attack was over at noon, the bank would need some time to ensure that everything was back to normal before they reopened.

Craig says Li, Yang, and Wu are all at the PRC Embassy. They undoubtedly are reviewing the results of the attack. Craig says Tony wants me to find out what they've discussed before he's back from Chiang Mai tonight.

I go into my bedroom while the others wait in the living area. I lie down and start trying to connect with Wu about an hour ago. The meeting is already over, so I back up an hour and start there.

They're all sitting in a conference room, with Li at the head of the table.

"There were reports in the Bangkok Post today about the operational problems at Krung Thai Bank. Do you think they know what happened?" asks Li.

"No, there was not a trace left of the malware. The bank will conclude it was a bug in their system and will waste a lot of time trying to find it," says Wu.

"What about the Bank of Thailand?" asks Li.

"They also will never figure it out," says Wu.

Our tech is too good to be detected by the Thais or Americans.

Wu says, "Everything worked as planned."

Just as I knew it would.

"Both Krung Thai and Bank of Thailand banks were all shut down. We set up regular transfers between embassy accounts at Bangkok Bank and Siam Commercial Bank. The transfers did not happen as scheduled. Also, we wrote small checks on a regular schedule that were deposited at the same time each day. There was a break in the check-clearing pattern on the day the system was under attack."

You should show me some appreciation.

"Yes, you have achieved something significant for China. We are now ready to implement our plan in the U.S. Is everything ready?" asks Li.

"Karlsson and Kleiner are ready," says Yang.

"Okay, I want you both to go to Washington, D.C., and put the plan into effect as soon as possible. I want Wu to program the devices personally to prevent any mistakes," says Li.

Thank goodness! Yang would only screw it up.

"I want the attack to take place within a week. Yang, take more cash in the diplomatic pouch in case you need it. Come to my office, and I'll give you the cash," Li says. "Yang, make sure your two agents here in Bangkok are eliminated quickly."

"Arrangements have been made, sir. It will happen tonight," replies Yang.

"Good. The Chiang Mai attack on the American intelligence agent, Mr. Russell, failed. So far as we can tell, the Thai police have not connected the dead operative to us. I would still like to see the American eliminated while he is here in Thailand. He was too curious about the ATMs, and we don't know exactly what brought him to Thailand. And he also apparently brought a small group of American agents with him who he has met with several times at the Shangri-La Hotel. He must have received some specific intelligence on our plans in order to make the trip to Chiang Mai, so it's in our interest to neutralize him now. He seems to know too much.

"Yang, the men assigned to eliminate your two mercenaries may take whatever measures are necessary to eliminate Mr. Russell. And find out what you can about the other American agents. Keep them under surveillance, and install bugs in their hotel rooms if you can. We may need to deal with them quickly, too."

"Yes, Deputy Chairman," says Yang.

Now we're getting into a shooting war with American agents? This could be very dangerous. It would probably be better to wait until our operation is over. Still, I'm not going to disagree with Deputy Chairman Li.

"Get back to Beijing as quickly as your business here is finished," says Li.

I bring myself back to the present and review what I've found out. So China was responsible for the Chiang Mai attack on Tony. Then it was smart for Tony to make arrangements to stay at the Ambassador Debowy's residence when he returns to Bangkok. He'll be safer there than in a hotel. Unfortunately, Li now knows we're here, but he doesn't know exactly what we're doing. And he doesn't seem to know about me — not yet, anyway.

But it bothers me that the motorcycle attack wasn't mentioned. That probably means the Chinese weren't involved; was it the Russians?

I go out to the living area and share with the others what I've learned. As usual, Craig frowns and then says he needs to talk to Tony, so he goes to his room with his phone in hand.

In a few minutes, Craig comes back to the living area.

He says, "The situation seems to be getting more dangerous. Tony doesn't want to spook them into calling off the U.S. operation, so we should lay low. Tony will be back in touch with us when he gets to the Ambassador's residence tonight.

"With the threat level higher and Li's plan moving along, we need to be ready to leave Bangkok on short notice. It appears it'll be at least two days before Yang and Wu will be prepared to fly to Washington, D.C., and we'll be flying there, too."

CHAPTER 40

Even though Li has left Bangkok, we decide to have our last meal the next day at Le Normandie, in the hotel, which feels safer than going out. Our flight to D.C. is at 12:20 a.m., and we all still have yet to pack.

We arrive at Le Normandie precisely at 7:00 p.m. We are escorted by the maître d' to our table by the window. The view is straight out of a movie. Lights are twinkling on the teak rice barges converted into boats for dinner cruises. They lumber along awkwardly, being quickly passed by the river taxis still taking workers home from a long day in the city.

The restaurant is again filled with lovely flowers and is not busy this evening. Craig allows me to order the wine. I order two Bordeaux wines: Chateau Pape Clement Blanc 2010, a white blend, also Chateau Montrose 2016, a red blend. They are exquisite; thank you, Tony!

We all order caviar et oursin for an appetizer, as sort of a celebration of finally leaving Thailand for home. We like Bangkok, but we're all ready to get back to the United States of America. Karen orders turbot for her main course, Angie requests féra, Craig asks for Wagyu beef, and I ask for roasted milk-fed lamb.

Our last dinner is fantastic, but we decide to skip dessert. We go back to the room to finish packing and take quick showers before Chief Parker picks us up in an embassy van at 9:30 p.m.

At 9:20 p.m., Chief Parker calls to tell us he's going to come up to our suites and escort us downstairs, just in case. I worry he might know something that we don't. I think those motorcycle guys might still be a threat, and now we have Li's people watching us and they could be a threat. In a couple of minutes, Chief Parker and another CIA officer arrive at the suite. He tells us to call the bellman to get our luggage. The bellman comes quickly and takes the luggage downstairs. Craig goes to the front desk and checks us out while we wait nearby with Chief Parker and the other officer, then we all climb into the van.

On the drive to the airport, Chief Parker collects our weapons. He's brought a portable gun safe for that purpose. Fortunately, the traffic is not too bad, and we get to Suvarnabhumi International Airport a little ahead of schedule. A porter takes all the luggage at the curb, and we proceed quickly to the ANA counter. Chief Parker and his assistant accompany us to make sure we get safely through security. There is a short line for business-class passengers at the ticket counter. The ticket agent takes a lot of time checking our passports. We are questioned by security officers as we stand in line; this is standard practice for flights from Asia to the U.S.

Finally, we get our boarding passes and head to security. Since we're in business class, there's an exclusive line for us, and we get through quickly. Craig nods to Chief Parker, who waves goodbye, and we proceed to the Thai Airways lounge, which ANA business-class passengers can use to wait for the flight.

The time now is 10:30 p.m., so we have a while yet before boarding.

I start looking around the lounge, and I think I see a familiar face, not anyone I know but someone I think I've seen before. The stranger is Thai or Chinese. He has a round face, black hair, and glasses — just like half the male population of Bangkok — but there's something about him that has the hair on my arms standing on end. I ask Craig, but he thinks I'm mistaken, but my stomach's queasy feeling won't go away. I suspect we're being followed, and I don't like it. I file this guy in my memory as Unknown Person #1.

After we land in Tokyo and then take off for the second leg of our flight, I need to use the restroom, and the ones behind us are closer, so I walk back. Seeing the lavatory is occupied, I wait there, my eyes roaming around the plane. I notice sitting in seat 18H is Unknown Person #1, and that horrible, sinking feeling returns to my stomach. He seems to be reading something, though I can't see if it's a book or an electronic device. Just then, the person in the restroom leaves, so I go in.

As I come out of the restroom, I look back to the passenger in seat 18H. He doesn't seem to be paying any attention to me, but that could be a ruse. As soon as I get back to my seat, I try to mentally connect with him. In a few seconds, I see a laptop on his tray table. The screen shows what appears to be a presentation. The top-right corner of each page has the logo of the World Health Organization. The presentation is about the WHO vaccination program among the Thai hill tribes in northern Thailand. He's editing the presentation. Finally, he goes to the title page, which says, "Report on the WHO Vaccination Program in Northern Thailand" by Dr. Piyanit Tharmaboonchaiyat. The presentation has a date that is two days in the future. He must be going to D.C. to make a presentation. Obviously, Unknown Person #1 is not a threat to us. I sigh in relief.

CHAPTER 41

THE NEXT DAY, after a sweep of the suite in the AKA White House furnished apartments, Tony calls Craig to say that Yang and Wu have arrived and are staying at the Washington Hilton.

Tony says, "We're waiting for Hua Shuang to pass the flash drives to Allison Murphy, which may happen today or tomorrow. Yang will first go to the PRC Embassy to deliver the flash drives to Hua — after they're first programmed by Wu Min."

All we can do is wait for the chain of events to unfold.

Tony then says, "Grant, I still want more information on those Hong Kong accounts."

I suddenly realize that during the rush to get information from Wu Min about the malware failure, I never told anyone about the list of companies making payoffs or about Beijing Consulting Services. I tell Tony, who is pleased. I promise to give him the list of companies later today.

Tired of being cooped up, Karen, Angie, and I decide to walk over to the White House and see if we can catch a glimpse of the President or any dignitaries entering or leaving the compound. Craig, as usual, thinks we should try to minimize going out as an entire group, so he stays in the suite.

Fortunately, Tony had loaner weapons delivered to us shortly after arrival at AKA. So I get a government-issued Glock after all, if only for a few days. We all strap on our weapons before leaving.

We exit the AKA at around 11:00 a.m. The weather is bright and sunny, and the temperature is about seventy degrees. It's delightful in May compared to the hot, humid weather coming in another month. We walk along H Street and turn on 17th Street for one block until we reach Pennsylvania Avenue. In front of the White House, Pennsylvania Avenue is now a pedestrian mall; closed to vehicular traffic since the Oklahoma City bombing in 1995. We stand on the sidewalk with the other tourists, taking selfies and photos with the White House in the background.

After about ten minutes, we've had enough and cross the street to Lafayette Square, where there's the usual cadre of protesters. We stroll through the park, only stopping to inspect the equestrian statue of Andrew Jackson at the Battle of New Orleans. It was cast in 1853 and was the first equestrian statue in the world to be balanced solely on the horse's hind legs. We marvel at how that was done with the technology available at the time. Obviously, the sculptor had developed his talent to the highest level achievable. I am envious of the satisfaction he must have felt when the statue was unveiled; the crowd would have been amazed at his accomplishment.

On the other side of Lafayette Square, we walk past the Hay-Adams Hotel and I wonder if Tony is watching us from his room.

Later that evening, Tony phones in, and Craig puts him on speakerphone.

Tony says that Hua and Wu Min met with Allison Murphy at Fyre. They both had their Nordstrom bags and made an exchange. Wu Min apparently explained the arming of the malware.

"We think that Li is paranoid that something will go wrong with arming the malware, and he's not taking any chances. So he insisted that Wu explain the procedure to Allison Murphy. That unnecessarily exposes Wu Min, but apparently, Li is willing to take the risk," explains Tony.

Craig asks, "When will the arrests be made?"

Tony responds, "We believe our case will be stronger if Kleiner and Karlsson are arrested on their way into work with the flash drives on their person. So we'll wait until tomorrow morning. Once they're arrested, we'll take Allison, Yang, and Wu Min into custody."

I shake my head, as I'm sure Kleiner and Karlsson will never try to bring the flash drives through security.

"What about Hua?" asks Craig.

"He definitely has diplomatic immunity, so we won't bother with him. Anyway, he really isn't involved in the larger scheme," says Tony.

"Don't Yang and Wu have immunity, too?"

"Our legal staff has been researching this, and we don't believe they do. Yang and Wu are not diplomats and are not assigned, even temporarily, to the embassy. Careless work on their part, but this is a renegade operation, so mistakes will be made."

I assume Tony and his group are more professional than Li and Yang, but now I wonder if this could happen to me. I don't believe I had diplomatic immunity in Thailand, though I never thought about it. Tony did, but that's Tony taking care of Tony.

He ends the call by telling me Hua, Wu, and Allison

Murphy met at 1:15 p.m. yesterday and asking me to review the meeting.

After I go to my room, I lie down and begin to concentrate. Fairly quickly, I begin to see images of Allison and Hua.

Hua says, "Allison, this is Wu Min. He is an expert on the software and will explain what needs to be done."

Wu says, "I will give you step-by-step instructions. The malware will be on a flash drive. To eliminate mistakes, I have already programmed the start time, which is Monday at noon. The next time the flash drive is connected to a computer, a screen will come up with an 'Execute' field in the menu. At that point, highlight 'Execute' and hit 'Enter' twice, and the worm is activated and will start at the time that was set. Any questions?"

"So, when I give these devices to my agents, I tell them all they need to do is connect the flash drives, allow the malware to load, highlight the 'Execute' field, and hit 'Enter' twice. Right?"

"Yes."

Allison says, "I don't know how they'll get the malware into their own systems, but it might not be directly from the flash drives. It might be using an intermediate device. In that case, would they need to do anything differently?"

Wu says, "No, we have considered that possibility, and once the malware is activated, it can be moved from one device to another without any adverse effect on its function. Just don't hit 'Enter' until it is loaded into the target computer."

"How soon will the malware begin its attack?" asks Allison.

"It won't take long; within a few minutes after the 'Start' time, the effects will be noticeable."

Allison asks, "What if, for some reason, the malware is not loaded until after the programmed start time?"

Wu answers, "Then it'll automatically wait 24 hours before activating. We prefer that the software is activated at noon."

"Is there any chance it'll be detected?"

"No, we've tested it in many environments, and it's never been detected until it's too late."

"How long does it take to load the malware?" Allison asks.

I don't like all these questions. It seems that she's questioning my expertise.

"Less than a minute, usually about thirty seconds."

"Okay, I've got it."

Allison says, "I expect Kleiner and Karlsson will ask for more money. They've had time to think about it and might be getting cold feet."

Hua says, "But they think they're only loading monitoring software to catch some embezzlers, right?"

"That's what they've been told, but I think they're smarter than that," replies Allison.

Hua says, "We anticipated that, and there's more cash in the Nordstrom bag, along with the flash drives. There's $50,000 each for them if you need that much. And another $100,000 for you. But nothing can go wrong."

She nods her head and says, "Nice to have met you, Wu Min."

"I'm looking forward to seeing the results."

Then, Wu Min bows slightly to Allison. She returns the bow.

Hua and Allison exchange their Nordstrom bags, same as before. They all nod and shake hands before they leave the restaurant.

After a few seconds, I come back to the present. I go out to the living area and tell the crew what I've learned. I add that Allison asked when the attacks would be initiated, and Wu said Monday at noon. I ask Craig when I'm going to see Karlsson in person.

Craig says, "Let's call Tony and ask him." He dials Tony's number.

"Tony, Grant wants to talk with you," Craig says, and hands me the phone.

"I thought I would see Karlsson, so I'm ready in case he doesn't have the flash drive on him when he's arrested, and we need to find out what evasive action he's taken," I say.

"Well, I've changed my mind. If the Chinese are watching Karlsson to make sure he's not compromised in some way, I don't want them to spot you or any of us before Monday. They might decide to abort their attack or choose another target. We want to get our hands on that malware. But you can be there for the arrest if you want," he says.

"Okay, that's almost as good, I guess."

Well, at least I have something to look forward to on Monday. It's going to be a long weekend.

I don't like it and think it was a mistake that I could not make contact with Kleiner or Karlsson. Instead, I try to decide how I would get the flash drives into these secure operations. One thing is for sure. I wouldn't try to bring a flash drive through the security checkpoint, and I figure Kleiner and Karlsson won't either. So what will they do instead?

I guess we'll find out on Monday.

We sit around the rest of the day, mostly watching TV and reading. Tony calls at 5:30 p.m. to say Allison Murphy went to New York and met with Kleiner. It appears she passed the flash drive, but they're not sure if she gave him more money or not. Murphy's on the way back to D.C. now. He expects she'll meet with Karlsson tomorrow to make another flash drive handoff.

CHAPTER 42

It took her nine days, but Special Agent Justine Aebischer finally has a lead on Ryurik Vetrov. She'd already confirmed Mr. Ryurik Vetrov is still living in the city. Unfortunately, he hasn't been at home since she arrived in New York last week.

She and Special Agent John Tyson are meeting this morning. Not only has John been helping her with the Devereaux case — specifically, finding out everything he can about Ryurik Vetrov — but Justine also feels safer with John than any other agent she knows. He's the size of an NFL lineman and looks meaner, but he's actually a teddy bear. He's a graduate of North Carolina A&T, a historically all-black college where he did actually play football.

She asks John, "What did you find out about Vetrov?"

"I'm told he's a rich jerk, about fifty-seven years old. All the oligarchs are starting to get up in years. He made his money in Russian nickel, palladium, and copper mining."

"Does he speak English?"

"Yes, but I'm not sure how well. He probably has difficulty when it suits him. And I hear he's connected with the Russian mafia, which means he's used to getting his way. He also has ties to powerful people in the Russian government, as do all the oligarchs."

"Is he married?"

"Yes, he has a least one wife, a few ex-wives, and many girl-friends. I imagine when you have that much money and have already done anything and everything you ever wanted to do, you get easily bored."

"Do you know where Vetrov has residences?" asks Justine.

"He has residences in St. Kitts, Manhattan, London, and Saint-Tropez. By the way, he doesn't live at The Dakota any-more. He moved to the south end of Central Park, at 157 West 57th Street — the One57 building. He's moving up in the world — literally. He bought a unit on the 67th floor overlooking the park. It's one of the groups of new skyscraper condo buildings along Central Park South that's being called Billionaire's Row."

Justine says, "Good work, John."

Based on the evidence already obtained in Paris, Justine had already decided to seek a search warrant for the FBI to examine the residence of Mr. Vetrov, as well as any safe deposit boxes he may have rented. Since they don't know where he has a safe deposit box, they decided to list all the major banks in New York and private safe deposit box rental locations. And since the search warrant included so many locations, it requires the intervention of FBI Director Lambert to obtain it.

"I really doubt he would keep expensive jewelry in St. Kitts or Saint-Tropez. New York and London would be more likely because secure storage is available, and there would be more occasions for his wife to wear it," Justine says.

"Then I would suggest requesting a search warrant for the London residence through Interpol. The pendant might not be in Manhattan. You might also try to get a blanket warrant for any bank or private safe deposit boxes he might have in London, too," John says.

"Good suggestion, I'll start the process now. I need to call the Director about the New York search warrant and I'll get his approval to request the Interpol warrant. Then, we'll wait until Vetrov returns to New York," says Justine.

CHAPTER 43

Tony let me know yesterday that Angie and I will be going this morning to Karlsson's workplace, The Clearing House, to arrest him. They expect Karlsson to arrive at his usual time of 8:00 a.m., but we will be there early. We are to meet Special Agent Robinson, who Angie knows. They have arranged for me to have a temporary badge and an FBI windbreaker.

Angie says, "As long as we're in D.C., you're going to be Special Agent Mark Grant."

That catches me by surprise. But after a second or two, I say, "That's clever, did you think of that?"

She says, "No, that was Tony's idea."

I smile.

Maybe he does have a sense of humor!

When we arrive at The Clearing House in McClean, Special Agent Robinson is waiting.

Angie says, "Hi Steve, it's been a while. This is Mark Grant. Do you have his badge and ID?"

"Yes, and here's his FBI windbreaker, too."

I shake hands with Robinson, take my ID case with the badge from him, and put on the FBI windbreaker.

"Where will we wait?" Angie asks.

"We're going to wait in a room next to the screening area," he says. "We're going to have two agents at the screening station with the regular security employees. Our guys will do the screening and then bring him into the room where we're waiting. We hope to find the flash drive on him, but who knows?"

At 7:55 a.m., we can see Karlsson approaching security through a one-way window that looks out into the screening area. Karlsson has a small backpack with him. He's relatively tall, medium build, short blond hair, glasses, about forty years old. After Karlsson puts his cell phone in a locker and takes the key, he inserts his ID into a scanner, which beeps and allows him to pass through the turnstile. He then enters the area where the body scanner and X-ray machines are located. He doesn't seem to be nervous, but he appears to notice some guys there he hasn't seen before. He waits in line while two people go before him. When he gets to the front of the line, he empties his pockets, takes off his belt, watch, and shoes. He puts them in a tray, which passes through the X-ray along with his backpack. Then he steps into the full-body scanner. The attendant waves him through and over to the side.

They tell him they need to do some additional checks. He doesn't appear to be bothered by this. The attendant pats him down and doesn't find anything.

"We need to talk to you, sir. You can get your things first," says the security agent — actually an FBI agent. He points Karlsson to the room where we are waiting. After Karlsson puts on his shoes, belt, and watch, he grabs his backpack, and the agent escorts him into the room.

"Mr. Karlsson, I'm Special Agent Robinson of the FBI. These are Special Agents Reynolds, Grant, Chandler, and Wells. We received a tip that someone would try today to bring malware into the secure area to infect the check-clearing systems, and your name was mentioned. Do you have any kind of computer storage device with you, sir?"

"No, definitely not," says Karlsson. "Who accused me, Agent?"

Agent Chandler says, "You indeed have access to the check-clearing system software, right?"

Karlsson says, "Yes, but so do a lot of other people."

Agent Chandler asks, "So you deny this allegation, correct?"

"Absolutely," says Karlsson.

"Then, we'll take you to one of our facilities for further questioning and examination of all the items in your possession."

"Are you arresting me?" asks Karlsson.

"No, sir, not yet, anyway," says Agent Chandler.

Karlsson doesn't say anything but sits quietly with a scowl on his face.

"All right, then, Agents Robinson, Wells, and I are going to escort you out of here and take you to the other location. If you cooperate, we won't need to handcuff you, but we won't hesitate if you don't. We're going to stop and get your cell phone from the storage locker on the way out. Any questions?" says Agent Robinson.

"No," says Karlsson.

"Okay, then let's go. Give the cell phone locker key to Agent Chandler," says Robinson.

"Isn't that like a search? Don't you need to have a warrant for that?" says Karlsson.

"We don't suspect you have the malware on the phone, so what's the problem?" says Chandler.

"My private information is on the phone, and I don't agree for you to go through it," says Karlsson.

"Well, in that case, we'll leave the phone here for now," says Agent Chandler.

Karlsson looks relieved. Angie and I look at each other. We can't imagine why Karlsson is so worried about the phone. Maybe I can find out later.

Agent Robinson nods at us as Karlsson is escorted out by the other agents. Angie and I wait until they are gone.

She says, "What do you think?"

"Well, I should be able to make a mental connection with him. The big question is, where did he hide the malware? At least he proved me right — there was no way he would try to bring a flash drive through security. Tony won't be happy."

"That's for sure," Angie says.

Once we're in the car and on the way back to AKA, I call Tony and tell him what happened.

"Tony, Karlsson didn't have the flash drive on him," I tell him.

"Yeah, I heard," he replies. "Do you think you can find out where he's hidden it?"

I say, "I think so. I'll let you know as soon as possible. What about Kleiner?"

Tony says, "The same thing, no flash drive."

"I was afraid of that. What about Allison Murphy?"

"We arrested her at home. She claims not to know anything, as expected. We recovered the Nordstrom bag used in the exchange and expect to find Hua's fingerprints or DNA on the bag, which will link her to the Chinese. We also recovered $100,000 in cash. The FBI may trace the numbers on the bills back to China, but they're not sure yet. And we told her we know about Kleiner and Karlsson. That got her attention, but she still won't talk," Tony says, with some exasperation in his voice.

"Do you want me to go to New York to see Kleiner?" I ask Tony.

He says, "Not yet, let's see what happens."

"Okay, I'll let you know as soon as I know anything more about Karlsson," I tell him.

"All right, let me know. Bye," says Tony.

"What did Tony say?" asks Angie.

"He says we have three people in custody but don't know any more than we did yesterday," I reply.

"He should have listened to you and checked them out with your help in advance," she says.

"Well, we're no worse off, as I see it. We've got them in custody. It's just a matter of time before we find out what they did with the flash drives," I say.

"What about Yang and Wu Min?" she asks.

"I don't know, he didn't say anything about them."

"Can't you connect and see where they are?" she asks.

"Yeah, I can do that." It'll be a good way to distract myself while I wonder what happens if we can't get our hands on those flash drives.

When we arrive back at AKA, Angie tells Craig what happened with Karlsson while I try to connect with Wu, Yang, and Karlsson.

Wu is sitting by himself in an interrogation room.

How did they know about the flash drives? Did Yang slip up, or was it Allison Murphy? What happens now? Why do they deny me diplomatic immunity?

Well, that answers the question about Wu. He has been arrested, and they are in the process of trying to get him to talk.

Now I decide to see what's going on with Yang.

Yang is also sitting in an interrogation room, facing several FBI agents.

The agent in charge says, "Mr. Yang, do you want an interpreter, or can we talk with you in English?"

Yang replies, "I want an interpreter from the embassy, and I want to talk to the Minister, Hua Shuang."

So Yang is also stonewalling.

Now I can give my full attention to Karlsson. I connect with him quickly. He is sitting at a table in an interrogation room as well. He's watching two agents who are looking through the items they seized from him.

Karlsson says, "I really don't care if you go through my things, but how long will it take?"

Special Agent Robinson says, "It doesn't make any difference if you care or not. You insisted on a search warrant, so we showed you we have one. We'll be here as long as it takes for us to find the flash drive or for you to tell us where it is."

They look through the backpack — there are some snacks, several computer language reference books, a small screwdriver, and a comb. The agent looks them over and puts them back. Then one of the agents picks up a clear plastic bag containing car keys and Karlsson's watch. He inspects them but doesn't even take them out of the bag.

Karlsson breathes a sigh of relief.

Thank God they didn't notice the watch!

I'm surprised. I know a flash drive won't fit inside the watch. And it's not a smartwatch, so he can't have downloaded anything onto it. But since he's so concerned about the watch, it needs to be checked out thoroughly.

I call Tony. After he answers, I tell him, "The FBI needs to check out Karlsson's watch. He was concerned about it and was relieved when they weren't interested in it."

"Okay, I'll let them know. Thanks!"

Craig tells me the New York FBI field office decided to carefully surveil Kleiner after receiving the flash drive from Allison Murphy. They saw that he dropped off a package to FedEx on Friday. So when he didn't have the flash drive on him when he reported for work on Monday, they decided to trace the package.

They found it was shipped to the JPMorgan Chase office, disguised as being sent from an approved equipment supplier, addressed to a technician in the computer services department. They executed a search warrant and found the package, delivered to his accomplice co-worker. They found the flash drive. Kleiner confessed to sending it. He's flipped on Allison Murphy, saying she hired him to install monitoring software to catch an embezzler.

Special Agents Robinson and Wells again talk with Karlsson.

"Mr. Karlsson, we're going to search your premises and your workplace if you don't cooperate. And we're going to find out what's on your phone that you're trying to protect. You know we have a search warrant, so we're not playing games. You can have an attorney if you like. Do you want to call one?" asks Wells.

"No, I don't need one yet. If you're not going to arrest me, then let me go."

"We haven't decided yet what we're going to do. You are

aware, aren't you, of 18 U.S. Code §1030, which covers illegal activities involving protected computers? Under this statute, the penalty is a minimum of ten years and up to twenty years of prison time per count. If I were you, I would cooperate and tell us about your involvement with Allison Murphy," says Robinson.

Karlsson just sits stiffly and stares straight ahead.

"While you're thinking about that, we're going to take another look at your things. Did you know your watch has a dead battery?" says Wells as he looks over Karlsson's watch.

"Yes, I noticed it this morning. I was going to get a new battery after work today," replies Karlsson.

"Don't worry, we're going to save you the trouble. Agent Robinson is pretty good with watches, and he has a set of watch tools. We just need to see exactly which battery this watch takes," says Wells.

Special Agent Robinson checks the black G-Shock watch for a model number. He says, "Model GD400-9."

He looks it up on his phone and finds that it takes a CR2016 battery.

"You're in luck. We happen to have one," says Robinson, as he begins to remove the screws from the back of the watch.

After he removes the four screws, he removes the back cover. But when he opens the watch, he doesn't find a battery. Instead, there is a micro SD card in the battery slot.

"Well, this is interesting — a micro SD card instead of a battery. No wonder it wouldn't run. How do you explain that, Mr. Karlsson?" asks Agent Robinson.

Karlsson glares at him.

"Apparently, you went to a lot of trouble to transfer the malware from the flash drive to the micro SD card. Oh well, it was a lot of wasted effort, but it was a brilliant way to avoid detection, except that it didn't work. I think you've got a lot of explaining to do, Mr. Karlsson," says Agent Wells.

"Okay, I think I'd like to call an attorney now," says Karlsson with a worried look on his face.

⁓

Yang and Wu were arrested at their hotel by the FBI. Several more flash drives were found in Wu's personal effects. They both claimed diplomatic immunity, which the FBI denied. The PRC Ambassador has already filed a strong objection with our Secretary of State.

It's expected they'll be charged under the federal statutes, which covers illegal activities involving protected computers. There will also be other charges under terrorism and national security statutes. They're looking at a long time in jail, so there'll be a huge motivation for them to cooperate.

Tony says he doesn't know what will happen next, so we should stay in D.C. in case we're needed. The DNI, the CIA Director, and the White House are still considering what to do about Li, since they consider him an active national security threat. Obviously, holding Yang in custody will be a significant concern to Li when he finds out, and we don't know how he might react.

It occurs to me that the arrests this morning are not really the end of the mission; the next steps against Li will be more critical and more tricky to achieve. I was expecting a nice vacation after squelching the Plan 23-2 threat, but this will continue for who knows how long.

I don't like that these arrests don't bring this case to an end, but I have a lot invested in it now. I want to help bring it to a successful conclusion. In a way, my credibility is on the line. If Tony and the others don't think I'm worth it, they'll cancel our agreement. I don't want that to happen without the Devereaux investigation being completed.

A few hours later, Tony calls again. Yang is willing to cooperate, but not Wu. Actually, Allison Murphy, Kleiner, and Karlsson are almost irrelevant now. The real battle concerns Li, and Yang can help us, but he wants to be released in return. Tony says he'll call later with updates.

About 4:00 p.m., Craig gets a call that a message was delivered for him at the front desk. After Karen and Angie come over to our room as my protection, Craig heads down.

A few minutes later, he comes back with a sheet of paper folded into thirds and stapled with his name printed onto a sticker on the outside. The front desk receptionist had told him a young guy delivered it, probably a bicycle messenger; she had never seen him before.

He puts it on the table, and we all take a look. It's not inside an envelope, so there's no need to worry about a powdery substance or another type of contaminant inside — unless it's impregnated into the paper. Craig shakes the folded paper, grasping it between two spoons, and nothing falls out, so it appears safe to open. He gets a knife from the kitchen drawer, pries open the staple, and pulls it free. He unfolds the paper and sees the following typed message:

"Concerning Wu Min. Meet at 5:00 p.m. today at Stratford Park on the basketball court. No weapon. Look for a yellow bag. Come alone or no information. Important. Don't be late, or I leave."

Craig says, "I think I should go find out what this is about."

Worried this could be some kind of trick, I say, "I don't think it's a good idea."

He says, "Why not?"

But before I can answer, Karen says, "Because you won't

have a weapon, it's kind of a remote area, and you don't know how many of them will be there. They know who you are, but you don't know who they are. And what information could they have about Wu Min that would be of any value to us? We already have Wu Min. And we have Grant, who can get any information we need."

I say, "Wait a minute. I can't get information from someone I don't know about."

Craig says, "Yeah, maybe there's someone at the PRC Embassy who doesn't like Wu and wants to make sure he's put away for good. The embassy staff are just pencil pushers anyway — nothing to worry about. I'll call our backup agents and have them follow me. I'll let them know when I get downstairs to the car, and I won't leave here without them. If we notify the FBI, they'll be late getting to the park, and we'll lose this contact. And I'll call you as soon as I make the rendezvous."

It worries me that someone knows who we are and where we're staying.

And what if they know about me?

Craig is insistent on going to the rendezvous with the backup agents, and we all reluctantly agree. However, I'm afraid something is going to go very wrong.

After Craig leaves, I ask, "Why would Craig do that, instead of letting the FBI check this out?"

Karen says, "Because the contact obviously knows him on sight. And Craig isn't going to let a little danger scare him. That's just the way he is."

At 5:00 p.m., the rendezvous time, I begin pacing the room. "How long before Craig calls?" I ask.

Angie looks at me from her perch next to the window. She's been watching the street for signs someone is watching our apartments. She says, "It depends on how long he talks with the contact, I guess."

Karen says, "We better start thinking about what we're going to do if we don't hear from him." I watch as she fiddles with her gun, as if making sure it's still there in the holster or maybe subconsciously protecting Craig. After all, they've worked together for years.

I say, "Well, we could try calling the trailing agents — or Tony. But let's call or text Craig first."

By 5:15 p.m., we still haven't heard from him. At this point, I can tell Karen and Angie are starting to worry as much as I am that something's gone wrong. We call and text him several times with no answer.

We wait until 5:30 p.m., and then Karen calls Tony.

"Tony, an anonymous note was delivered to Craig here at AKA to meet someone at Stratford Park at 5:00 p.m. to get important information about Wu Min. Craig left by himself and was taking the trailing agents with him. But it's 5:30 p.m., and we haven't heard anything," says Karen.

Tony says, "What the hell was he thinking? Let me call the trailing agents. Have you talked to them?"

"No, not yet. We wanted to let you know first, in case something went wrong."

"Okay, let me make a few calls, and I'll let you know what I find out."

Tony calls back in five minutes.

"The trailing agents say Craig never left AKA; they've been waiting across the street to follow him. I told them to go into the parking garage underneath the hotel to see if the car is still there. I'll let you know. And you three stay put," he says angrily.

Tony calls again ten minutes later.

"The trailing agents found the rental car in the garage, and Craig's phone is lying on the front seat. We have to assume Craig's been taken. There's nothing to do now except wait for a call or a note from the kidnapper. If Craig's been abducted, we'll receive their demands shortly."

As we wait, I ponder why they've abducted Craig. It could be to draw away some of my protection. If so, then we could potentially be attacked at any time.

I blurt out, "Angie, Karen, we'd better be careful. With Craig out of the way, we might be the next targets. Check your weapons and stay ready."

Tony finally calls Karen back about an hour later, and we all listen to the speaker.

"I've just received an e-mail, which says:

Mr. Russell,

We will release Mr. Clayton after Yang Kexin and Wu Min are safely back in China. If not, Mr. Clayton will die. We want to see Yang and Wu's photos with their boarding passes, passports, and the details of their itinerary. Also, photos showing them in their seats on their flight preparing to leave the U.S. before any further communications. You have until 12 noon tomorrow.

Arief

Tony says, "The e-mail was sent from arief@bahaya.id, which means nothing to any of us. FBI and DHS experts are working to find the origin of the e-mail, but I'm doubtful they'll find anything helpful. Whoever took Craig was smart, luring him to the garage by himself, and then leaving his phone in the car to prevent being tracked.

"The FBI is sure the perpetrators got my e-mail address from Craig's phone. The FBI will be checking the garage surveillance video if there is any. The garage has controlled access to vehicles, and Craig didn't leave the garage in our vehicle or on foot — so how they got in and out is a mystery."

I don't like that Tony isn't telling us what he's going to do if Craig can't be located and rescued. The clock is ticking, and there's a noon deadline tomorrow for Yang and Wu to be on a plane back to China.

We wait and wait. It's now 8:00 p.m., and we've heard nothing. Karen, especially, is upset. I see her wiping her eye with a tissue.

Come on, Tony!

Tony calls — "We've struck out on the source of the e-mail. The e-mail domain is registered in Indonesia, but that means nothing. Arief used a VPN, so there's no way to know where it originated. Our experts determined that bahaya means 'danger' in Indonesian. And the name Arief means 'smart and wise.' Arief, whoever he is, seems to be taunting us. I'll let you know if and when we hear more. We don't intend to let Yang and Wu get on any plane."

"Tony, you're not saying you're willing to sacrifice Craig, are you?" I ask angrily.

"No, I didn't say that, but we can't just let Yang and Wu waltz out of here. I've got to go now. I'll be in touch. Bye."

Tony's last comment creates a lot of concern among us. Karen turns worried eyes to us. "Tony's really putting Craig in a lot of danger by denying any hope for a deal with the kidnapper." Angie and I both nod.

Angie, seeing Karen's reaction, now seems agitated. She says, "Let's go down to the garage and see what we can find."

None of us have a better idea, so we go.

When we get to the garage, we go straight to the car. I say, "There's his phone on the seat." When I try the door, it's locked.

We use our phone flashlights to look around the vehicle. Angie goes around in front and finds a key fob against the wall in front of the car; actually, not a key fob but a smart key.

She says, "I found the key!"

The smart key has a soft, flexible rubber case, so it wouldn't make much noise if dropped on concrete.

Karen says, "Craig must have dropped it or more likely thrown it away when he was attacked. Why would he have done that?" Angie and I shrug our shoulders. We have no idea.

My eyes roam around the garage, and I try to visualize Craig's attack. Across the aisle, I notice something partially hidden behind one of the cars. I walk over to take a look, and when I get closer, I realize it's a man's body!

"Karen, Angie, come here, quick!"

They're there in seconds. Karen says, "Thank goodness, it's not Craig."

"Do you think Craig shot him?" I ask.

"No, because the trailing agents would have seen him lying there when they came to look for Craig. It must have happened later," says Karen.

But who is it? The body is face-down partially between the car and the wall. It's a man, but that's all we can tell until Angie rolls him over.

It's Unknown Person #1 from the Bangkok flight! What's he doing here, and dead? Karen examines him. He's been shot twice in the chest. She finds a gun next to his body. She says it hasn't been fired, so it's his gun; someone must have surprised him.

I recall my earlier thought that Craig's kidnapping might have been to draw my protection away. But if that's so, this guy was waiting to ambush the three of us, but someone got him first. Who and why? Well, that's a question that's going to have to wait.

Suddenly I have an idea.

"I should be able to access Craig's memory and find out what really happened," I blurt out. They both light up at the thought.

I don't know why I didn't think of this before! Too upset, I guess.

Karen says, "Why don't we get in the car, and you can relax in the back seat and try to connect with Craig. Then we'll decide what to do."

I ask them to remind me exactly when Craig went to the car. Angie thinks it was about 4:30 p.m. I try to engage with Craig at that time.

I see an image of Craig getting off the elevator in the garage and walking toward the car. As he approaches the car, he hits the remote, and the doors unlock. Just at that moment, two men jump out from behind the car with guns drawn.

"Hands up," says a tall Chinese man holding a gun.

Craig puts his hands up.

I can't believe I walked into a trap.

"Okay, okay," Craig says.

Out of the shadows steps another man. I instantly recognize the square face, the slits for eyes, the powerful build, and the menacing look; it's Yang's bodyguard!

The tall man says, "Give me your phone. Slowly put it on the ground and slide it over here."

Craig does as he says.

The tall man and the bodyguard both follow the phone with their eyes as it slides across the floor. As they watch the phone, Craig is still in a stooped position and discreetly flips the smart key over against a rubber bumper mounted on the wall. It barely makes a sound as it hits and drops to the floor; they don't notice; they're focused on the phone.

I hope Grant can figure out what happened.

The tall man picks up the phone and looks at it. He says in Chinese to the bodyguard, "It's locked."

The bodyguard says, "Get the code."

The tall man says, "What's the unlock code?"

Craig considers this for a moment.

If I don't tell them, they'll just beat me until I give it. Besides, I suspect they want it if I get a call or a text, which they can answer with their demands.

"022846."

The tall man unlocks the phone. In Chinese, the bodyguard says, "Get the contact info for Tony Russell and AirDrop it to our phones." The tall man apparently does it because the body-guard smiles and nods while looking at his phone.

The tall man opens the door, puts Craig's phone on the seat, manually hits the door lock button, and closes the door. He checks to make sure the door is locked.

The tall man says, "Stand up and turn around with your hands behind your back."

Craig complies.

The bodyguard pats him down, then plastic-ties his hands together and puts tape over his mouth. For good measure, he also tapes his hands.

The tall man says, "Move over here." The bodyguard opens the doors on a white cargo van parked a few spots away. "Now get in and lie down," he tells Craig.

Craig struggles to get in and lies down in the back. The bodyguard ties his feet to the utility rails on the inside of the van.

This is not how I wanted to spend my Monday evening!

The tall man gets in the driver's seat and the bodyguard in

the passenger seat. The bodyguard watches to make sure Craig doesn't move.

The gate opens automatically, and they pull out onto H Street. Craig can't see anything from his position in the back, so there is no reason to pursue this any longer.

I come back to the moment and tell Karen and Angie what I've seen. I suspect the tall man had checked in to the AKA, which would have gotten him garage access with his room key. We need to ask Tony to check on this later, but it doesn't matter now. I speculate the bodyguard cannot speak English and that the tall man is probably a PRC Embassy employee. Therefore, any communications between the kidnappers and us will depend on the tall man.

Karen's phone rings, and it's Tony.

"I answered Arief and told him we wouldn't do anything to respond to his demand until I know Craig is alive and well. In a few minutes, I received a reply: 'Mr. Craig says he likes sugar.' I responded, "I think you like bourbon better."

So Tony knows that Craig is alive, though under duress, and Craig knows that we know it — if Arief passed on the message.

Tony also says that the FBI, DHS, and NSA experts have made no progress on tracking the source of the e-mail.

I ask to talk with Tony and tell him what I saw.

When I'm done, I say, "The bodyguard was with Yang at the Met, so I think I might be able to probe his memory. If I can, then maybe I can metaphorically ride along with him to where they're holding Craig."

Tony says, "Okay, great! When you're certain you know the location, let me know, and we'll send an FBI team."

"Tony, one more thing. We found a dead Chinese or Thai in the parking garage near our car. He was on our flight from Bangkok. I'm guessing he was a Chinese agent and was waiting to ambush us when we came to check on Craig. He must have delayed until after the trailing agents checked out the garage looking for Craig, then snuck in to wait for us. But then someone got him. This is getting so confusing."

"We'll see if we can learn anything from the garage cameras. We'll send a cleanup crew to get the body, too."

I respond, "Okay, bye."

I tell Karen and Angie what Tony said about mentally making the trip and then sending the FBI team, but they don't like it. Karen says, "That could take hours. You would have to follow along their entire trip to know every turn between here and there. Then it would take the FBI just as long to get there. Why don't we just go ourselves?"

Angie says, "We can decide when we get there whether to wait for the FBI or do something ourselves if Craig's in danger. We've all got weapons."

Out loud, I say, "Okay, that sounds like a plan." But inside, the prospect of putting myself in that much danger terrifies me. Still, Craig is in danger, and if the FBI can't get to him in time . . . I shake my head.

If I can help save him, I have to do it. After all, he's saved me twice from being killed.

Angie volunteers to drive, Karen sits in back, and I'm in the passenger seat. I try to connect with the bodyguard at the time they're leaving the garage.

I say, "This is why Craig ditched the key — so we could use the car. Let's go!"

CHAPTER 44

Closing my eyes, I try to find the moment the bodyguard leaves the garage in the van with Craig and sync it up with Angie's driving.

"I've never done this before, so I might have issues giving you directions in time," I say — with my eyes still closed.

"I can handle it," Angie says. We slowly turn right from the garage onto H Street and make another right turn onto 17th Street. I tell her to turn left onto New York Avenue and get onto the E Street Expressway. She does this smoothly. I have to jump ahead about thirty seconds and then tell her to get in the left lane for I-66 West. I'm getting the hang of this now.

From what I can tell, we stay on I-66 for a while. Opening my eyes, I ask, "Where could they be taking him?"

"A lot of major foreign embassies have a property in rural areas of Virginia or Maryland for staff retreats or just a place to get away from D.C. during the hot and muggy summer months."

We drive for over fifty miles, then the van takes Exit 18 for VA-688 toward Markham, Virginia. We follow suit and turn right onto Leeds Manor Road. We are definitely in rural Virginia now. I notice the bodyguard regularly turns and checks on Craig, who lays quietly in the back of the van. After only about three more miles, the van slows and turns onto Apple Manor Road.

I say, "Angie, turn right at the next intersection."

It's almost dark, and there are barely any buildings in sight, mostly horse farms, and those are few and far between. After a short distance, the van turns right again onto Audubon Trail, and I tell Angie to do likewise. A sign says Dead End, No Outlet.

"Stop now!"

We stop in the middle of the road. Ahead, we can see where the road ends.

"I saw the van turn into the driveway just ahead on the left," I say.

At the end of the road, we can see a gravel entrance to a field on the same side of the road.

"Let's park the car over there, off the road."

She slowly drives to the field entrance and parks the car, partially behind some scrub trees and bushes. About three hundred yards away is the house where I saw the van turn in. The property is bounded by a white fence enclosing large pastures on both sides of the driveway. The mailbox says 40 Audubon Trail.

"We should call Tony," I tell Karen and Angie.

"It'll take them hours to get here," says Karen.

"Let's call, but then let's try to see what's going on in there," says Angie.

Karen doesn't look happy but says, "Okay, we'll call Tony, then decide."

"Grant, you better call him. He doesn't know we're here."

I call Tony. He answers, saying, "Where is he?" He's not on speakerphone, but it's so quiet out here we can all hear him.

I tell him, "40 Audubon Trail, somewhere off I-66."

After a minute, he says, "It's out by Markham. Okay, we'll

have agents there in about an hour. Describe the location the best you can."

"The best I can tell, it looks like an old horse farm. There's a large white house on the driveway's right, a detached garage at the driveway's end farther back than the house. Then, there are stables on the left of the driveway across from and slightly behind the house. The house is about a hundred yards from the road, surrounded by large trees. There are no other houses anywhere close."

Tony says, "Okay, then just sit tight, and we'll let you know what happens when the FBI gets there. Bye."

I say, "Well, he didn't even give me a chance to tell him we're here. Ha, ha!"

Angie's grip tightens on the wheel as she looks at the house. "An hour's a long time. Let's get closer and see what's going on. If Craig's in trouble, waiting for the FBI team could be a mistake."

I'm not so sure, but we all agree.

I suggest we walk along the fence line on the property's edge, then cut across the back. We probably can look in a window without being seen. At least we can see if the van is here, perhaps in the garage.

We creep along the fence line bordering the adjoining property until we are well behind the house. Then, along the outside of the fence where it turns at the corner of the pasture, further back than the garage. We go around to the opposite side of the house and shine a phone flashlight in the window. The garage is empty. The tall man has probably gone for food.

We slowly make our way to the back door of the stable, out of direct sight of the house. Karen opens the door and briefly shines in her phone flashlight; the stable is also empty. There are maybe a dozen stalls, with horse tack strewn about and a few bales of hay.

Angie says, "If Craig's here, he's being held by the body-guard. One of us should take a look inside the house. I'll do it, and you two can provide cover from the garage."

She slowly makes her way to a window at the back corner of the house and looks in. Then she crouches low and moves to another window. Then she quickly and stealthily makes her way back to the garage, while I hold my breath the entire time.

She whispers, "Craig's tied up in a chair in the kitchen. He looks okay, but his mouth is taped, and the bodyguard is sitting at the table watching him. Fortunately, he was facing the other direction and didn't see me. I don't think Craig saw me, either. The tall man wasn't there so far as I could tell."

Her brows furrow as she glances back at the window. "It might not be good when the FBI team shows up. The bodyguard doesn't speak English; he may panic if they can't understand them, and Craig could get killed. And if the tall man comes back, there'll be two of them to fight off the FBI team. That's got to be more dangerous for Craig."

"Well, there are three of us and only one of him, so we ought to be able to do something," Karen says, looking at the two of us.

I can feel myself trembling. I know this could end very badly. But it might be our best chance to free Craig.

I say, "Let's see if we can lure the bodyguard away from the house. Then one of us can go in and cut Craig loose."

Karen says, "But what about the bodyguard? He won't go very far away from Craig."

Angie says, "If we can get him to go into the stable, we can lock him in long enough to get Craig away from here."

The stable has sliding doors at both ends, with latches to keep the doors shut and a padlock hasp on the outside of the doors.

Karen finds an old walking stick leaning in the corner, and

I see a bucket of rusty metal items, including what appear to be rail spikes.

I take two of the spikes and slide one into the hasp on the stable's rear doors. It works perfectly to lock the door.

I tell Karen, "Go over to the garage on the side nearest the house and break the window with the walking stick. Make as much noise as possible, then hide behind the garage. That should draw the bodyguard out of the house. We'll leave the door to the stable open, and hopefully he'll go inside to investigate. When he does, we'll shut the door and spike it. I'll text you when I want you to break the window."

Angie positions herself behind the fence near the stable corner with her weapon drawn and the spike in her waistband. I take a position behind a large tree along the driveway about fifty feet from the stable. When it appears we're all in place, I text "Now" to both Karen and Angie.

Karen shatters the window with a huge crashing sound. The light quickly goes out in the kitchen.

I draw my weapon, holding it steady, and wait. I hope I don't have to shoot, but I will protect myself or our team.

I can't see Angie, but I know where she's hiding. Karen should be back behind the garage by now.

After a few minutes, I think I see a shadow slowly moving around the corner from the front of the house toward the garage. My weapon feels like it weighs a ton, but I steady it with both hands.

Just at that moment, a vehicle turns into the driveway, bathing the entire area in light. My heart races as Karen, standing next to the garage on the side nearest the stable, is suddenly exposed. The bodyguard sees her and takes several shots but misses. Angie and I both fire at him, and he falls.

I feel queasy at the thought that I might have been the one

who shot the bodyguard. I never expected to be in that sort of situation, and I don't like it, but what else could I do?

The vehicle backs out of the driveway and tears off down the road. The driver must have seen there were several of us, and he probably saw the bodyguard fall. He also may have thought if three of us were here, more were on the way.

The bodyguard doesn't seem to be moving. Karen and Angie come running to me.

"I'll stay with the bodyguard, you guys get Craig," Angie says before turning back to the guy on the ground with her gun out, just in case.

I say, "Okay, let's go."

Karen and I go through the back door, using our phone flashlights to find our way. Karen finds a knife in a kitchen drawer, and I remove the tape from Craig's mouth.

"Nice to see you guys again," he says with a smile. "Who got shot?"

Karen says, "The bodyguard," as she cuts his hands and feet loose. He rubs his wrists and stands up a little awkwardly but quickly gains his balance. "Let's get out of here."

We go out the back door and tell Angie, "Let's go!"

We work our way along the fence line back to our car and head back toward I-66.

"We need to be careful. The tall man might be hiding along here somewhere," I say, my gun gripped tightly in my hand. I notice Karen keeps hers out as well while Angie drives.

We get back to Apple Manor Road and see a bunch of cars and flashing lights ahead. When we get closer, Angie pulls over. I can see the tall man in handcuffs standing outside his vehicle. The FBI team arrived at just the right time, and I breathe a sigh of relief. Thank goodness!

❧

After we're back at AKA, we hear from Tony.

"You should have waited for the FBI team, but I'm glad you didn't. Anyway, we weren't able to learn anything from the security cameras in the AKA garage. Craig's kidnappers blinded the cameras with wasp spray — the aerosol can shoot a stream over 20 feet. It left the lenses a blurry mess. But we got lucky and found a security camera across the street from the garage entrance. It shows that your Unknown Person #1 walked from the sidewalk down the ramp into the garage after our trailing agents left the garage. Then a couple of minutes later, a woman followed him into the garage with a large purse slung over her shoulder.

"Within a minute, she came back up the ramp and walked down the street in the opposite direction. We think she's the one who shot Unknown Person #1. NSA has analyzed the video using facial recognition and identified the woman as the Russian agent Irina Rachkova."

Tony continues, "By the way, we identified your Unknown Person #1 as Chang Fan, one of Li's bodyguards in Bangkok, but he's also a former MSS agent. The reason he looks familiar is that you probably saw him with Li at the Oriental Hotel."

Tony's last comment jogs my memory. Now I remember — the same round face with glasses peeking around the corner in the Authors' Lounge. So why did Li send him to D.C.? I suspect it was to have another resource here that he trusted if something went wrong that Yang and Wu couldn't handle.

And why did the Russians kill Chang? It seems they did it to protect me! But why? So they could kidnap me later? This whole situation is getting more and more complicated.

CHAPTER 45

THIS TIME, WE have three FBI special agents waiting for us when we arrive at the Jackson-Evers airport. One of them drives our car, and we ride to Natchez with the others in their van. We arrive back at the office a few minutes after 10:00 p.m., the day after we freed Craig. We go inside for a few minutes to get our own weapons, then Karen and Angie go with me back to Wexford House. I can't see anyone, but I can almost feel the backup agents following us and ensuring our safety.

The next morning, I smell bacon frying in the kitchen. Miss Doris greets us with a big smile and a full pot of coffee.

"Mr. Grant, I wondered if you were ever coming home!"

"Miss Doris, you know I'm always happiest when I'm back in Natchez," I respond, happy to see her after what seems like months away.

She had prepared a full breakfast, and Karen and Angie ate more than they wanted, not wanting to hurt her feelings.

I ask her, "What's been happening in Natchez while I've been gone?"

"There's another attempt by the school board to get the funding to build a new high school. The *Natchez Democrat* has been publishing a series of articles with all the popular viewpoints, for and against. I'm for it, but it probably won't happen. It'll create a lot of controversy in the next few months, though," says Miss Doris.

"We have a gift for you, Miss Doris. I'm sorry it's not wrapped, but airport security wouldn't allow a wrapped package," I explain.

She excitedly opens the box, unwraps the tissue paper, and sees the Benjarong vase. A big smile lights up her face, and she carefully picks up the vase from the box.

"It's lovely, thank you all so much. I can't wait for my friends to see it. I bet there's not another one between here and New Orleans!"

I say, "It's as special as you are, Miss Doris!" She hugs the vase and carefully wraps it, and puts it back in the box. "I won't let Joe touch it," she says.

When we arrive at the office later, Craig is already there. His phone rings almost as soon as we walk in the door. Tony must have some sort of ESP, too.

Craig puts the call on speaker, and Tony's voice booms through the room. "The current situation is that we have stopped the attack on our financial system, at least temporarily, and we have the perpetrators in custody. However, the driving force behind it, Deputy Chairman Li, is still free in China. We know about his scheme, but he doesn't know that. He's probably been told that Yang and Wu are in custody. No doubt he's wondering how we learned about Plan 23-2 here in the U.S. Li will feel the need to respond to Yang and Wu being taken into custody. He's probably making contingency plans in case Yang and Wu flip.

Given all that, we've decided to offer Yang a deal. If he cooperates fully, we'll let him return to China if he promises to expose Deputy Chairman Li's scheme to President Xiong.

"But allowing Yang to return to China will pose some risk, as we'll lose control of him. To be sure of his intentions, we need Grant to find out what he really thinks when we make the offer, and then monitor him afterward if he has a change of heart. We'll interrogate him again later this morning. If all goes well, we'll make the offer after lunch. So Grant, plan to search Yang's memory beginning about 1:00 p.m. this afternoon, noon your time."

"No problem, Tony," I say.

After a pause, Tony continues, "Wu Min is a different situation. We plan to keep him here. His hacking and malware skills are too dangerous to allow him to go back to China. We might give him generous privileges if he cooperates and gives us information about APT10 that we can use to counter their efforts. We aren't sure yet if we want him to know that we realize he set up the Hong Kong accounts. The PRC Ambassador has filed objections about the arrest of Yang and Wu. We haven't responded yet except to say they were involved in a scheme to cause harm to the United States, and we've determined they don't have diplomatic immunity."

Angie says, "Why don't you wait and see if Yang or Wu volunteer information about the bribery scheme? If they mention it voluntarily, then you'll have some indication they're sincere in their cooperation. Besides, any mention of bribery will show we have some deeper intelligence operation in place, and you probably don't want them to know that. Grant's involvement should be shielded at all costs."

Tony says, "Yeah, that makes sense. We'll press Yang and Wu only on Plan 23-2, though we won't let them know that we know the code name. Talk to you all later. Bye."

While I wait for the Yang offer to occur, I research the cost data for comparable gems to those Sammi offered. I'm especially interested in the pink padparadscha sapphires from Madagascar and the spessartite garnets from Nigeria, and the blue zircons from Cambodia. Not many dealers offer these stones, which I'm sure Sammi already knew. I wish I could turn back the clock to when this was all I had to worry about — the price of gems — instead of China maybe wanting to rub me out!

At 1:00 p.m., I figure the meeting's probably over, and I tell the crew I need some quiet time to connect with Yang, so they leave my office and go next door. I quickly connect with Yang and get the image of him in an interrogation room at Chesapeake. There are two men in suits sitting across the table.

"Mr. Yang, I'm FBI Special Agent Carl Greer. This is Mr. Ye Chao, he is an interpreter if you would like this interview to be conducted in Mandarin." Agent Greer is a typecast mid-forties portrait of authority and competence.

Yang says, "Yes, Mandarin."

"Mr. Yang, you have talked several times to Special Agent Roman Muzik. He tells me you have denied everything. Is that right?" Ye Chao translates. Yang nods his head, yes.

"Mr. Yang, we have Mr. Wu Min and others in custody, and we have been interviewing them. And they've been talking to us. You should know that when we get corroborating information from two independent sources, we consider it to be true. If you tell us something completely different, it damages your credibility. Now, we know you've made several trips recently to the United States, bringing sealed diplomatic packages each time. We believe you brought cash and computer equipment in the pouches. The purpose of bringing these items was to facilitate an attack on the United States' financial system. Is that right?"

Yang just sits quietly.

Someone must've talked. How do they know about the pouches?

"Mr. Yang, you are not a citizen of the United States. Therefore, you do not enjoy the legal rights of our citizens. And you are not a diplomat, so there's no diplomatic immunity. There are U.S. laws with significant penalties for the type of attacks that you and your associates attempted. You all will be subject to charges under 18 U.S. Code §1030, which covers illegal activities involving protected computers, as defined by U.S. law. Under this statute, the penalty is a minimum of ten years and up to twenty years of prison time per count. There'll also be other charges under terrorism and national security statutes. You likely will be facing prison time of more than a hundred years."

Greer watches him intently, and Yang forces himself not to fidget.

Agent Greer's piercing eyes make me nervous, and I don't like this prison talk. When is the embassy going to get me out of here?

"Mr. Yang, while we know you were the lead person facilitating this operation, we believe there were others higher in the PRC government who authorized the attack. We want to know who in China authorized the attack and the details of the overall plan. If you cooperate with us, we may be able to influence the prison sentence to reward your cooperation."

So they are willing to trade incriminating information on Deputy Chairman Li for a reduced sentence. I wonder how much reduction? Does Li deserve my loyalty if it means the rest of my life in prison?

"We'll give you time to think about this." Special Agent Greer and Ye Chao get up and leave the room.

I'll give Deputy Chairman Li until tomorrow to do something to help me. Then I'll consider assisting the Americans if they offer a serious deal. I wonder what Wu Min is telling them.

I come back to the moment and tell the others what I learned, then call Tony and tell him as well.

Tony says, "We'll make Yang sweat a while before talking with him again. We aren't getting anywhere with Wu. Allison Murphy is cooperating, but she doesn't know anything that we don't already know. I want you to find out what Hua is thinking about all this. He may be in contact with Li."

"Okay, Tony. I'll let you know. Oh, I was wondering — what'll happen if the Chinese can pull off the attack by alternate means? I mean, how will the U.S. respond?"

"Grant, since you could find out if you really wanted to know, I'll tell you. We would retaliate with our own cyberattack on them. We would shut down their electrical grid, their transportation network, including trains and airports, their water system, and military command and control. We have already infected their systems, and all we have to do is trigger our own cyberattack. It would help us if Wu could confirm a few technical aspects of their systems, but we're basically ready to go."

"But wouldn't that escalate to armed conflict?"

"We don't think so, but it could, especially if the Russians get involved. They might try to take advantage of the situation by taking over part of Ukraine or Belarus or the small Baltic countries. But don't worry about that. You only need to worry about the Plan 23-2 threat," says Tony.

"I'll let you know about Hua," I reply.

"Grant, soon, okay?"

"Yes."

I go back to my office, lean back in my leather desk chair, and put my feet on the desk. The thought crosses my mind that if I'm going to be doing this often, Tony needs to buy a comfortable couch for my office. But then I begin to concentrate on connecting with Hua. I decide to start searching the morning after the arrest of Yang.

I work my way through fifteen-minute segments for most of the day. About 3:00 p.m., Hua has a call to come to the PRC Ambassador's office. Ambassador Han Zemin is sitting behind his desk with a frown on his face. Hua sits down in front of the Ambassador and starts to make small talk. Han puts up his hand, signaling him to stop.

"Hua, I talked to Deputy Chairman Li this morning. I told him Yang Kexin and Wu Min have both been arrested by the Americans. I told him the Americans said Yang and Wu were involved in a scheme to harm the United States. He said he doesn't know anything about that. He says Yang and Wu were here to meet with embassy staff to better understand recent political developments in the United States. I know they met with you. What can you tell me?"

Obviously, Deputy Chairman Li didn't have the approvals for Plan 23-2. I must follow his lead.

"Ambassador, it is just as Li has said. They wanted to know about the mid-term elections and how social media was being used in the political process. Also, they wanted to learn about electronic voting methods at the precinct level."

If he asks about Allison Murphy, I am sunk.

"Hua, I am told Yang brought diplomatic pouches into the embassy on several recent trips. What do you know about that?"

"Ambassador, I have no knowledge of that. Who reported this?"

"Never mind. Maybe the report was mistaken. But I may have more questions for you later."

I should never have cooperated with Yang without the Ambassador's approval. Why haven't the Americans tried to detain me? Maybe I'm next.

I call Tony with Craig, Karen, and Angie listening.

"Tony, Hua has been meeting with Ambassador Han, who is confused by what he has been hearing and seems to be suspicious of Hua. Han talked with Li, who says Yang and Wu were exclusively at the embassy to find out about American politics. Hua agrees that's all they talked about, and he doesn't know anything about any diplomatic pouches. Now Hua's scared that he's going to be dragged into this. The most important thing is that Li denies knowing anything and apparently will not give Yang and Wu any help."

"Okay, we'll continue as planned. Yang will probably flip and help us, so that's good. We'll let you know what happens next."

I say, "Okay, bye."

This is getting complicated. I don't see what Li has to gain by not at least trying to help Yang and Wu. But if he does, then he will risk incriminating himself with President Xiong.

Going off of Li's reaction, it's clear Craig's kidnapping attempt was orchestrated by Yang's bodyguard, not by Li. I assume that means the Chinese still don't know about me. If they haven't discovered me yet, then that means they weren't behind the assassination attempt by John Demarge. But if they weren't, who was — Russia, Iran, or someone else?

The idea that more adversaries might know about me escalates my concern.

CHAPTER 46

WEDNESDAY, MAY 22
NATCHEZ, MISSISSIPPI

THE NEXT MORNING, I ask Craig, "How long will this phase last? Will we really let Yang go back to China?"

Craig says, "I think only a few more days. If we don't move quickly, then there may be other developments that muddy the water. We don't know the true state of President Xiong's health, so we don't want to wait too long. Yes, I think we'll let Yang go back if it helps oust Li. More importantly, he's our window into what the Russians are doing."

I say, raising my eyebrows. "No, I'm your window, so Tony better not take me for granted."

Craig says, "Yes, you're right. It's too easy for us to forget. Sorry about that." A look of chagrin passes over his face, and I settle back into my chair. It's easy to feel underappreciated and overused by Tony sometimes.

"By the way, we'd like to set up shop in the upstairs of your carriage house for some of our crew. They'll be better able to protect your home. We think you can rent it out as an apartment and be within Natchez zoning laws. It'll take some work to get it set up, but Tony'll pay for everything. What do you think?"

After Demarge, the Nissan, the motorcycle guys, and Craig's kidnapping, I think more security would probably be a good idea. I nod and say, "Yes, that sounds fine. But you've got to pay rent so that everything is legitimate, say, $1,000 a month plus utilities. After everything that's happened, I agree more security would be a good idea."

Craig says, "Tony might not like paying rent, but okay."

I don't like the invasion of my privacy, either, but better safe than sorry. Maybe all this security can be scaled back later.

"I'll have to think about how to explain it to Miss Doris. She'll be suspicious if she sees a lot of people coming and going."

Craig says, "We can add a door and stairwell in the back so our people can enter from the alley and not be seen from the house. Besides, there's parking in the alley, so that's a logical reason to add another door."

"I'll let you know in a few days," I say.

I decide to resume my research on pricing the precious gemstones I'm considering purchasing from Sammi. I decide that Sammi's prices are reasonable. I could press him to accept a lower price, but I decide against it. I want him always to consider me first when he has unique gemstones. I send him an e-mail with a list of the gemstones I'd like to buy. I ask him to e-mail me copies of the GIA colored stone reports. After I review them for the specific gemstones he's offering, I'll wire him the payment, and then he'll ship to me via Brink's, as we've done before.

After the message is sent to Sammi, I can return my attention to what's happening with the China conspiracy.

I go through the connecting door to Suite 302 and find Craig sitting at the desk and Angie and Karen at their desks with their laptops open.

"Anything new?" I ask no one in particular.

Craig says, "Tony says they have had another session with Wu this morning, and Tony wants you to check it out. They began at 8:00 a.m. our time."

I turn around, go back to my office, and close the connecting door. I recall the thought about the couch and go back and tell Craig. He says, "Okay, order what you want." I go back with a smile and sit down in my office chair and lean back.

Wu is sitting at a table in the small interrogation room. Agent Greer and Ye Chao are sitting across from him.

"Mr. Wu, I tried to explain yesterday the difficult situation you're in. We have others in custody, and they've been talking with us. We have a good picture of what you and the others were trying to do. It's important for us to understand the details of the plan, including who approved it. If you cooperate, we will be willing to reduce your prison sentence substantially," says Agent Greer, who has a very stern look on his face as he speaks.

Before I agree to anything, I want to know how much they will reduce the sentence.

"How much will you reduce the penalties?"

"It depends on how much you cooperate, but it could be very significant," says Greer.

"What exactly do you want to know?"

Let's see what they are after.

"Who approved the malware attack?"

If I finger Deputy Chairman Li, I may eventually be in physical danger. Still, maybe that is a risk worth taking rather than spending the rest of my life in jail.

"If I tell you, what is that worth?"

"We can't say until we examine the entirety of what you tell us and how much of it we can corroborate."

So this will be a cat-and-mouse game. Unfortunately, I am the mouse, but maybe I can make Deputy Chairman Li the mouse instead.

"Deputy Chairman Li authorized the attack, but that's his job. He's in charge of our cyberattack unit, among other responsibilities. He's a member of the Politburo Standing Committee, our highest political body."

"But wouldn't the Politburo Standing Committee have to approve something as important as this?" asks Greer.

"I don't know, but I assume they would, yes."

But the Deputy Chairman did this on his own.

"Since the plan failed, we assume he will blame you and Yang," says Greer. "By the way, why did you have to personally come to the U.S. to execute the plan?"

"Because we were unable to penetrate the firewalls and other cyber protections. Therefore, we needed to arm the malware manually immediately before it was uploaded into the computer systems, and I have the expertise to do that."

"But you weren't going to actually load the malware in the system?"

"No, but the malware had to be armed to start and stop exactly when we wanted."

"You wanted it to stop?"

"No, but we had the capability if we wanted to use it that way."

"Will you be willing to talk to our cyberwarfare experts to explain the technology and strategies you are pursuing in APT10?" Greer asks.

"Would that help reduce my sentence?"

"Yes, it would be an important consideration."

"Since that would be giving away national secrets, I need to know exactly how much my sentence will be reduced so I know if it's worth the risk."

I hope I have some leverage. They obviously want to know our capabilities and plans.

Greer's eyebrows raise, somewhat incredulous. "Since you're facing a hundred years in prison, I would think that you wouldn't worry too much about divulging that information," says Greer.

"Yes, but if I tell you, what prevents the United States from sentencing me to the hundred years in prison anyway?"

"We would be willing to sign a plea agreement that would be binding."

"But you can say I didn't fulfill my end of the bargain."

"The final plea agreement would only be signed after you give us all the information we require."

"Then you are asking me to trust you, is that it?"

"Yes, but you really don't have any choice, do you?"

No, I don't, but I don't want them to know I'm thinking that.

"Then I want a complete list of everything you want to know, and I will consider it."

Greer nods. "Okay, fair enough."

I'm going to have to give away our technology, the details of the plot, and incriminate Yang. I will hold onto the information on the crypto accounts. I will hold onto that as a final bargaining chip in case I need one.

Agent Greer and Ye Chao get up from their chairs and leave. The door latch buzzes when opened, then makes an ominous clunking sound, as if an exclamation point, as it closes after them.

I go over to Suite 302 and tell Craig I'm ready to share what I've discovered from Wu.

He calls Tony and puts him on the speakerphone. "What is he thinking, Grant?"

"He wants to make a deal, but he wants to know what he's going to get. He's trying to negotiate with Greer. He wants a list of information that we want and what we're willing to give him to get it. He's afraid of Li and probably others in the Chinese government. He'll give what we want, but he wants a written agreement. That's about it, really."

"Okay, that's good to know. Thanks! We're interviewing Yang again later this afternoon. I'll let you know what time. It's very important that I know what he's thinking."

I go back to Suite 301 and start researching leather sofas. I finally decide a leather recliner will be better for my purpose. I tell Craig I want to order a Hancock & Moore leather recliner, but it's expensive. I already have the matching desk chair, so I tell him that's what I want. He says go ahead and order it. I'm happy — for now.

⁓

Later in the afternoon, Craig says, "They're finished with Yang. Tony wants to know what you can find out."

He leaves my office, and this time I hold my head in my hands with my elbows on the desk and close my eyes, trying to concentrate.

Yang is sitting at the same table, with Special Agent Greer and Ye Chao facing him.

"Mr. Yang, have you decided if you will cooperate?" Greer asks.

"It depends on how much the sentence will be reduced," Yang says.

"That depends on how completely you cooperate and if we can corroborate any of what you tell us, but it could be a very substantial reduction."

"How do I know you will keep your word?"

"Unfortunately, you are not in a position to know in advance, but I can tell you in all sincerity we are honorable people. We will sign a written plea agreement, but only after you give us the information and we have the chance to evaluate it," says Greer.

It seems Deputy Chairman Li has done nothing to get me out of here.

"I might say that we may be more honorable than your superiors. Listen to this audio recording of a telephone call from your Ambassador to our Secretary of State."

"Mr. Secretary, this is Ambassador Han Zemin. I am calling about Yang Kexin and Wu Min, the two Chinese citizens you have arrested. As you know, they are PRC government employees. I have been assured that if they were involved in a plot to attack the United States financial system, it was on their own initiative and not an act approved by the People's Republic of China." Greer turns off the recording.

So Deputy Chairman Li is going to let us take the rap for his mistake. That's it, I will incriminate him with all the details.

"That's not true. We were ordered to make the attack by Deputy Chairman Li, as I told you before. I will cooperate. Tell me what you want to know."

"What was Li trying to accomplish?"

"The Deputy Chairman says President Xiong is very ill with lymphoma. Li wants to succeed him, but he's not the front-runner. He decided a successful attack on the United States would help his chances. But just in case, he has also been bribing members of the Politburo Standing Committee and other lower, but influential, officials to support him in his quest to succeed President Xiong."

"How do you know this?"

"Because I am the one who facilitates the payments and solicits the funds for the bribes."

"Will you give us a list of officials involved?"

"Yes, of course."

"And tell us the source of the bribe money?"

"Yes, definitely."

"Then, there will be a substantial reduction in your prison sentence if you give us that information."

I hope Li is starting to feel the pressure, not knowing if I will talk or not. I feel less pressure now.

"We'll talk to you again later, Mr. Yang," says Greer. He and Ye Chao leave the room.

It seems Yang wants revenge. That probably bodes well for him cooperating. I tell Craig and the ladies what I heard and saw; they agree that Yang seems to want revenge.

We decide to call it a day.

When we arrive at home, Karen and Angie go upstairs to freshen up. Miss Doris is in the kitchen cooking; she looks up and smiles. I am a little nervous. I don't want to mislead her, but I know I must.

I say, "Miss Doris, you know I rented an office to a new financial company in town. One of the partners is looking for a place to live, and I'm thinking about renting him the upstairs apartment in the carriage house. It won't take much work to get it back in shape. He can park in the alley, so it won't bother us at all."

She studies my face for a moment, purses her lips, then says, "Mister Grant, I have known you since you were a child, and I can read your face. Houseguests for five or six weeks, renting out office space that's been vacant for thirty years, long trips out of the country with your guests, internet technicians here multiple times, carrying around that gun under your shirt — don't think I didn't notice — and now you want to rent out the carriage house? I know something's going on, and you'll tell me when you want me to know. In the meantime, don't spend any effort trying to fool me. I'll do whatever you need to make things work, just tell me. And I won't say a word to anybody, even Joe."

I am shocked to hear Miss Doris talk like this. I feel so stupid, but I decide if I tell her what's going on, I will put her in more danger. I may have to tell her sometime, but not today.

"I know you'll do whatever I need, Miss Doris; you are truly family. I'll tell you when I can."

I decide not to tell the others about Miss Doris's suspicions. I know that I can do whatever I need to do, and she won't ask any questions. And she might already be in danger just by being here. The thought that I've brought her into this mess . . . I really feel so bad — and stupid.

That damned Tony!

CHAPTER 47

THE NEXT MORNING, before heading into the office, Karen and I go over to the Natchez City Hall on South Pearl Street, only a few blocks from Wexford House, to the Office of Inspections. We tell Mr. Robert Pursell, the department head, what I want to do with the carriage house, and he tells me it's okay with the Inspections Office; I'll need an inspection permit when the contractor is ready to begin work. However, he says that I'll need to talk to the City Planning Department. I walk around the corner and check with City Planning. Since this is a historic property, Mr. Roger Moore says I'll need to make an Application for Certificate of Appropriateness to add a rear door to the carriage house. He doesn't foresee a problem getting it approved.

Back in the office, I'm discussing the carriage house renovation specifications with Craig, Karen, and Angie when Tony calls. He tells me he wants to know what Deputy Chairman Li is thinking now. He asks that I check his thoughts and actions beginning from about 8:00 p.m. last night, which would have been during office hours in Beijing. I wonder if I can do it from that distance — Beijing is over 7,000 miles away!

The others retreat to Suite 302, and I lean back in my office chair and concentrate on Deputy Chairman Li. Fairly quickly, I begin to get images. Li is in his office, as Tony suspected, at 9:00 a.m. He is by himself.

Li is thinking about the situation regarding Yang and Wu.

I have no choice but to let Yang and Wu face punishment. Wu had a bright future but bad luck. And luck must be involved because the Americans had no way to know about Plan 23-2. Once this episode is finished, we need to find out how we were compromised. The Americans must have recruited a spy within APT10.

Li looks through the stack of papers on his desk. Most of them deal with foreign security matters, but he can't take his mind off Yang and Wu.

What happens if Yang tells what he knows? He's the most dangerous to me. But what would the Americans do with the information? Would they rather blackmail me or expose me?

I should destroy the ledger book with the records of the bribes and the crypto accounts. I can't take the chance that it might be found if my office is searched. But I must have the ability to access the information. Perhaps I can hide it somewhere else.

Ah! The app Wu Min installed on my phone. I'll take photos of the ledger pages before I destroy them. Then I'll store the images in a hidden folder. Let me see if I can create an encrypted file.

Li plays with his phone, trying to remember how to find and use the hidden app. He finds it and then has to remember how to encrypt a photo and hide the file. He gets the ledger book from the safe and takes a photo of the accounts summary page. He then goes through the steps to create an encrypted file and folder. He gets to a point where he needs to enter a password.

What can I use as a password that I won't forget but will be sufficiently strong? I can't write it anywhere, so what can I use that I know I won't forget? The combination to the safe! That's it, so simple and secure!

He enters R27-L16-R33 and hits enter.

Li makes sure he can access the hidden folder and the photo file. He then takes photos of the other pages in the ledger, encrypts them, adds them to the folder, and makes sure he can access everything. When he's satisfied, he rips the pages from the ledger and puts them through the cross-cut shredder under his desk. He then puts the ledger back into the safe and empties the shredder bin into a large brown envelope with a metal clasp. With a pen knife, he cuts numerous slits on both sides of the envelope before putting on his coat and telling his secretary he's going to take a walk.

Li walks toward Yingtai, an island in the South Lake. Along the way, he stops and picks up a rock, which he puts in the envelope and seals it.

When he reaches the bridge to Yingtai, there are only a few people out walking. He crosses partway over the bridge, looks around, making sure no one is watching, and drops the envelope into the water. It floats for a second or two, but as the air inside escapes through the slits, it starts to sink. After five seconds or so, it disappears entirely under the water, and there are no more bubbles.

Now, let them search.

Satisfied, Li walks back to his office.

Once he arrives, he opens the safe. He takes out the bundles of money and puts them in a briefcase. After he's removed the silencer, he puts the gun in his center desk drawer just in case he needs it quickly.

Now, if the safe is searched, all they'll find is an empty ledger book. I'll get rid of that later. And I can show my cooperation by opening the safe without any objection. I'll decide later where to hide the money, but for now, I'll take it to my home. It would be hard to explain why I have so much U.S. cash here in the office.

After I report my findings, Craig calls Tony, and he's pleased but concerned.

"If we tell the Chinese about the hidden app, the password, and the hidden encrypted folders, we'll be disclosing too much about our intelligence capability," Tony says.

Tony and the other officials in D.C. will have to decide what and how much to share.

Li may be able to fool the Chinese authorities and blame Yang and Wu, thereby retaining his power. Then he'll probably try to get revenge for us stopping his attack. I need to do all I can to help Tony get Li out of the way permanently. In the meantime, I'll be very cautious.

Tony calls Craig again later in the afternoon. Craig puts him on the speaker so we can all hear what he has to say.

"Yang has provided the list of politicians that Li has bribed and the amounts as best he can remember. Yang has also told us what he knows about the source of the bribe money, the sham consulting company, and the companies dependent on state contracts. Plus, what he knows about the crypto accounts in Hong Kong, but he doesn't have much about that. He says Wu knows those details.

"Wu decided to cooperate, and met with our cyber experts and shared the details of the malware with them. He also has discussed other projects APT10 is developing and the technologies they are using. Our people say he will be very useful to us if he continues to cooperate. He hasn't mentioned the crypto accounts yet. We're trying to decide how to squeeze that out of him.

"Now we're considering what to do with Yang and Wu. We think if we want to take down Deputy Chairman Li permanently, we'll need to provide a credible witness to the Chinese. We're going to talk to Yang about him being that witness later today.

"We won't free Wu, he's too dangerous, but if he continues to cooperate, we'll be lenient. We need to show him we're going to honor our promise to reduce his sentence, so we're presenting a plea agreement to him today.

"Grant, we need you to be ready to inform us what Yang and Wu think after we talk with them."

"I'll be ready, Tony," I reply.

Then Tony says, "One more thing — the NSA found that Irina Rachkova has left the country. She left Dulles on a British Airways flight only three hours after Craig was kidnapped. She's traveling on a British passport as Emily Beth Chapman. We didn't find out until she was already in London. And who knows where she is now, probably in Moscow."

With Rachkova gone, I wonder if the Russians assigned another agent to protect me from the Chinese. And if so, why? Do they want me for themselves?

We say our goodbyes, and Craig puts his phone away.

As long as I'm with Craig, Angie, and Karen, I feel safe, so I'm going to try to go about my business. If I worry about every little thing, I'll go crazy.

When I get back to my office, I find that Sammi has e-mailed the GIA reports, so I spend time reviewing them. Once I satisfy myself that everything is all right, I decide to go downstairs to the bank and wire the money. I let Tony know, and he says okay, but Karen needs to go down with me. Angie wants to go along, so we all three ride down the elevator and enter the bank through the lobby entrance.

When we enter the bank, the branch manager, David Feldman, greets us. I introduce Karen; Angie already knows him. He asks how he can help me today. I tell him I want to make a wire transfer from my business account to Siam Trading Company in Bangkok, which I have done in the past.

He says he can take care of that for me and asks the amount. I tell him and notice out of the corner of my eye that both Karen's and Angie's jaws drop when they hear the six-figure number. I just smile and shrug my shoulders. David hands me the wire transfer form to sign, and I quickly scrawl my signature. He says he'll be happy to help the ladies with any banking transactions while they're visiting Natchez. We thank him and go back upstairs.

When we arrive back at Suite 302, Craig says Tony has called and wants me to check out Yang's thoughts beginning at 3:00 p.m. our time; they've made the offer. I go back over to Suite 301 and start my usual routine. I lean back in my chair and try to connect with Yang. Very quickly, the images begin to materialize in my mind.

Yang is again sitting in the interrogation room, and Special Agent Greer and Ye Chao are there.

"Mister Yang, we've corroborated most of what you told us with what we have heard from Mr. Wu. We're ready to make an offer. You can think of it as sort of a trade. We're prepared to send you back to China in exchange for cooperating with PRC officials in prosecuting Deputy Chairman Li for his crimes — meaning the bribery scheme and attacking the United States without proper authority. However, if you agree, then we must also obtain the agreement of Chinese officials. We think President Xiong will want to get rid of Li Zhang Yong from the communist party and the government. Are you ready to do this, or would you rather stay in the United States in prison?"

There's no doubt. Putting Li in prison would be sweet revenge.

"You really don't give me much choice, but how do I know I won't face serious trouble of my own when I return to China?"

"We believe President Xiong is a man of his word; that is all we can offer."

"When you can assure me that President Xiong has agreed, I will go back."

"We'll let you know and bring a formal plea agreement for you to sign."

"That's fine."

The only fear I have is that President Xiong will die before this is over, and then Li will be able to eliminate me once and for all. Even so, this agreement is my best choice.

Once we fill Tony in, Craig says we might as well call it a day. Since it's a Thursday and still early, I ask the crew if they'd like to eat somewhere special tonight.

"It's called H. D. Gibbes & Sons. The place was a shuttered 130-year-old country store in a small town of about fifty people, less than two hours from here, on the way to Jackson, in Learned, Mississippi. The family inherited the property and decided to turn it into a restaurant on the weekend. They serve steaks, fish, lamb, and other dishes that can be grilled. They have long tables set up inside the store, and they serve the food on paper plates. You can bring your own wine or even hard liquor. They have coolers with bottles of beer, and you get what you want and show the number of caps when you're finished, and they charge accordingly, on the honor system. And they usually have entertainment. But they only take cash or checks."

Angie says, "It sounds like fun."

Karen and Craig agree. So we head out, stopping on the way to pick up some wine. We head up the Natchez Trace Parkway, and it takes only a little over ninety minutes to get there, but only because Craig is a fast driver. I notice he's also careful to watch if we are being followed. The town of Learned is only about two miles off the Natchez Trace. We pull in just before 5:00 p.m., which is when they open. And there's already a group of people waiting outside in the heat.

In a few minutes, we're seated at one of the long tables, we open our wine, and Craig gets a beer. They offer us some cups for our drinks, and we are all set.

We all order something different — lamb chops, filet mignon, redfish, and rib-eye steak with sides of salad, green beans, baked Idaho and baked sweet potatoes. Everything was served on disposable plates, so it was a very different experience from the fancy restaurants in Bangkok — but the food was excellent, and so was the ambience!

CHAPTER 48

Justine just got word from John Tyson that Vetrov is scheduled to land at Teterboro Airport today. They're arriving from St. Kitts via Miami, so they've already cleared passport control and customs.

Teterboro Airport in New Jersey is the largest private airport in the country. It's where all the corporate jets and those owned by wealthy individuals fly into if their passengers' destination is Manhattan. It's no more than an hour away from Lower Manhattan, so Justine has a little time before he arrives. She and Special Agent John Tyson are already on their way.

As John drives, Justine stares out the window at the scenery, wondering when and how the Devereaux pendant got from Natchez to Paris in the first place. She'd discovered from Interpol that M. Lang and M. Rousseau, as well as their spouses, are all deceased, so those leads became dead-ends.

She tries to come up with different scenarios. One way

would be for the thief to have taken it to Paris. Another way would have been for the thief to have sold it to someone who then took it to Paris. In that case, the purchaser might not have known it was stolen, that is, if there was fraudulent paperwork involved. But who could have gotten away with providing dishonest paperwork, when there would have been a tremendous amount of money involved in the purchase?

Oh well, she decides to continue this thought experiment later.

"Is his wife on the plane?"

"No, the passenger manifest lists two females we haven't identified, but not his wife. Also, a male we don't know, and his personal assistant, Viktor Zlobin," says Agent Tyson.

They arrive at Teterboro about thirty minutes before the Vetrov plane is scheduled to land. Justine and Agent Tyson go inside the Meridian Terminal and ask for the terminal manager.

When the manager comes out from her office, Justine says, "I'm Special Agent Justine Aebischer, and this is Special Agent John Tyson, FBI. We're here to meet the incoming Vetrov flight, tail number P4-RV1. We'd like to talk to Mr. Vetrov about an investigation we're conducting, and we booked two conference rooms here at your terminal. Can you show us the rooms? Also, can we arrange to be at the bottom of the steps when the passengers deplane?"

The manager, a friendly, dark-haired woman in her forties dressed in a dark blue suit with a Meridian logo on the jacket, introduces herself as Andrea Newby. She says, "Sure, let me show you the conference rooms." They take the elevator to the second floor. The adjoining conference rooms are just a few feet down the hallway.

They look into both rooms, which each have a large conference table with chairs for eight people. John says, "These look fine. We'll want to talk with Mr. Vetrov separately, while the other passengers wait in the other conference room. Then we may want to talk with one or two of the others. There will be two other agents and an interpreter meeting us here at any moment. Do you know who will be picking up the Vetrov party?"

"They normally use Luxor," Andrea says.

"Can you tell Luxor they won't be needed today?" Justine asks.

"Yes, I'll do that. I'll tell them Mr. Vetrov has made a change in his plans. It happens."

"And is there a third conference room or office if we need it?"

"There's a smaller conference room for four next to the other rooms. It's not booked, so you can use it if you need it," Andrea says.

They take the elevator back down to the lobby, where Andrea goes to the service desk and asks the status of Vetrov's plane. The customer service agent tells her they're landing in about five minutes and will park over by the hangar. Andrea tells her to change spots and park them in front of the terminal.

Andrea says, "I'll walk you two out to the plane. The others can wait inside. We don't want too many people out on the apron for safety reasons."

Justine responds, "Okay," and John nods. John says to Justine, "Agents Clark and Miller are waiting. And Ms. Plieva, our interpreter, is here, too."

Justine says to John, "Tell them to wait here until we come inside, then the agents can take the remainder of the party to the conference room upstairs on the left. Ms. Plieva can go with Mr. Vetrov and us to the conference room on the right."

While John talks to the others, Justine purses her lips, considering how to approach Vetrov about the case.

When Agent Tyson comes back, Justine says, "I'm not going to tell Vetrov what we're looking for except that it's jewelry. The first thing I want to know is the whereabouts of Mrs. Vetrov. If she's at home in Manhattan, we'll go there and search. If not, we'll play it by ear. We don't want Vetrov to somehow signal his wife and have her move the Devereaux pendant to a new location."

John says, "That makes sense."

The terminal manager walks up to them and says, "The plane has landed and is taxiing in now. It should be here in a couple of minutes. The ramp crew is outside waiting. As soon as the plane is parked, we'll walk out."

They stand near the door, watching for the plane. After about two minutes, they see the gleaming G650ER approaching the Meridian Terminal. The ramp crew starts signaling the aircraft into position in the spot closest to the terminal. Then the pilot shuts down the engines.

Andrea says, "Let's go." They walk out the door and head toward the plane, which is only about a hundred feet away. When they arrive, the airstair is being lowered to the ground. Once in place, the cabin attendant sticks her head out, looks around, and then goes back inside.

In less than a minute, passengers start to descend the stairs. The first is a young man in casual clothing, turning his head and talking to two attractive young women, dressed in stylishly casual clothes, who follow behind. Justine notices the young man has a concealed weapon, so she assumes he's probably a bodyguard. When they reach the ground, Agent Tyson identifies himself and tells them he will escort their group into the terminal. The young man hesitates but follows John.

Then two older men emerge from the doorway. The first man is short and stocky with straight, sandy hair, wearing dark glasses and casual clothes that are obviously expensive. The light-cream pants have a sharp crease, and Justine wondered who in St. Kitts would even know how to iron such a crease, or if they did know, why would you want that? The man behind is a little taller, a little younger, has long, dark, wavy hair, and is also wearing dark glasses and expensive clothing. Justine decides the older man must be Ryurik Vetrov.

When the first man reaches the bottom of the stairs, Justine steps forward and says, "Mr. Vetrov, I'm FBI Special Agent Aebischer" and displays her badge. He acts confused and turns to look at the second man, who speaks to him in Russian.

Then the second man says, "Mr. Vetrov wants to know what you want. I'm his assistant, Viktor Zlobin. His English is not very good."

"We want to speak to him about an investigation we're conducting. He's not suspected of anything, but he may have information that will help us."

"Mr. Vetrov wants to know why you met him at the airport," Zlobin says.

"Because we didn't know if he was going to his residence or to the Hamptons to visit friends, or somewhere else. We didn't want to wait around at his residence when we knew we could meet him here." Zlobin translates this for Vetrov, who nods.

"Okay, then I will assist him, as he may need help to communicate during the interview," says Zlobin.

"We have our own translator, Mr. Zlobin. The investigation is confidential," says Justine.

"As you wish. I'll be here if you need me." He then speaks to Vetrov, who shrugs his shoulders. Justine wishes she could see his eyes behind the sunglasses.

They walk into the terminal, ride up the elevator, drop off Zlobin at the conference room with the others, and then go next door to their room. Agent Tyson and Zita Plieva were waiting. Justine introduces them, and Vetrov asks where Zita was from. Zita says, "Gatchina, outside St. Petersburg."

Vetrov says, "I know it well."

Zita translates for Justine the conversation with Vetrov

about her hometown. Justine smiles but is momentarily confused. Justine knew that Zita was from Krasnogorsk, outside Moscow. Then she realized Zita probably decided it was prudent not to give Vetrov any personal information.

Justine says, "Mr. Vetrov, we are investigating a theft of jewelry that happened many years ago. We have information that you may have purchased it. You wouldn't have known it was stolen, of course. We would like to know if you keep any expensive jewelry at your residence or anywhere else in Manhattan, perhaps in a safe deposit box."

Vetrov looks at Zita as she translates. He says, "I really don't know. I've purchased many pieces of jewelry over the years. What exactly are you looking for?"

Justine ignores his question and asks, "Where is your wife?"

He says, "She's in London, I think."

"Can you find out?"

"Yes, I'll do that if you wish." He gets his phone and starts to make a call.

Justine says, "Please text instead of call. Ask her only where she is." Zita translates.

After sending a text, he says, "London, she's there at home."

"Okay, tell her you'll call her later."

He texts again. "I told her."

"We're going to take you and your party to One57. Your friends can wait in the lobby or at the Park Hyatt while we search your premises. Here's the search warrant," Justine says, holding a folded paper in front of him.

Vetrov looks at Zita Plieva. Zita takes the warrant from Justine, opens and reads it, and then speaks in Russian to Vetrov, explaining the warrant.

Frowning, he says, "Okay, let's get it over with."

Zita translates for Justine, who stands up and says, "Then let's go."

CHAPTER 49

As they cross the George Washington Bridge, Justine asks Vetrov, "If you have a safe, are you going to open it, or do I need to call a locksmith to meet us there?" Zita translates.

Vetrov laughs. "I have nothing to hide. I'll open it."

When they arrive at the One57 entrance on West 58th Street, the valet parks their van at the hotel. They enter through the discreet One57 entrance and wait just inside for the others to arrive. Soon, the other agents, Clark and Miller, arrive with the other passengers. Justine, John, Clark, Vetrov, and Zita go through security and up to the 67th floor. Agent Miller stays with the others downstairs.

Using a biometric scanner, Vetrov unlocks the entry, and they all enter.

"Where do you want to start?" he asks.

"Where is the safe?" Justine asks.

"It's in the master dressing room." He waves toward the hallway on the other side of the living room. "I'll show you."

They walk through the living room with an entire wall of twelve-foot glass windows looking out over Central Park. Justine pauses for a moment to take in the view. "Unbelievable," she mutters.

When they reach the master bedroom, they walk through and into the dressing room. The safe is on the floor against the far wall.

Vetrov says to Ms. Plieva, in Russian, "Can you wait in the bedroom a minute? I have the combination hidden in here, and I would rather not have you know where it is." Zita translates to Justine.

Justine says, "Then you can hide it somewhere else later, but I'm not leaving. And make it quick."

After a few seconds, Vetrov has a piece of paper in his hand that he retrieved from under some clothes on a shelf and says, "Okay." He then bends down, spins the dial, and opens the safe. When it opens, she motions him out of the way and begins to look through the safe. There are eight trays; each one is about eighteen by twelve inches and two inches deep. She takes the trays out one by one. There is no jewelry, only cash, and various documents. After she had removed all the trays, she again looks closely to see if she had missed anything, but there's no jewelry.

She says loudly, "No jewelry, so we'll have to go through the entire apartment."

John says, "That doesn't make sense. No jewelry, none?"

"Nope," Justine says, shaking her head.

Then she stops and asks Vetrov, "Does the building have safe deposit boxes for the tenants to use?" Again, Zita translates.

He says, "I think they might, or maybe that's the building in London. It's hard for me to keep the buildings straight."

Since he isn't sure whether the building has safe deposit boxes, they all make their way to the manager's office on the 21st floor. Justine introduces herself and asks the manager, Zaida Fontanez, whether Vetrov has a safe deposit box in the building.

Zaida replies, "Hello, Mr. Vetrov," smiling at him. "Yes, he has one. Usually, though, Mrs. Vetrov or Mr. Zlobin are the ones who access the box."

"Mr. Vetrov would like to access his box. He's helping us with an investigation." Zita translates, and Vetrov nods.

Zaida stands up from her desk and waves them over to the large vault door. "Mr. Vetrov and I will need to pass the biometric scan to get into the vault." She puts her hand on the scanner until it beeps, and the screen shows "Pass." Then she points to the scanner; Vetrov puts his hand on it, and the screen shows "Pass" again. She then opens the vault door, and they enter a small room with an entire wall of safe deposit boxes. On the other wall is a machine that looks like an ATM. "This is the key safe." He has to pass another biometric scan on both of his irises within one minute of the biometric hand scan. Once the iris scan is complete, a key is dispensed. Zaida then puts her face in front of the scanner. Another key comes out.

Ms. Fontanez hands a key to Vetrov and walks over to the bank of safe deposit boxes. She finds the box that matched the key number, though it was coded with letters and numbers corresponding to the box. Vetrov's box was #14, but the key was marked K41, with the coded meaning of 11 (K being the 11th letter of the alphabet) plus 4 minus 1. The code is simple enough, but maybe it would slow down a thief, who somehow got access to the keys, just long enough to be caught.

Zaida shows Vetrov which box is his and where to put his key. When hers is also in the lock, she turns both keys, and the door pops open. She then pulls the box out of its slot and hands it to him, gesturing to the small table to the right of the key safe. He puts the box down on the table and sits in the chair.

Justine says, "Go ahead and open the box, then take out one item at a time." Ms. Plieva translates, and he nods.

The first several items are envelopes, which he opens and pulls out the documents. Justine, standing next to him, quickly dismisses these with a wave of her hand.

Then he pulls out a small flat case and opens it. Inside is a diamond bracelet. Justine again waves her hand, and he sets it aside. He opens a small jewelry box; inside is an emerald ring, and he puts it aside. Next is another flat case. He opens it, and Justine gasps when she sees the large ruby pendant surrounded by diamonds. It's hanging from an 18k gold mesh chain. "Spectacular," she says, "That's what we're looking for."

The others lean in to see the pendant. There are murmurs, especially from Zita, who says something in Russian. Zaida must've been used to seeing the elegant jewelry the residents store in their safe deposit boxes and shows no reaction. John is wide-eyed with curiosity.

Justine examines the pendant a little closer. The ruby is cushion cut and surrounded by a double row of diamonds — too many to easily count — maybe fifty. The markings on the back of the setting included the French eagle and the Mellerio hallmark, as expected. It matches the description of the Devereaux pendant. The gold mesh chain, which is the ideal size and style to match the pendant, has the letters FOPE engraved on one side of the clasp. She assumes it is the chain designer's name.

Justine says, "Mr. Vetrov, I'll give you an Evidence Property Receipt for the pendant. The gold chain is yours, however. And you are free to go. Thank you for your cooperation." Ms. Plieva translates all this, and Vetrov nods.

Vetrov replies, through Ms. Plieva's translation, "Please give the gold chain as a gift to the owner of the pendant to compensate for the twenty-plus years my wife has enjoyed wearing it. Either my insurance company or I will sue Sotheby's for selling me a stolen item, so I am not unhappy. My wife will enjoy being able to buy something new."

"I will pass along the gold chain to the owner if that is your wish," Justine says. After writing out a receipt and giving it to Vetrov, she adds, "If you need help with your insurance company or attorney, please call me, and I will be happy to explain the situation to them."

Zita translates, and Vetrov nods.

Justine says, "Thank you for your cooperation, Mr. Vetrov. We'll be going now." Agent Tyson, Agent Clark, and Ms. Plieva also say goodbye. As they leave, Zaida Fontanez instructs Vetrov on what he has to do to replace his safe deposit key in the key safe.

Zita Plieva takes the van with Special Agents Clark and Miller back to Teterboro, where she had left her car. Justine and Agent Tyson get in their own vehicle. As she and John pull away from One57, Agent Tyson says, "Vetrov wasn't such a bad guy after all."

Justine replies, "I doubt Sotheby's will be saying the same thing when he's through with them. And look at it from Vetrov's standpoint. What would he gain by not cooperating with the FBI? I wouldn't be surprised if the FBI has future dealings with Mr. Vetrov, and he probably expects that — he's no dummy."

Tyson just shrugs his broad shoulders.

Justine laughs, then calls FBI Director Lambert to let him know they recovered the pendant from Vetrov. He instructs them to head to the closest bank, put the pendant in a safe deposit box, and bring him the keys and a photo of the jewelry.

Justine is thrilled to have recovered the pendant, but her mood changes when she realizes she still doesn't know who stole it or how it got to Paris.

CHAPTER 50

Tony sits back in his chair to consider what to do next. FBI Director Lambert had just called to tell him Special Agent Aebischer recovered the Devereaux pendant. He never thought the FBI would be able to find a stolen piece of jewelry after ninety years. That was enough to ruin his day.

He made a call on his mobile phone to CIA Director Kohl.

"Mr. Director, this is Tony. I've just heard from Director Lambert that the FBI found the Devereaux pendant. You remember the Markey deal, right?"

"Yes, I remember. So what's the problem?"

"If the FBI finds the thief, then the whole mystery is solved. And if the thief wasn't Markey's great-grandfather, his family name is cleared, and he might just quit on us. I think the possibility of clearing the family name is what has sustained his cooperation," Tony says.

"So what do you propose to do, Tony?"

"Director Lambert says he'll slow-walk the rest of the investigation, but only if you agree. That'll keep Markey on our team, at least for a while."

"Will Markey find out what we're doing?"

"No, Director Lambert says he can make sure that doesn't happen."

"Yes, but can't he search our minds and find out what we're doing?"

"He can, but that's against his ethics, so he won't — unless someone tells him we're slowing down the investigation."

"Okay, then, you have my approval. Do you want me to tell Director Lambert?"

"Yes, sir, if you don't mind," Tony says.

"I'll tell him, but it's your responsibility if something goes wrong, Tony."

"I understand, sir."

So if Grant quits, it's my fault? Well, I need to string him along, at least until we have this China situation under control.

CHAPTER 51

Justine is sitting at her computer, going over the clues she has on the Devereaux case. She's resumed her thought experiment on the various theories of how the pendant might have gotten to Paris. Then her phone rings, interrupting her thoughts.

As soon as she answers the call, Director Lambert says, "Agent Aebischer, have you shared your good news with Markey?"

"Not yet, sir. I've been too busy."

"Well, you can go ahead but make sure he understands it's going to take a while to establish ownership," Lambert says. "And one more thing — we don't want to discover the identity of the thief very quickly, if at all. I can't explain, except to say it involves national security. Don't mention that to Markey, either. Let him think everything is proceeding as fast as possible on that part of the investigation. And let me decide what to share on any future update before you talk with him. You can go ahead with the investigation, but we don't want it to officially come to an end any time soon. You got that?"

Justine doesn't hesitate to say, "Yes, sir. I understand. You mean go slow and don't share any new developments without talking to you first."

Why would he tell me to do that?

"That's right, Agent Aebischer. Goodbye."

Justine sits and thinks a few minutes about what FBI Director Lambert just told her. She can't figure it out. But she knows she must follow orders, and that's what she'll do.

With a small shrug, she places a call to Grant.

"Hello, Grant Markey," he says softly.

"This is Agent Justine Aebischer, Grant. I have some good news. We've recovered the Devereaux pendant."

"Really, where, how?"

"It was in the possession of the person who bought it in 1995 in an auction house in Paris. We found it in a safe deposit box in Manhattan. But it will take a while to go through the legal procedures to verify the lawful owner. And since all this took place over a period of ninety years, it might not be easy or fast."

Grant says, "I understand. Can I ask a favor? I don't want the FBI to announce they've found it until I decide what I want to do with it, assuming I get it. And to make that decision, I want to know who stole it because that might influence my thinking."

Then there won't be an announcement for a very long time, since I was ordered to drag out my investigation.

Justine responds, "Yes, that's fine. We usually don't make announcements in cases like this, though the pendant's value might justify an announcement. I'll take steps to make sure there's no announcement. By the way, I'm going to text you a photo."

There's a pause in the conversation while she sends the

photo, then Grant says, "Beautiful, amazing! The color is intense! Just like I envisioned from the black-and-white photos."

"If you want to come to New York, I'll arrange for you to see it," Justine says.

"No, that's okay, I'll wait. What about the investigation of the thief? How's that coming?"

Let's see how good a liar I am.

"Well, we know the pendant was repaired by a jeweler in Paris in 1973. That's as far back as we've been able to go. The 1973 owner is deceased, and we haven't discovered any of his family members or friends who might have any information. But we're working on it."

I wonder if he'll believe me?

"Okay, keep me updated," Grant says.

"Definitely," Justine says. "Goodbye!"

Justine takes a moment to think about what both Director Lambert and Grant Markey had just told her. Then she makes her decision.

I have to go ahead with my investigation. If I discover the thief, the Director can decide to withhold that information from Grant, but I'll have done my job. If I slow down, it won't be consistent with my promise to Grant.

Her thoughts go back to how the pendant got to Paris. An idea suddenly pops up in her head, and she excitedly turns to her computer.

CHAPTER 52

PRESIDENT WILLIAM CAMERON, National Security Advisor Preston Blackwell, and the State Department interpreter for Mandarin, Terri Hopton, meet in the Situation Room a few minutes before 8:00 p.m. A call had been arranged with President Xiong for 9:00 a.m. in Beijing to inform Xiong of Deputy Chairman Li's involvement in the plot against the U.S.

CIA Director Kohl had said it was possible that to avoid the appearance of cooperating with the U.S., President Xiong might not act on the information they were about to give. But, he said, on the other hand, President Xiong might be happy for an excuse to get rid of Li while he has the chance.

It was a risk President Cameron was willing to take.

The phone rings, and the President picks up. Ms. Hopton and Mr. Blackwell are listening on their own phone extensions.

"Good morning, Mr. President," Cameron says.

"Good evening, Mr. President," Xiong says.

"Mr. President, thank you for taking my call on short notice. We have a serious situation that I want to tell you about." After a small pause, Cameron continues with, "We discovered and prevented a cyberattack on our financial system by agents of the PRC — Yang Kexin and Wu Min — with several paid accomplices. The plan was fully in motion, but we stopped them before it was implemented. However, we have plenty of evidence, and they are under arrest."

Xiong responds, "Mr. President, are you sure? Neither the Politburo nor I have authorized any such attack. It would not be in our interest to do so. We are too dependent on the functioning of a strong financial system in the United States. We are competitors, but we would not be so foolish to do something that would hurt us as much as you." Hopton translates into English.

"Yes, Mr. President, we agree. That is why I'm sharing this with you. Our information from Yang is that Deputy Chairman Li initiated the attack. He felt that by harming the United States, he would gain support among politicians and the public in China so that he could increase his chances of succeeding you in the future. Yang also told us that Li is bribing high-ranking officials in China to ensure his succession. And he has given us a list and provided details on how the bribery scheme worked," Cameron says.

He continues, "We respect the right of the PRC to have its own succession process, free of corruption, and we hope you respect ours."

Xiong responds, "Yes, of course. If this is true, I will severely punish Deputy Chairman Li. Will you share your evidence with us?"

Cameron replies, "We'll do better than that. We'll release Yang to your custody if that will help bring Li to justice."

"I would like that very much, Mr. President. General Wei Li Jie will act for me. I will talk to the General immediately."

"Please have the General contact Secretary of State Morrill to work out the details. I will talk to the Secretary immediately after this call," Cameron says.

"And what about Wu Min, Mr. President?"

"We are going to hold Wu here. He was involved in developing the cyberattack, and we need to know more about the details."

"I understand, Mr. President."

"Thank you again for taking my phone call. Please let me know if there is anything else we can do to help your investigation. And if you take action against Li, then we don't plan to retaliate against the PRC. I hope to see you again soon."

"Thank you, Mr. President. Goodbye."

Once Xiong disconnects, Cameron asks Blackwell and Hopton, "Did either of you notice anything unusual? You've been on calls with Xiong before."

Blackwell says, "He sounded exhausted." Hopton nods.

The President nods thoughtfully. "Yes, I agree. We might not have much time to stop Li. We need to expedite Yang's return.

"Preston, please fill in the Secretary of State and the others on the details of this call. And tell them we need to speed up the transfer of Yang and help the Chinese as much as possible — but without giving up anything that will divulge our sources and methods, of course."

CHAPTER 53

AS HE READS the President's phone call's briefing, Tony hopes Li didn't have a source in President Xiong's office. If Li was warned that Yang is returning to help bring him down, he might try to intercept him or even try to harm the General. They were getting closer and closer to taking the Deputy Chairman down. Tony doesn't know what he'd do if Li somehow got away with it.

A notification on his computer grabs Tony's attention, and he sees a secure e-mail from Secretary of State Morrill. It says, "General Wei contacted me and said President Xiong has asked him to conduct the investigation of Li's conduct. He wants all the evidence and the complete statement of allegations sent to him in writing. The General has asked us to put our information in a sealed U.S. State Department diplomatic pouch and give it to the PRC Ambassador. He'll put the unopened State Department pouch inside a PRC Embassy diplomatic pouch for transmission to General Wei. If both pouches are still sealed when the General receives them, he'll know there's been no tampering. Please let me know when we can have the information for the pouch."

Tony calls FBI Director Lambert. "Mr. Director, I think we should include the plea agreements from Yang and Wu in the package we're sending to the General. The plea agreements are actually confessions. When will they be available?"

"We're meeting with Yang and Wu today and expect to get their signatures," Lambert says.

Tony says, "Then there's nothing for us to do at the moment."

"Yes, that's right, but we'll need your man to verify they intend to honor the agreements," Lambert says.

"He can do that. Let us know when they're signed."

Tony ponders the situation. They should send the General all the evidence they have, which will incriminate Li, but nothing more. Therefore, the Yang plea agreement will be necessary. However, the Wu plea agreement contains the provision that he will provide the United States with information on Chinese cyberwarfare technology. It's best if the Chinese don't see that agreement. Therefore, that section should be redacted, or a separate statement that only addresses Li's involvement should be prepared for Wu's signature. He decides a separate statement from Wu will be better.

Picking up the phone, he makes some calls to see if he can make that happen.

CHAPTER 54

FRIDAY AFTERNOON, WE get a call from Tony to update us, saying that President Cameron and President Xiong have been in contact.

"General Wei contacted Secretary Douglas Morrill and asked that we send him all our evidence by diplomatic pouch. We're going to send everything we have, including Yang's plea agreement, once he signs it. Also, a statement from Wu with his assertion that Li is behind the attack. Neither Yang nor Wu has signed these documents yet, but maybe today. Until they do, there is nothing else to do but wait," says Tony.

Then he adds, "I wish we had a way to know the exact instructions President Xiong has given the General. Well, we can't have everything."

A couple of hours later, Tony calls Craig again.

"There's been a snag. Yang agrees with the plea agreement, but he wants the Chinese authorities to grant him immunity in China if he goes back and cooperates in the Li investigation. We need to contact the General to see if this can be worked out. We'll let you know, but it might take a day or two. There's nothing new on Wu's situation."

Tony's comment about the General starts me thinking. I've noticed the information I'm getting from Yang and others has been getting clearer and more complete as time goes by. Maybe it's because I'm developing my telepathic ability with practice. Anyway, I wonder if I could use a connection I already have as a sort of portal for a new connection with someone else contained in that memory. I wonder if I can connect with the General if I already have a connection with someone he knows, perhaps with Deputy Chairman Li. Since they are both on the Politburo Standing Committee, they must occasionally meet on political matters.

I ask Craig to find out through our CIA assets in Beijing the dates and times of any meetings between Li and General Wei. He says he will inquire.

While he figures that out, I call Miss Doris about cleaning the carriage house. She says she will get some of her friends to come over and do the cleaning this week. She says she will go out there today and see what needs to be done. I tell her a contractor might come by to take a look at adding a back door and an inside stairwell. She says she'll show the contractor around.

Craig comes over to my office and says Tony has received a reply to the request for information on when Li and the General's meetings have taken place. The most recent meeting was about a month ago. Craig gives me the date and time. He has information on other meetings if I need it.

I lean back and try to establish a connection with Li. It doesn't take long for images to emerge. They are seated in a location I've not seen before, probably the General's office. I notice quite a few framed photos on the wall of men in uniform, plus plaques and awards that have the five-starred red flag of the PRC on them. Li and the General are seated at a conference table in the large office. A large desk is nearby. General Wei is slightly taller-than-average in height, medium build, in his early fifties, with jet-back hair and a military bearing. He is wearing his PLA green uniform containing three stars with a semicircular wreath on his shoulder and collar insignia. This indicates his rank as a senior general, the highest PLA rank, known as Shang Jiang. I read that he has been a PLA officer for over thirty years and has been tested in many difficult situations as he advanced through the ranks.

General Wei says, "Mr. Deputy Chairman, I understand we have been asked to make a recommendation to the Standing Committee. Specifically, how to handle the social unrest and threats that are being made along our border with Kyrgyzstan."

Deputy Chairman Li says, "Yes, General, I believe we should continue and even escalate our crackdown of the radicals in the Uyghur minority. They are the ones who are increasing the unrest."

The General says, "Mr. Deputy Chairman, our policy of increasing pressure on the Uyghur population does not seem to be working. Why don't we try a new approach? We allow religious education for the Hui Muslims. We allow them to fast during Ramadan, wear veils, and build mosques. Why shouldn't we allow the same for the Uyghurs?"

"Because they are a racial minority, General, not just a religious minority. They want to push the ethnic Chinese out of the Xinjiang region."

As the General and the Deputy Chairman continue their discussion, I get a strong feeling that Li both hates and fears the General. I have not sensed such strong emotions during my mental connections before. The mental connection with Li must be very robust during this session. I've heard and seen enough for now.

I decide to find out if I can connect directly with General Wei even though I've never seen him in person. I try to go to where I've left off in the meeting between the General and Deputy Chairman Li. Before long, I start to get images. This time, I can see the Deputy Chairman sitting across the conference table. His square, pockmarked face is slightly red, and his eyes are narrowed to slits.

The General says, "Mr. Deputy Chairman, unfortunately, the Uyghurs are responding by resisting. And our troops are not comfortable with the overly repressive policy."

Li says, "Can't we keep discipline among our troops?"

"Discipline begins in the heart, Mr. Deputy Chairman. The troops must believe in what they're doing. We've been able to keep discipline by rotating the troops to other border regions so they are not stationed in the Xinjiang region for too long."

"I would like to see more extreme measures. The Uyghur leaders must be eliminated, and their families must suffer."

Li has an obsession with force, though he doesn't understand the consequences of using it.

"I wouldn't escalate at this time. Rather, I would deescalate and see what happens."

Li's face gets even redder.

"I would never recommend such a thing, General."

"Then I suggest we each present our views to the Standing Committee and then the entire group can debate and decide, under the General Secretary's leadership."

"As you suggest, General."

I consider what just occurred — my ability to connect through a surrogate, not by direct exposure. This opens the possibility of making connections with anyone, anywhere, based on the theory of six degrees of separation. I decide not to share my successful experiment with Tony just yet. I'm not sure I understand all the implications — positive and negative.

When next I see Craig, he tells me he's had a crew at Wexford House today installing surveillance cameras around the house's exterior and on the carriage house. They'll run the fiber-optic cable over to the carriage house tomorrow. Craig says the camera and sensors can be monitored from here at the office or anywhere we have access to our secure network. And, yes, he says they removed the bugs from the house!

CHAPTER 55

It's a Saturday, but we decide to be available if anything happens in Washington. I think it is an excellent time to clean my Glock. Before I get the supplies from the closet and start to work, I tell the others what I'm doing. They decide that's a good idea and clean theirs, too. I suggest we go to Pearl and get in some target practice today. The ladies agree, but Craig decides to stay at the office and then later go over to the carriage house with the contractor.

We head out to Crosshairs but stop in Jackson at Three Little Pigs for lunch. I am in food heaven with my pulled pork barbecue sandwich. It takes about another thirty minutes to reach Crosshairs. As usual, Randy is there behind the counter and is happy to set us up with several boxes of expensive ammunition to expend. We are all happy that Tony'll be paying. Angie is the most accurate shooter in our group. After about an hour and over a thousand rounds later, we head back to Natchez.

We stop by the office to check in with Craig. He says there's been another development. The United States has offered to send both bodyguards' bodies back to China, and they have accepted. Simultaneously, as a goodwill gesture, we have released the tall man, Wang Jin, but expelled him from the United States. China denies they ordered Craig's kidnapping.

I decide to try to connect with General Wei again, but this time when he's meeting with President Xiong. We know he met or talked with Xiong shortly after President Cameron's phone call. So I start at about the time I estimate President Cameron called President Xiong. I sample General Wei's memory in half-hour increments. In preparation, I have searched for photographs of President Xiong, so I'll know for sure when the General is meeting with him in person.

After searching for about an hour, I see the General's secretary giving him a message that President Xiong requests a meeting with the General in an hour — at the President's office in Zhongnanhai. The General walks from the West Compound over to Qinzheng Hall on the South Lake's north end.

"Come in, General, please take a seat," says President Xiong.

The President is a distinguished-looking man in his late sixties with the obligatory coal-black hair. The tired look in his eyes confirms that the information on his declining health from Deputy Chairman Li is probably accurate.

"I received a call this morning from the President of the United States. He says they foiled a plot to attack their financial system and arrested Deputy Chairman Li's assistant, Yang Kexin, and Wu Min, a high-level manager in APT10. They have admitted their guilt and blamed Li for planning the unauthorized attack to boost his standing. But here's the worst part — Li also has a scheme in place to bribe members of the Politburo Standing Committee and others in the Politburo to back his candidacy to replace me when I retire. The President says while the United States doesn't agree with our policies, they agree we have the right to our own succession process, free of corruption. I believe he's sincere.

"I've told the Americans you'll investigate these allegations on my behalf. They'll let Yang return to China because he's promised to cooperate in the investigation. They want you to contact their Secretary of State to work out the details. If these allegations are true, we need to systematically and quietly eliminate Deputy Chairman Li and the other people involved in the bribery scheme. Do you understand, General?"

"I do, Mr. President."

"Even though the attack was not authorized, I'm concerned the Americans were able to find out, and we didn't even know about it ourselves. The Americans must have cultivated informants in our most sensitive and secretive organizations; we need to find them. I also assign you that task, General. You may use any means to wipe them out. You might start searching for information by using the sleepers we have recruited inside the CIA.

"I'm also concerned that Wu Min will tell the Americans about our portfolio of cyberattack plans and about the technology that enables them. Please initiate plans to silence Mr. Wu."

"I understand, Mr. President."

So, the Chinese government really didn't authorize the attack! They'll be leaving no stone unturned to find out how the United States knew about it. That means they want to know about me, though they have no idea I exist, not yet, anyway. That thought sends a chill up my spine. I'm still not going to tell anyone I'm able to connect with the General. I have to consider whether disclosing this new capability puts me in even more danger. And right now, I believe it does.

CHAPTER 56

LIKE CLOCKWORK, TONY calls Craig just as we're finishing our morning coffee.

"I'm putting you on the speaker, Tony," says Craig.

"Alright, I want to bring you up to date. We've put together a package of information to deliver to General Wei. We included the transcript of Yang's confession, the details Yang gave us about the bribery scheme, the incriminating statements about Deputy Secretary Li, and copies of the signed plea agreements. Grant sent me confirmation yesterday that Yang intends to abide by the agreement. We put all that information in a sealed United States diplomatic pouch and took it to the PRC Ambassador at their embassy. Our representative watched him seal the unopened pouch inside a PRC diplomatic pouch, addressed to General Wei, and it was sent on a flight to Beijing last night. We didn't provide anything from Wu; we haven't finalized anything with him yet.

"We didn't tell Yang everything we included in the pouch. So he may divulge more or less to the General. We'll let them sort that out. We also didn't include any information about the ledger book or the combination to the safe. So far as we know, Yang doesn't know about the ledger. We decided telling them might let them know more about our intelligence capability than we want them to know. If the General is as smart as we think, he'll figure out the missing pieces. We just wanted to give him enough info to confront Deputy Chairman Li.

"We'll send Yang back to China this afternoon with a security escort. Wu has been cooperating, but we haven't decided to present him with a plea agreement yet. We need to continue his interrogation before we decide on the terms. We have people watching in Beijing so we can know when the General moves against the Deputy Chairman. That's the current status, any questions?" concludes Tony.

"So, we just wait for further developments, right?" I ask.

"That's about it."

I decide to check in on the General to see if I can find out what he's planning. I go back to my office and sit down in my new recliner. I decide to start at 8:00 a.m. yesterday in Beijing. The General is in his office in Zhongnanhai. He asks his secretary to get Minister Hua Shuang in Washington, D.C., on the phone. It's 8:00 p.m. in D.C., so she probably calls Hua on his mobile phone. She tells the General that Minister Hua is on the line.

"Minister Hua, I am sure you are aware Yang Kexin and Wu Min were arrested by the Americans. I have been asked by President Xiong to handle the situation. The Americans are releasing Yang, but Wu is still in jail, and it appears they're not going to release him. He's one of our most valuable resources in APT10. He knows all our cyberwarfare plans and technologies. We must not let the Americans get that information. Is that understood?"

"Yes, General. He's being held in a maximum-security facility. The only option we have is to neutralize him if we can. I believe we can do it, but it will be expensive."

"Spare no expense, Minister Hua. Get it done quickly and let me know when it happens."

I decide I should switch to connect with Hua to understand his plan and abort it if I can. I get images from Hua just after he completes his phone call with the General.

Again, someone in power is putting me in a bad situation with others in authority. The General probably doesn't know I was helping Yang and Wu. And now I'm being asked to arrange Wu's murder. I'll have to get in touch with our U.S. Triad contact. I'll contact Lee Tai immediately.

A few minutes later:

"Lee Tai, this is Minister Hua Shuang. We need you to do a job. One of our people, Wu Min, is being held at the Chesapeake Detention Facility. He has information we don't want to be shared. We need to neutralize him as soon as possible."

Lee says, "Chesapeake is a maximum-security facility. It'll be expensive, but it can be done. Do you know if Wu Min is being allowed to mix with the other prisoners?"

"I think he's being held separately," says Hua.

"That's good because that means he's being brought food directly to his cell. We can arrange to poison him. I need to make some phone calls to ensure a guard is assigned to Wu Min's cell block willing to do this for a price. Of course, the guard will not know he's giving a lethal dose. We may be burning our bridges at Chesapeake for quite a while, so it'll cost you plenty. Understand?"

"Yes, please move quickly on this; we'll pay 50% more than your last job," says Hua.

"And I have another request. Allison Murphy is in the same facility. We need to silence her, too," adds Hua.Lee says, "Okay, but this extra assignment will cost you double. I'll let you know when it's done."

Hua says, "Yes, that's fine."

It'll be worth it. I want to tie up loose ends, and Allison is the only one who knows about my involvement. I don't want to be deported back to China.

I call Craig over to my office and tell him what I found out from Hua, but nothing about the General. Later in the day, Tony tells us that Wu Min is being moved to Fort Meade, the headquarters of U.S. Cyber Command, and the Secret Service will be protecting him.

"Tony, what about Allison Murphy? She's in danger, too."

"Grant, Wu has a lot to offer us. Allison Murphy has nothing. She sold us out."

"But Tony, you can't just let them kill her."

"We'll do what we can, but we're not going to move her. It's the Chinese at fault, trying to kill one of their own."

"So I guess she's just a pawn to be taken off the board."

"Yeah, that's a good way to look at it," says Tony.

I saved Wu, but likely not Allison Murphy; she has no usefulness to us. Their attitude — Tony, Li, the General, and probably all the decision-makers — about the cheapness of human life makes me feel sick to my stomach.

CHAPTER 57

We're all still waiting to see what happens in Beijing. I've just gone to sleep when my phone rings. It's Tony!

"Grant, sorry if I've wakened you, but we really need to know what's happening in Beijing with Yang. Will you please try now to see what you can find out?"

"Okay, Tony. I'll let you know."

I'm half asleep, but I decide to explore Yang's memory in thirty-minute increments, starting two hours ago.

Yang is being taken from Yidongyuan by car at 10:00 a.m. Surprisingly, he's in handcuffs. It seems that General Wei wants to intimidate Yang, making it clear he better fully cooperate. The sky has a yellow haze, and it's a little difficult for Yang to breathe; this is a typical Beijing late spring day. The traffic is heavy as they head along the 4th Ring Road and then the Jing-cheng Expressway toward Zhongnanhai.

I don't know why they need to handcuff me. Where would I go, and how would I escape? They promised me immunity if I cooperate, and that's what I intend to do. My biggest fear is that Deputy Chairman Li will intercept me.

I fast-forward by half an hour and find that Yang has arrived at the West Compound in Zhongnanhai. The MSS agents remove his handcuffs, and he steps out of the car.

We're at the back of the main building; they obviously don't want me to be seen entering. I'm feeling very anxious. I'm not sure if they'll keep their end of the bargain.

The MSS agents escort Yang to the elevator, and they go up to the fifth floor. When the elevator door opens, one of the agents goes into the hallway to make sure it's clear. He waves the other agent out, and they go two doors down the hall.

I assume they're worried Li might have his men waiting to kill me.

They quickly enter the office, and the secretary says, "Mr. Yang Kexin, the General is waiting for you, let me tell him you're here." Yang enters the General's office while the MSS agents wait in the outer office. The General is sitting at his desk in his crisply pressed uniform.

The General says, "Yang Kexin, please sit down. I want to hear everything. I have read the file sent by the Americans. It does not reflect well on the Deputy Chairman, or upon you. Please tell me about the bribery scheme first. What was your involvement?"

I need to be careful and tell the truth, but I don't have to tell him everything. The Americans can only have told him what I told them.

"Deputy Chairman Li used me as the go-between with all the participants. I think this was so, if necessary, he could easily deny everything. Those involved in taking bribes seemed to understand. They could also deny ever talking to Li about a bribe."

The General asks, "Why did you cooperate? You know this is illegal."

"Because the Deputy Chairman promised I would be handsomely rewarded if he succeeded President Xiong. And, to be honest, I was afraid of him."

"I have a list here of those you say were involved. Please look at it and tell me if it is correct and complete."

He looks at the list the General presents to him. "Yes, it's complete."

"Was anyone contacted who declined to participate?"

"Yes, I'll give you their names. I'm trying to remember."

"Why were these particular people selected?"

"Some of them had already expressed support for the Deputy Chairman. He suspected the others needed money or were susceptible to a bribe for other reasons."

"What can you tell me about the secret accounts?"

"I don't know much. They were set up by Wu Min at a bitcoin exchange in Hong Kong with identities of peasants whose identity papers were purchased in the rural areas."

"How were the bribes to be paid?"

"Again, Wu Min knows the details. But my understanding is that bitcoins were being used to open accounts at commodity exchanges to buy gold in Singapore and Canada under a different set of fake names. Eventually, these accounts were turned into local currency, and the funds were to be withdrawn by those bribed."

"Do you know who has the records concerning these accounts?"

"No, but I suspect the Deputy Chairman kept detailed

records somewhere. He always wanted to be in control of the details."

"How would the persons being bribed know how much had been deposited in their bitcoin account?"

"The Deputy Chairman had me deliver the account information and passwords to each person so they could check the balance directly with the bitcoin exchange at any time."

"Did you make copies of this information?"

"No, I only delivered sealed envelopes, which he told me contained this information. I would have never had the opportunity to copy the information."

The General says, "Yang Kexin, I hope you're telling me the truth because I'm going to send you to take a lie detector test. Is there any answer you wish to change?"

"No, General, I'm telling you the truth."

"We'll see about that later. Right now, we're going to take a walk."

I think he believes me; otherwise, I would be sent back to Yidongyuan. I wonder what he's up to now?

The General gets up from his desk, picks up his uniform hat, and walks to the outer office. He says, "Captain Chen, Lieutenant Tang, we'll go to Deputy Chairman Li's office now. You know what to do. Please escort me and Yang Kexin."

The General and his entourage walk from the West Building to Building B in the West Compound. This is where Deputy Chairman Li's office is located.

CHAPTER 58

I SWITCH OVER to connect with General Wei instead of Yang.

The Deputy Chairman's secretary announces the General is here to see him. The Deputy Chairman invites him into his office.

"Please take a seat, General. What brings you to see me?"

The General stares at Li for a moment before answering. He doesn't seem to expect anything.

The General says, "I came to arrest you."

Li regards him coolly. "Under whose authority?"

"Under my authority as the head of the MSS and the direction of President Xiong."

"And what are the charges, General?"

"Treason, extortion, and bribery, Deputy Chairman. And the misuse of government resources to wage a cyberattack against another country without authorization. Also, the extortion of funds from companies who require the support of government agencies under your control."

"And what is your evidence, General?"

"We have the testimony of Yang Kexin and Wu Min, who were captured by the Americans during the execution of the cyberattack."

"Ha, Yang, and Wu must have been forced to create this fantasy by the Americans. Surely, you have more evidence than this, General."

"I'm expecting you will provide the evidence, Deputy Chairman."

Li looks quizzically at the General.

"And how do you expect me to do that, General?"

"Before we get to that, I brought someone to see you, Deputy Chairman."

The General rises from his chair, goes to the door, and waves in Yang. He enters and sits on the other chair in front of the desk.

Li is obviously surprised. I'm glad — that means he hasn't made plans to deal with this development.

"Yang, so I see you have lied your way out of captivity from the Americans," Li says.

Yang looks very uncomfortable, shifting around in the chair and showing perspiration on his forehead.

"No, Deputy Chairman, I told the truth."

"What is the evidence of your so-called truth?"

"The flash drives and the money that was paid to the operatives in America. The Americans have confiscated those items. Wu Min and I could never have raised that much money ourselves. And we have no motive for coordinating a cyberattack on our own. We were under your orders."

"Well, that's a fantasy. Maybe you were under the General's orders?"

Yang is obviously agitated; his face is red, and the perspiration on his forehead is becoming more noticeable. Li has a fierce look on his face, as if he would like to get his hands on Yang.

The General says, "Deputy Chairman, this is a complex scheme. There must be records of the transactions. I imagine you kept records to maintain some control over those who took the bribes. And also, those who gave you the money to fund the bribes, as they were both illegal acts which they would not want to be exposed. Therefore, I suggest you open your safe, as that is the logical place to start the search."

I don't think Li would be stupid enough to leave incriminating evidence there when he heard Yang was arrested. However, I agree with Yang that Li would have written documentation. So the question is, where has he hidden his records? We need to find them. Li has too many friends in the Politburo. And if I can get the right evidence, in China the death penalty applies to embezzlement and treason. And in this case, the treasonous use of national resources for the cyberattack on a foreign country might qualify for the death penalty, too. The Court of the People's Procuratorate will decide the sentence, though President Xiong will unofficially have influence, I'm sure.

General Wei is making it his mission to eliminate Li one way or the other. He sees it as his obligation to his country. This is a little surprising because it's also in his personal interest, but he doesn't seem to see it that way. I go back to the memory where I left off.

"Yes, of course, General, I have nothing to hide."
But now Li's face has a worried look.
Deputy Chairman Li bends down and opens the safe.
The General calls in Captain Chen and tells him to search the safe. The Captain finds nothing. The General asks Li to provide the combination to the safe, as they may want to search

it for hidden compartments later. The Captain records the combination, R27-L16-R33. The General tells him to try the combination to make sure it is correct; it works.

The General tells the Captain to search the desk. The Captain looks through the drawers but finds nothing. Then, he searches the bookcases, the seat cushions, and everywhere in the room with the help of Lieutenant Tang, but they find nothing. The General sends them to the outer office. Yang appears to be more uncomfortable. Deputy Chairman Li now has a smirk on his face.

The General says, "You are very clever, Deputy Chairman. However, it is inconceivable that you would destroy your records. Please give me your phone."

Deputy Chairman Li frowns and hands his mobile phone to the General. The General examines it, checking the apps and the settings.

He says, "Deputy Chairman, APT10 is not the only organization that has loaded applications onto mobile phones for special purposes. The MSS has a Special Operations Unit that has shown our top officials how to hide encrypted files onto these phones."

He plays with it for less than a minute until he finds the hidden files.

"Deputy Chairman, I have found your hidden files. Now, if you would be so kind, please give me the password."

"If there are files on the phone, I didn't put them there. Perhaps Wu Min or Yang added them," says Li, who appears even more nervous and agitated. His face is red, and he glares at Yang.

The General pauses and thinks for a moment.

He must have used a password that he would be sure not to forget. He wouldn't want to write it anywhere that it could be found. It had to be complicated and not very easy to crack. Yes, the combination to the safe would be perfect.

The General looks at the combination on the slip of paper that Captain Chen left on the desk. He enters R27-L16-R33. The files open, and the General smiles.

"Deputy Chairman, I can see your files now. The members of the Politburo, the list of payments, the donors, the account numbers — everything."

"General, that doesn't prove anything. Yang, or Wu, or someone else — even you — could have planted those documents on my phone."

"Deputy Chairman, how do you explain this receipt? The receipt says, 'I, Yang Kexin, acknowledge receipt of $200,000 from Deputy Chairman Li on this date for the purpose of carrying out Plan 23-2.'"

At that moment, Li pulls out a pistol from a hidden shelf under his middle desk drawer.

"I don't have to explain anything. I only have to say you threatened me, and I defended myself. And unfortunately, I had to kill you."

"Deputy Chairman, the two MSS officers outside will tell a different story. They know we're not armed. Besides, your dream of becoming President and General Secretary is now over. Your plot will be exposed no matter what you do."

Li sat forward in his chair, pointing the pistol at the General, then at Yang, back and forth with a confused and angry look on his face.

The General says, "Deputy Chairman, now you have to decide whether to kill me out of jealousy or fear — or Yang out of revenge — or yourself out of guilt and shame. If you think the evidence is weak, you can take your chances in the Court of the People's Procuratorate."

Now I decide to switch over to Li to see and understand things from his perspective.

Li says, "I have reason to kill you both — Yang, because he failed to complete the operation, sold me out, and does not deserve to go free. And you, General, because you are the only one standing in my way when I am so close to my goal. You're right; most of my life, I've dreamed of being the Chinese people's supreme leader. But I made my choices, and now I have to face the consequences."

Deputy Chairman Li waves the pistol in his right hand slowly back and forth, trying to decide what to do. The General sits stiffly, while Yang cowers in his chair.

I think, as if talking to Li, "Just kill yourself. It's better than spending the rest of your life in prison, or being executed and shaming your family."

Suddenly, Li puts the pistol to his own temple and pulls the trigger.

Then the images disappear because Li is dead. So I connect with Yang.

Blood, skull fragments, and brain matter are everywhere, and Li is slumped over the left arm of his chair.

The sound of the gunshot brings Captain Chen and Lieutenant Tang running into the room, weapons drawn. The General says, "Lieutenant, please escort us back to my office. Captain Chen, you are in charge here."

Along with the Lieutenant, Yang and the General hurry out of the Deputy Chairman's office while Li's secretary sobs.

I'm stunned. Not because Li killed himself, but because it was like my thoughts actually caused him to do it! But I was searching Li's memory, so I'm confused. What I saw must have been in the past, which I couldn't influence. Or was it? No, it couldn't have been because I can't connect with dead people. So I must have been able to access Li's mind in real time, communicated directly with him, and he must have heard my voice in his head. This is something entirely new, and I am definitely not going to let Tony know I can do this until I've thought through all the ramifications.

I call Tony.

"Li is dead, he shot himself in the presence of Yang and the General. They were able to get Li's bribery files, which he had stored in hidden files on his phone."

Tony says, "Thanks, we'll see what we can find out from our sources in Beijing. I'll let you and the others know as soon as we find out. It might not be until the morning."

CHAPTER 59

SHORTLY AFTER WE arrive at the office, Tony calls Craig and says the CIA has received word that something significant happened inside Zhongnanhai yesterday. But they haven't yet been able to corroborate my story. They also have been informed there have been arrests of some prominent politicians, likely those taking bribes from Li.

There is nothing for us to do now but wait, so we decide to close the offices and go to Wexford House to check on the carriage house apartment renovation. Craig follows us after picking up another agent, Lloyd Hart.

When we arrive, we go inside the house, greet Miss Doris, and all walk over to the carriage house. The metal exterior door has been added, facing the alley, and the inside stairwell is almost finished. The fiber-optic cable has been run from the main house to the carriage house and into the second-floor living area. I also notice new cameras on the carriage house and on the main house as well. It appears the entire perimeter of the house can be monitored. I wonder what other sensors they've installed.

I introduce Miss Doris to Craig, and he introduces all of us to Lloyd. Craig and Lloyd have decided Lloyd will be the carriage house tenant. Craig tells us Lloyd is his new partner in Canal Street Investments, Inc.

Miss Doris says her friends have cleaned the apartment, and everything does look spotless. The new furniture and appliances have been delivered. We check out the renovated apartment; everything is in order. The computer equipment will not be installed until the apartment is occupied. Lloyd says he'd like to move in tomorrow, and I agree. Miss Doris tells him to let her know if there's anything he needs. Craig and Lloyd leave, and the rest of us go back to the main house.

While we're waiting for dinner, I play the Steinway square piano, which I haven't done in a long time. Karen and Angie seem to enjoy listening. Craig returns for dinner so that we can all wait together for more news from Tony.

Miss Doris prepares another fine meal for us. She doesn't say much, but I can tell she's wondering about Lloyd Hart and what his presence means, and why Craig is here. She knows I'll let her know when I'm ready, whenever that may be.

Tony calls after dinner and says there was an announcement in Beijing that fifteen Politburo members have resigned, including four from the Standing Committee. Political observers consider it to be a routine housecleaning of the Communist Party hierarchy. Nothing has been announced concerning the death of Deputy Chairman Li. Tony expects that announcement will be coming soon. We must continue to wait for further developments, and Tony asks Craig to remain with us.

An hour later, Tony calls Craig again. Craig puts Tony on the speaker.

"There is big news from Beijing. It was announced that

Deputy Chairman Li died suddenly of a heart attack. Second, there have been five new members elected to the Politburo Standing Committee. Third, President Xiong has resigned for health reasons. And General Wei has been temporarily appointed President of the People's Republic of China and General Secretary of the Communist Party. In other words, there has been a clean sweep."

I ask, "So, that means our mission is finished?"

Tony says, "Yes, it appears so."

Then Tony adds, "There's one more thing — Allison Murphy is dead. Her food was poisoned at Chesapeake. We weren't able to stop them."

Hua was trying to protect himself from Allison Murphy, giving evidence of his involvement, and he was successful. And both Li and the General had already given orders not to leave any tracks. Even though Hua has diplomatic immunity and wouldn't face trouble like Yang and Wu, he really didn't want to get deported back to China.

My life has changed so much in the three months since Tony first called me. I'm not sure how to feel now that the mission is over. I wonder if I no longer have to worry about hitmen and motorcycle gunmen, but I wince as I realize the answer.

I say, "Okay, what do we do now?"

Tony says, "We celebrate! But we're also going to be watching to see if the succession in China is challenged. We don't think it will be. There'll be a formal election in a few months. It appears the General is fully in charge. We eventually expect the Politburo members who resigned to be arrested."

Based on what I've learned, I expect General Wei to take full control. He'll root out all those associated with Deputy Chairman Li. I'd like to share the details of everything I know, but I won't. Suppose Tony finds out I have access to the General's memory — and may have real-time access to any subject's mind. In that case, I will never — ever — get my life back, so I decide to keep quiet.

CHAPTER 60

JUSTINE REVIEWS HER Devereaux investigation notes. A lot has happened in the last eight days. Despite being told to slow down, the investigation actually sped up due to a lucky break. Now she has to decide what to do with the information she has. She wants to follow orders from her Director. Still, she wants to keep her promise to Grant and her integrity as an investigator.

She decides to call FBI Director Lambert.

"Director Lambert?" she says when he answers.

"Yes, Agent Aebischer. I hope this is important. We're a little busy handling the China situation."

"I need some direction because of new information on the Devereaux case," she says.

"Well, what is it? I mean, the new information," he says.

She hesitates slightly before saying, "I've solved the case."

"I told you to slow down," he says sternly.

"I know, but sometimes if you get a break, the case just works itself out. And I know it's mostly circumstantial, but with all the people dead after ninety years, that's the best we can do."

"Tell me about it," says Lambert.

Justine begins, "I kept wondering how the pendant got to Paris. It didn't make sense unless there was a connection to Natchez. So, I reviewed all the information I could find on the people interviewed in the original investigation.

"I found that the wife of the senior bank teller, William Hopkins, was a second cousin of Devereaux. So I have to assume Hopkins and Devereaux knew each other. Then I found that Hopkins was a cousin of Antoine Rousseau of New Orleans, the owner of the coffee brand Café Chicorée. People in New Orleans might not have had any money during the Depression, but they were still buying their chicory coffee, so Rousseau had money.

"Then the big break came when I checked the tax records of West Feliciana Parish, Louisiana, which includes St. Francisville. They showed that Devereaux was delinquent on his taxes for the Chantilly Plantation in 1931 and 1932. But the taxes were paid up just before the land was set for a delinquent tax auction by the parish in 1933. So, where did he come up with the money? I think he arranged to 'borrow' the pendant with Hopkins's help, and planned to return it later. But John Markey ruined the plan when he checked the safe deposit box and found the pendant was missing.

"I believe Devereaux paid Hopkins to take the pendant from the safe deposit box and then to introduce him to Mr. Rousseau. Hopkins had access to the bank master key, and he probably knew that John Markey kept his own safe deposit key in his desk. It took both keys to open the box. And he had the chance to take Markey's key at an opportune time — long enough to remove the pendant and return the key.

"Then Devereaux borrowed money from Antoine Rousseau, just like he borrowed from John Markey, using the pendant as collateral. The plan had to change when the pendant was discovered missing, so Devereaux converted the loan into a sale with additional money changing hands. Likely, Antoine Rousseau didn't know the pendant had been taken or that Devereaux had pledged the pendant for a loan from John Markey. The theft was extensively reported in newspapers throughout Mississippi, but only sketchily reported, if at all, in New Orleans.

"Hopkins was paid for his role in cash from the Rousseau loan proceeds. And he kept it hidden, so there was nothing unusual going on in his bank account for the investigators to see.

"After some time had passed, Antoine Rousseau showed the pendant to his brother, Pierre Rousseau, a wealthy Parisian bond dealer. And Pierre Rousseau bought the pendant from his brother, took it to Paris as a gift for his wife, and kept it there for almost forty years until he sold it to M. Georges Lang in 1973. Pierre Rousseau was eighty-four years old in 1973 and died two years later, so maybe he was just winding up his affairs when he sold it. And neither he nor his brother had any idea what it was worth until he sold it.

"All this is conjecture, based on the circumstantial evidence. But this theory is the only one that's consistent with the facts," Justine says.

"Why weren't these facts discovered when the case was first investigated?"

"Because at that time, the only suspicious connection would have been Hopkins's wife being related to Devereaux. But investigators didn't have access to data like we do today, so they probably didn't know, or maybe because Devereaux himself wasn't a suspect, they never looked for a link."

"Your theory probably wouldn't stand up in court, but this isn't going to court. Can you pull this together with all the evidence and documentation into a report for Grant Markey?"

"Yes, of course. But when can I share it with him?" Justine asks.

"I'll get back to you on that," Director Lambert says.

"Okay, then I'll wait," Justine says.

Justine feels justified in following her leads. And she had the feeling that the Director agrees.

Maybe I'll be allowed to tell Grant soon — maybe even tomorrow!

Tony's sitting in his office, wondering what's going to happen next. Then Director Lambert calls Tony. When Tony answers, Lambert says, "Agent Aebischer believes she's solved the Devereaux case. At least as far as circumstantial evidence can take it."

"I thought we all agreed to slow-walk it," Tony says.

"Yes, but she got lucky. You know how investigations go."

"Yeah, but we've got to keep Markey on the team."

"Tony, you squelched the Chinese plot, and Li is out of the picture. Nothing's going to change that. So you're going to have to tell Markey sometime. Why not now? It's as good a time as any. And if he finds out you tampered with the investigation, you're going to lose him anyway," Lambert says.

There are only bad choices here. In either case, I might lose Grant. But it's probably better if we tell him.

"Yeah, I guess you're right. What did she find out?" Tony says.

After FBI Director Lambert gives him a summary, Tony says, "Okay, she can tell him. I'll let Director Kohl know. Thanks for calling."

"I'll tell her to wait until she's finished her written report. It'll likely be Monday," says Lambert.

Then I have some time to decide how to handle Grant if he says he wants to quit. Well, I still have to decide on the rewards for the successful conclusion of the case. Maybe I should juice his bonus!

CHAPTER 61

My phone rings, and I see it's Justine's number.

"Grant speaking."

"Hello, this is Agent Aebischer. I've finished the investigation. I've taken it as far as I can, considering all the people who were involved are dead — and we can't interview any of them."

"What did you find out?" I ask anxiously.

This is what I've been waiting for, but it doesn't sound like I'm going to like the conclusion.

She tells me exactly what she told Director Lambert a few days ago. When she's done, she says, "Unfortunately, it's a circumstantial case because we don't have any hard evidence to show Hopkins's or Devereaux's involvement. But the fact they were related by marriage and had connections to the Rousseau family is too much of a coincidence."

I say, "Well, this a shock!"

So Devereaux took his own pendant — but only intended

to borrow it! And my great-grandfather's trusted employee was in on it.

"Unfortunately, it's not how I was hoping this would work out. I hoped the pendant would be recovered and returned to the Devereaux family, and my great-grandfather's name would be cleared."

And I would be out from under a cloud here in Natchez.

"But I can't give the pendant to Devereaux's family if he took it — and sold it twice. My great-grandfather is cleared, as far as I'm concerned. But if there's no direct evidence, then it doesn't seem right to smear Hopkins and Devereaux, though they probably deserve it."

Justine says, "I'm sorry I couldn't do more."

"Justine, I really appreciate what you were able to do in such a short amount of time. The pendant will be back in the family — assuming the legal process confirms I'm the rightful owner. But once I have it, what can I do with it? I have a lot of choices — from selling it to donating it to a museum. I've got a lot to think about."

And it seems that whatever I do, I can't do publicly. That'll just revive the old controversy. I'd rather keep a low profile.

Justine says, "I've put everything in a report with all the evidence I've collected — and with all the details all spelled out. I'll send it to you as soon as I get off the phone. When you want to see the pendant, I can meet you in New York and show it to you. I'd suggest you start thinking about where you're going to store it when you take control. It's too valuable to keep just anywhere."

"Okay, I'll be thinking about that, and let me know if you have any suggestions. Thank you again, so very much," I reply.

"Since you ask, I actually do have a suggestion for a location near you. The Security Center in New Orleans is in the old Federal Reserve building. They have very secure vault storage. We've used them for temporary jewelry storage in the past. Goodbye, Grant. I'm happy I was able to help."

"Thank you, Justine."

The worst part is that Tony has fulfilled his promise to complete a full investigation. Now I can't use that as an excuse to quit! But on the other hand, I don't feel like I have to continue, because the investigation is over. That gives me the upper hand. So there, Tony! I feel better already.

CHAPTER 62

THE NEXT DAY, Tony calls to tell us the situation seems to be under control in Beijing, with General Wei entirely in command. It's time to celebrate, and he wants to meet us in Baton Rouge, Louisiana, tonight at 6:30 p.m. We should come dressed for a nice dinner and a celebration.

I ask Craig, "Why Baton Rouge?"

Craig says, "It's lower profile than New Orleans and less chance that someone will spot Tony. And he can fly directly to the Baton Rouge airport from D.C. in two and a half hours on a private jet."

Tony has arranged a private dinner at Mansurs on the Boulevard, the best seafood restaurant in Baton Rouge, he says. It's an easy drive for us, only a little over two hours straight down U.S. 61, forty miles past St. Francisville.

We arrive at Mansurs right on time, thanks to Craig's driving and his decision to leave fifteen minutes early. It's raining slightly, and we hurry from the parking lot to get under the long black awning running from the curb to the restaurant entrance.

Tony's already at the bar, discussing the wine list with the bartender, who Tony introduces as Mark Robbins, a retired former FBI agent who Tony knew from years ago. Tony says Mark knows more than he does about wines, and that's saying something.

The hostess shows us to the wine cellar, which Tony has reserved for our celebration dinner. As we're seated, the server brings champagne glasses and a bottle of Dom Perignon 2008.

Tony says, "Tonight, we celebrate! Here's to a successful mission with the best team I've ever assembled. Cheers!"

The server then brings appetizers and wine that Tony apparently had ordered earlier. There were oysters, crab cakes, and stuffed mushrooms. The server offered Hourglass Cabernet Sauvignon Napa 2007 or Aubert Sugar Shack Estate Chardonnay Napa 2017, both chosen by Tony with help from Mark.

We all order seafood from the extensive menu while discussing various situations and experiences during the recent mission. We all agree our best memories are from Bangkok, except for all of us being the target of gunshots, including Tony.

Though there are tasty choices on the menu, we all pass on dessert and order coffee instead.

Tony says, "When we first organized ourselves only a few months ago, we knew there was a serious national security threat of some kind, but we didn't know what sort or by whom. Since then, we've defeated the China threat, eliminated the person responsible, and exposed all of his cohorts in the bribery scheme. And we've helped install a successor to President Xiong that's at least not an enemy of the United States. We've also obtained detailed information on China's cyberattack plans and technologies, plus uncovered a Russian operation in China. And we did it all without China having a clue how we did it.

And Russia doesn't even realize that we know they were involved — and that they were hoping to benefit from Li's scheme.

"Now, for the fun part — the rewards. You put your lives on the line. Unfortunately, the public will never know because this was a covert operation. Craig, Karen, and Angie, you each will receive a cash award of half a million dollars. Grant, you will receive a cash award of three million dollars — we could not have possibly been successful without you. By the way, I would suggest you set up a separate bank account in Jackson, Baton Rouge, or New Orleans. Once that's done, let me know the details so I can wire the money. The others already have their accounts set up from prior operations."

I'm in shock! I can only stare blankly as I process the amount he just said.

Then, I say, "Wow, Tony, you meant it when you said I would be handsomely rewarded. I don't know what to say."

"Grant, just say you're going to continue working with us. Now take a couple months off and enjoy some vacation time. In case you're wondering, you'll continue to have a security detail and will stay on salary." Tony doesn't say anything more; he just sits and looks at me.

Oh, so he's expecting an answer.

I've been thinking about the choice I was going to have to make sooner or later. But now I realize the decision needs to be now! I'm thinking about the new friendships, the feeling of accomplishment and contribution, the excitement, the return of the Devereaux pendant, and the money — but also the danger. Okay, well . . .

"I'm in, Tony!"

For now, anyway!

Tony smiles but is still staring at me with those cold blue-gray eyes looking right through me.

I'm sure he can guess what I'm thinking, but hey, I know I've got options.

"That's great news, Grant! You're making the right choice," says Tony.

Yeah, actually, I feel pretty good about it. I've got three million reasons to feel good right now, plus doing something worthwhile for my country.

I smile and raise my glass.

"But I've got a question. Where is this much money coming from, surely not from the government?"

Tony doesn't seem to be surprised by this question at all. He was probably hoping I would ask.

Tony says, "The money is from a reward fund provided by major banks to counter cybersecurity threats.

"By the way," he continues, "there are going to be some other changes I need to tell you about." He pauses and looks around the table. I'm not sure if I can handle whatever other changes Tony might be planning.

Tony says, "Director Kohl is retiring. The President has asked me to take over as CIA Director. If I pass the vetting process, it'll be announced in several weeks."

Raising our glasses, we all congratulate him. I'm not sure I've ever seen Tony beam before, but he is definitely beaming. He's obviously very happy.

"So, in my new position, I have to give up my hands-on involvement with the team. But I've talked to Craig and Karen today about what we should do. Karen is going to take over my role for these kinds of operations. Craig likes the fieldwork, so he'll stay right where he is. And we'll renegotiate with the FBI to let Angie continue with the team. I'm sure Director Lambert will agree. So I think it's all going to work out just fine."

We congratulate Karen on her promotion and agree it's been a great adventure for all of us.

Then Tony says, "I hate to eat and run, but I need to get back to D.C. Craig, pay the bill and stay as long as you want."

Tony says goodbye to each of us and leaves the restaurant.

We sit around for a while talking, mostly with me asking questions.

"Are you always compensated this well?"

Karen says, "No, it depends on the job."

"Do you always get this much time off between assignments?" I ask.

This time Craig answers. "It depends on the length of the job. We've been on 24/7 for how many months? Tony wants us fresh for the next job."

Craig then says, "Tony didn't want to spoil the party, but you need to realize this might not be the last we see of the Chinese. Even though what Li was doing was unauthorized, they can't be happy our clandestine operation penetrated their internal organizations. They'll be working to find out how we did it and to put a stop to it. They may never find out, but they'll be trying. By the way, Grant, while we're on vacation, our backup team will be providing your security in Natchez or wherever you go for your vacation. That's one reason we wanted to get the carriage house operational."

We talk about where each of us is going on vacation. Craig is going to his place in Hawaii, which he had never mentioned before. Karen says she's going to the French Riviera with a friend. Angie throws out some ideas but nothing definite. The thought of an extended vacation is entirely new to me; I usually only take trips related to my business. I'm really clueless where I might go, but I do agree some time off to relax is a good idea.

CHAPTER 63

ABOUT FORTY-FIVE MINUTES after Tony departed, the team leaves the restaurant and heads toward their car parked across the lot, still discussing vacation ideas. Though the lot is still full, they're the only people outside, and their voices are the only sound in the semi-darkness of the lot.

Just as they reach their car, three figures dressed in black emerge from behind nearby cars on each side. They fire Tasers, hitting Craig, Karen, and Angie, who all fall to the ground, writhing uncontrollably. Another black-clad figure sneaks up behind Grant and jabs an auto-injector pen into his neck, and he slumps to the ground, unconscious. Immediately, an unmarked white cargo van turns into the lot, stopping next to the bodies on the pavement, and two men start loading Grant's body into the back of the van. As they do this, two large black Suburbans screech to a stop, blocking the exit, and turn on blue flashing lights. Several men jump out with automatic weapons fitted with silencers and shout, "FBI — step out of the van — put your weapons on the ground — and put your hands above your head!"

The cargo van's driver does as he is instructed and steps away from the vehicle as several FBI agents rush around to the back of the van. Caught by surprise, the figures at the back immediately get on the ground and are handcuffed.

The van's passenger also lays her weapon on the asphalt, but as she straightens up, her hand goes to her waistband, and suddenly she's shooting at the agents as she steps back partially behind the door. The agents return fire, then dive to take cover.

But the female passenger doesn't see the figure who circled around the row of parked cars until he is slightly behind her. As the agents directly in front have her attention, he raises his weapon, also with a suppressor, and shoots her from twenty feet with three quick shots, one in her head and two in her torso. The whole encounter, from start to finish, is over in less than twenty seconds.

Tony emerges from behind the car and checks the woman lying on the ground. It's the Russian agent, Irina Rachkova, and she's definitely dead. The fatal shot entered her skull just below the right eye socket, but above the prominent zygomatic arch — one of her lovely and distinctive high cheekbones.

Tony waves over one of the FBI agents.

"After you put those three in restraints, load them in the van along with her body. Move Grant to one of the Suburbans along with the three agents who were tased. One of you drive Craig's car, and let's head to the airport. The others can take the van, place the suspects under arrest for kidnapping, and take the body to the local morgue; we'll deal with it later. This is a federal case, and we'll confirm these are foreign agents, so don't worry about processing the scene. We've got it all on video."

The FBI agent nods and turns to give instructions to the other agents. Within two minutes, they're all gone, and no one from the restaurant knows that anything has happened right outside.

When they arrive at the Baton Rouge airport, they go to the Signature Flight Services facility, where Tony's plane is parked. By then, Grant had regained consciousness and is starting to feel much better.

Grant asks, "What did they inject me with to knock me out?"

"There's no way to know. The Russians are masters in creating those types of concoctions. You're just damn lucky they decided not to poison you. They really get off on that," Tony says.

Craig, Karen, and Angie had recovered enough from the tasing to be able to question Tony.

Karen asks, "Tony, we thought you were on your way to D.C. What happened?"

"I asked Craig to give Donnie and his backup crew the night off so they could have their own celebration. But I wasn't going to let you come to Baton Rouge without backup. So I arranged with the New Orleans and Baton Rouge FBI offices to work your backup detail and provide my security. When I landed at the airport, I saw a Gulfstream G650 parked over in front of the BTR Flight Center. That's not a plane you would expect to see in Baton Rouge, so it caught my attention. But then I noticed the tail number, P4-RV1, the same tail number I'd seen in Agent Aebischer's Devereaux investigation reports. I suspected immediately that the Russians were using Vetrov's plane for a covert operation. Russian oligarchs are sometimes 'requested' to assist the SVR or GRU; they really have no choice, and I don't blame them for cooperating. I decided the Russians must have known we were meeting at Mansurs, so with the FBI backup team in place, I let it play out."

"But why didn't you warn us?" Craig asks.

"Because it was obvious that if they were going to try anything, it would be to kidnap Grant and take him out of the country. They would've had no reason to use deadly force against any of you. While we were at dinner, the Baton Rouge agents found out that Vetrov's pilot had filed a flight plan from Baton Rouge to St. Kitts. So that's where they were planning to take Grant, then eventually on to Russia."

"But couldn't they simply have been planning to kill you, Tony, and then fly the assassin to St. Kitts? They don't exactly like you," Grant says.

"No, I'm not nearly as important to them as you, Grant."

"So who was the Russian agent that got killed, any idea? What happened? None of us saw anything," Angie says.

"It was Irina Rachkova. I shot her three times after she started shooting at our agents. She could have surrendered, but she made the wrong choice. We don't know when or how she got back into the U.S. Maybe Vetrov flew her in. But we won't find out from Vetrov, Zlobin, or the flight crew, because they took off just before we got back to the airport. Most likely, they had a trailing agent who saw what happened and alerted them to leave, but we don't know for sure."

"So the Russians were involved in this all along. How did they know we were coming to Baton Rouge tonight?" Grant asks.

"They must have had your offices bugged, or maybe they used sophisticated eavesdropping equipment they can point at a window and catch sound vibrations. Actually, that would be my guess. And they must have gotten the psychic evaluation that was stolen by C.T. Brasfield from Dr. Dehner. So it's likely they're the only foreign service who knows about your psychic skills."

"I guess I owe you for saving me, Tony."

"I couldn't let anything happen to my college buddy, right?"

CHAPTER 64

WHEN WE ARRIVE back in Natchez, Craig drops us off at Wexford House and heads off to his place. I ask Karen and Angie if they feel well enough to have a nightcap with me in the south parlor. They both agree, and I get three cordial glasses, and a bottle of ice-cold Limoncello kept for special occasions. Actually, I'm feeling pretty good; maybe it's the exhilaration of "dodging a bullet."

We sip our drinks and continue to discuss the Russian attack and our vacation plans, which we assume will have to be scaled back, but my mind keeps wandering.

Finally, I say, "There are some things that are bothering me. For instance, how can government employees accept private payments for just doing their job? Also, why were we never attacked again in Bangkok? And I'm wondering who really bugged Wexford House, since nothing ever came of it."

Karen says, "Grant, there are some things you deserve to know, and since we know you could find out easily enough yourself, there's no harm in telling you. Tony is not a CIA or FBI employee, nor are any of us; we're all government contractors. We all used to be government agents, but Tony left the CIA several years ago to set up his own private security firm, Russell & Associates, and we joined him. Well, he'll be a CIA employee again if he's confirmed by the Senate."

I shake my head at this news, and I'm frowning.

Tony is such a liar! I should have searched his mind from the very beginning. I'm too naive.

"The CIA, FBI, and other federal agencies don't want to be directly involved in all operations, especially those involving foreign threats. If things go wrong, it's better to have a paid contractor to take the fall. Contractors can do things that federal agents are not allowed to do. So the CIA and FBI subcontract with Russell & Associates to take on difficult cases where the risks are high. Tony is well compensated for the risk and treated as if he's still the CIA Deputy Director. The agency heads are insulated if things go wrong. And there seems to be no limit to the budget they have to hire contractors."

She pauses and seems to hesitate slightly before continuing.

"Tony set up the motorcycle shooters to give you a little scare so you would feel more dependent on us for protection and compliant with his instructions. And there were actually no bugs planted here in the house; that was Tony playing mind games."

That bastard! I knew Tony was that kind of person, but this? But, well, I have to forgive him for protecting me. Then I suddenly ask a question that I had been thinking about for a long time. "So, who are you guys, anyway? What are your real names?"

"Sorry, we can't tell you that for our own protection, even though you could easily find out by probing our minds. But we can tell you we worked with the CIA and FBI before joining Tony, just like we told you."

"Well, Craig told me about his hometown and his college years, so that must be his real identity."

She shakes her head. "No, he's just assumed the identity of the real Craig Clayton. But don't worry about it, we're all on the same team now. Actually, he's been dating Susan Emerson and asked her to go with him to Hawaii. She accepted, and he's delirious."

"Well, good for Craig or whoever he is!"

Angie says, "Tony's plan is for the team to stay with you indefinitely for your own protection. The Chinese and certainly the Russians are real threats to your safety, as are the other foreign intelligence services if you are ever found out."

Karen says, "On the bright side, after this success, Russell & Associates will get more plum assignments, and we'll be able to continue to earn big fees. But Tony will have to divest himself of his ownership in the business. There's no firm evidence that anyone but us, the agency directors, the Russians, and the President know about you. We might all be able to retire pretty soon after a few more of these big bonuses."

With that, Karen excuses herself for bed and goes upstairs.

Turning to Angie, I say, "This is making my head spin. I guess Tony thought if he told me he was running a private security operation, I would have told him to get lost. He's right. Now I've got a lot to think about and a lot of decisions to make."

But the more I think about it, I realize that the last few months have brought a meaning to my life that I'd been missing since Brooke passed. Yes, Tony lied to me, and he put me in a position where my life had been threatened more than once, but he also brought me work I enjoy and friends I enjoy doing that work with.

But before I can say anything, Angie takes my hand and begins stroking her fingers back and forth on the back of my hand. "No need to worry about that now. You're officially on vacation. Since you don't have any plans, go with me. I was thinking about vacationing in the Mediterranean, maybe in Mallorca, Formentera, or Corfu. But I guess now, maybe Jekyll Island, St. Simons Island, or Hilton Head would be more appropriate."

Angie's touch is more than something a friend would do. I'm sure now that she is interested in me as more than a friend, and not just frivolous flirting.

Barely louder than a whisper, I say, "Any of those places sound like a nice vacation spot. You know, I think I might learn to actually like this line of work."

I scoot closer to her on the couch; Angie smiles and runs her fingers through my hair. I take Angie in my arms, and we kiss passionately — for the first time, but definitely not the last.